MANGA SHAKESPEARE™

OTHELLO

ADAPTED BY

RICHARD APPIGNANESI

ILLUSTRATED BY

RYUTA OSADA

Amulet Books, New York

PUBLISHER'S NOTE: This is a work of fiction. Names, characters, places, and incidents are either the product of the author's imagination or are used fictitiously, and any resemblance to actual persons, living or dead, business establishments, events, or locales is entirely coincidental.

Cataloging-in-Publication Data has been applied for and may be obtained from the Library of Congress.
ISBN: 978-0-8109-8350-2

Originally published in the U.K. by SelfMadeHero
(www.selfmadehero.com)

Illustrator: Ryuta Osada
Text Adaptor: Richard Appignanesi
Designer: Andy Huckle
Textual Consultant: Nick de Somogyi
Publishing Director: Emma Hayley

Published in 2009 by Amulet Books, an imprint of Harry N. Abrams, Inc.

Printed and bound in China
10 9 8 7 6 5 4 3 2 1

HNA
harry n. abrams, inc.
a subsidiary of La Martinière Groupe
115 West 18th Street
New York, NY 10011
www.hnabooks.com

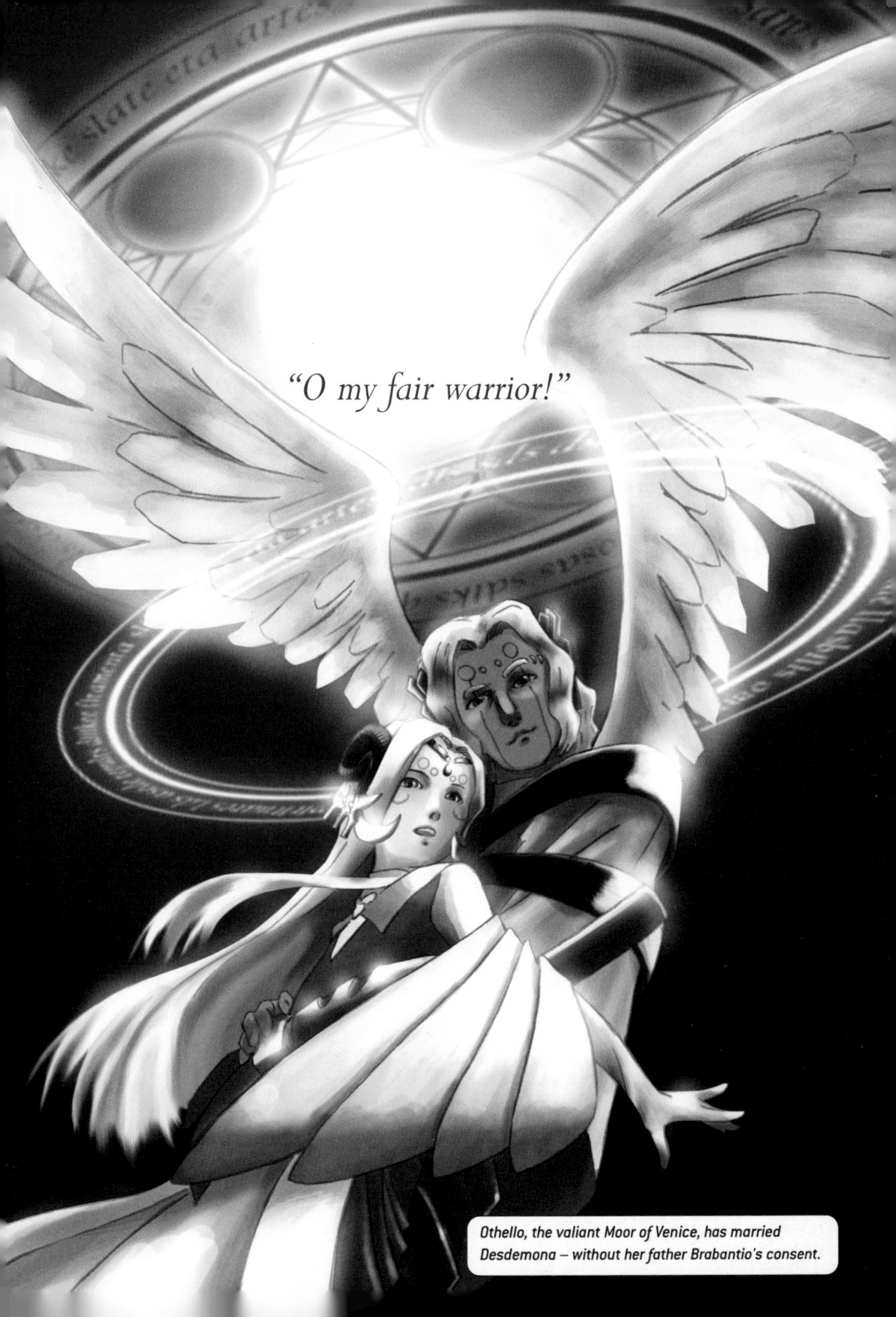
"O my fair warrior!"
Othello, the valiant Moor of Venice, has married Desdemona – without her father Brabantio's consent.

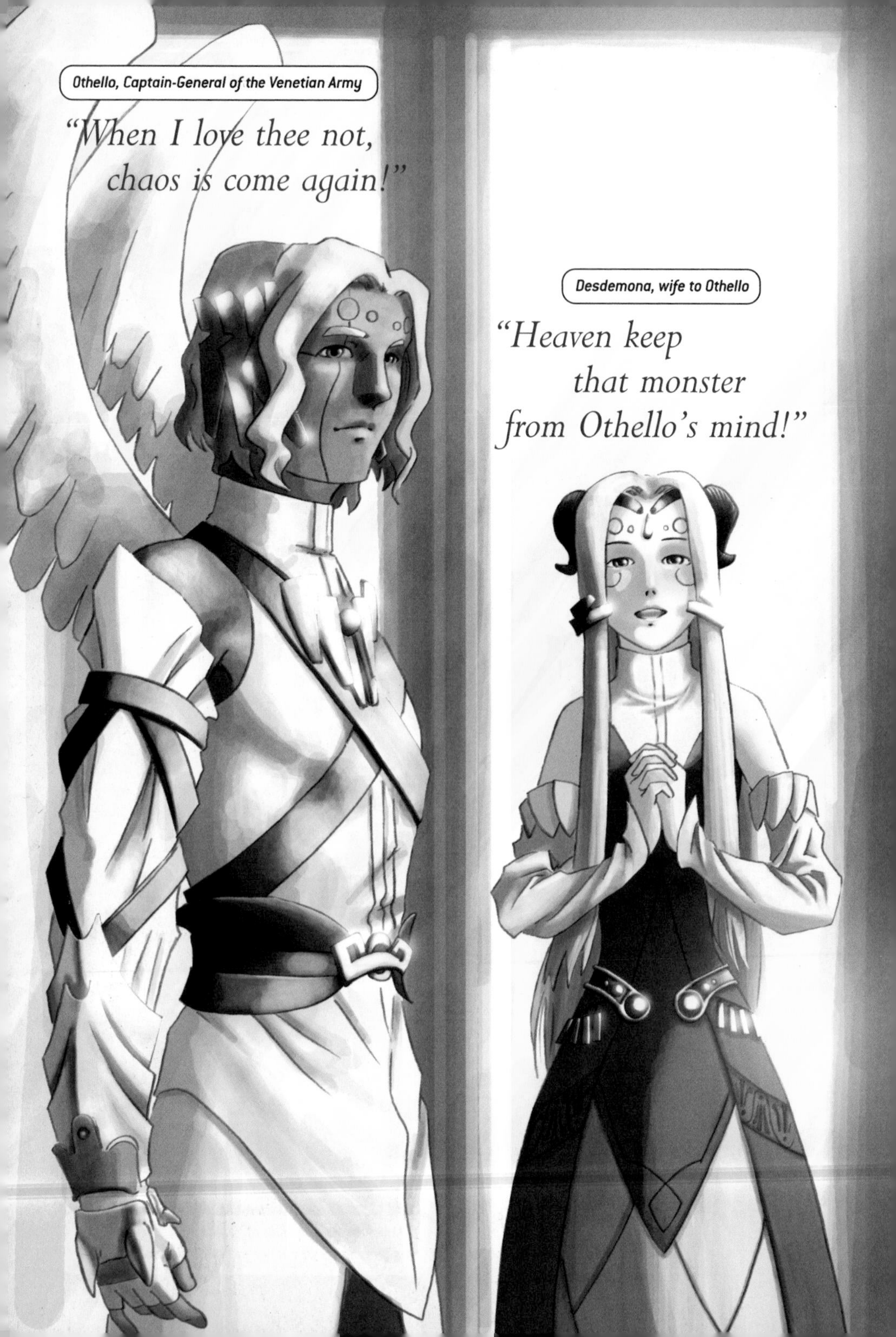
Othello, Captain-General of the Venetian Army
"When I love thee not, chaos is come again!"
Desdemona, wife to Othello
"Heaven keep that monster from Othello's mind!"

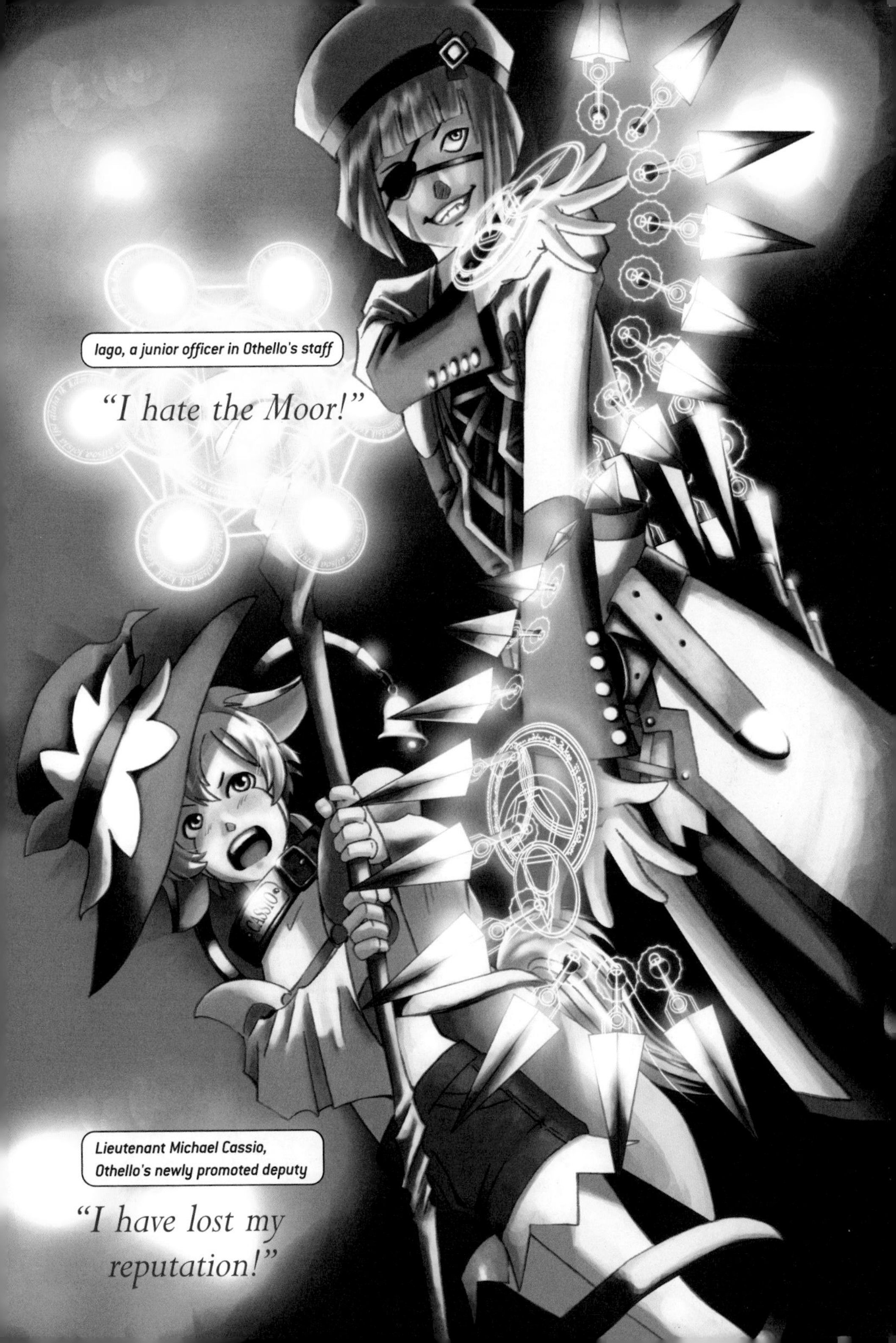
Iago, a junior officer in Othello's staff
"I hate the Moor!"
CASSIO
Lieutenant Michael Cassio, Othello's newly promoted deputy
"I have lost my reputation!"

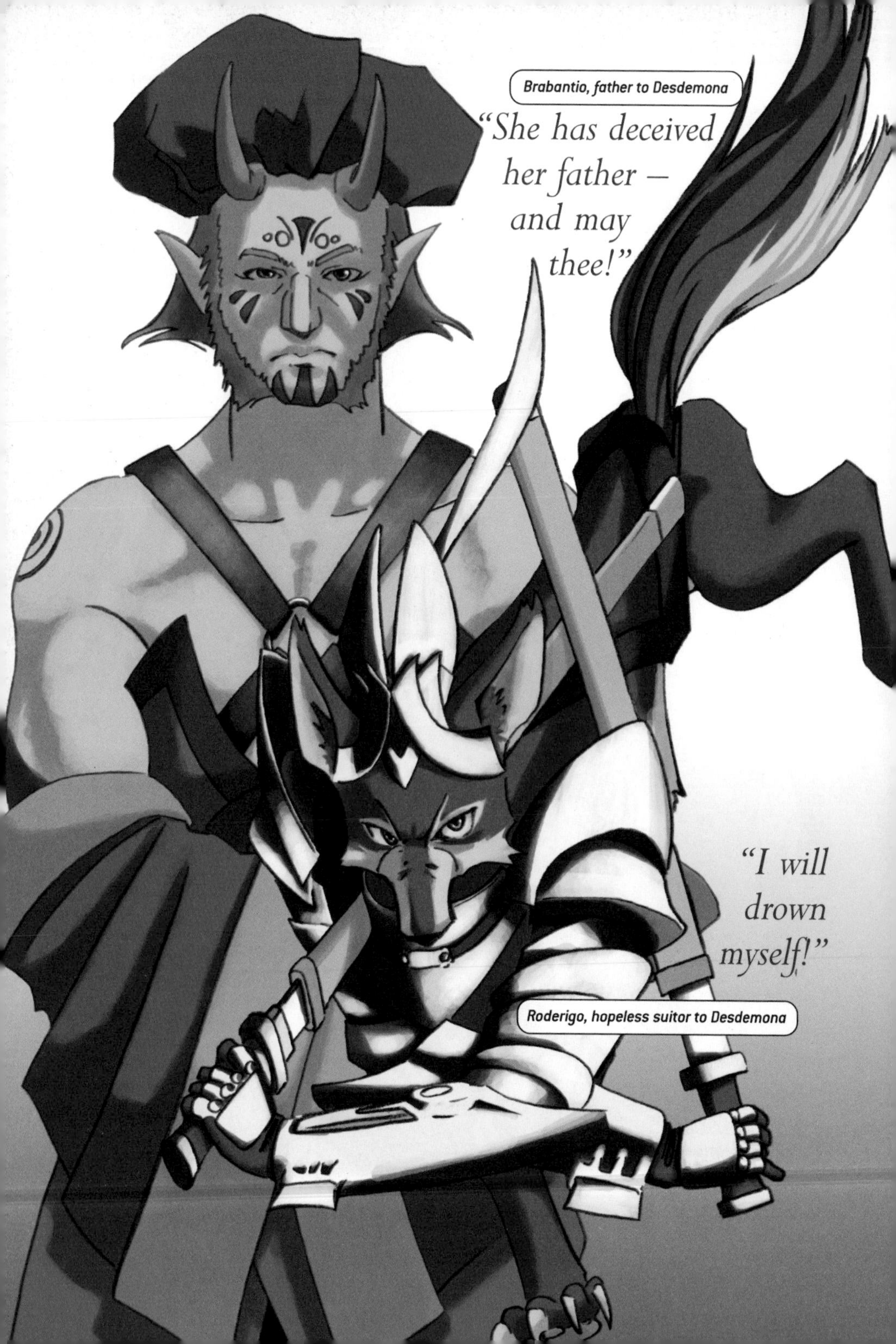
Brabantio, father to Desdemona
"She has deceived her father – and may thee!"
"I will drown myself!"
Roderigo, hopeless suitor to Desdemona

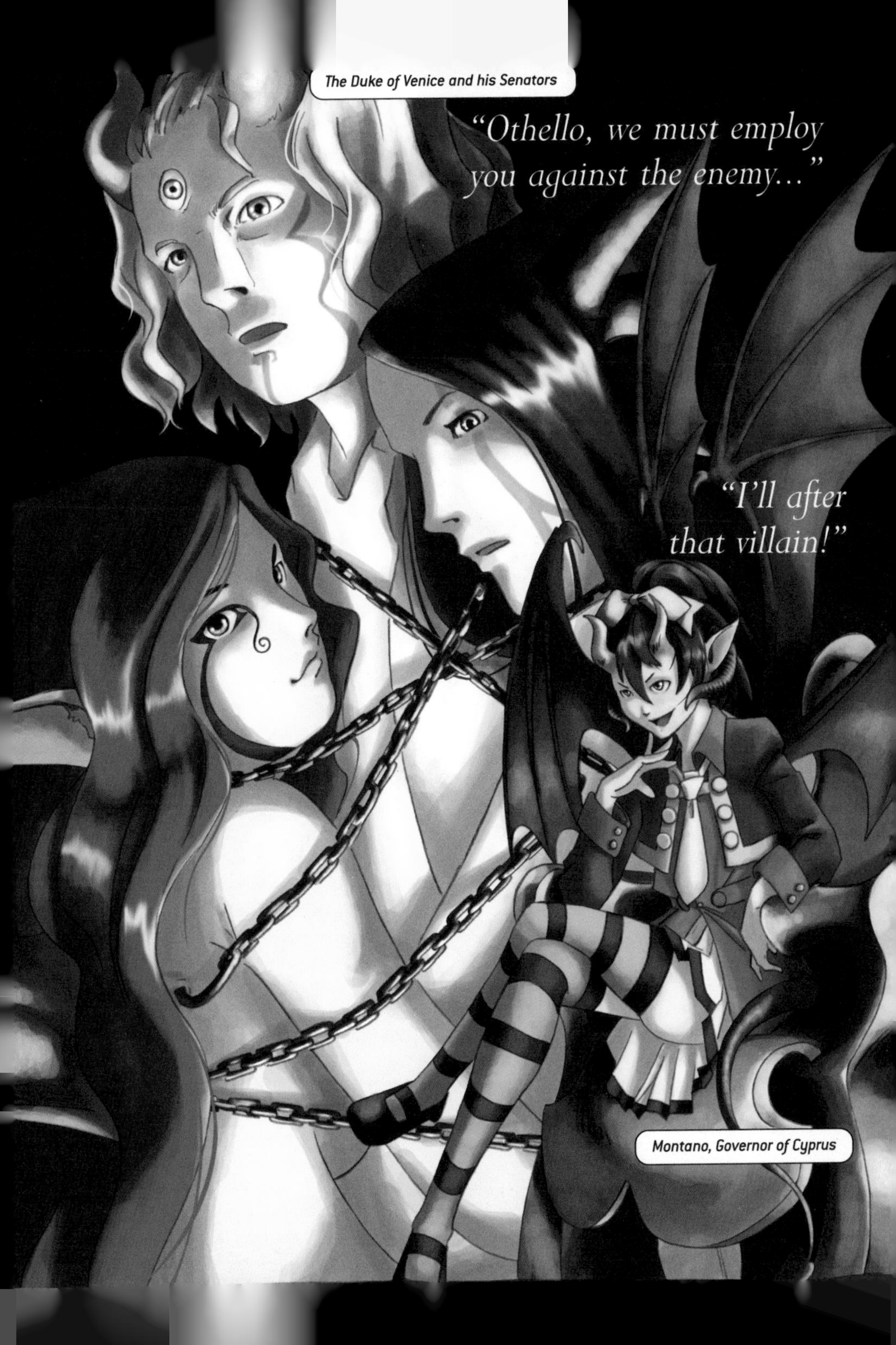
The Duke of Venice and his Senators
"Othello, we must employ you against the enemy..."
"I'll after that villain!"
Montano, Governor of Cyprus

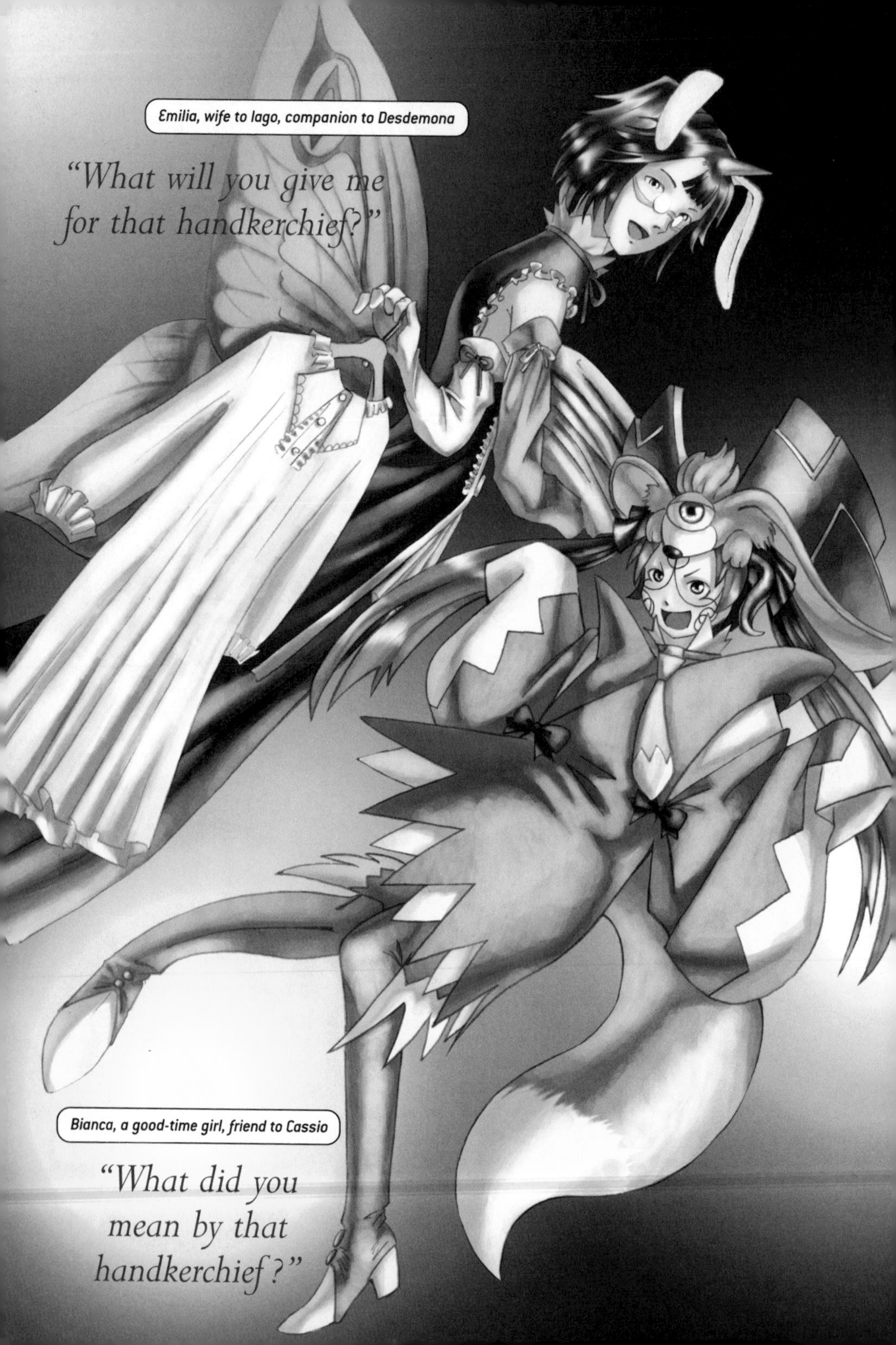
Emilia, wife to Iago, companion to Desdemona
"What will you give me for that handkerchief?"
Bianca, a good-time girl, friend to Cassio
"What did you mean by that handkerchief?"

Gratiano, a nobleman of Venice
"Poor Desdemona!"
Lodovico, a messenger from Venice
"This would not be believed!"

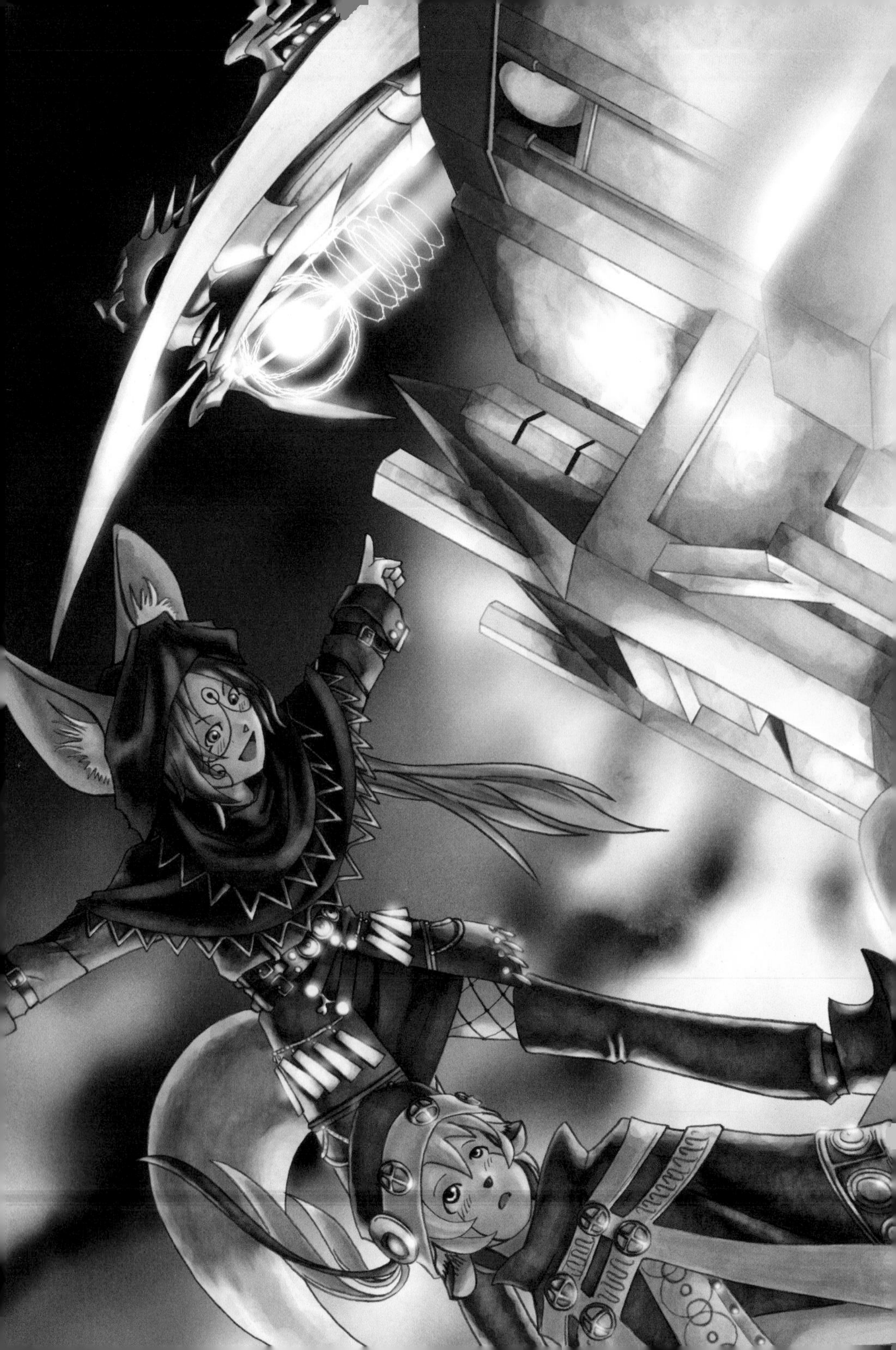

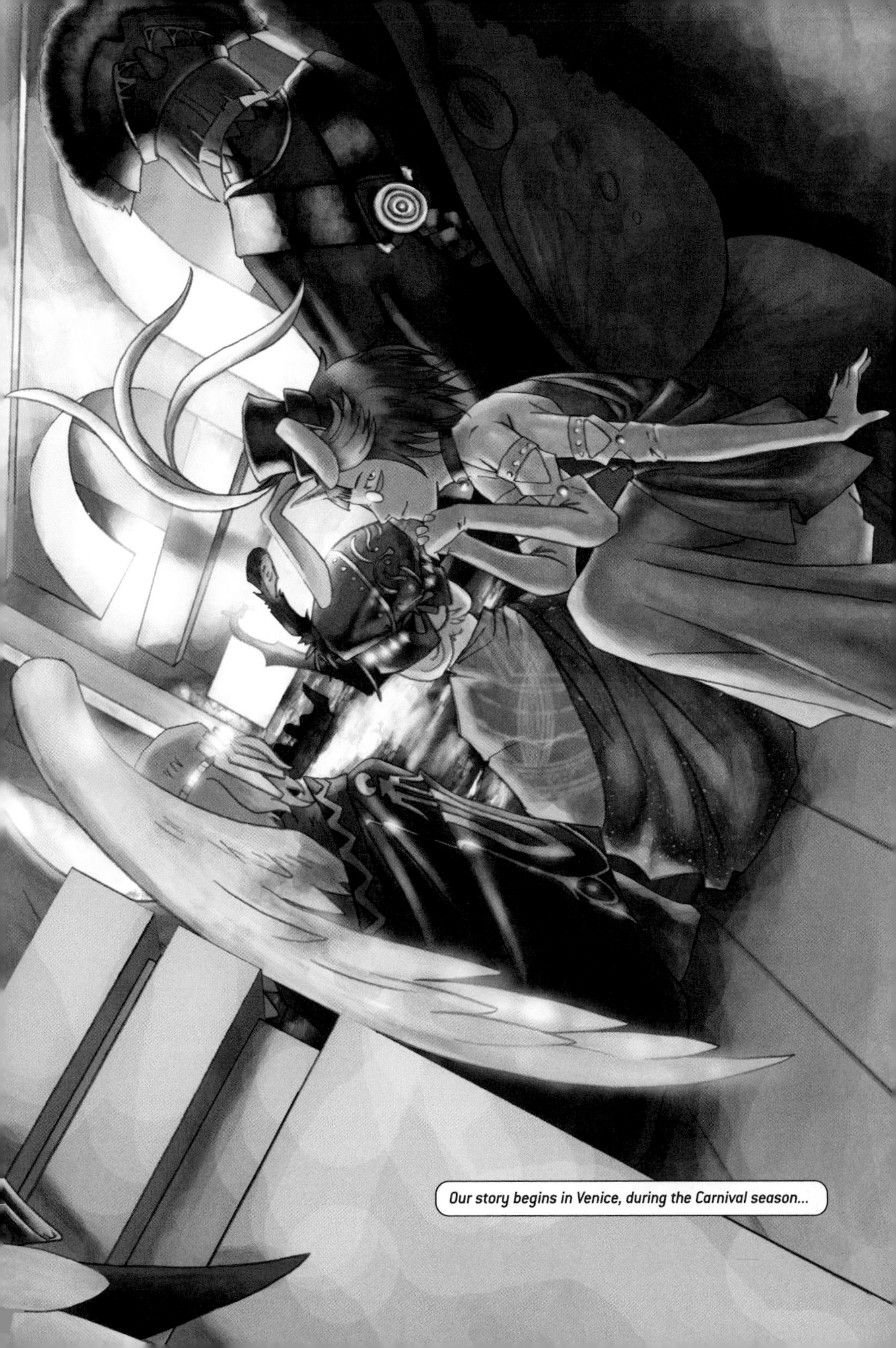
Our story begins in Venice, during the Carnival season...

VENICE AT NIGHT.
IAGO EXPLAINS TO RODERIGO HIS
GRIEVANCE AGAINST OTHELLO...

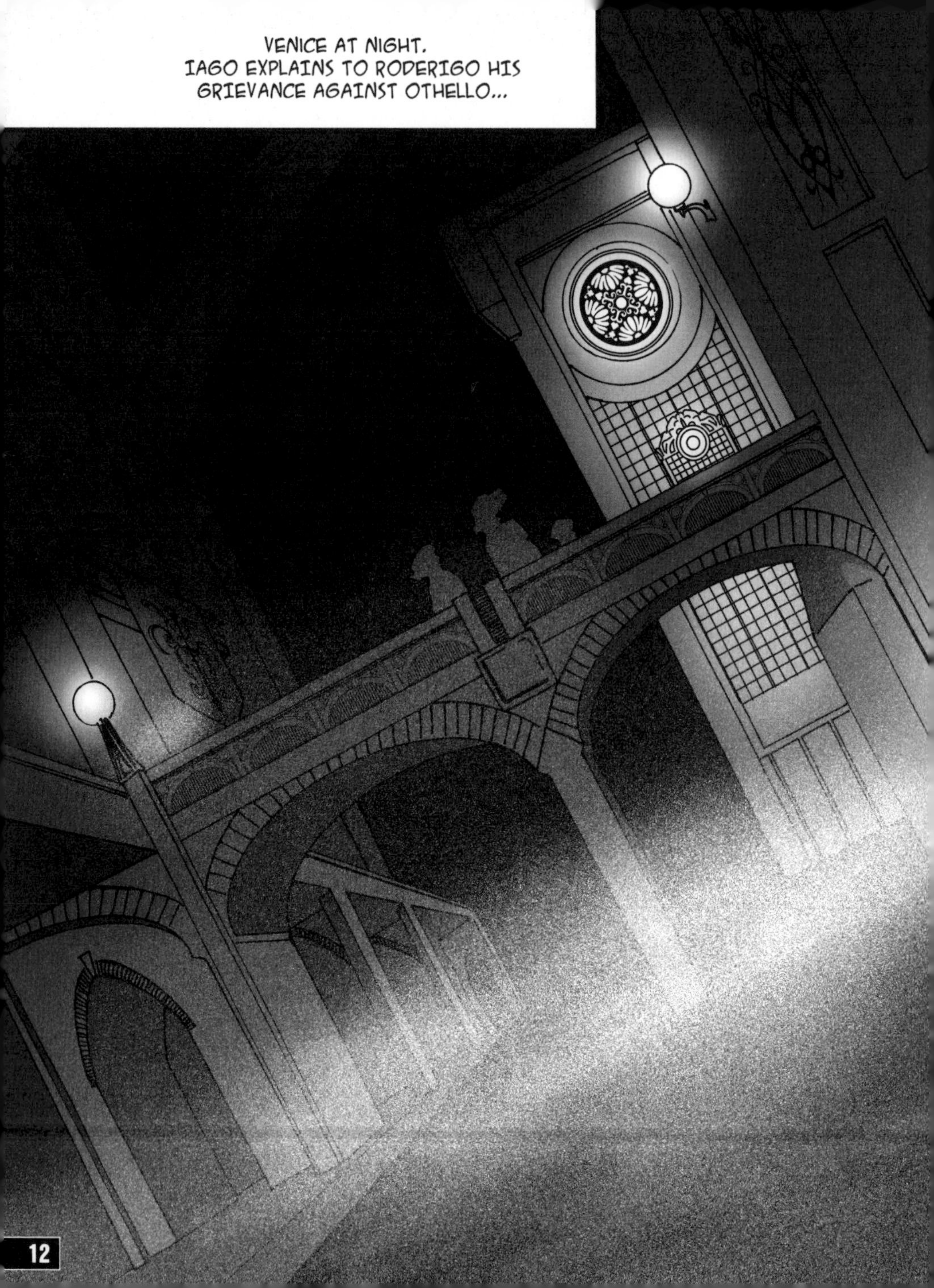

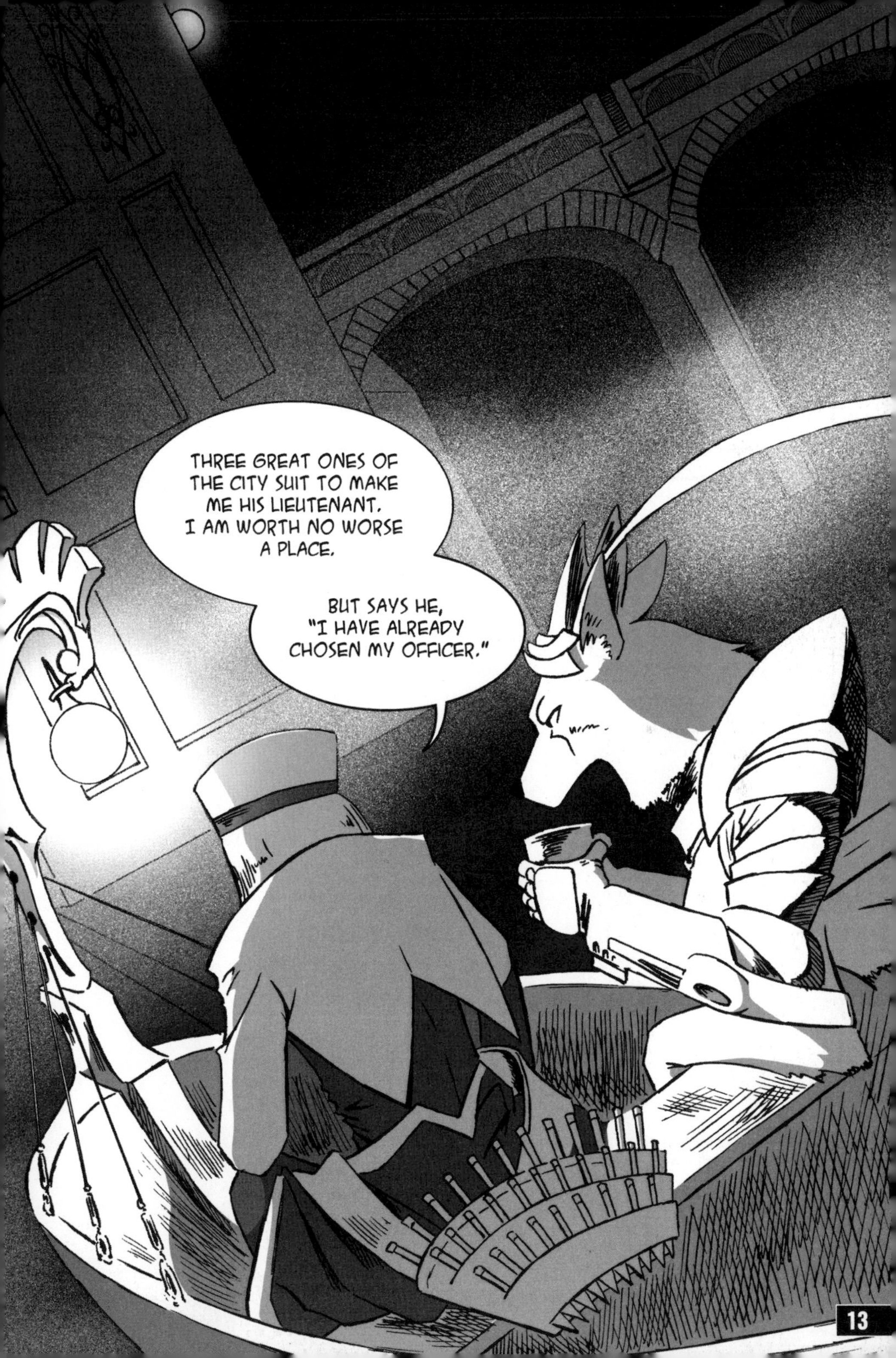
THREE GREAT ONES OF THE CITY SUIT TO MAKE ME HIS LIEUTENANT. I AM WORTH NO WORSE A PLACE.
BUT SAYS HE, "I HAVE ALREADY CHOSEN MY OFFICER."

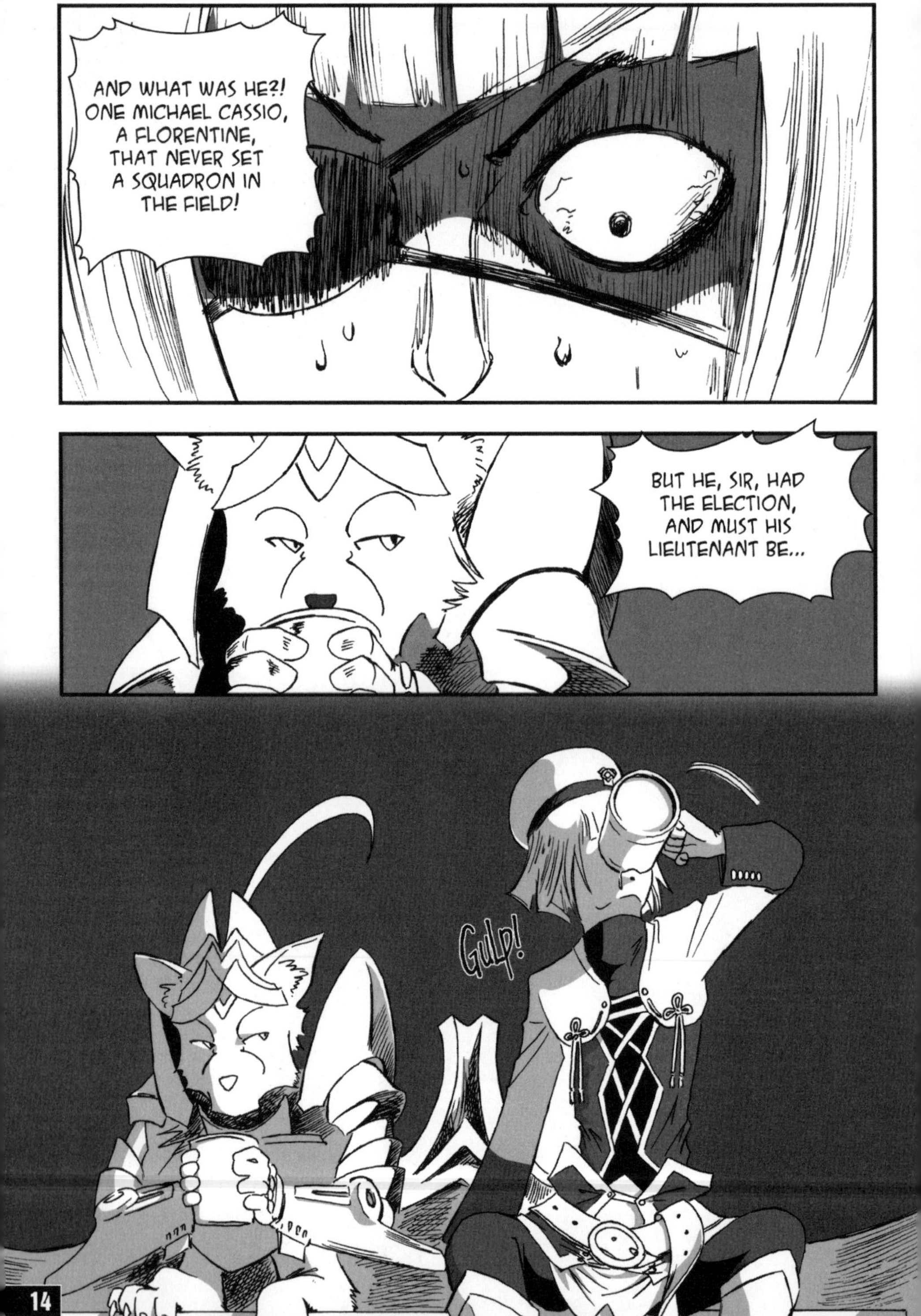
AND WHAT WAS HE?! ONE MICHAEL CASSIO, A FLORENTINE, THAT NEVER SET A SQUADRON IN THE FIELD!
BUT HE, SIR, HAD THE ELECTION, AND MUST HIS LIEUTENANT BE...
GULP!

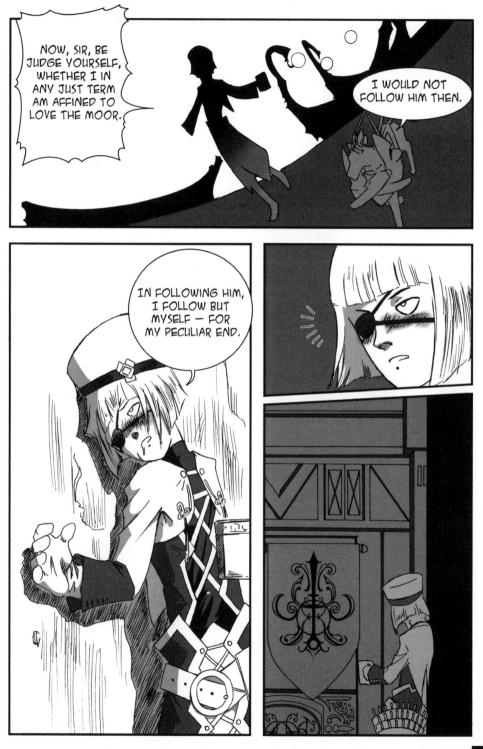

NOW, SIR, BE JUDGE YOURSELF, WHETHER I IN ANY JUST TERM AM AFFINED TO LOVE THE MOOR.

I WOULD NOT FOLLOW HIM THEN.

IN FOLLOWING HIM, I FOLLOW BUT MYSELF — FOR MY PECULIAR END.

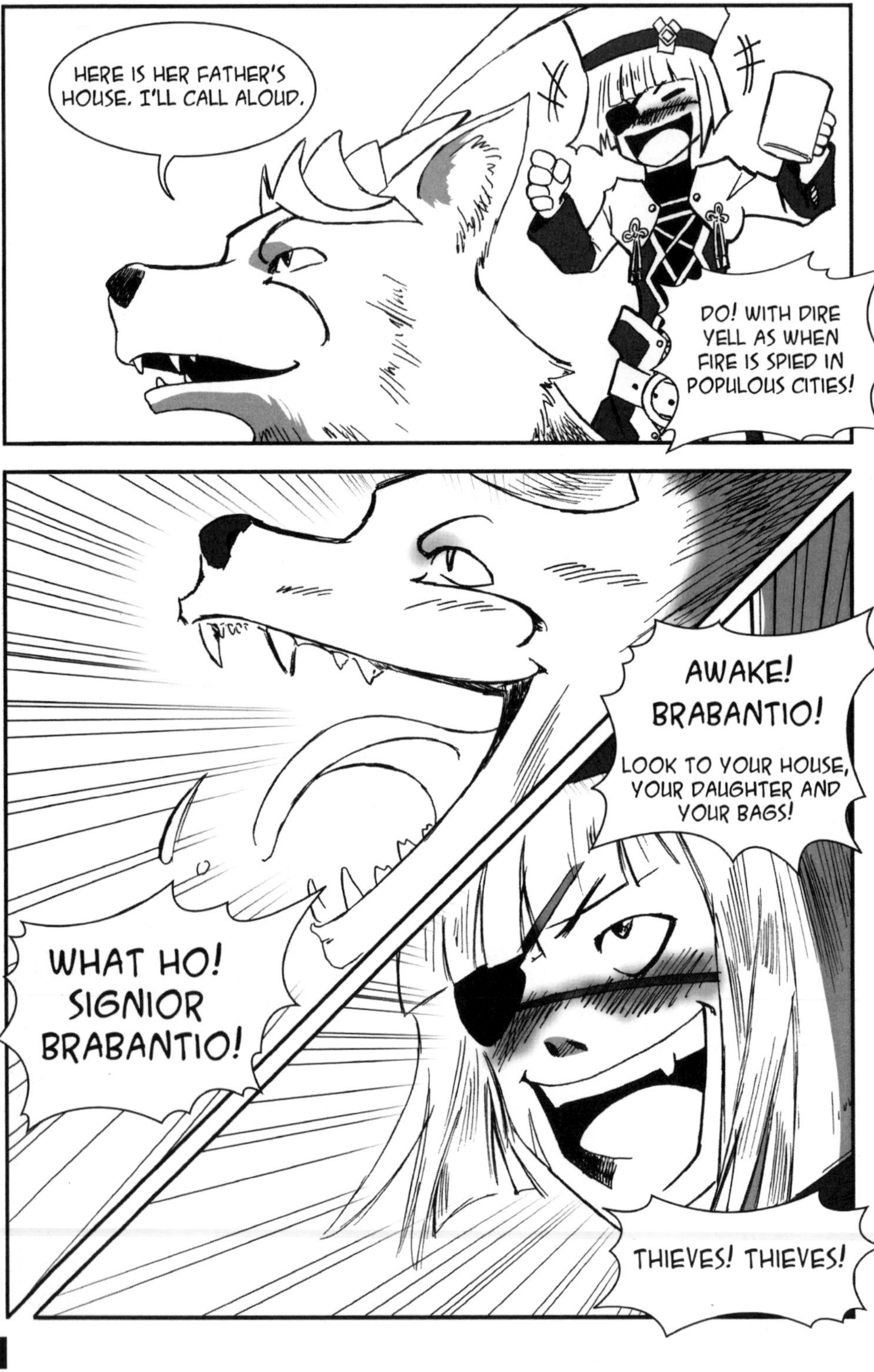
HERE IS HER FATHER'S HOUSE. I'LL CALL ALOUD.
DO! WITH DIRE YELL AS WHEN FIRE IS SPIED IN POPULOUS CITIES!
WHAT HO! SIGNIOR BRABANTIO!
AWAKE! BRABANTIO!
LOOK TO YOUR HOUSE, YOUR DAUGHTER AND YOUR BAGS!
THIEVES! THIEVES!

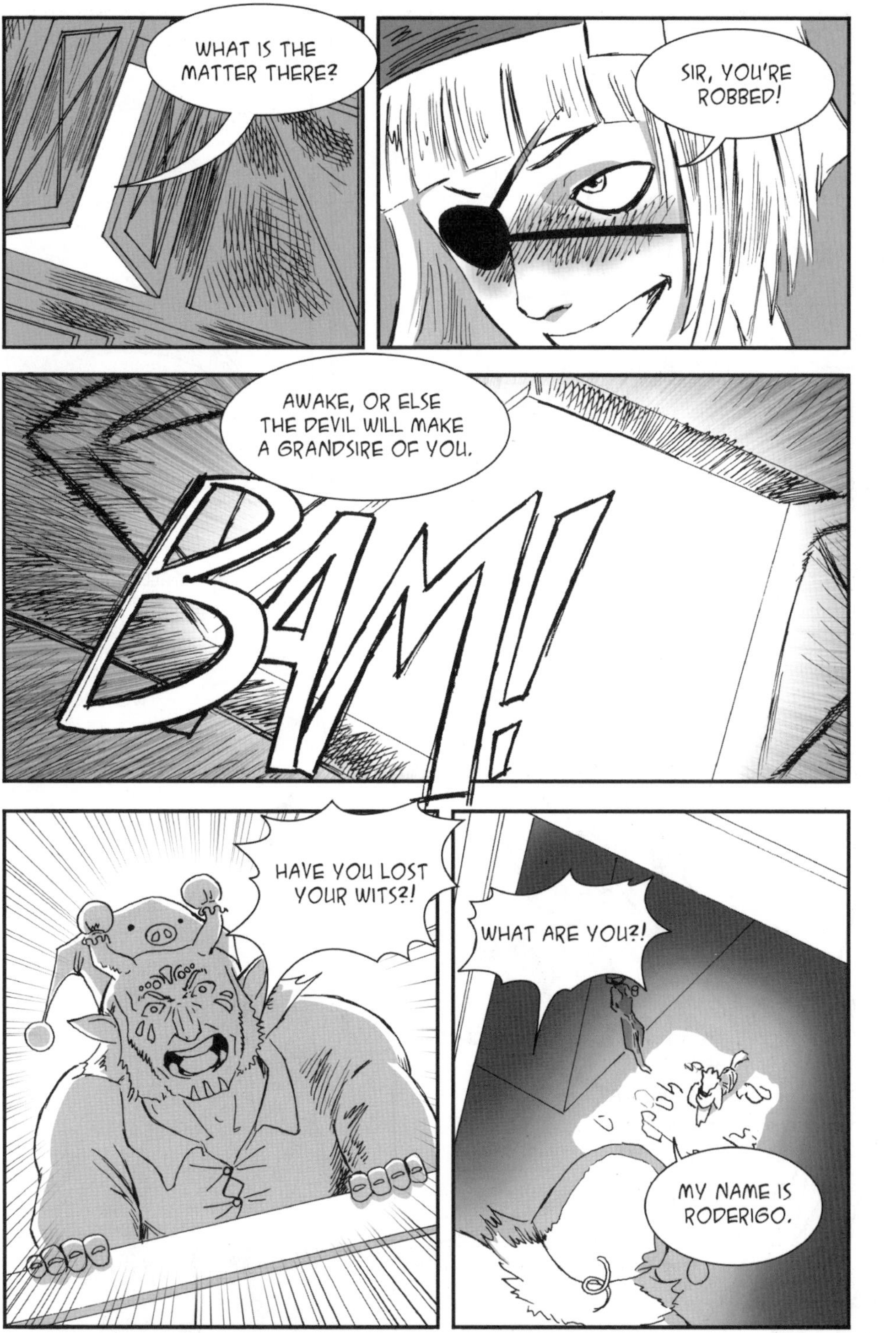
WHAT IS THE MATTER THERE?
SIR, YOU'RE ROBBED!
AWAKE, OR ELSE THE DEVIL WILL MAKE A GRANDSIRE OF YOU.
BAM!
HAVE YOU LOST YOUR WITS?!
WHAT ARE YOU?!
MY NAME IS RODERIGO.

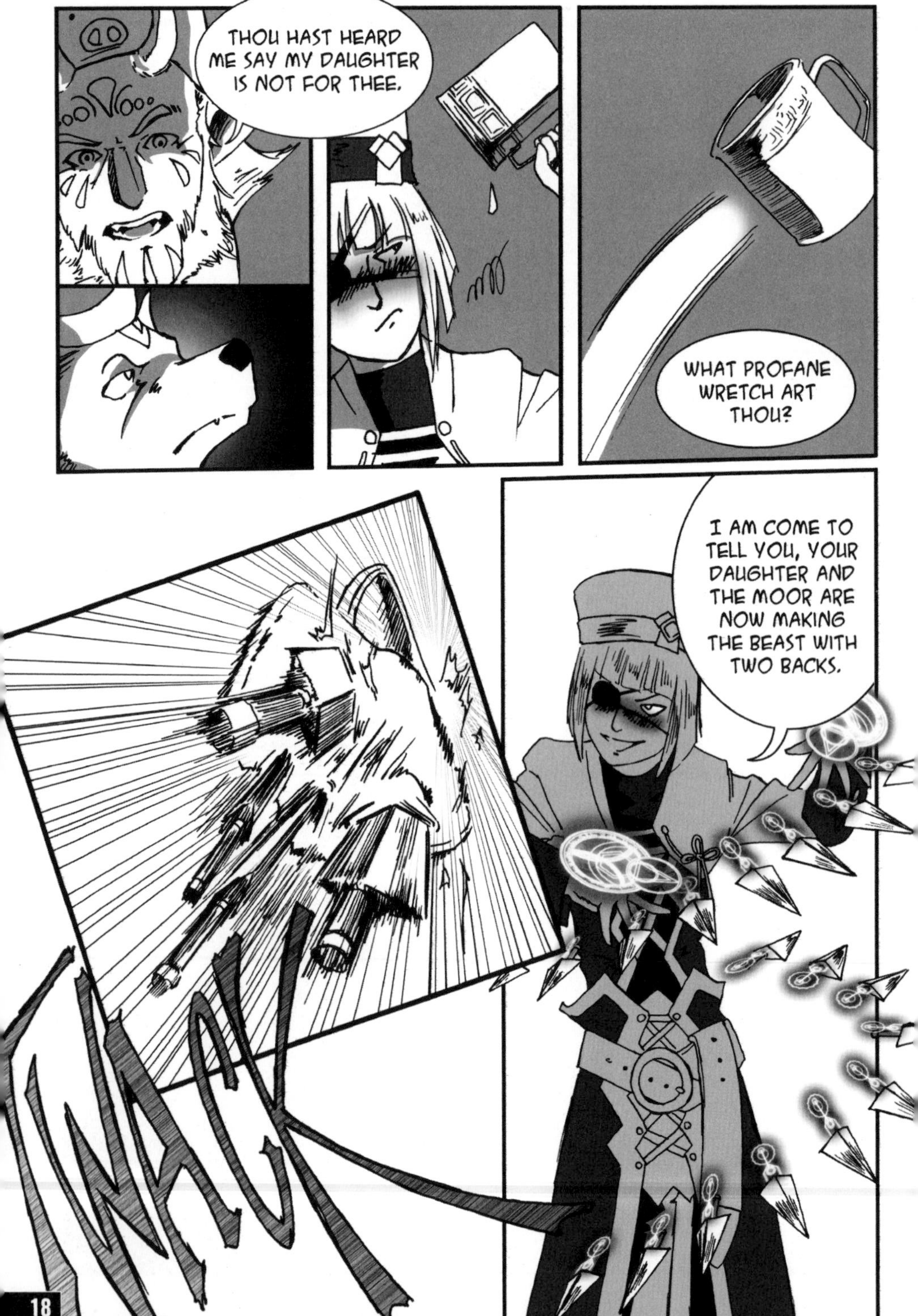
THOU HAST HEARD ME SAY MY DAUGHTER IS NOT FOR THEE.
WHAT PROFANE WRETCH ART THOU?
I AM COME TO TELL YOU, YOUR DAUGHTER AND THE MOOR ARE NOW MAKING THE BEAST WITH TWO BACKS.
WACK

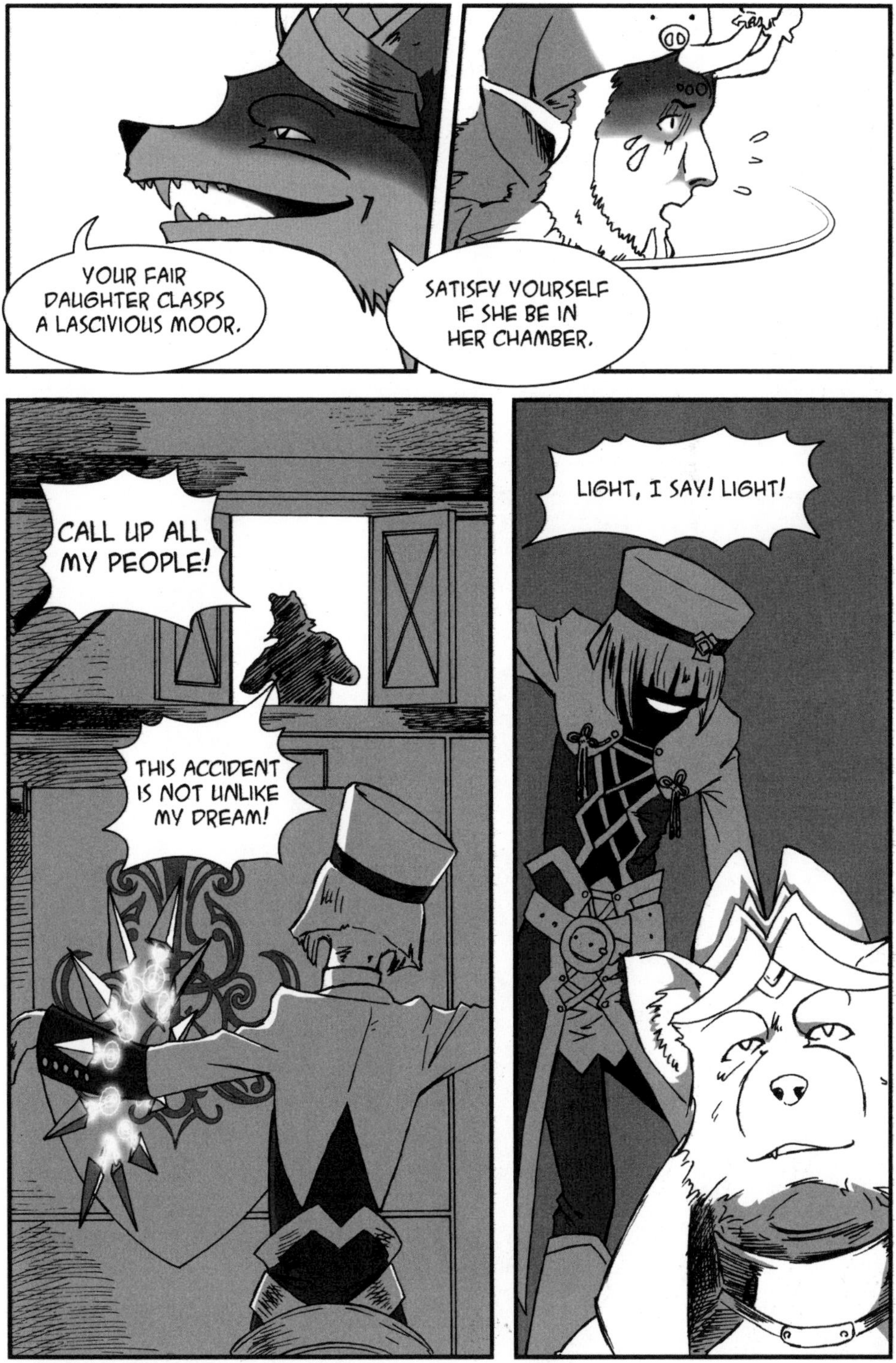
YOUR FAIR DAUGHTER CLASPS A LASCIVIOUS MOOR.
SATISFY YOURSELF IF SHE BE IN HER CHAMBER.
CALL UP ALL MY PEOPLE!
THIS ACCIDENT IS NOT UNLIKE MY DREAM!
LIGHT, I SAY! LIGHT!

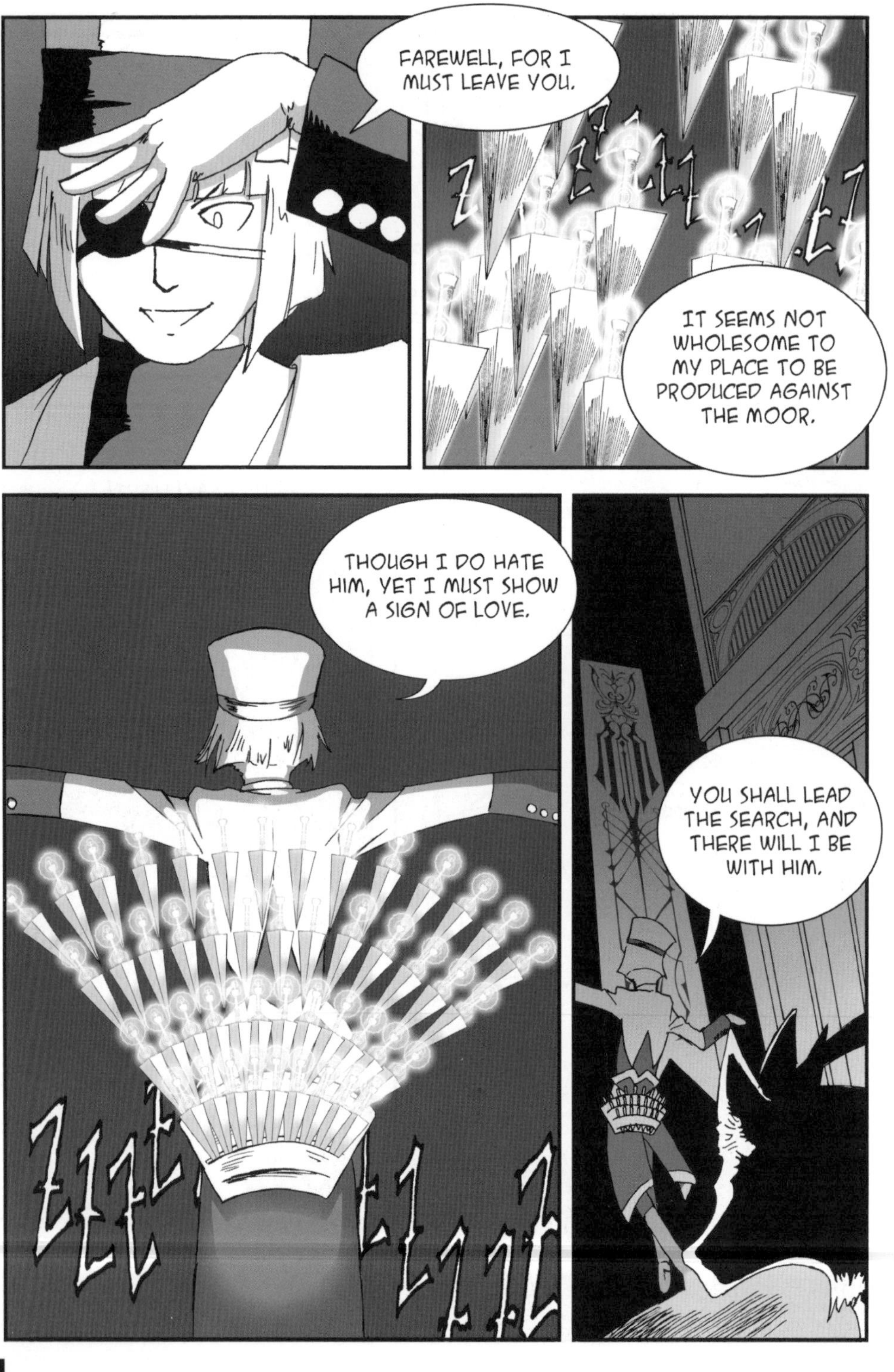
FAREWELL, FOR I MUST LEAVE YOU.
IT SEEMS NOT WHOLESOME TO MY PLACE TO BE PRODUCED AGAINST THE MOOR.
THOUGH I DO HATE HIM, YET I MUST SHOW A SIGN OF LOVE.
YOU SHALL LEAD THE SEARCH, AND THERE WILL I BE WITH HIM.

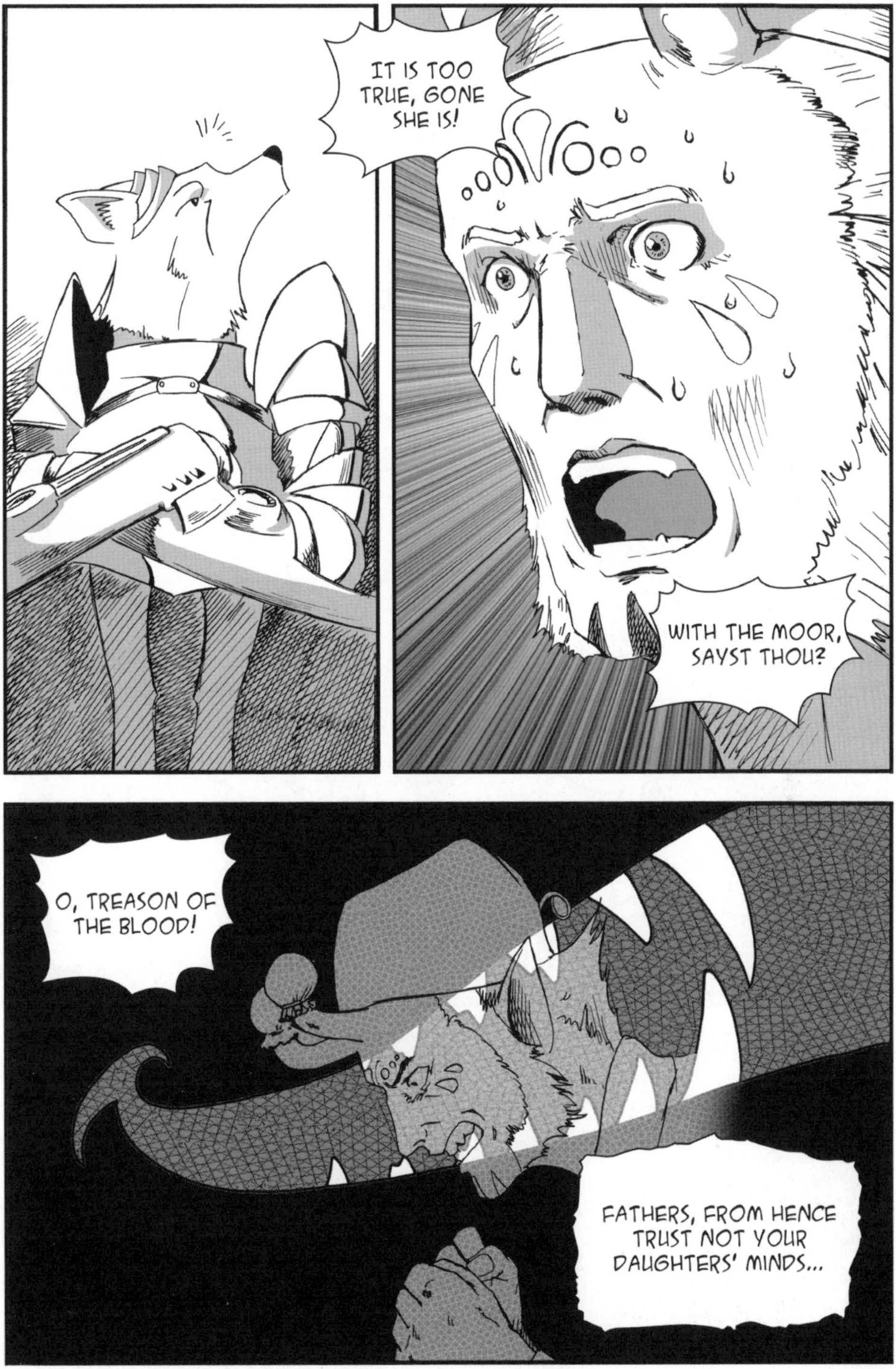
IT IS TOO TRUE, GONE SHE IS!
WITH THE MOOR, SAYST THOU?
O, TREASON OF THE BLOOD!
FATHERS, FROM HENCE TRUST NOT YOUR DAUGHTERS' MINDS...

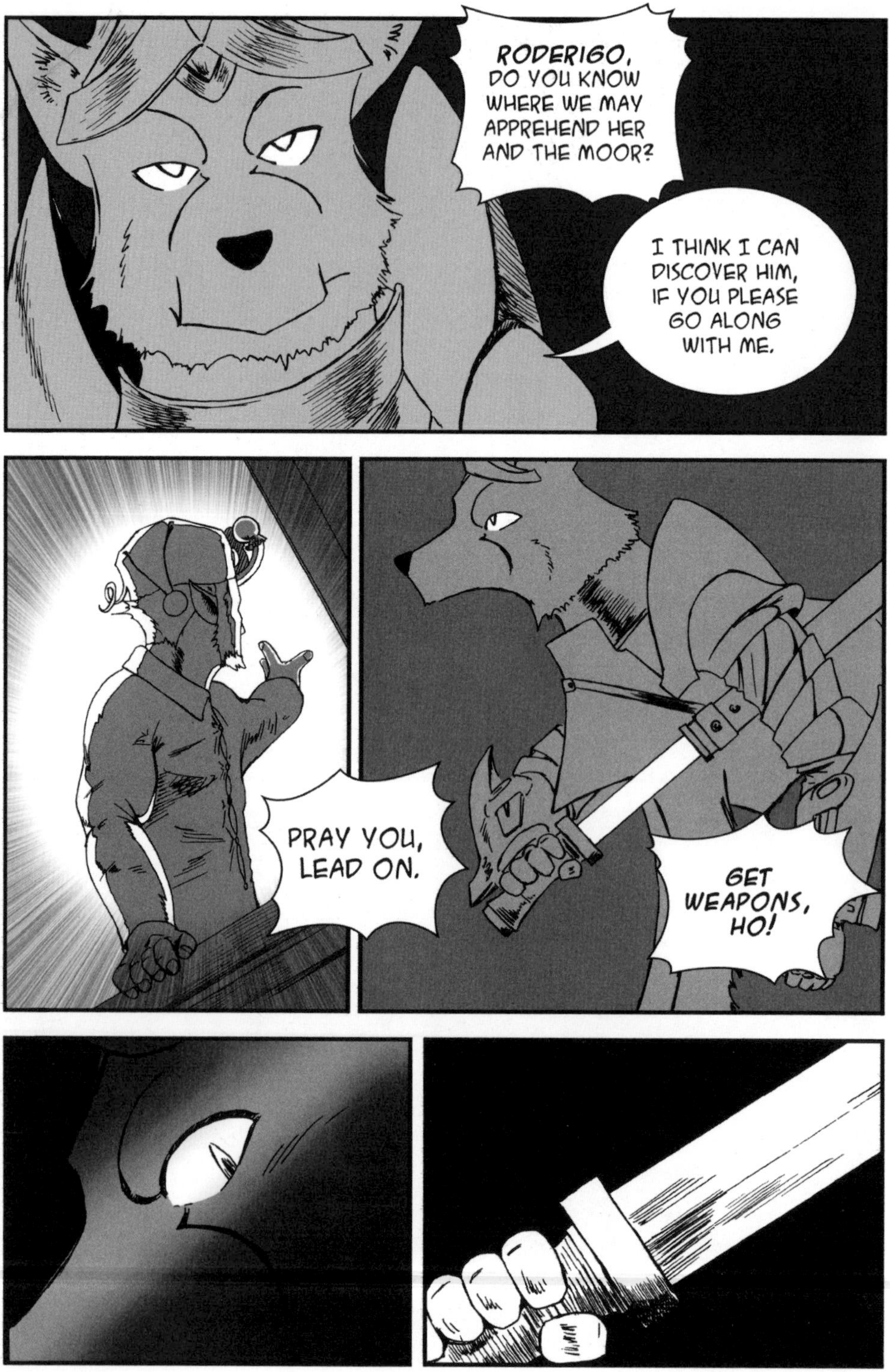
RODERIGO, DO YOU KNOW WHERE WE MAY APPREHEND HER AND THE MOOR?
I THINK I CAN DISCOVER HIM, IF YOU PLEASE GO ALONG WITH ME.
PRAY YOU, LEAD ON.
GET WEAPONS, HO!

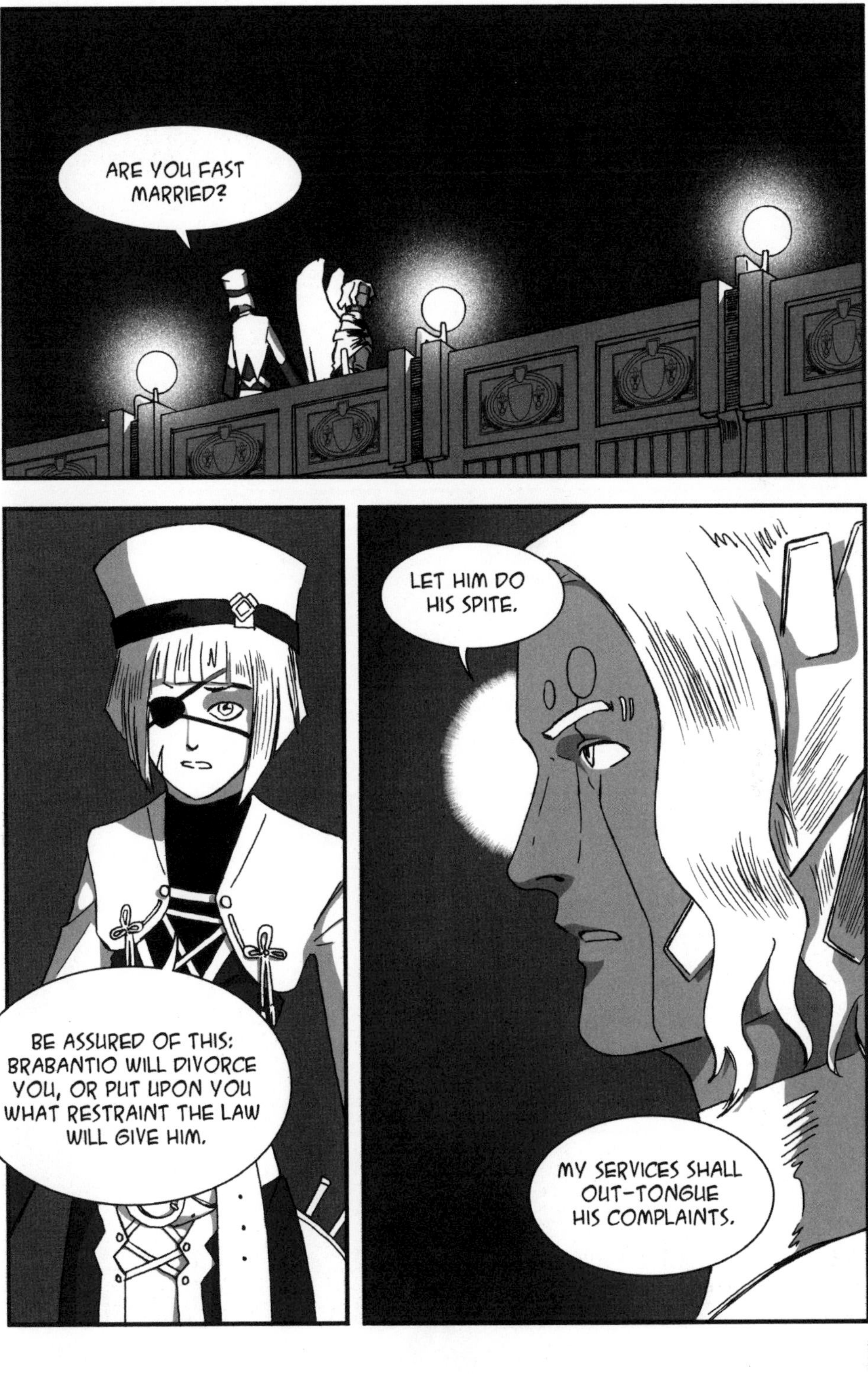
ARE YOU FAST MARRIED?
BE ASSURED OF THIS: BRABANTIO WILL DIVORCE YOU, OR PUT UPON YOU WHAT RESTRAINT THE LAW WILL GIVE HIM.
LET HIM DO HIS SPITE.
MY SERVICES SHALL OUT-TONGUE HIS COMPLAINTS.

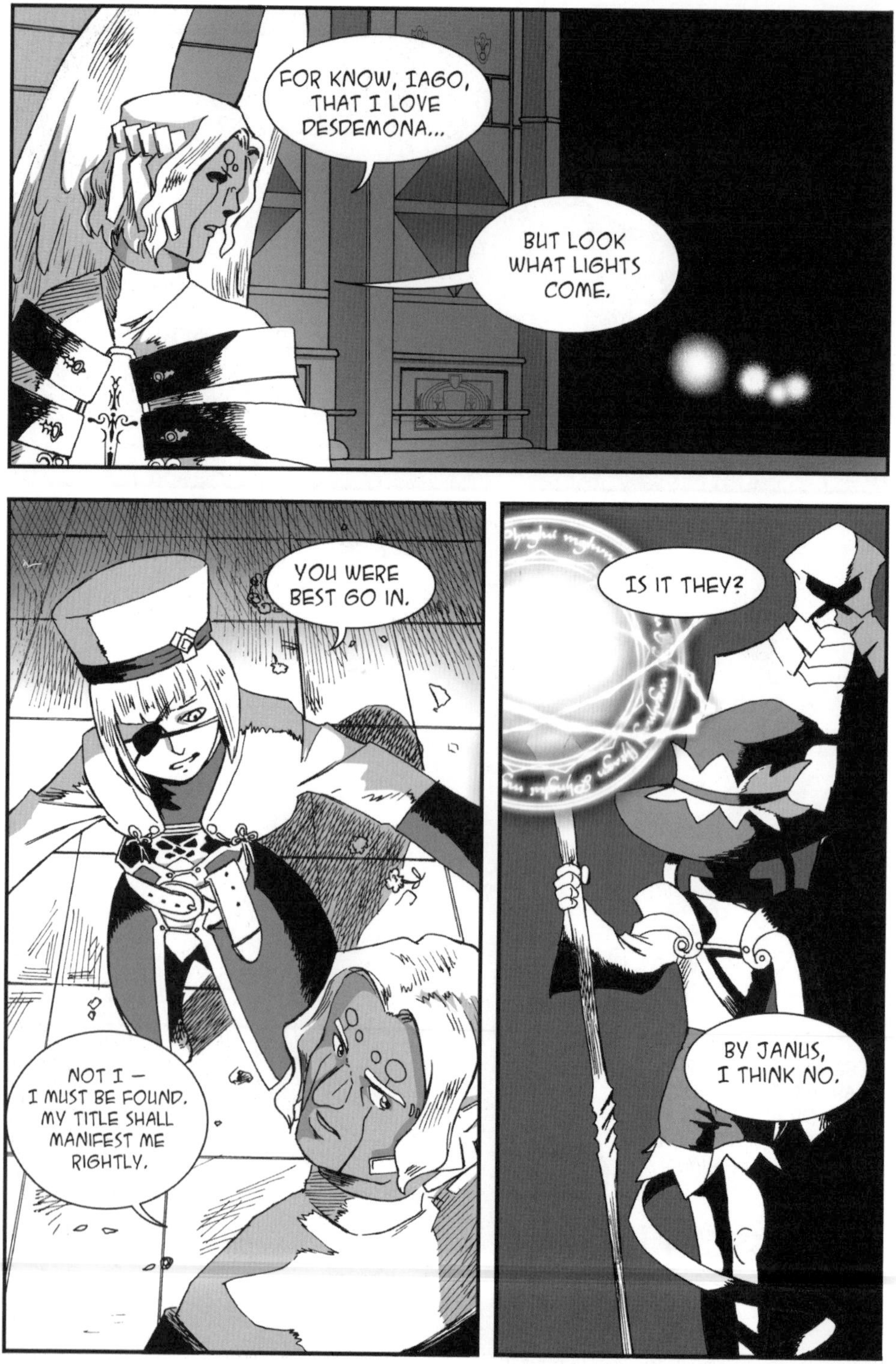
FOR KNOW, IAGO, THAT I LOVE DESDEMONA...
BUT LOOK WHAT LIGHTS COME.
YOU WERE BEST GO IN.
NOT I — I MUST BE FOUND. MY TITLE SHALL MANIFEST ME RIGHTLY.
IS IT THEY?
BY JANUS, I THINK NO.

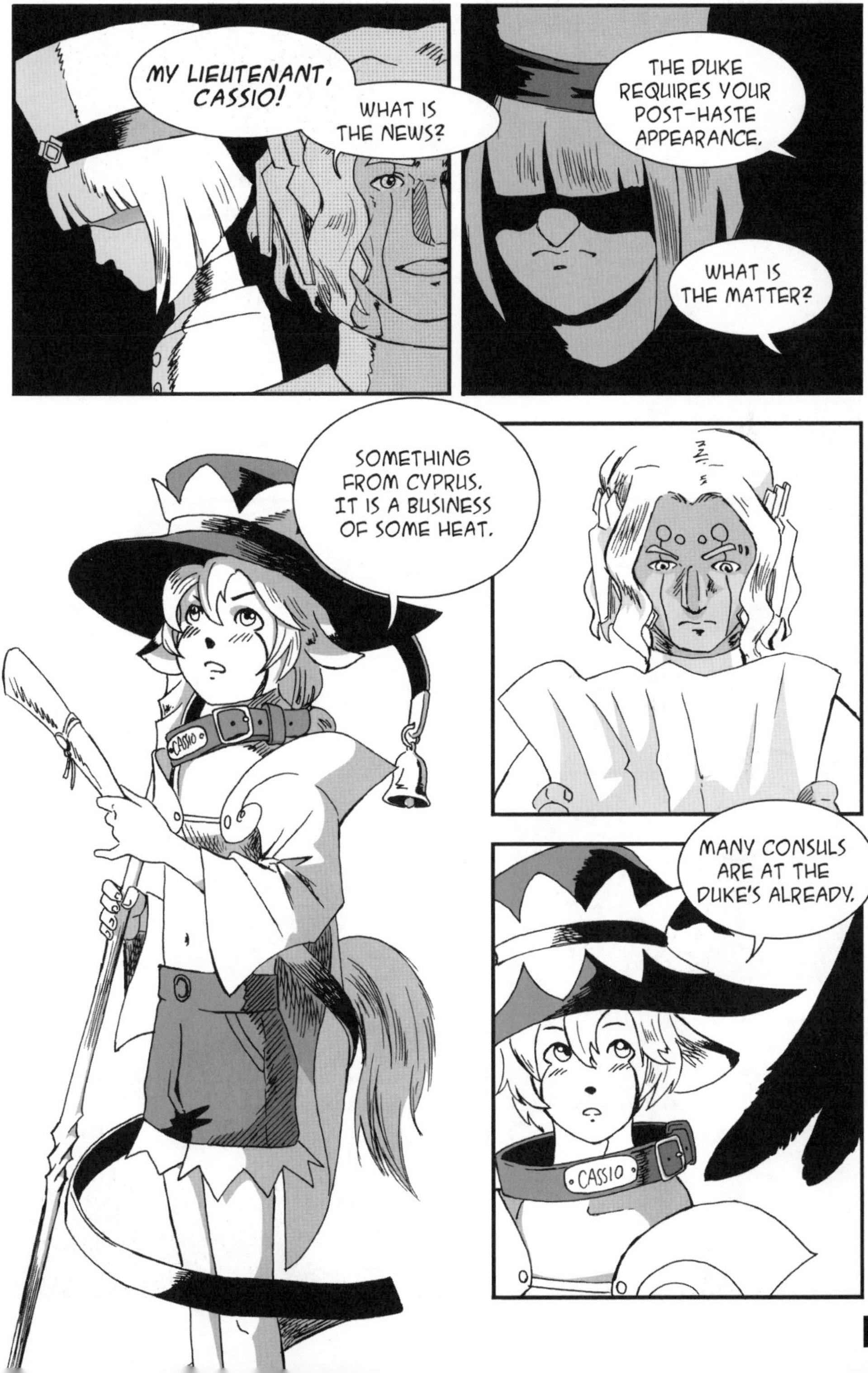
MY LIEUTENANT, CASSIO!
WHAT IS THE NEWS?
THE DUKE REQUIRES YOUR POST-HASTE APPEARANCE.
WHAT IS THE MATTER?
SOMETHING FROM CYPRUS. IT IS A BUSINESS OF SOME HEAT.
CASSIO
MANY CONSULS ARE AT THE DUKE'S ALREADY.
CASSIO

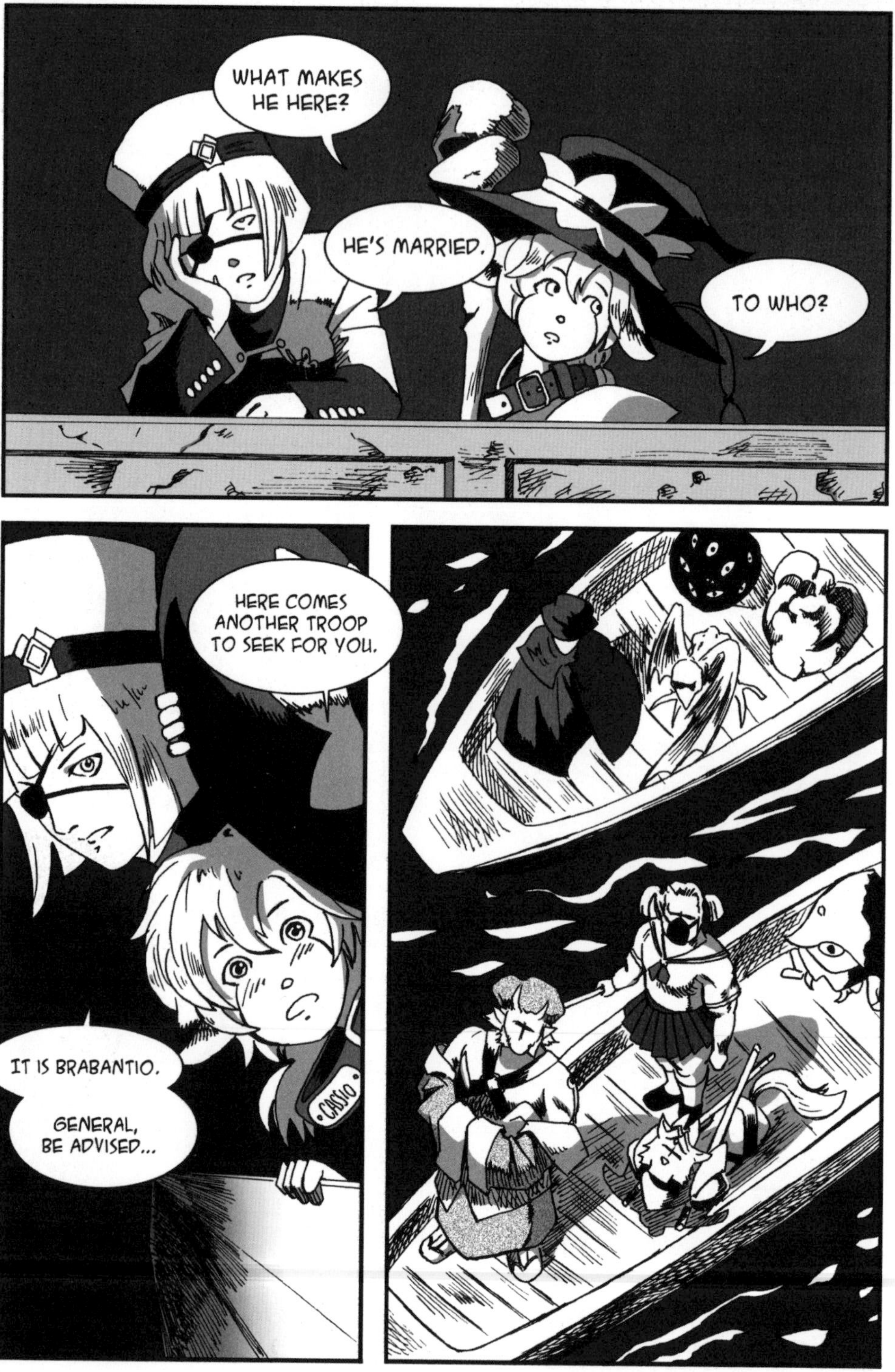
WHAT MAKES HE HERE?
HE'S MARRIED.
TO WHO?
HERE COMES ANOTHER TROOP TO SEEK FOR YOU.
IT IS BRABANTIO.
GENERAL, BE ADVISED...
CASSIO

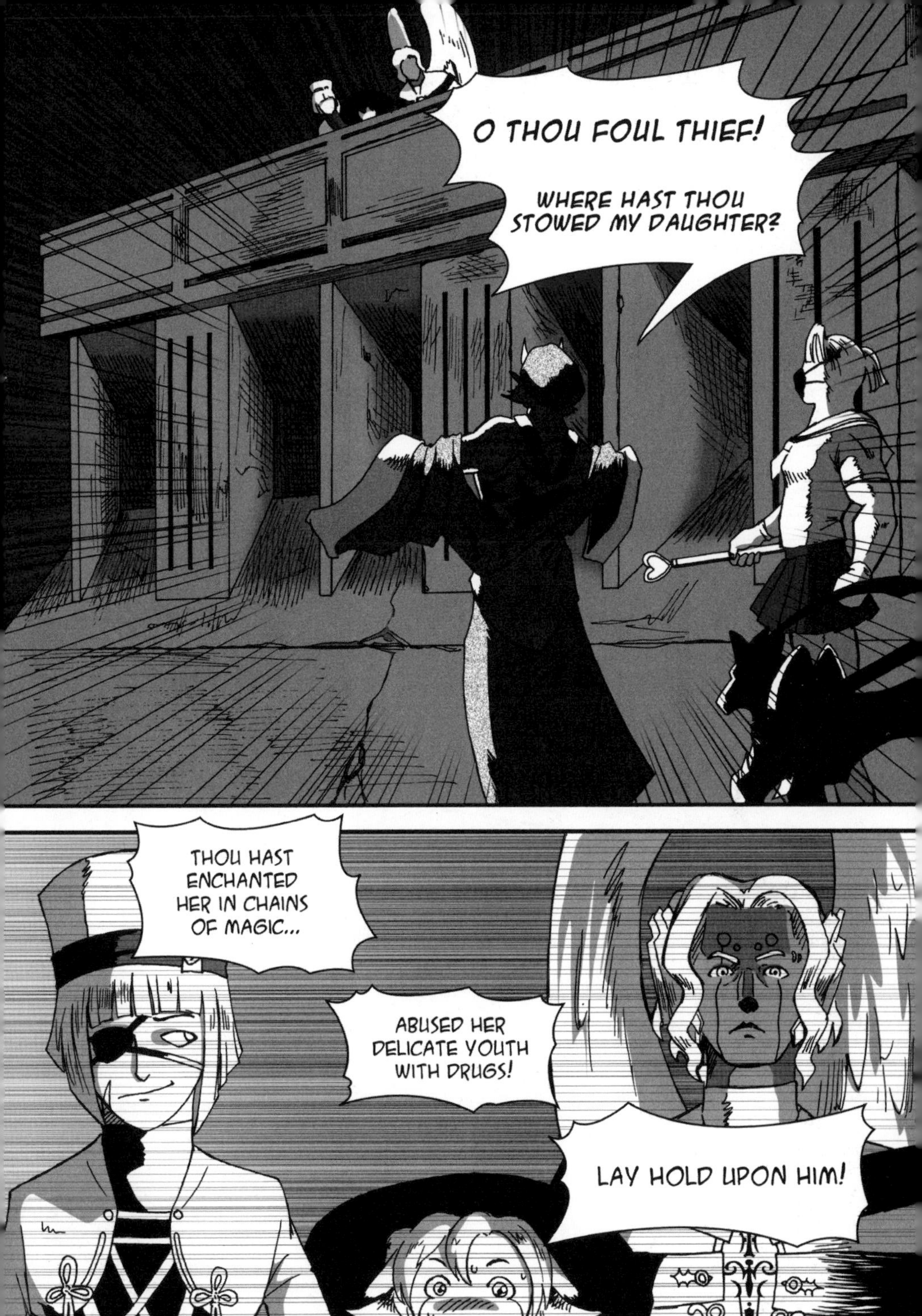
O THOU FOUL THIEF!
WHERE HAST THOU STOWED MY DAUGHTER?
THOU HAST ENCHANTED HER IN CHAINS OF MAGIC...
ABUSED HER DELICATE YOUTH WITH DRUGS!
LAY HOLD UPON HIM!

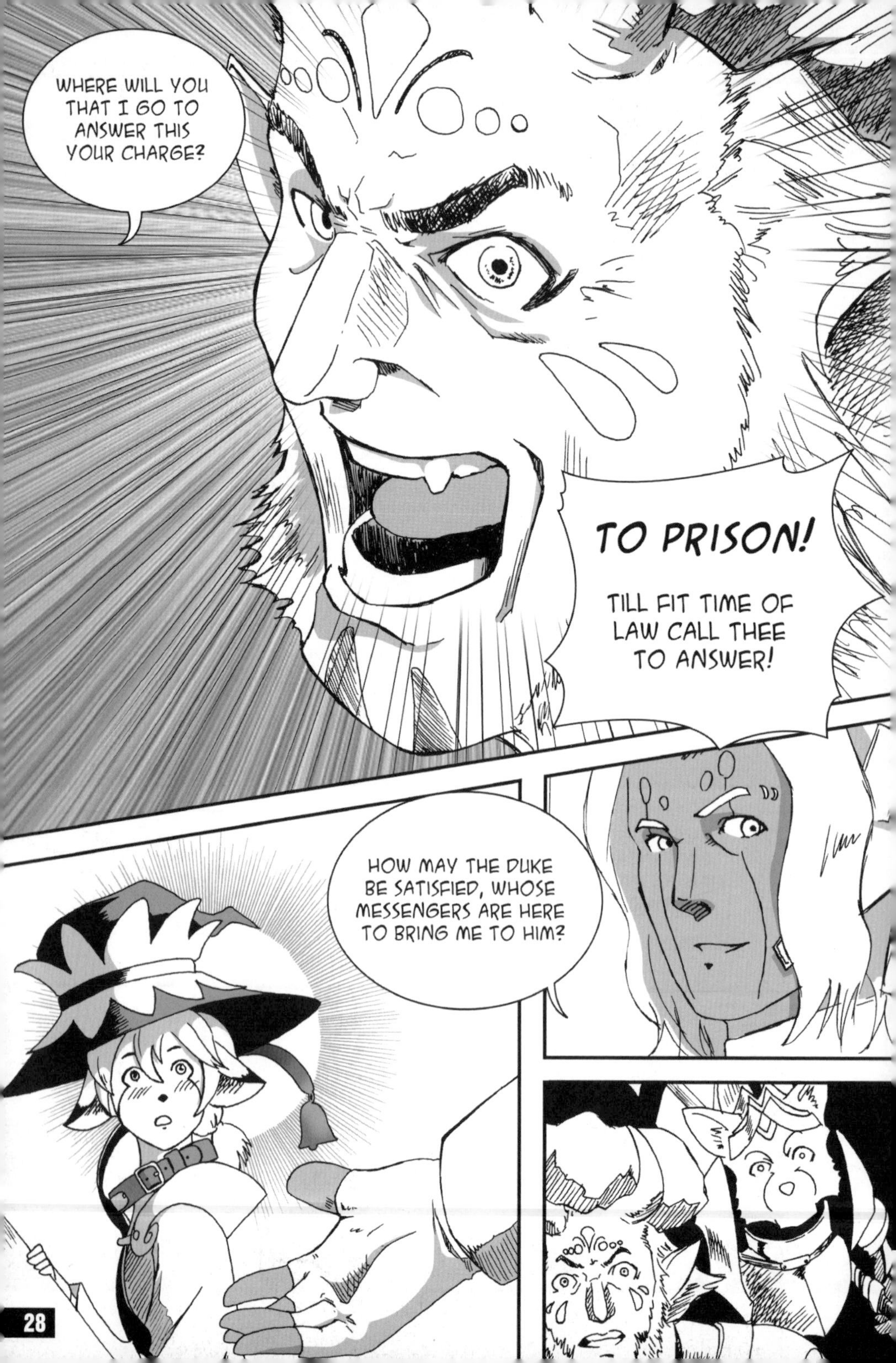
WHERE WILL YOU THAT I GO TO ANSWER THIS YOUR CHARGE?
TO PRISON!
TILL FIT TIME OF LAW CALL THEE TO ANSWER!
HOW MAY THE DUKE BE SATISFIED, WHOSE MESSENGERS ARE HERE TO BRING ME TO HIM?

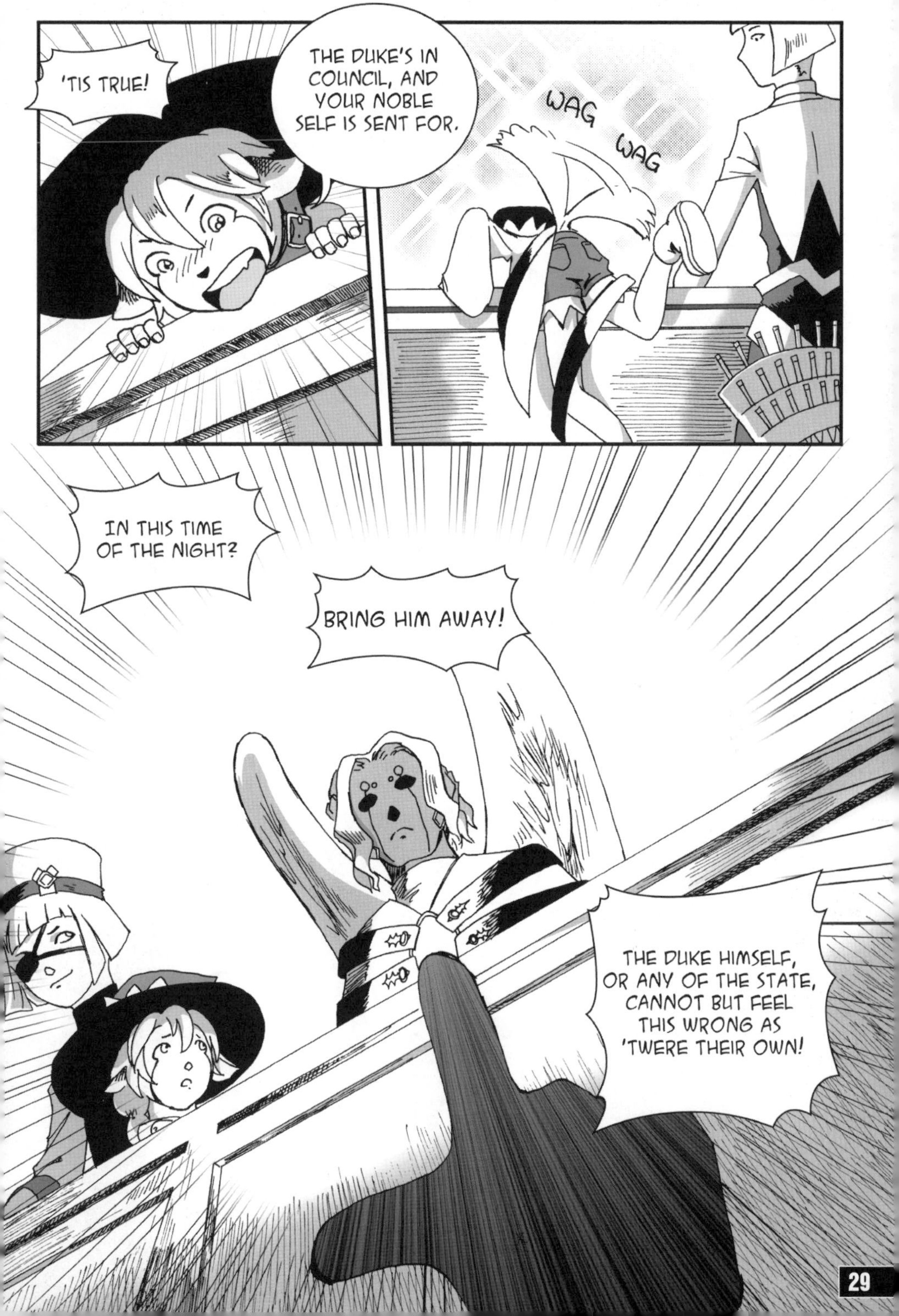
'TIS TRUE!
THE DUKE'S IN COUNCIL, AND YOUR NOBLE SELF IS SENT FOR.
WAG WAG
IN THIS TIME OF THE NIGHT?
BRING HIM AWAY!
THE DUKE HIMSELF, OR ANY OF THE STATE, CANNOT BUT FEEL THIS WRONG AS 'TWERE THEIR OWN!

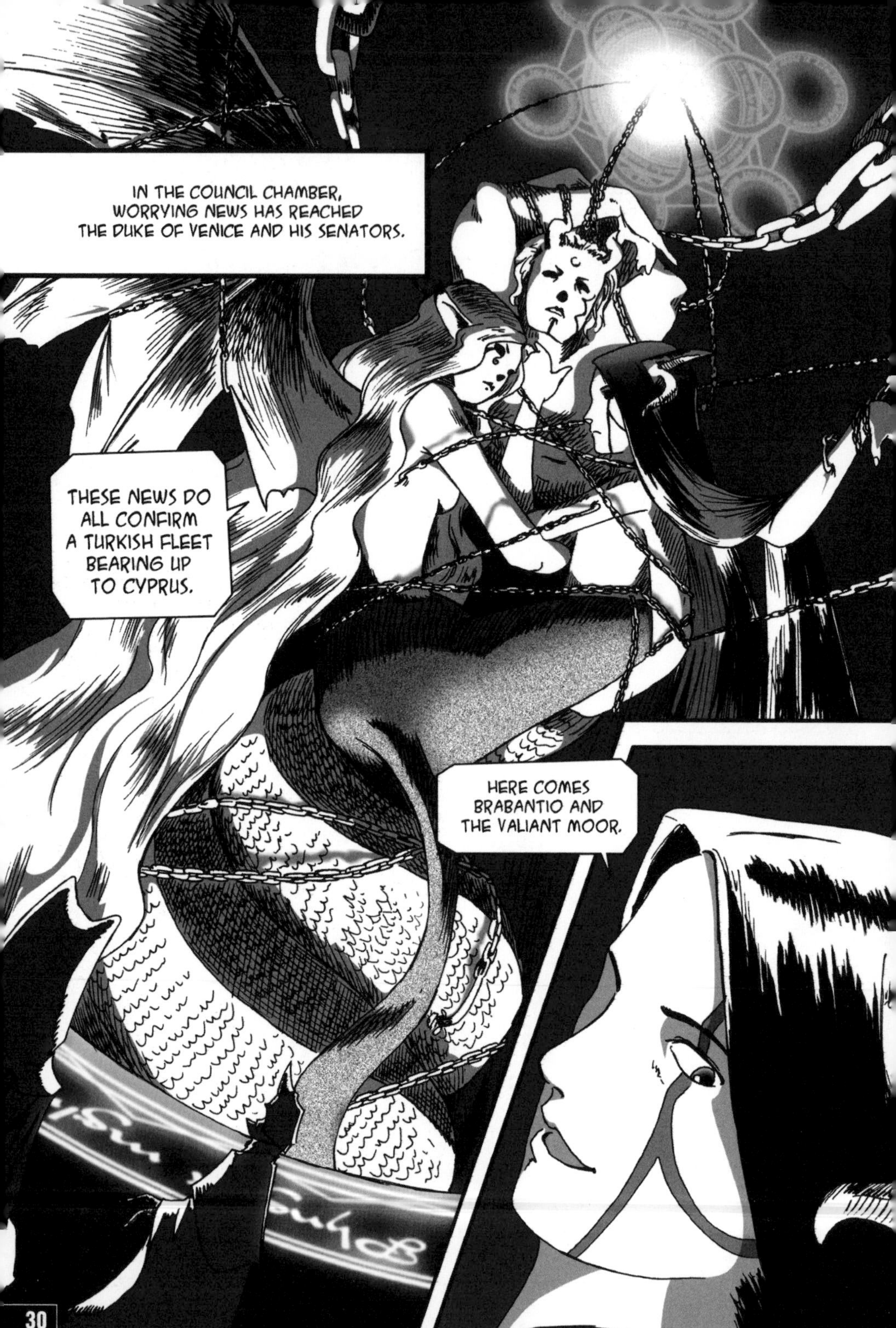
IN THE COUNCIL CHAMBER, WORRYING NEWS HAS REACHED THE DUKE OF VENICE AND HIS SENATORS.
THESE NEWS DO ALL CONFIRM A TURKISH FLEET BEARING UP TO CYPRUS.
HERE COMES BRABANTIO AND THE VALIANT MOOR.

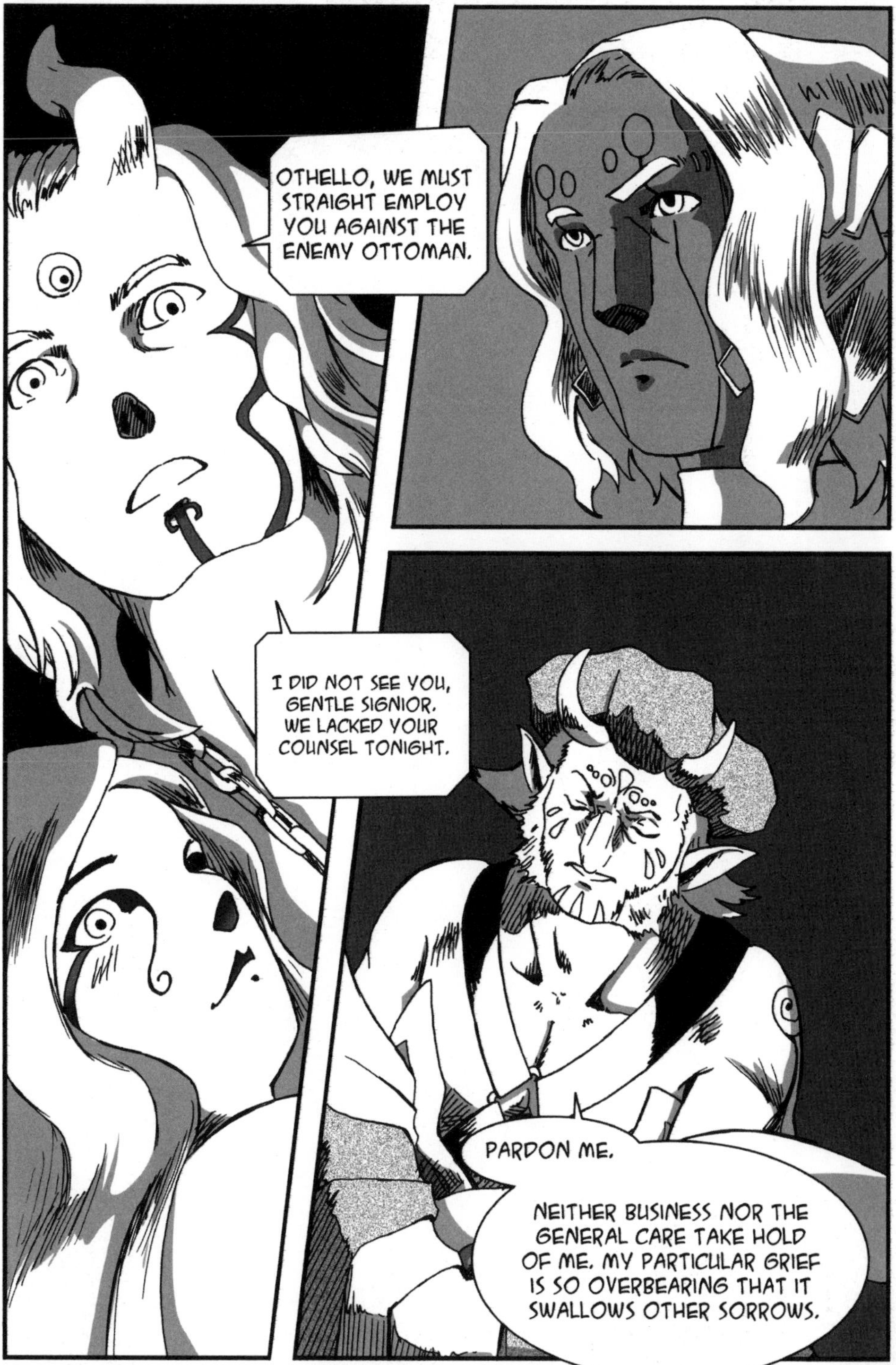
OTHELLO, WE MUST STRAIGHT EMPLOY YOU AGAINST THE ENEMY OTTOMAN.
I DID NOT SEE YOU, GENTLE SIGNIOR. WE LACKED YOUR COUNSEL TONIGHT.
PARDON ME.
NEITHER BUSINESS NOR THE GENERAL CARE TAKE HOLD OF ME. MY PARTICULAR GRIEF IS SO OVERBEARING THAT IT SWALLOWS OTHER SORROWS.

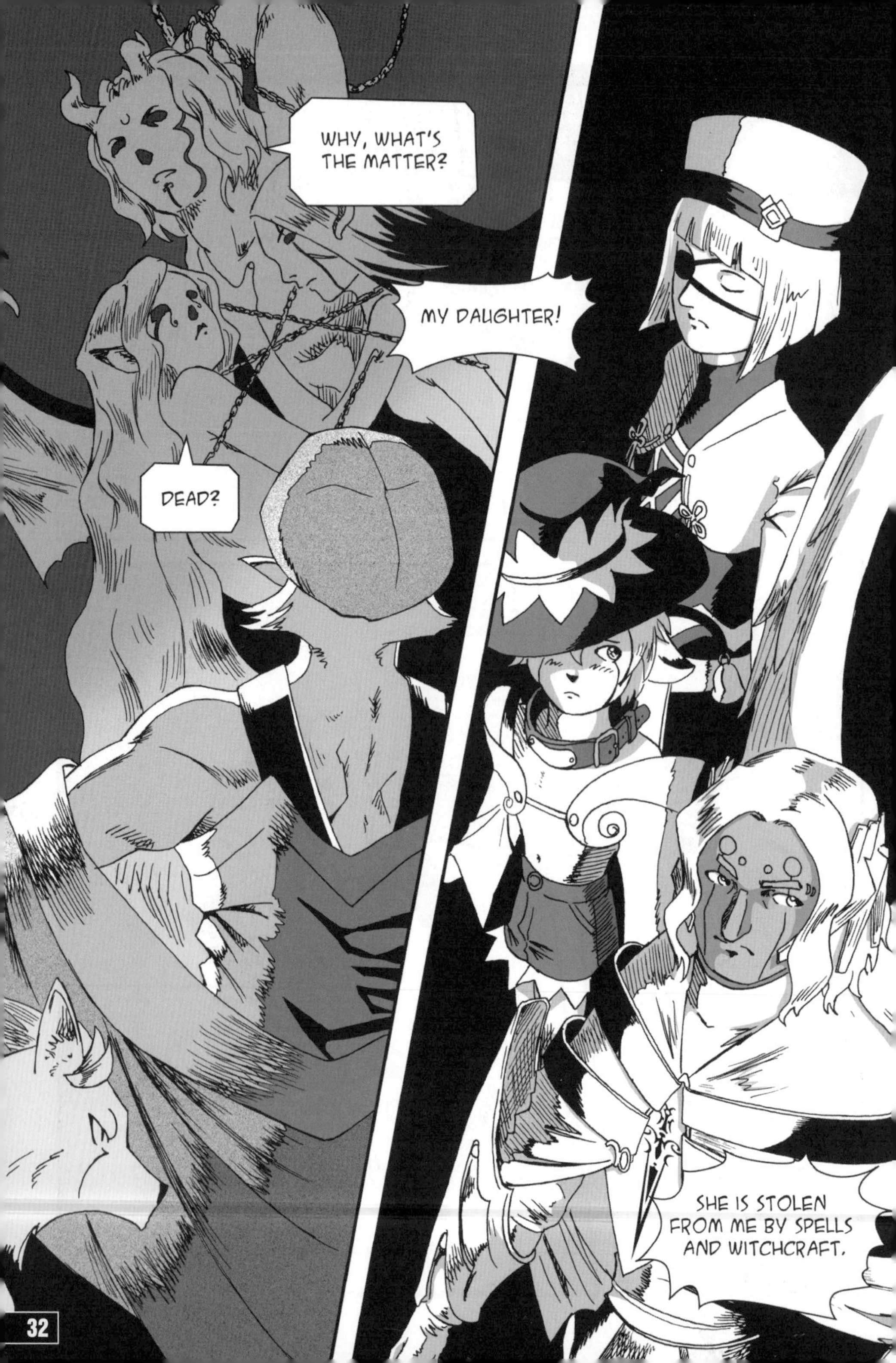
WHY, WHAT'S THE MATTER?
MY DAUGHTER!
DEAD?
SHE IS STOLEN FROM ME BY SPELLS AND WITCHCRAFT.

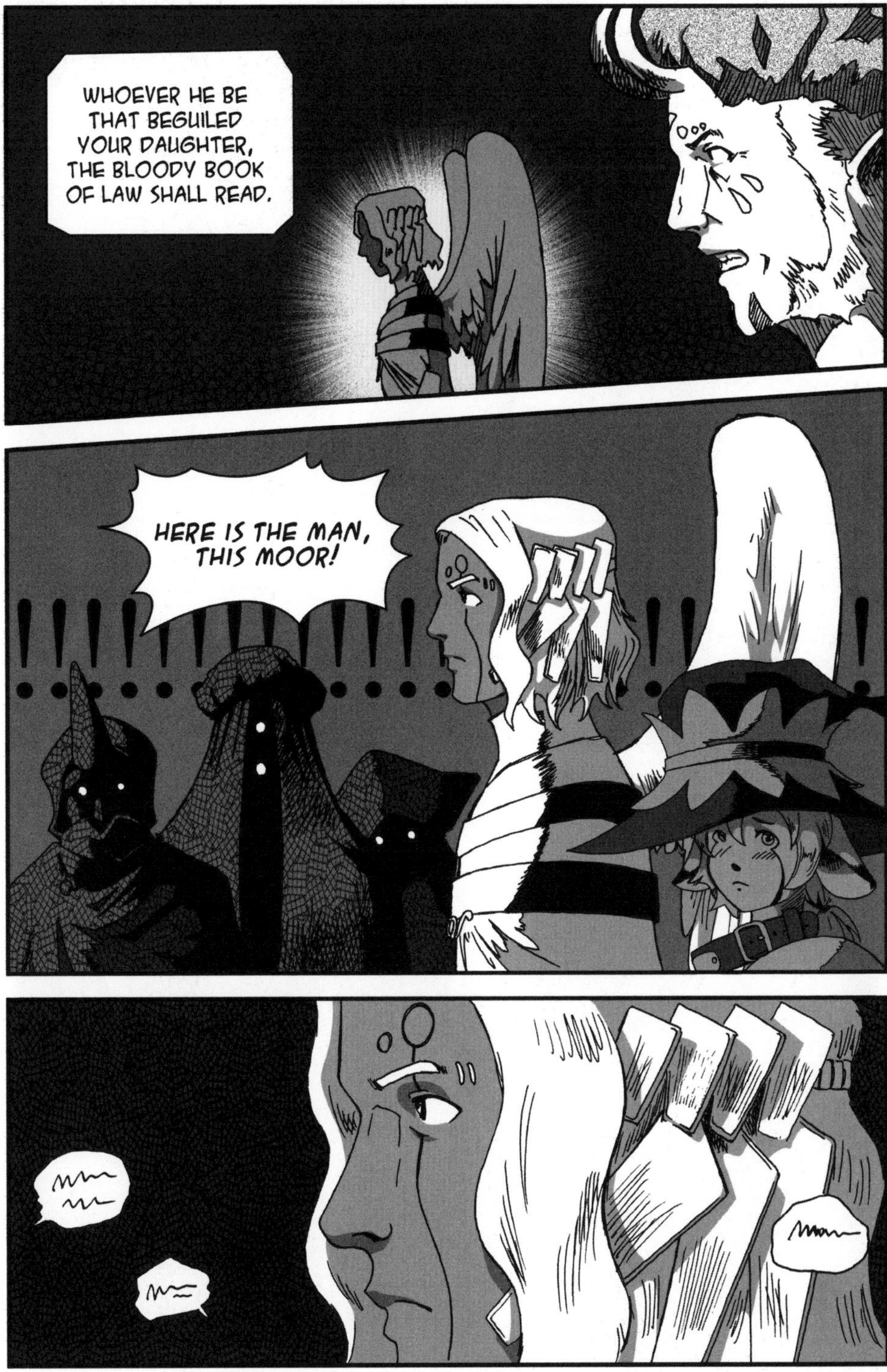
WHOEVER HE BE THAT BEGUILED YOUR DAUGHTER, THE BLOODY BOOK OF LAW SHALL READ.
HERE IS THE MAN, THIS MOOR!

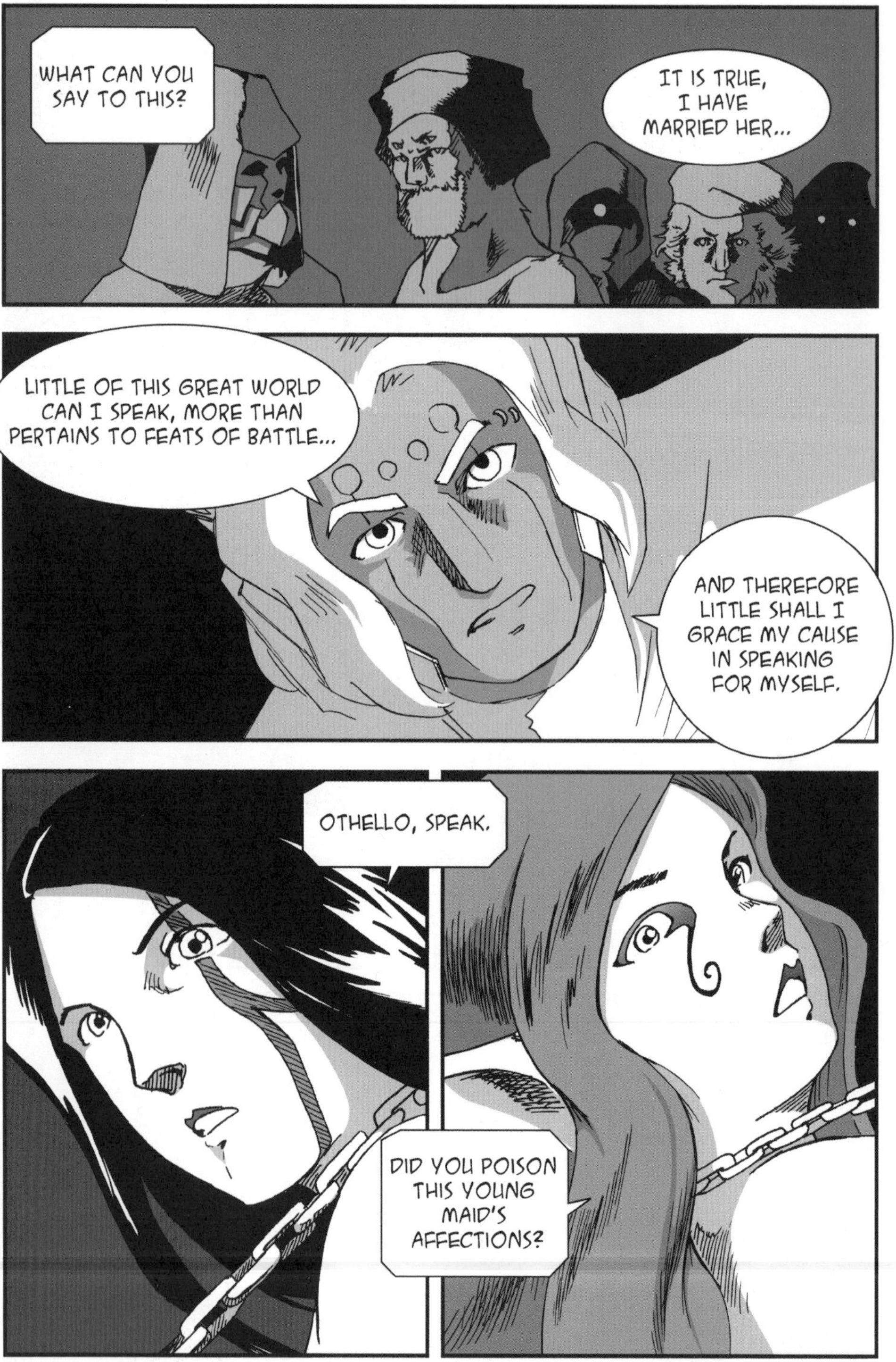
WHAT CAN YOU SAY TO THIS?
IT IS TRUE, I HAVE MARRIED HER...
LITTLE OF THIS GREAT WORLD CAN I SPEAK, MORE THAN PERTAINS TO FEATS OF BATTLE...
AND THEREFORE LITTLE SHALL I GRACE MY CAUSE IN SPEAKING FOR MYSELF.
OTHELLO, SPEAK.
DID YOU POISON THIS YOUNG MAID'S AFFECTIONS?

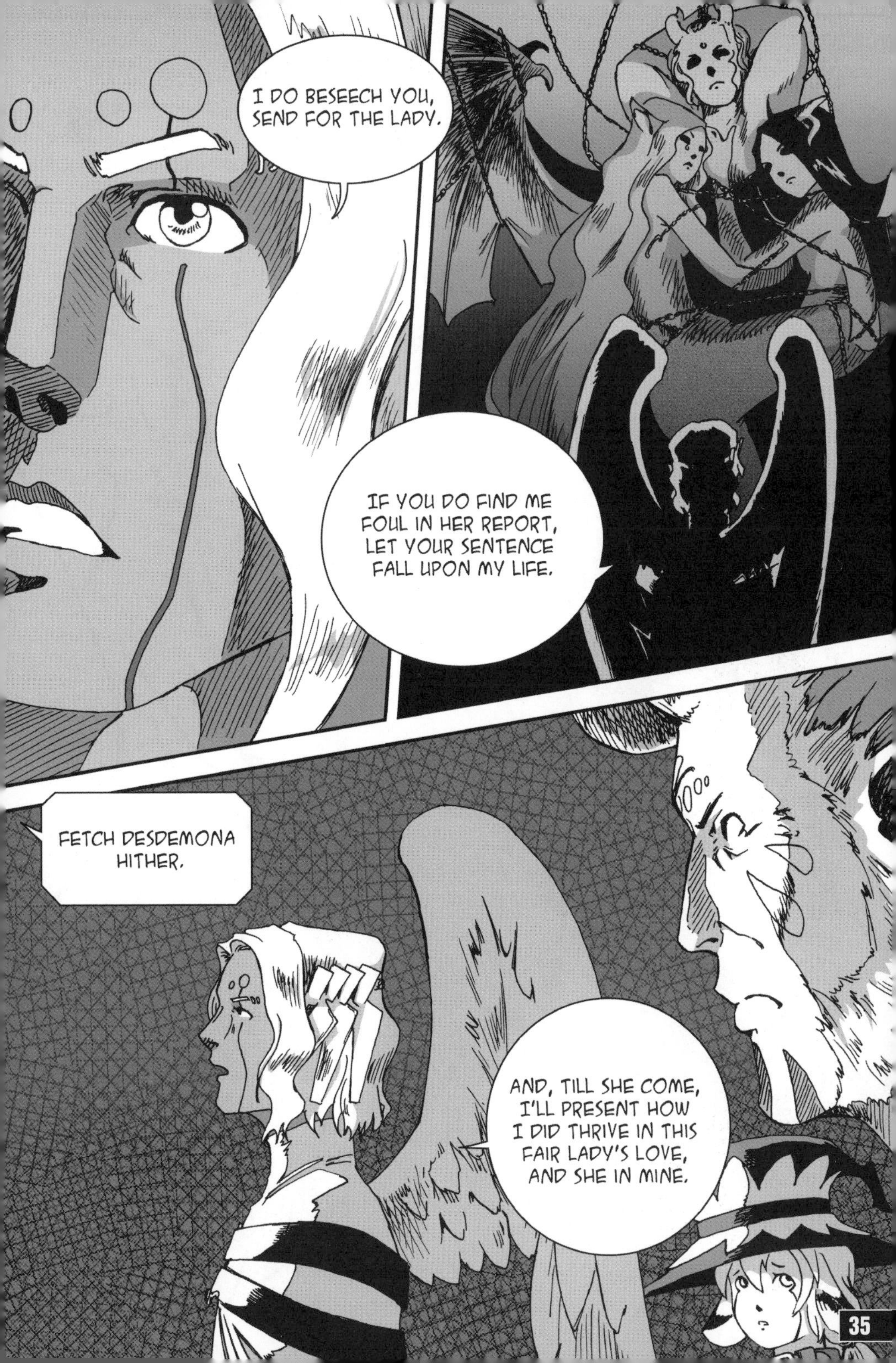
I DO BESEECH YOU, SEND FOR THE LADY.
IF YOU DO FIND ME FOUL IN HER REPORT, LET YOUR SENTENCE FALL UPON MY LIFE.
FETCH DESDEMONA HITHER.
AND, TILL SHE COME, I'LL PRESENT HOW I DID THRIVE IN THIS FAIR LADY'S LOVE, AND SHE IN MINE.

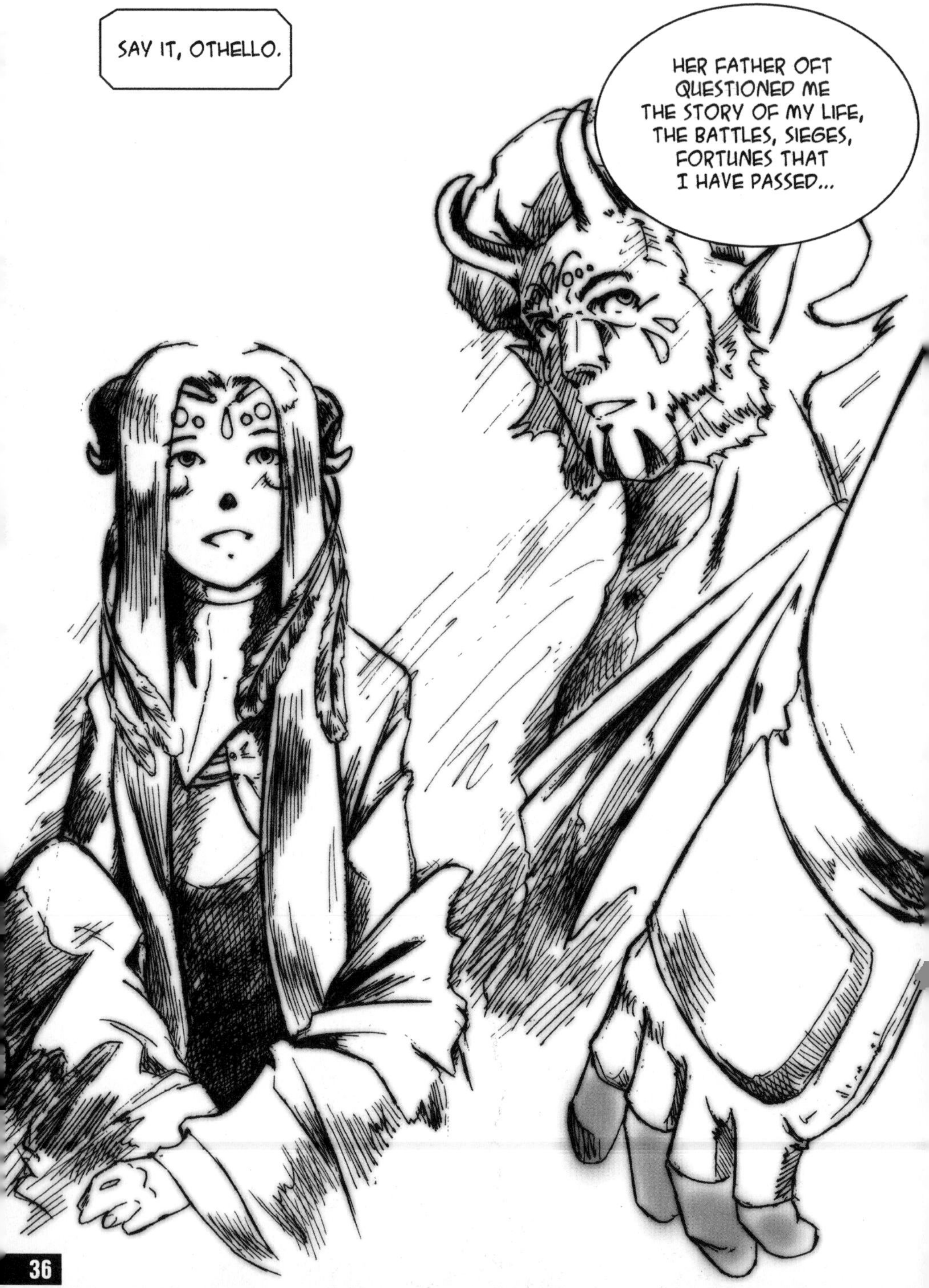
SAY IT, OTHELLO.
HER FATHER OFT QUESTIONED ME THE STORY OF MY LIFE, THE BATTLES, SIEGES, FORTUNES THAT I HAVE PASSED...

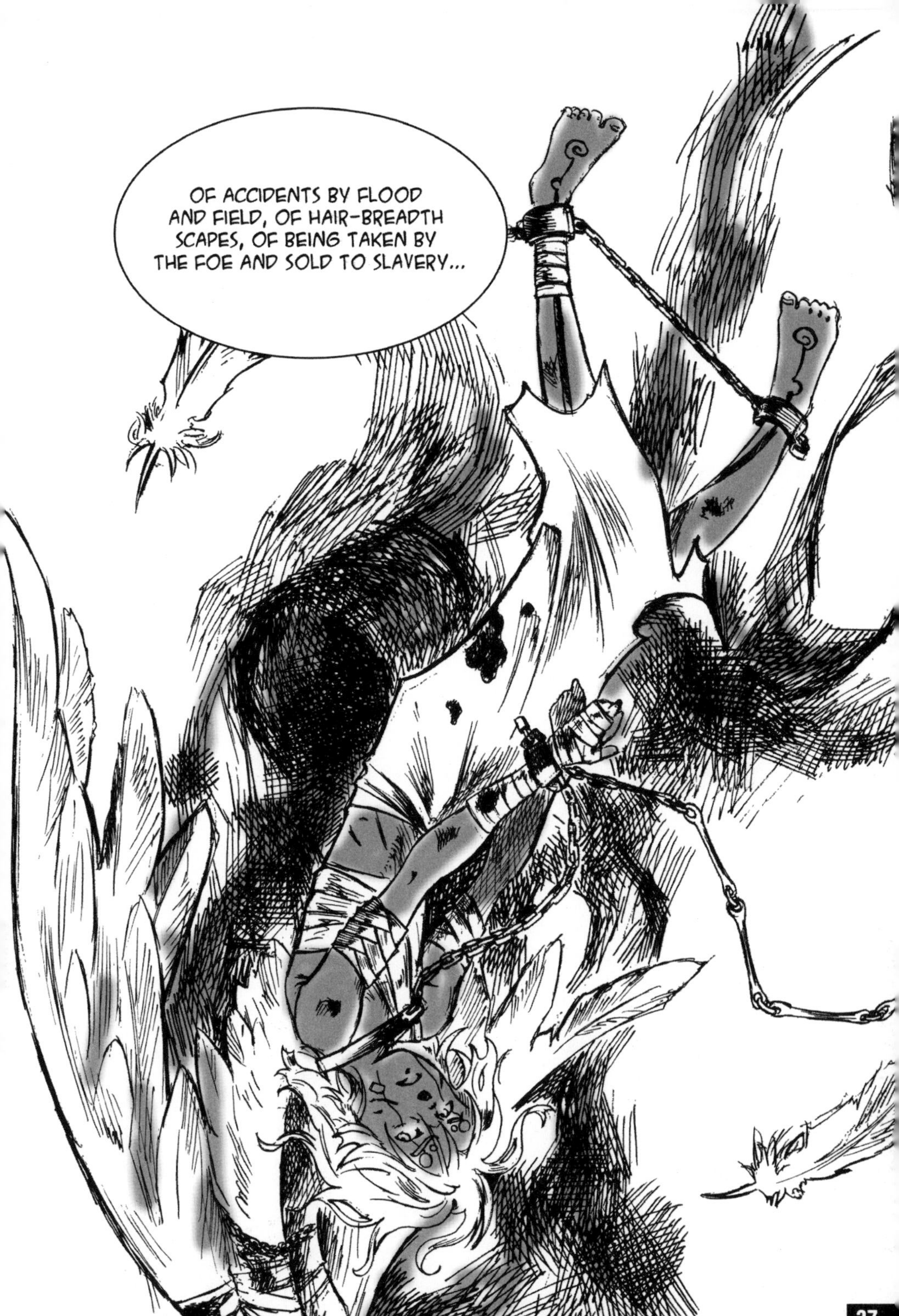
OF ACCIDENTS BY FLOOD AND FIELD, OF HAIR-BREADTH SCAPES, OF BEING TAKEN BY THE FOE AND SOLD TO SLAVERY...

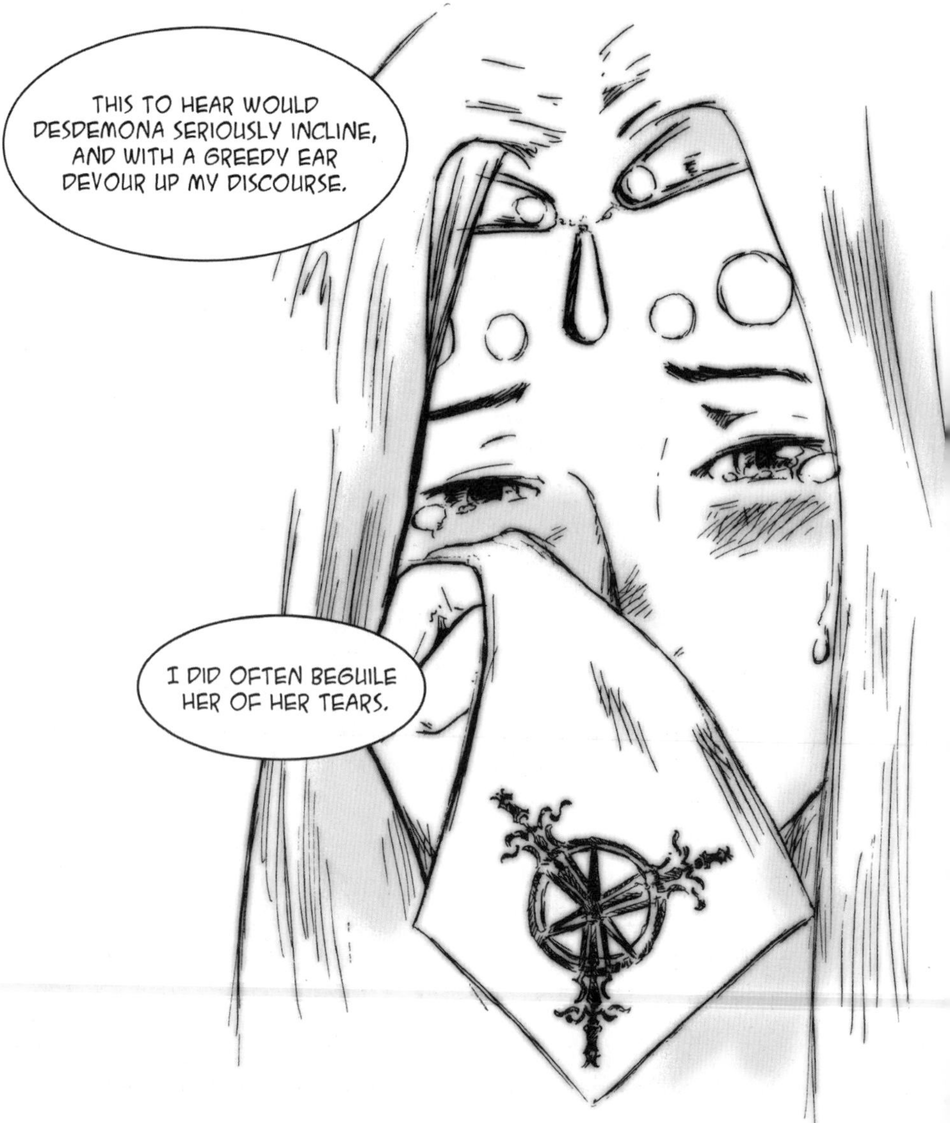
THIS TO HEAR WOULD DESDEMONA SERIOUSLY INCLINE, AND WITH A GREEDY EAR DEVOUR UP MY DISCOURSE.
I DID OFTEN BEGUILE HER OF HER TEARS.

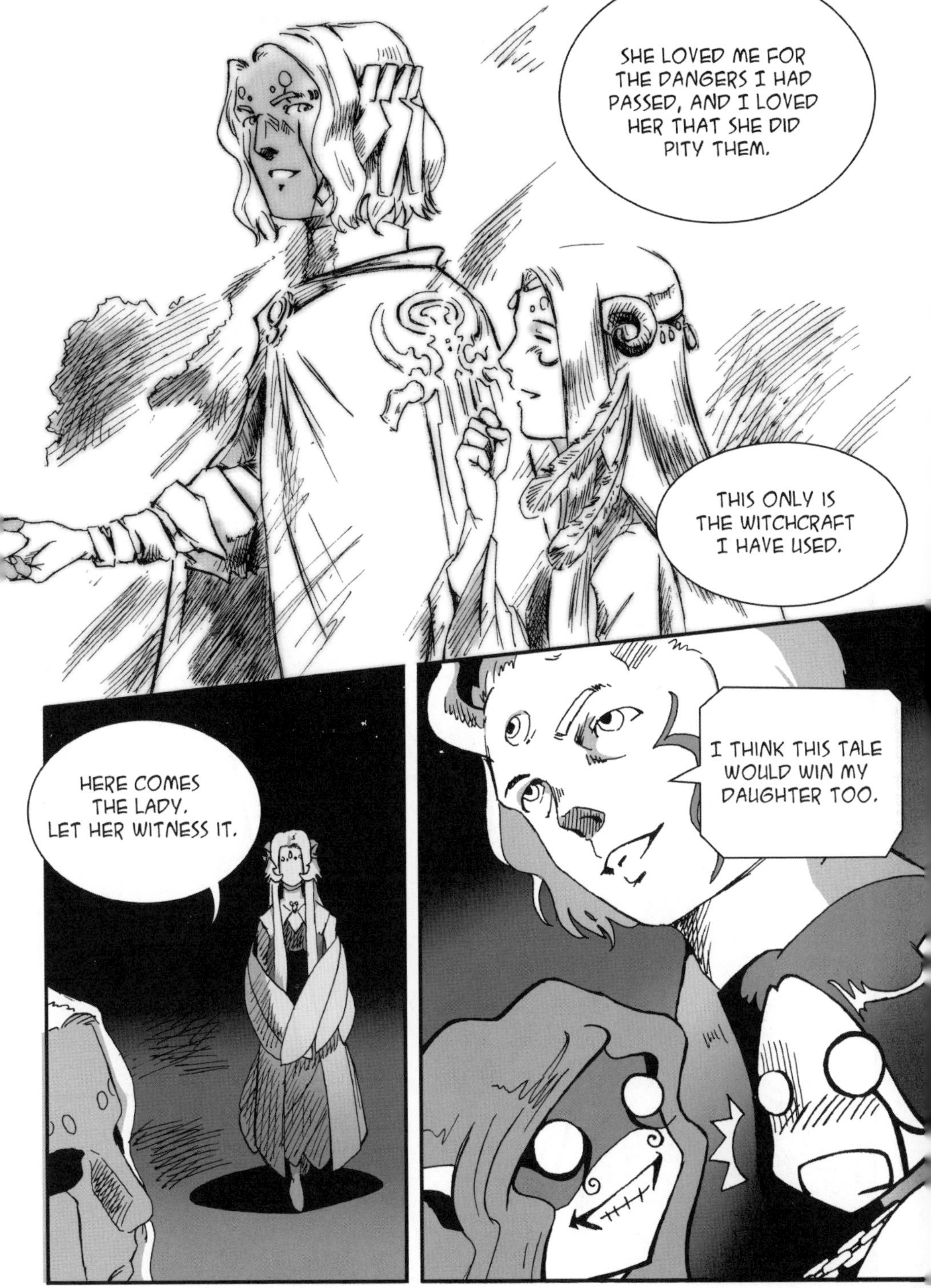
SHE LOVED ME FOR THE DANGERS I HAD PASSED, AND I LOVED HER THAT SHE DID PITY THEM.
THIS ONLY IS THE WITCHCRAFT I HAVE USED.
HERE COMES THE LADY. LET HER WITNESS IT.
I THINK THIS TALE WOULD WIN MY DAUGHTER TOO.

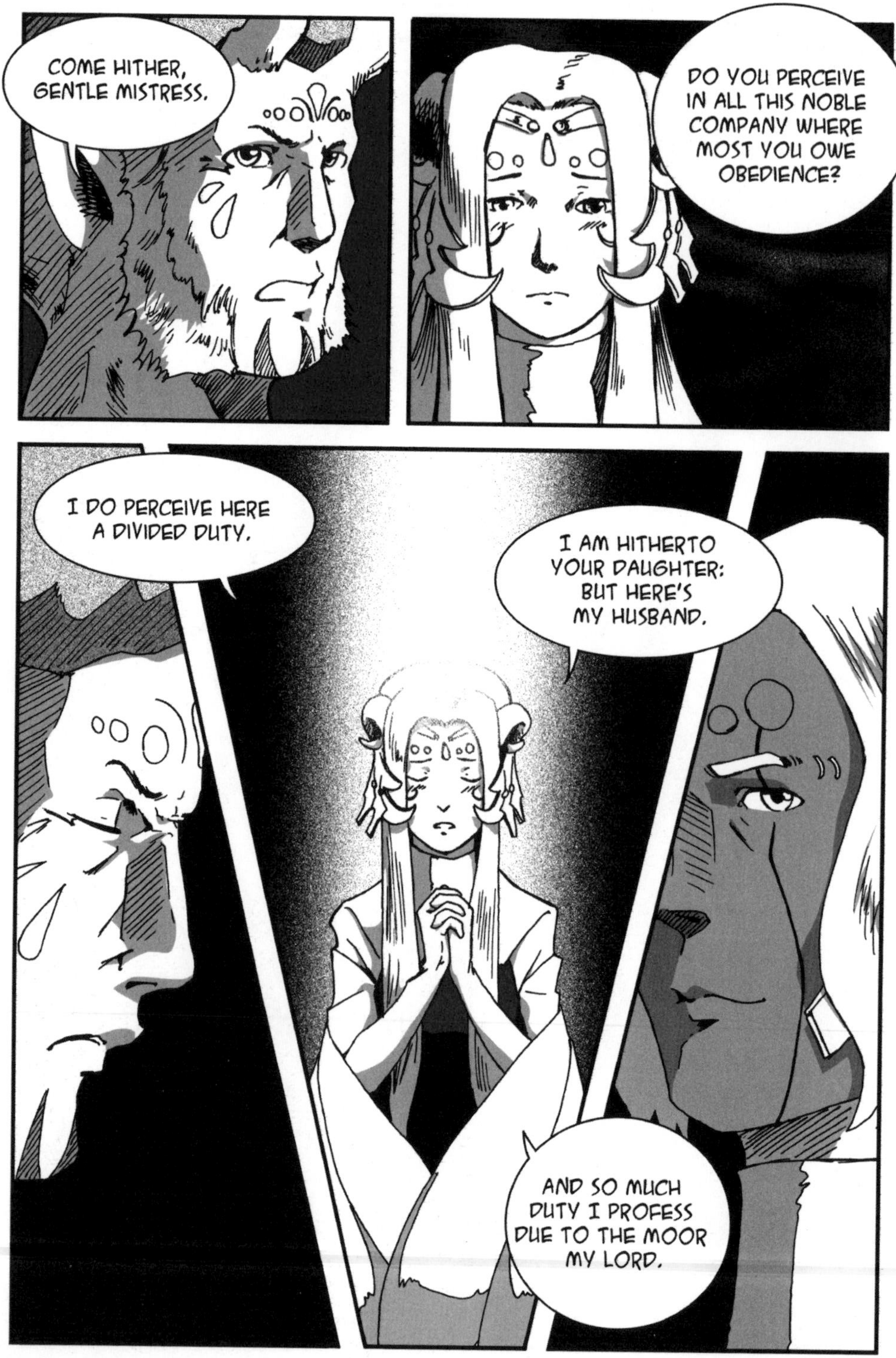
COME HITHER, GENTLE MISTRESS.
DO YOU PERCEIVE IN ALL THIS NOBLE COMPANY WHERE MOST YOU OWE OBEDIENCE?
I DO PERCEIVE HERE A DIVIDED DUTY.
I AM HITHERTO YOUR DAUGHTER: BUT HERE'S MY HUSBAND.
AND SO MUCH DUTY I PROFESS DUE TO THE MOOR MY LORD.

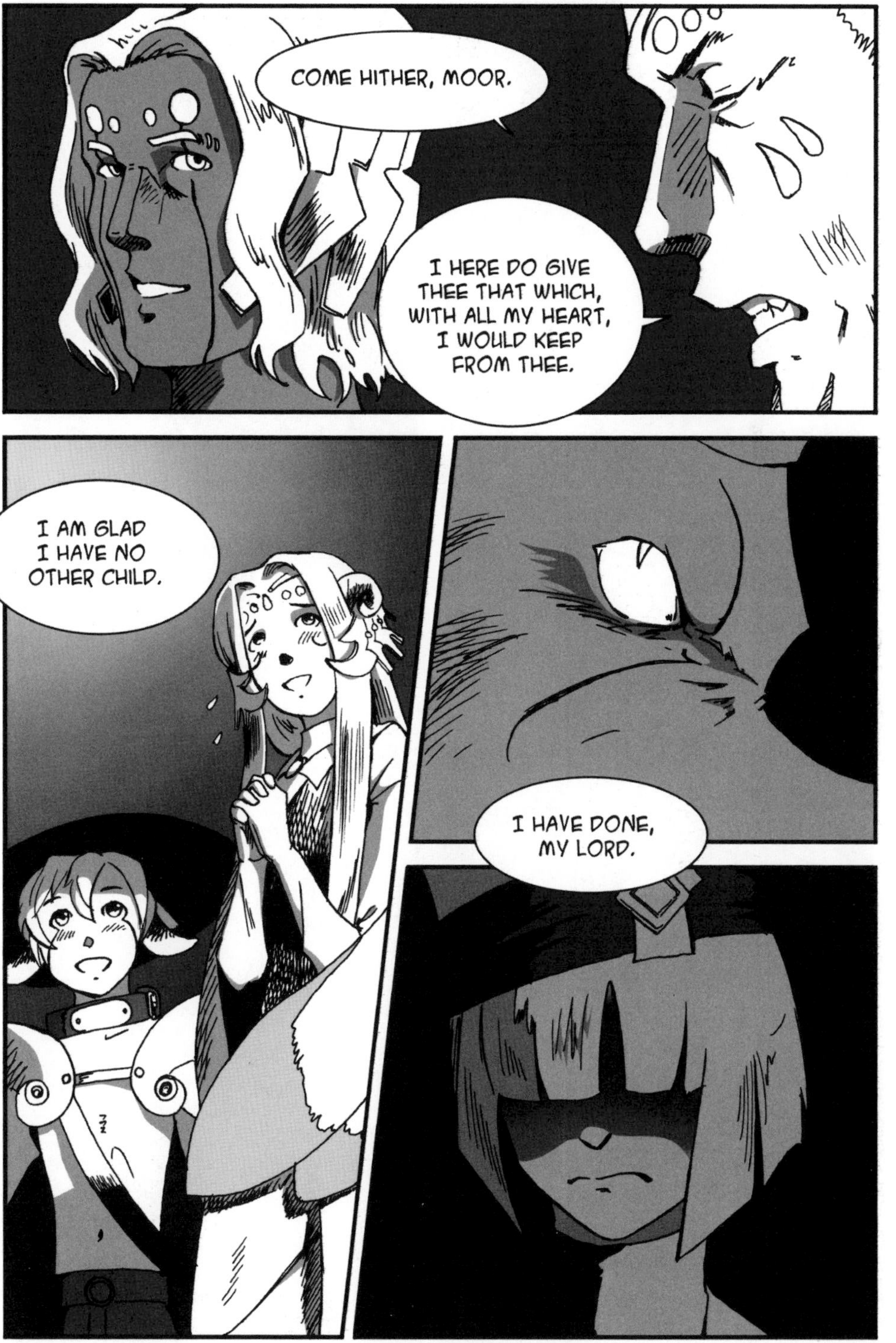
COME HITHER, MOOR.
I HERE DO GIVE THEE THAT WHICH, WITH ALL MY HEART, I WOULD KEEP FROM THEE.
I AM GLAD I HAVE NO OTHER CHILD.
I HAVE DONE, MY LORD.

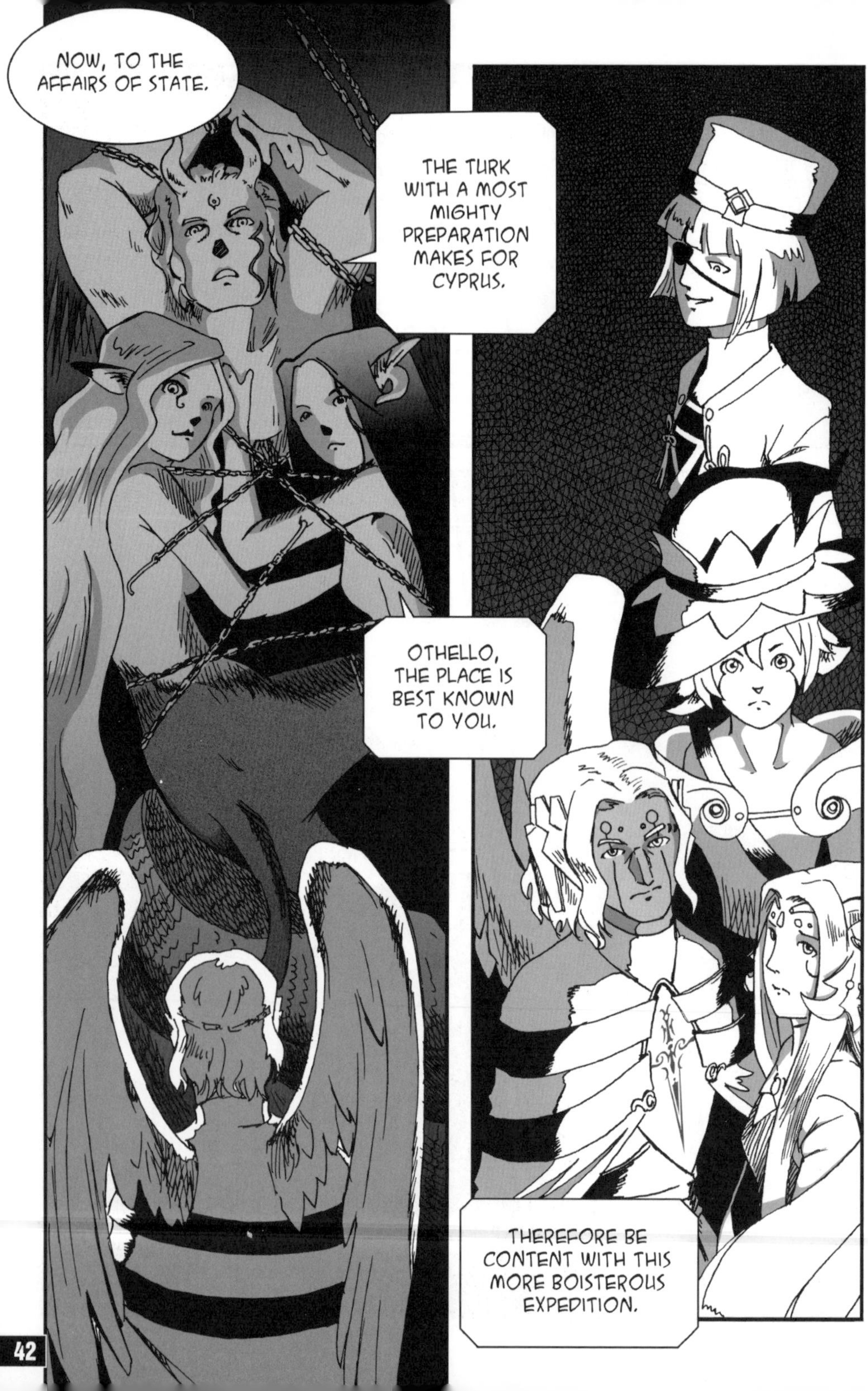
NOW, TO THE AFFAIRS OF STATE.
THE TURK WITH A MOST MIGHTY PREPARATION MAKES FOR CYPRUS.
OTHELLO, THE PLACE IS BEST KNOWN TO YOU.
THEREFORE BE CONTENT WITH THIS MORE BOISTEROUS EXPEDITION.

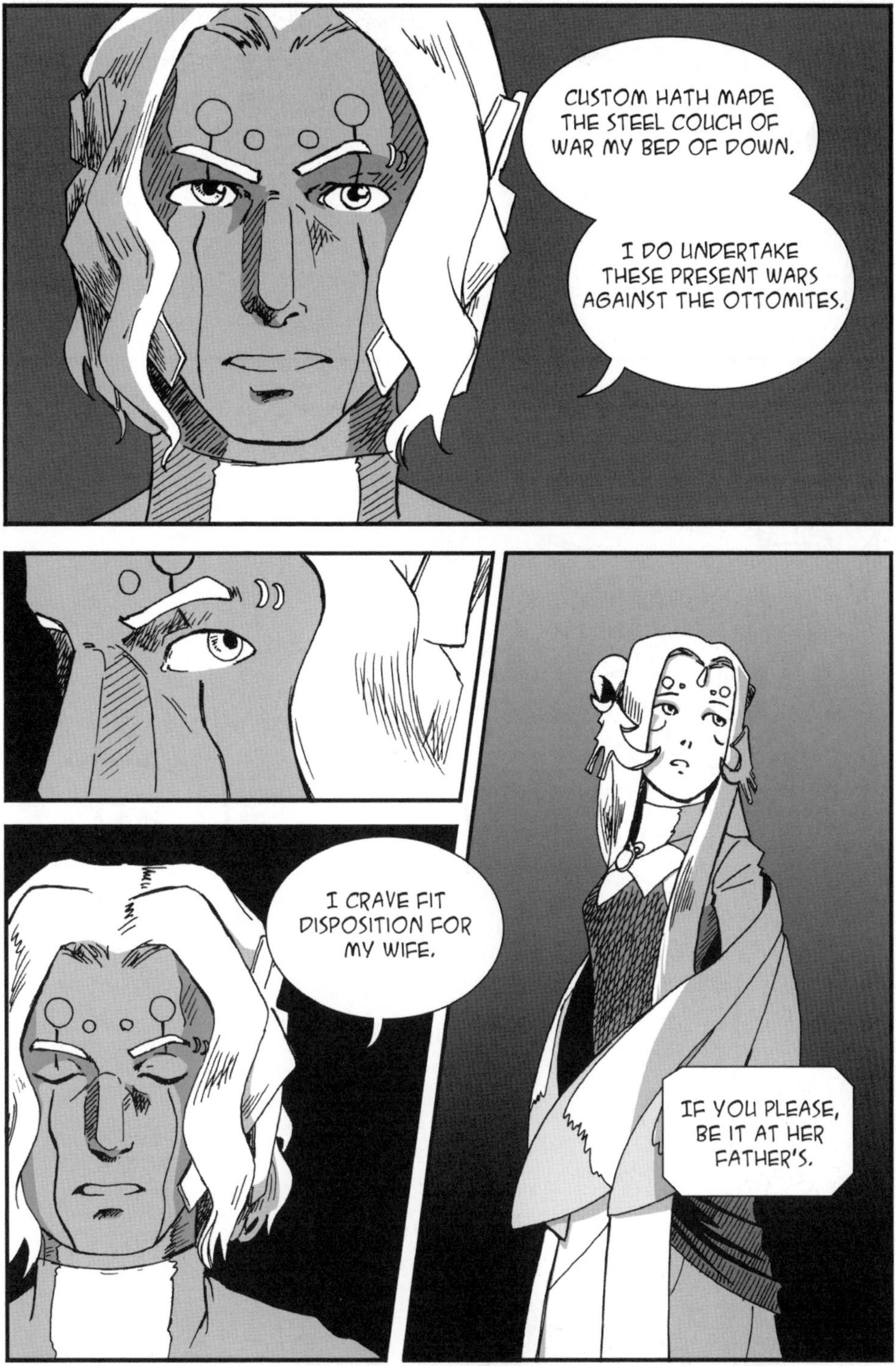
CUSTOM HATH MADE THE STEEL COUCH OF WAR MY BED OF DOWN.
I DO UNDERTAKE THESE PRESENT WARS AGAINST THE OTTOMITES.
I CRAVE FIT DISPOSITION FOR MY WIFE.
IF YOU PLEASE, BE IT AT HER FATHER'S.

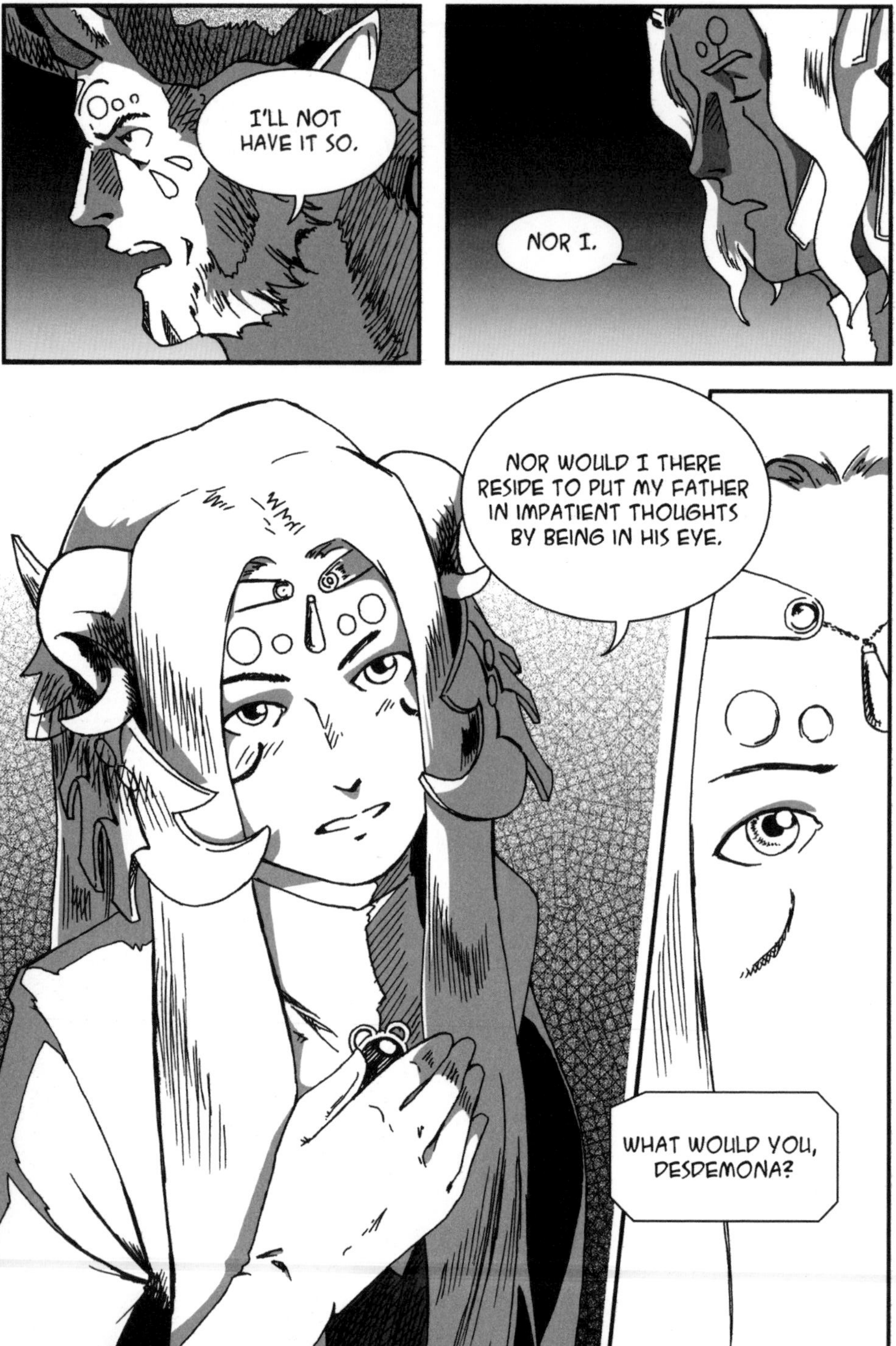

I'LL NOT HAVE IT SO.
NOR I.
NOR WOULD I THERE RESIDE TO PUT MY FATHER IN IMPATIENT THOUGHTS BY BEING IN HIS EYE.
WHAT WOULD YOU, DESDEMONA?

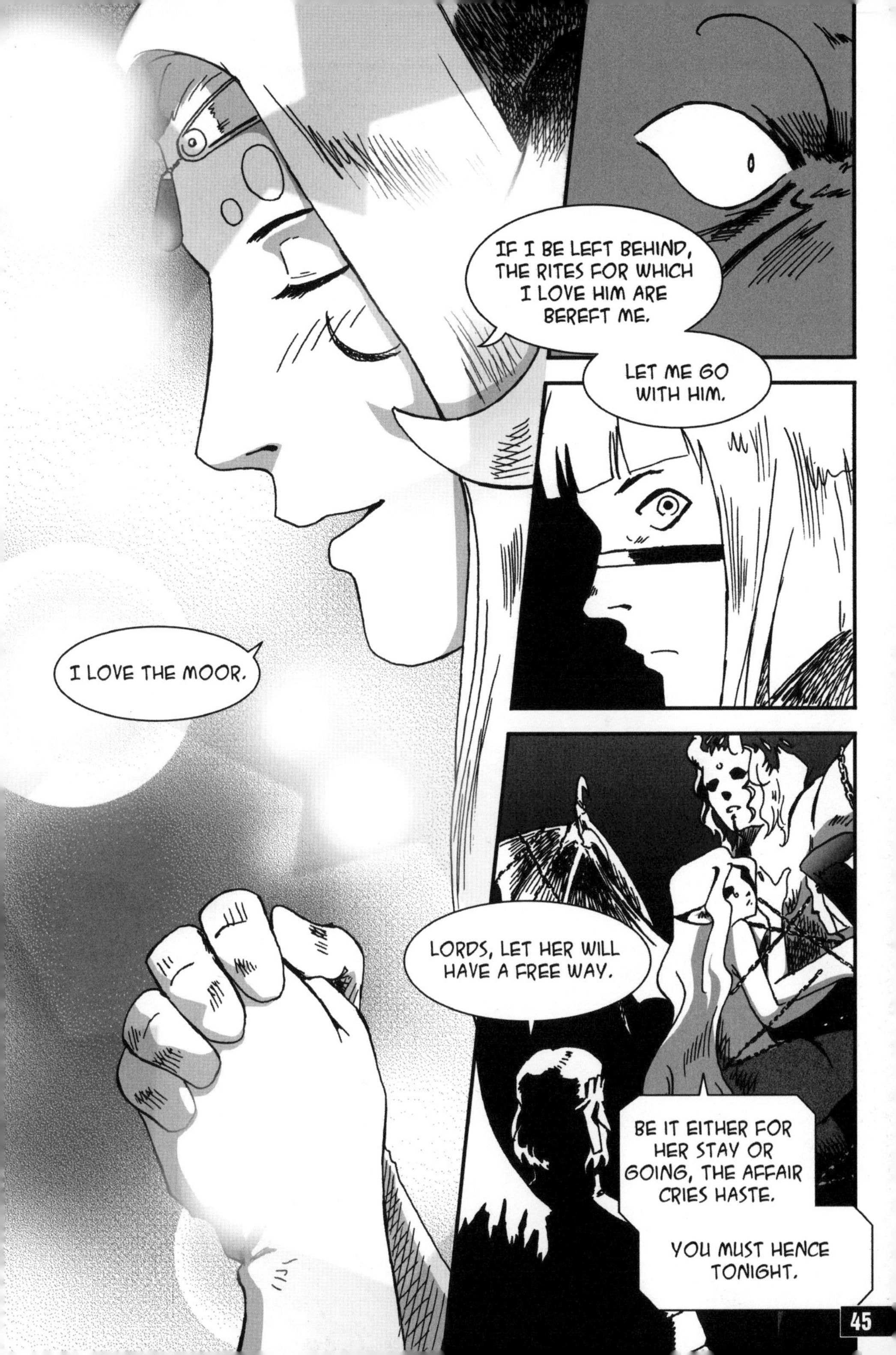
IF I BE LEFT BEHIND, THE RITES FOR WHICH I LOVE HIM ARE BEREFT ME.
LET ME GO WITH HIM.
I LOVE THE MOOR.
LORDS, LET HER WILL HAVE A FREE WAY.
BE IT EITHER FOR HER STAY OR GOING, THE AFFAIR CRIES HASTE.
YOU MUST HENCE TONIGHT.

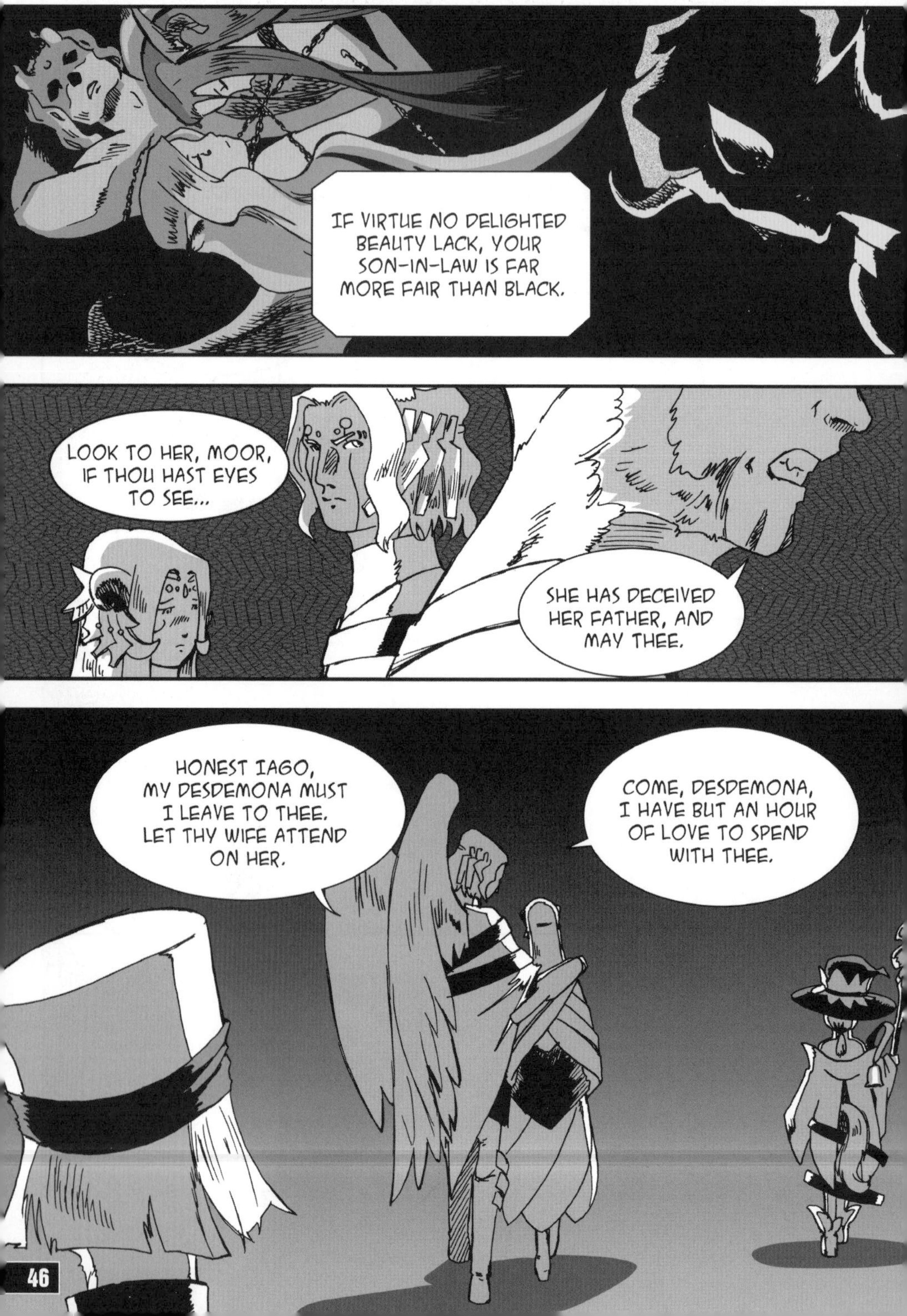
IF VIRTUE NO DELIGHTED BEAUTY LACK, YOUR SON-IN-LAW IS FAR MORE FAIR THAN BLACK.
LOOK TO HER, MOOR, IF THOU HAST EYES TO SEE...
SHE HAS DECEIVED HER FATHER, AND MAY THEE.
HONEST IAGO, MY DESDEMONA MUST I LEAVE TO THEE. LET THY WIFE ATTEND ON HER.
COME, DESDEMONA, I HAVE BUT AN HOUR OF LOVE TO SPEND WITH THEE.

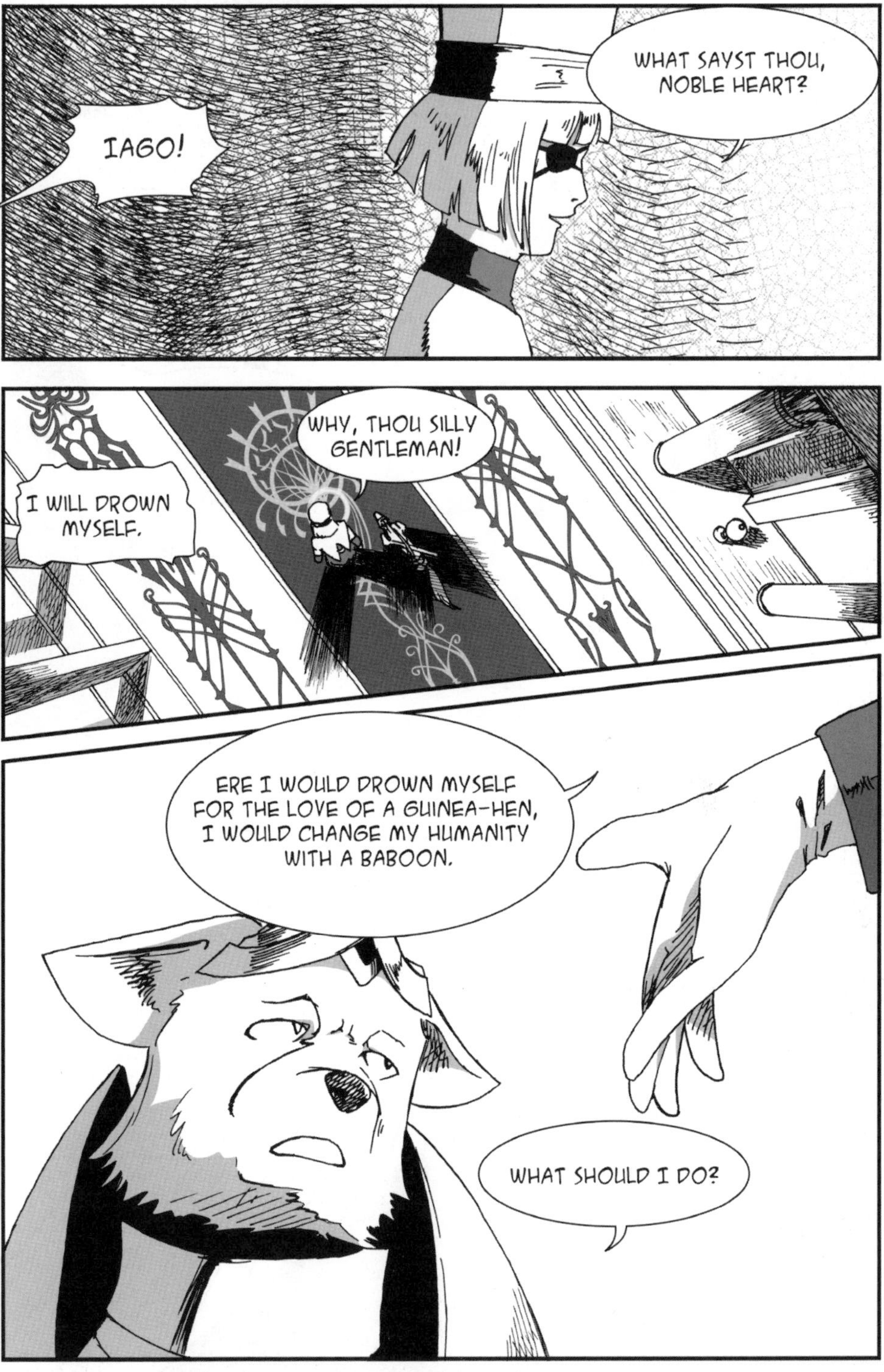

IAGO!
WHAT SAYST THOU, NOBLE HEART?
I WILL DROWN MYSELF.
WHY, THOU SILLY GENTLEMAN!
ERE I WOULD DROWN MYSELF FOR THE LOVE OF A GUINEA-HEN, I WOULD CHANGE MY HUMANITY WITH A BABOON.
WHAT SHOULD I DO?

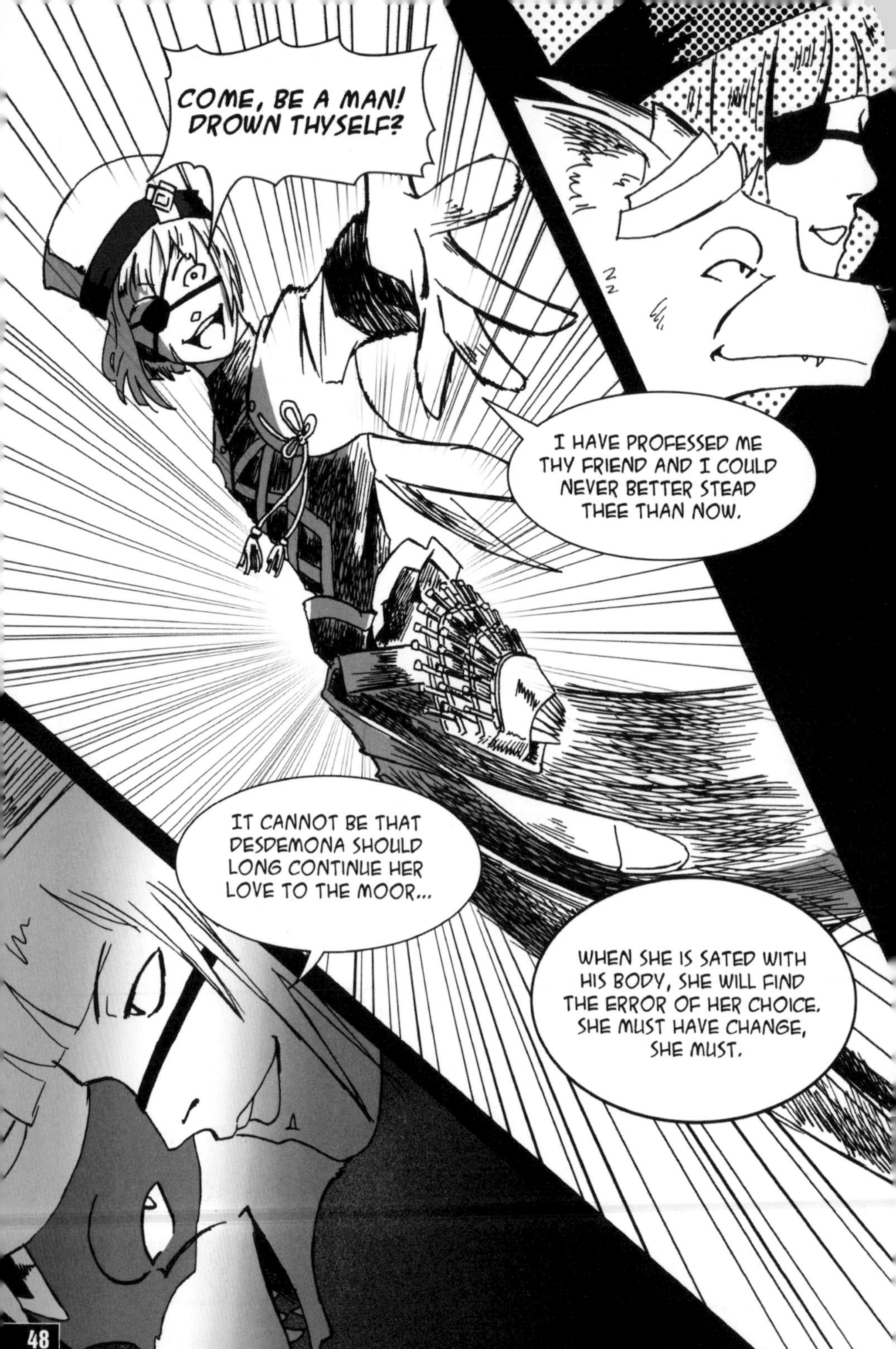
COME, BE A MAN! DROWN THYSELF?
I HAVE PROFESSED ME THY FRIEND AND I COULD NEVER BETTER STEAD THEE THAN NOW.
IT CANNOT BE THAT DESDEMONA SHOULD LONG CONTINUE HER LOVE TO THE MOOR...
WHEN SHE IS SATED WITH HIS BODY, SHE WILL FIND THE ERROR OF HER CHOICE. SHE MUST HAVE CHANGE, SHE MUST.

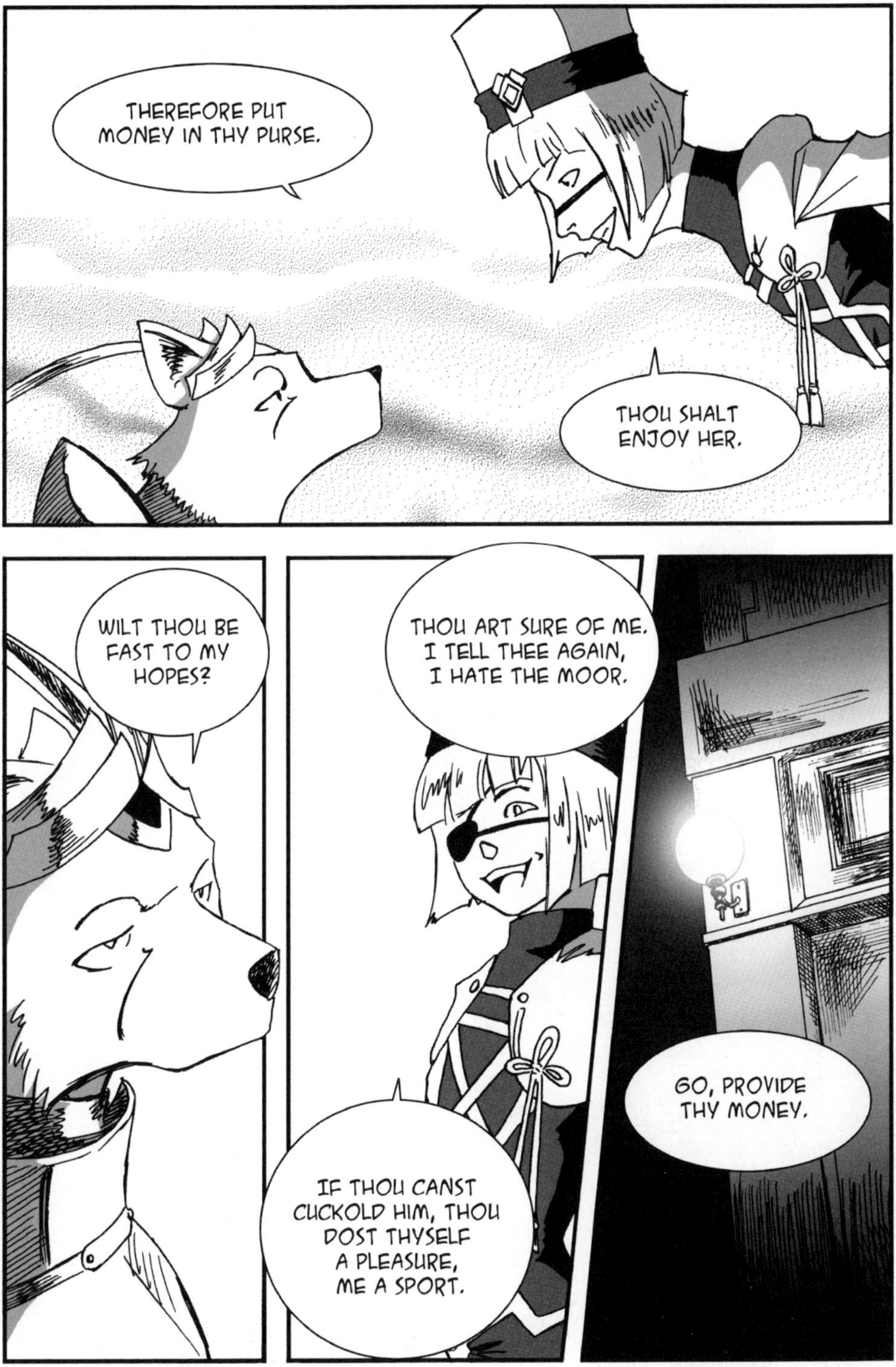
THEREFORE PUT MONEY IN THY PURSE.
THOU SHALT ENJOY HER.
WILT THOU BE FAST TO MY HOPES?
THOU ART SURE OF ME. I TELL THEE AGAIN, I HATE THE MOOR.
IF THOU CANST CUCKOLD HIM, THOU DOST THYSELF A PLEASURE, ME A SPORT.
GO, PROVIDE THY MONEY.

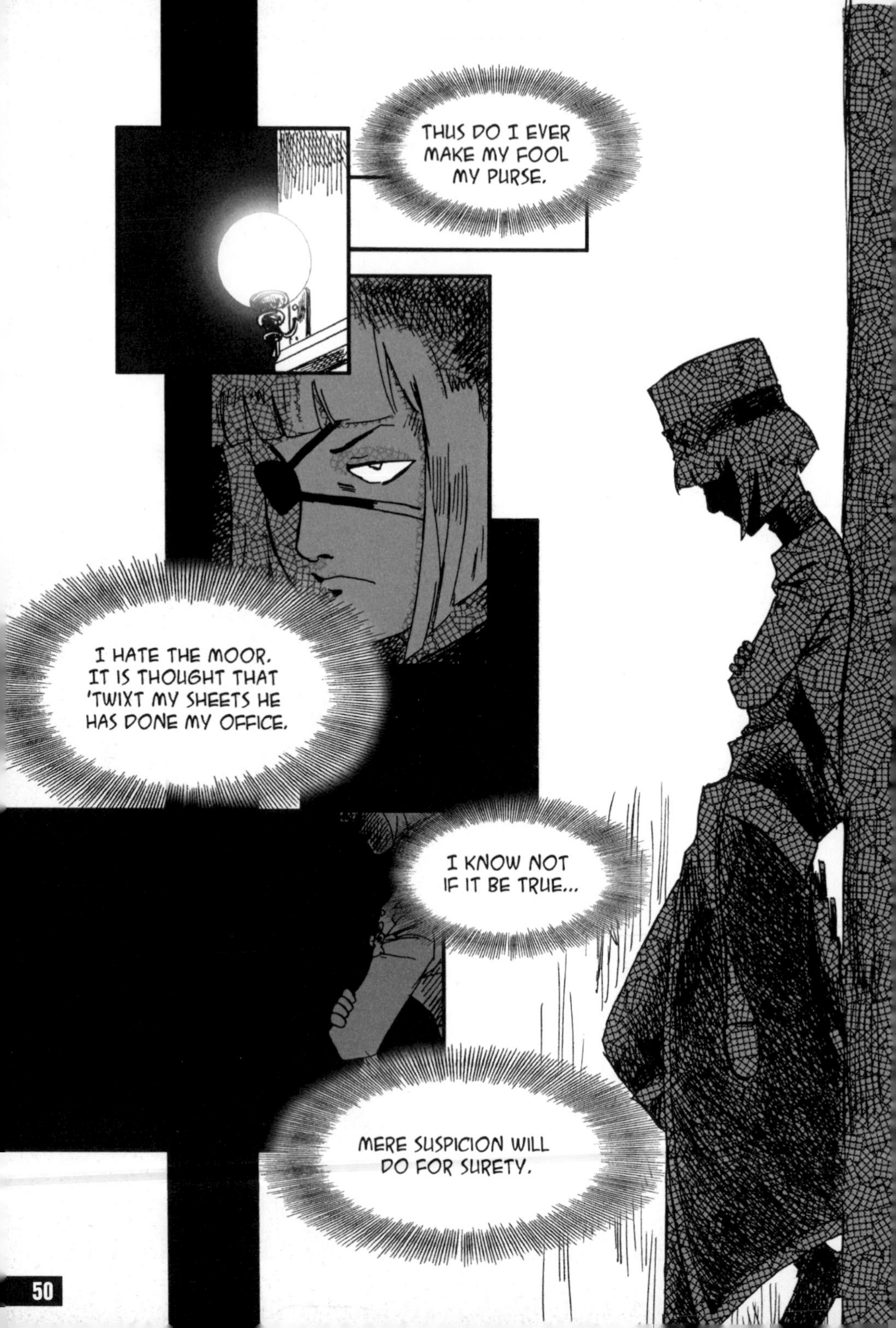
THUS DO I EVER MAKE MY FOOL MY PURSE.
I HATE THE MOOR. IT IS THOUGHT THAT 'TWIXT MY SHEETS HE HAS DONE MY OFFICE.
I KNOW NOT IF IT BE TRUE...
MERE SUSPICION WILL DO FOR SURETY.

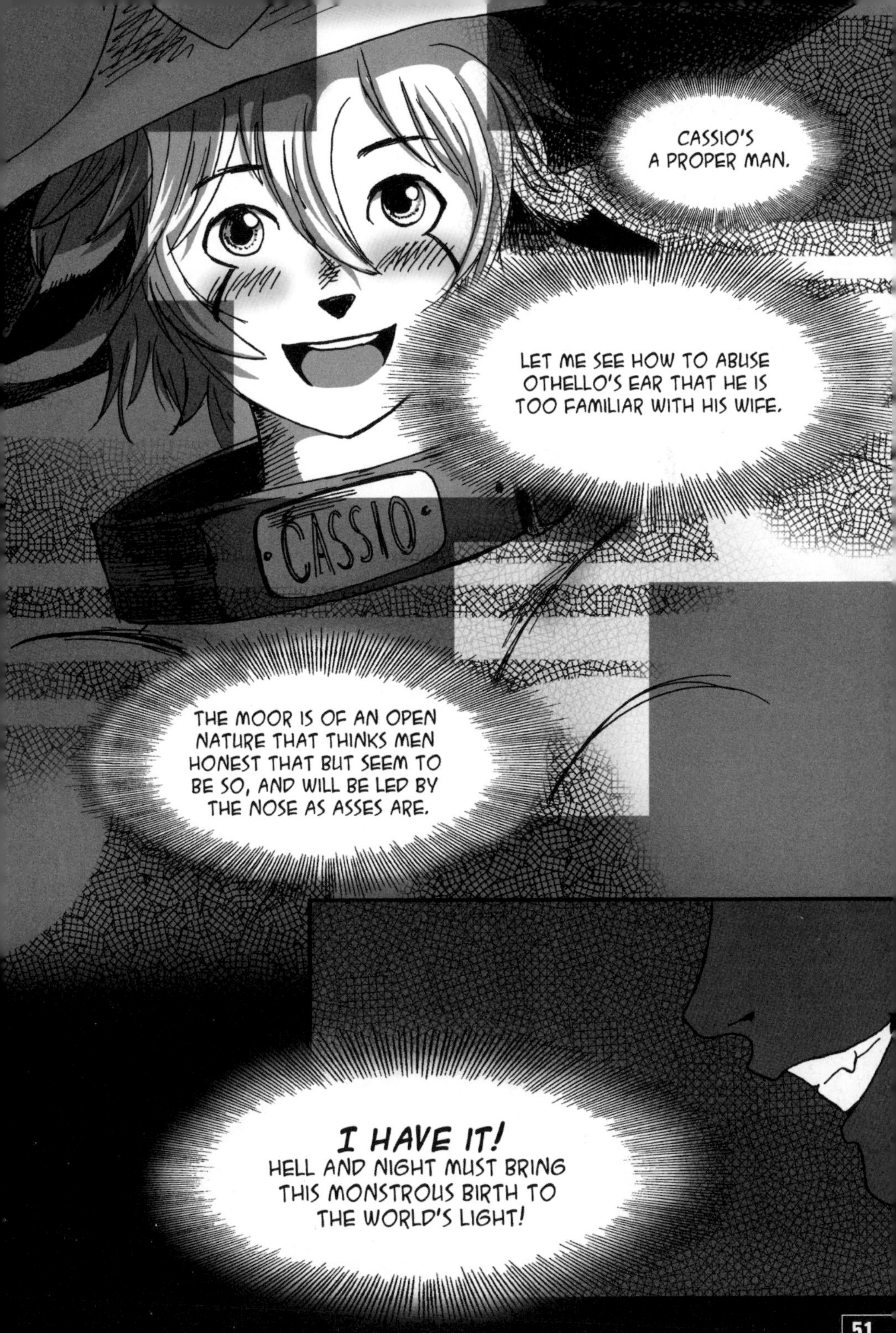
CASSIO'S A PROPER MAN.
LET ME SEE HOW TO ABUSE OTHELLO'S EAR THAT HE IS TOO FAMILIAR WITH HIS WIFE.
CASSIO
THE MOOR IS OF AN OPEN NATURE THAT THINKS MEN HONEST THAT BUT SEEM TO BE SO, AND WILL BE LED BY THE NOSE AS ASSES ARE.
I HAVE IT!
HELL AND NIGHT MUST BRING THIS MONSTROUS BIRTH TO THE WORLD'S LIGHT!

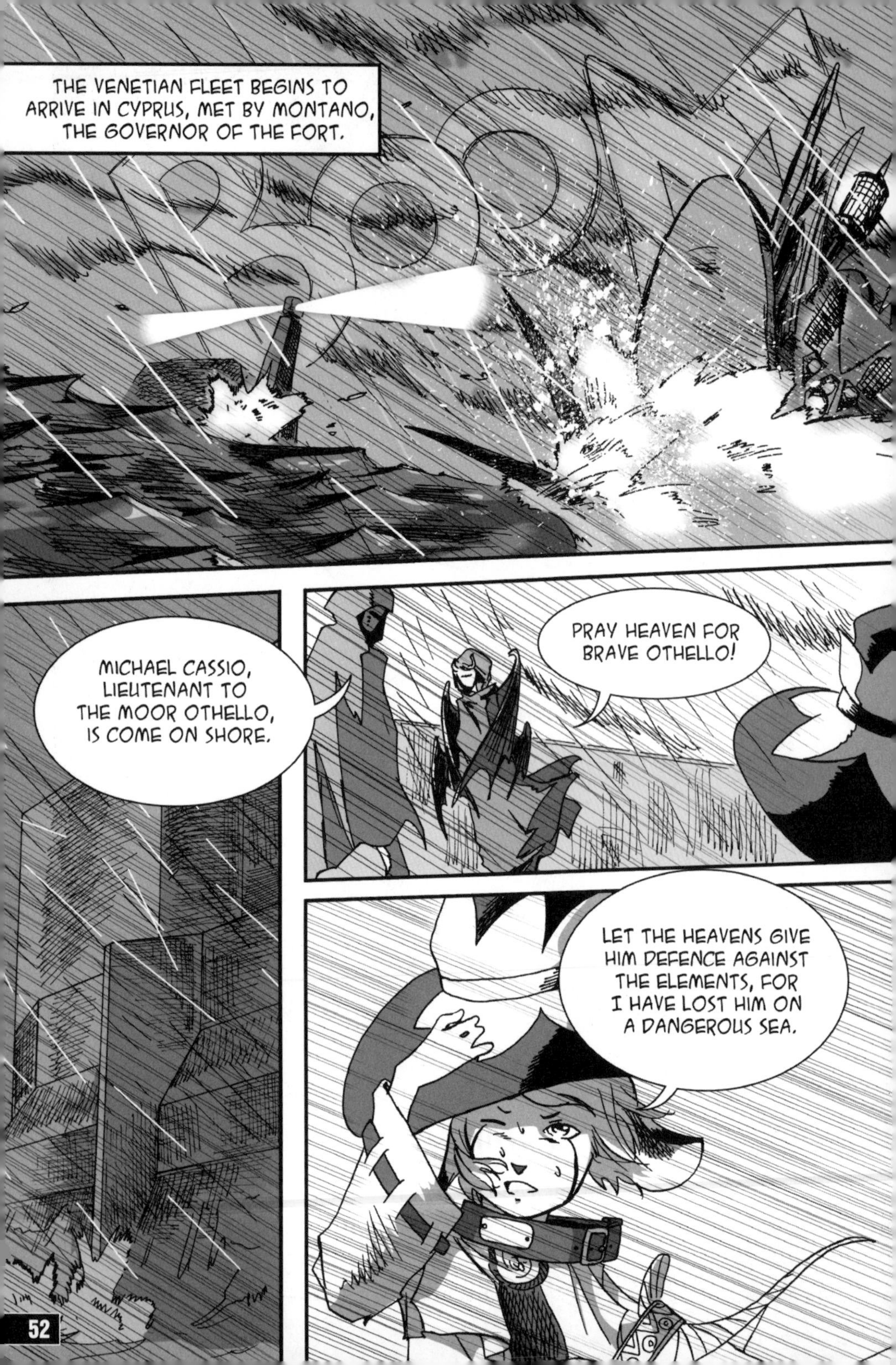
THE VENETIAN FLEET BEGINS TO ARRIVE IN CYPRUS, MET BY MONTANO, THE GOVERNOR OF THE FORT.
MICHAEL CASSIO, LIEUTENANT TO THE MOOR OTHELLO, IS COME ON SHORE.
PRAY HEAVEN FOR BRAVE OTHELLO!
LET THE HEAVENS GIVE HIM DEFENCE AGAINST THE ELEMENTS, FOR I HAVE LOST HIM ON A DANGEROUS SEA.

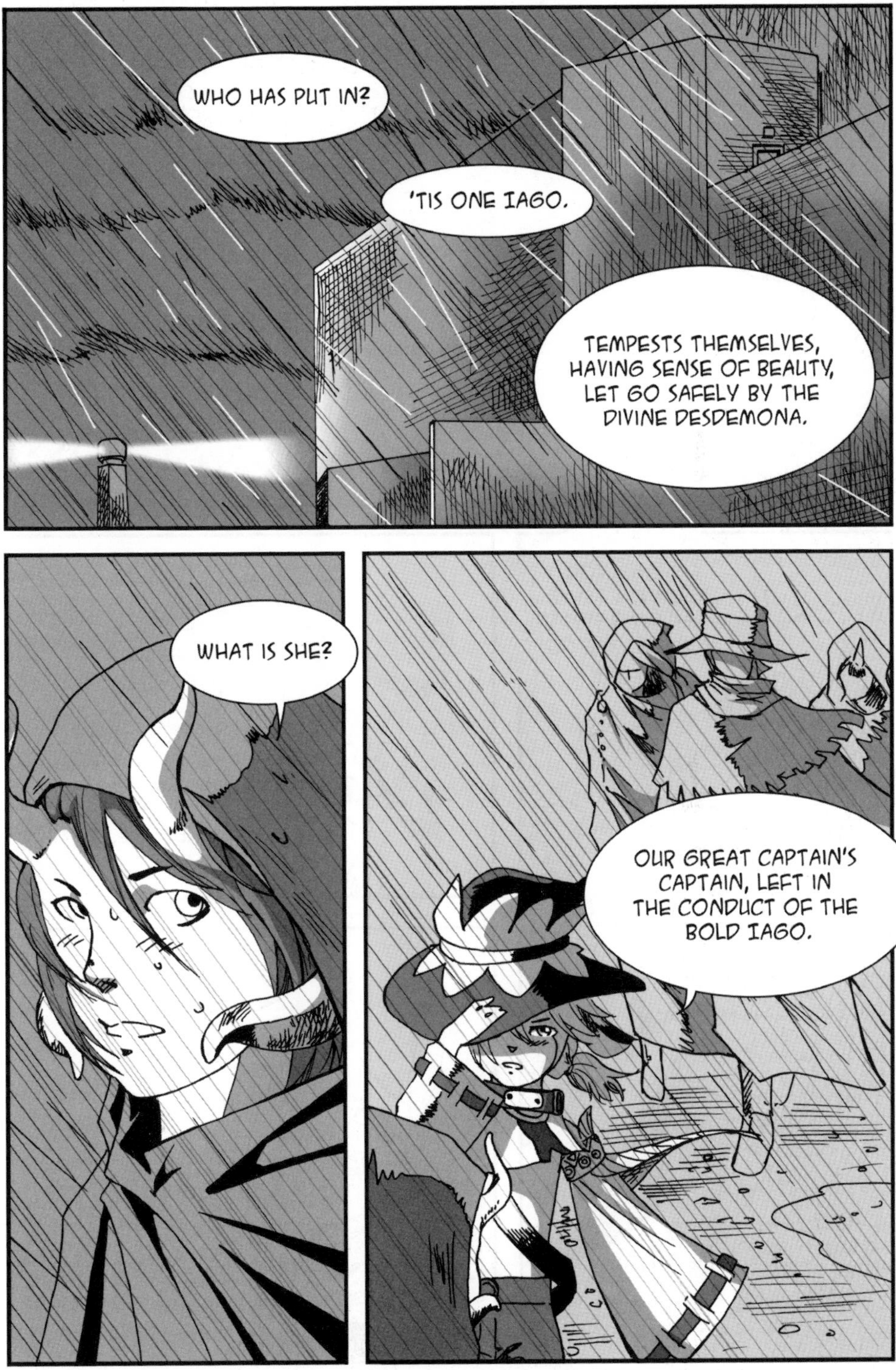
WHO HAS PUT IN?
'TIS ONE IAGO.
TEMPESTS THEMSELVES, HAVING SENSE OF BEAUTY, LET GO SAFELY BY THE DIVINE DESDEMONA.
WHAT IS SHE?
OUR GREAT CAPTAIN'S CAPTAIN, LEFT IN THE CONDUCT OF THE BOLD IAGO.

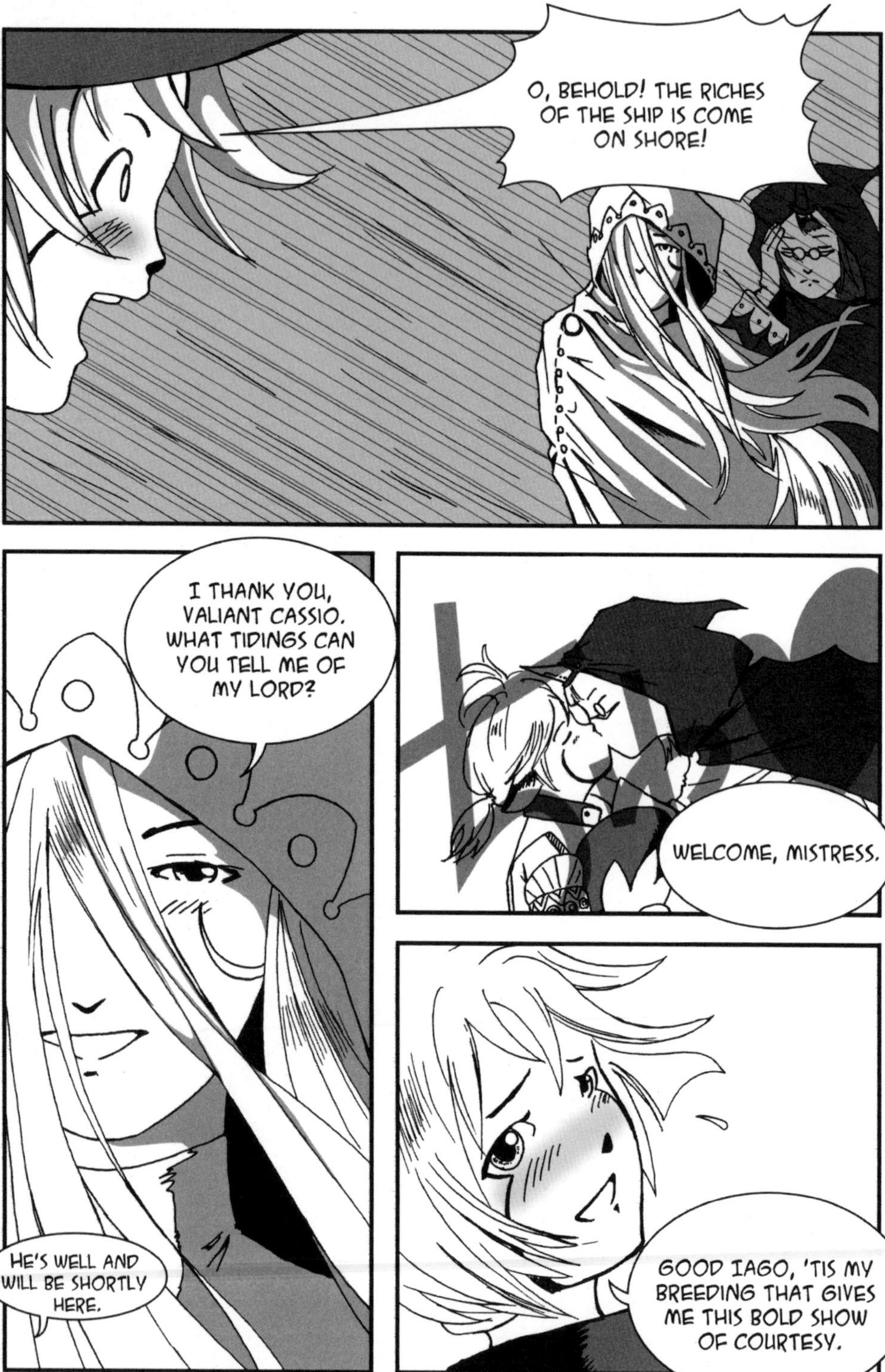
O, BEHOLD! THE RICHES OF THE SHIP IS COME ON SHORE!
I THANK YOU, VALIANT CASSIO. WHAT TIDINGS CAN YOU TELL ME OF MY LORD?
HE'S WELL AND WILL BE SHORTLY HERE.
WELCOME, MISTRESS.
GOOD IAGO, 'TIS MY BREEDING THAT GIVES ME THIS BOLD SHOW OF COURTESY.

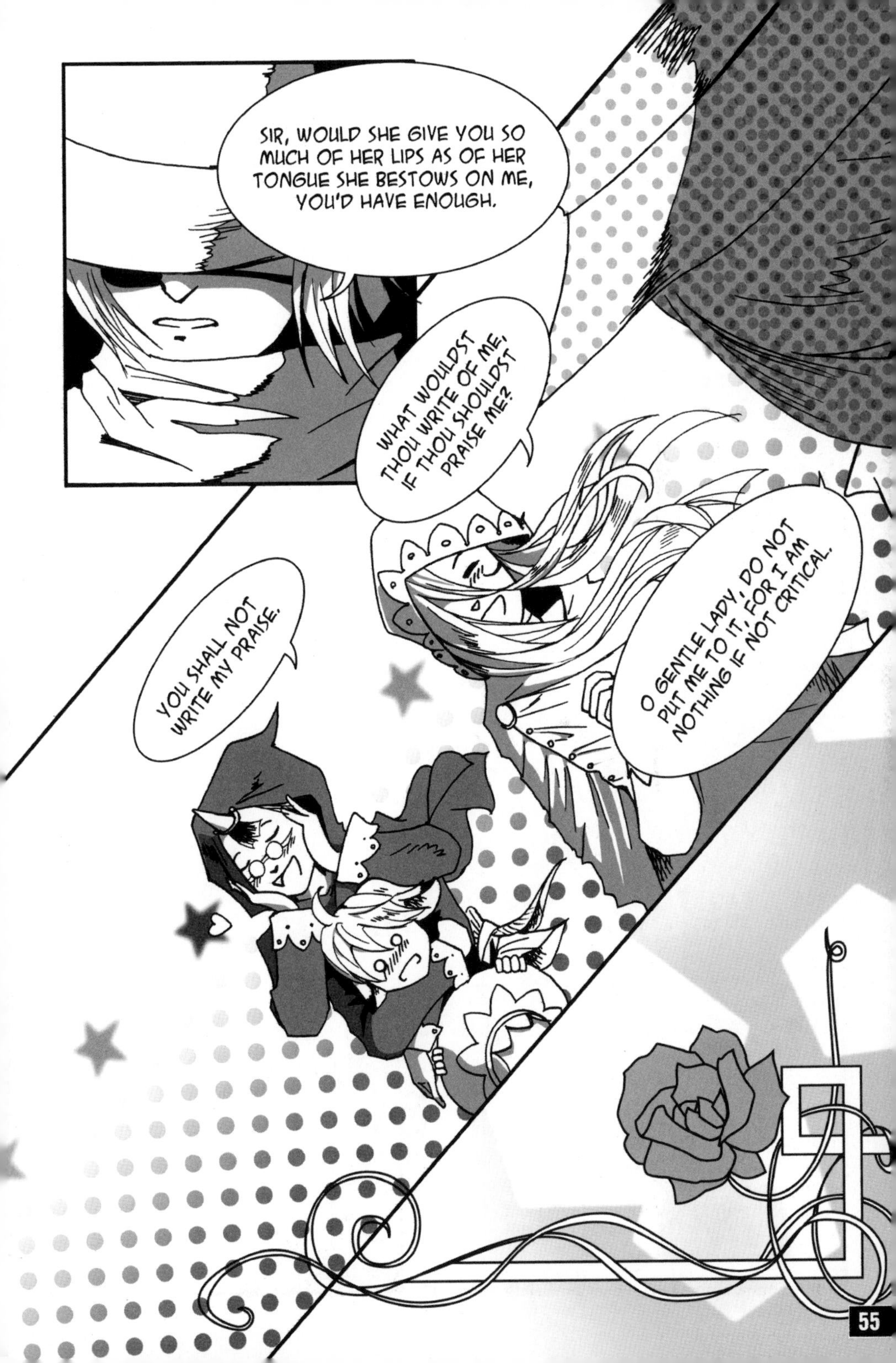
SIR, WOULD SHE GIVE YOU SO MUCH OF HER LIPS AS OF HER TONGUE SHE BESTOWS ON ME, YOU'D HAVE ENOUGH.
WHAT WOULDST THOU WRITE OF ME, IF THOU SHOULDST PRAISE ME?
O GENTLE LADY, DO NOT PUT ME TO IT, FOR I AM NOTHING IF NOT CRITICAL.
YOU SHALL NOT WRITE MY PRAISE.

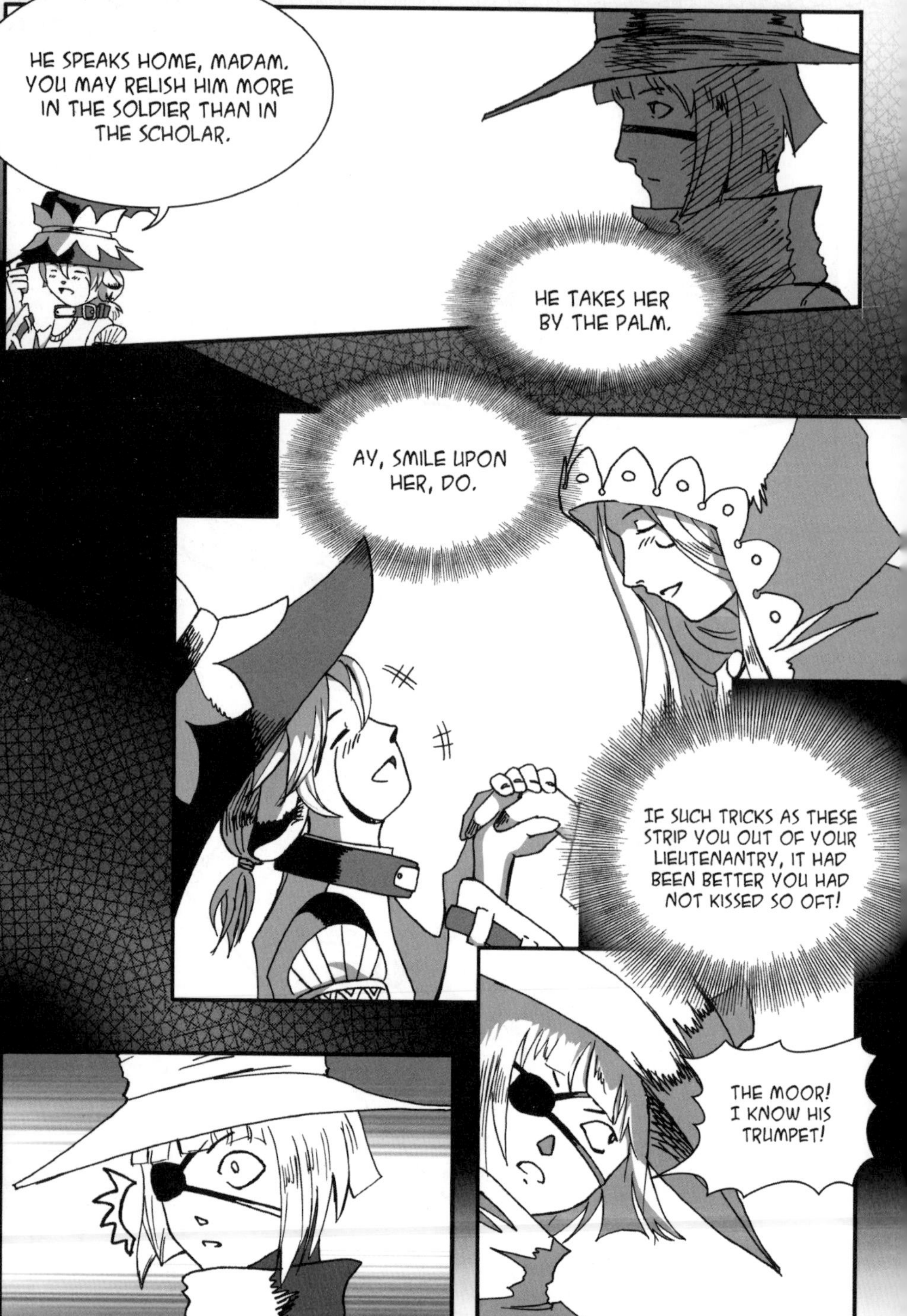
HE SPEAKS HOME, MADAM. YOU MAY RELISH HIM MORE IN THE SOLDIER THAN IN THE SCHOLAR.
HE TAKES HER BY THE PALM.
AY, SMILE UPON HER, DO.
IF SUCH TRICKS AS THESE STRIP YOU OUT OF YOUR LIEUTENANTRY, IT HAD BEEN BETTER YOU HAD NOT KISSED SO OFT!
THE MOOR! I KNOW HIS TRUMPET!

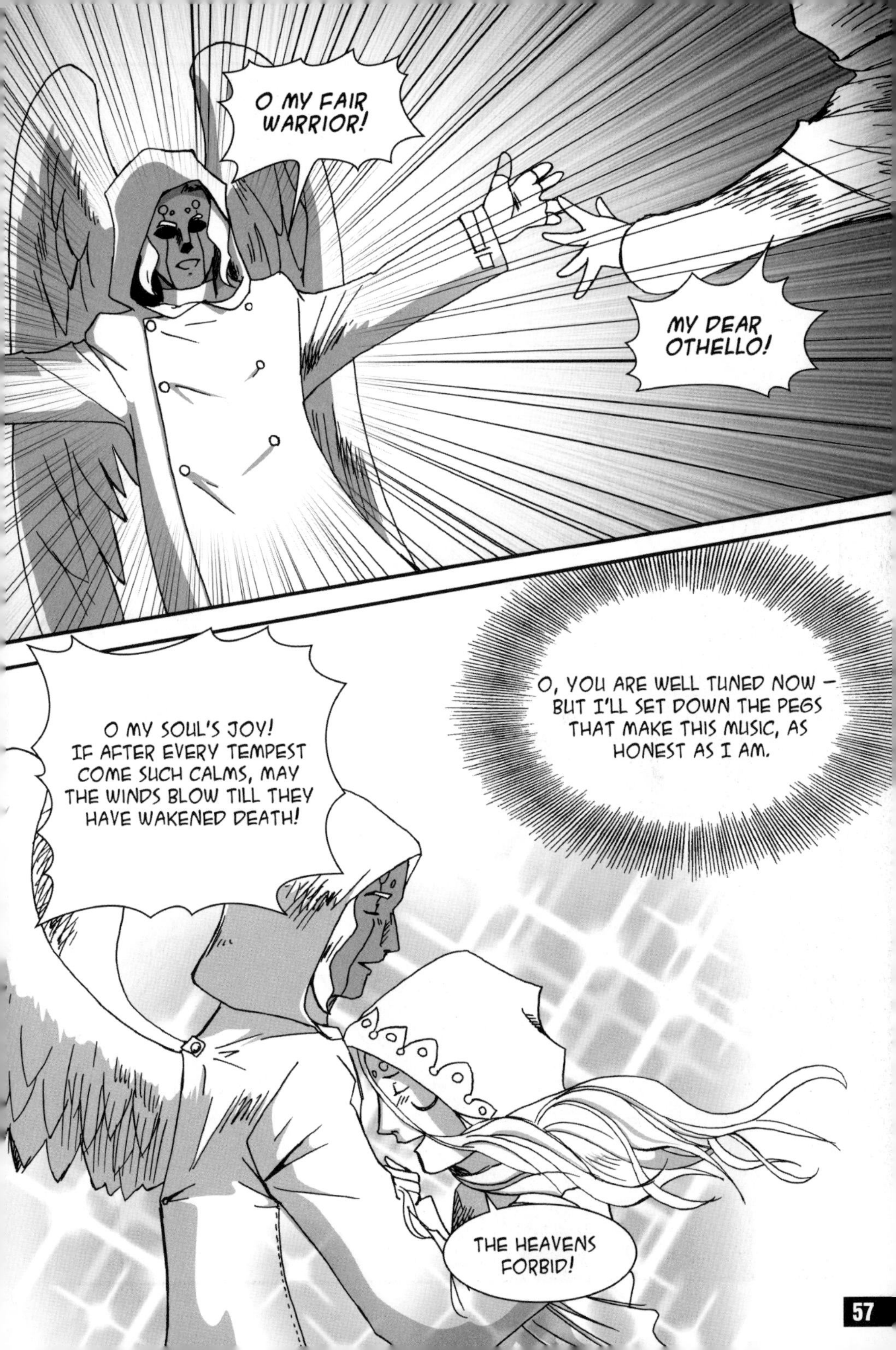
O MY FAIR WARRIOR!
MY DEAR OTHELLO!
O MY SOUL'S JOY! IF AFTER EVERY TEMPEST COME SUCH CALMS, MAY THE WINDS BLOW TILL THEY HAVE WAKENED DEATH!
O, YOU ARE WELL TUNED NOW — BUT I'LL SET DOWN THE PEGS THAT MAKE THIS MUSIC, AS HONEST AS I AM.
THE HEAVENS FORBID!

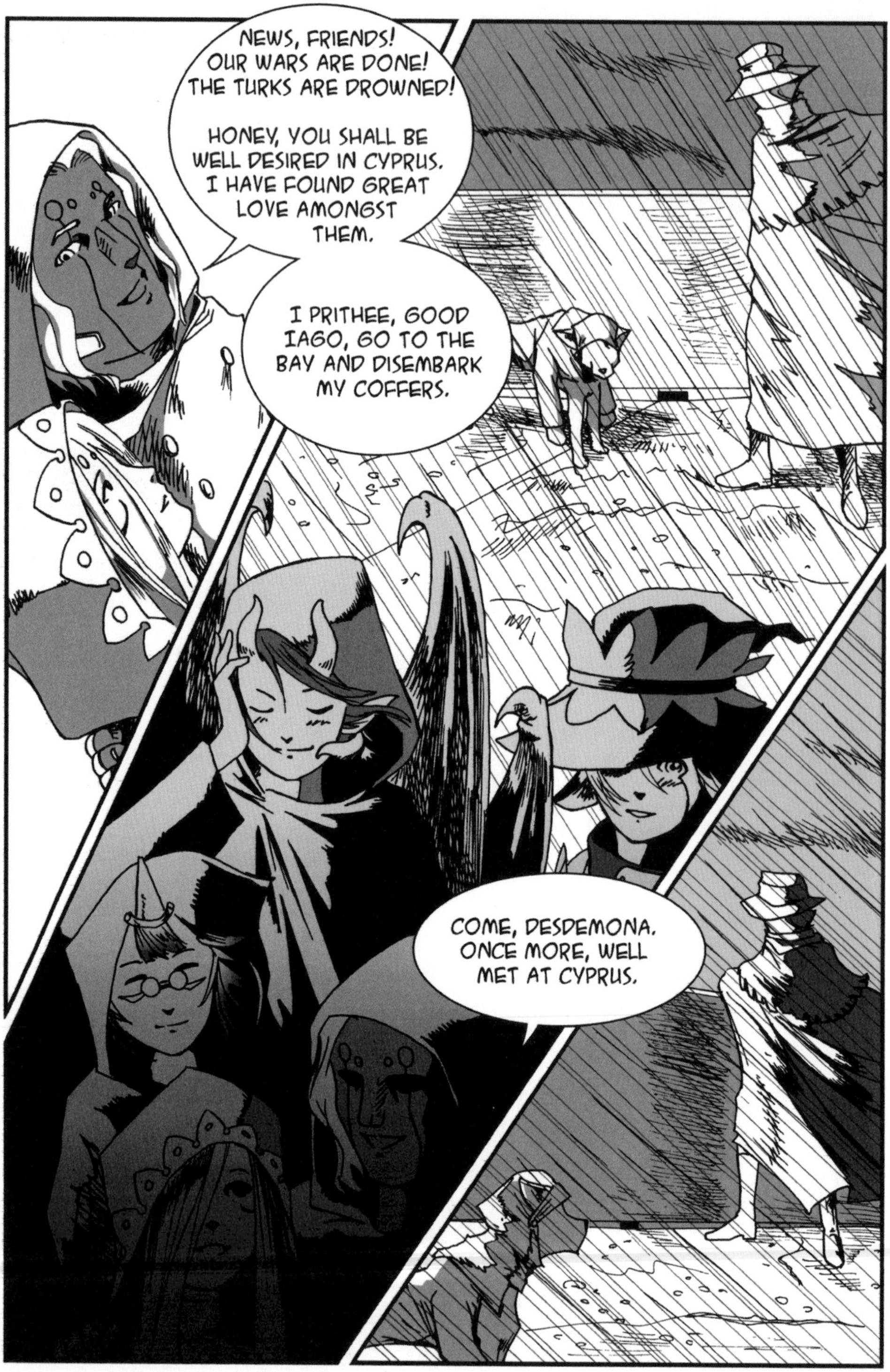
NEWS, FRIENDS! OUR WARS ARE DONE! THE TURKS ARE DROWNED!
HONEY, YOU SHALL BE WELL DESIRED IN CYPRUS. I HAVE FOUND GREAT LOVE AMONGST THEM.
I PRITHEE, GOOD IAGO, GO TO THE BAY AND DISEMBARK MY COFFERS.
COME, DESDEMONA. ONCE MORE, WELL MET AT CYPRUS.

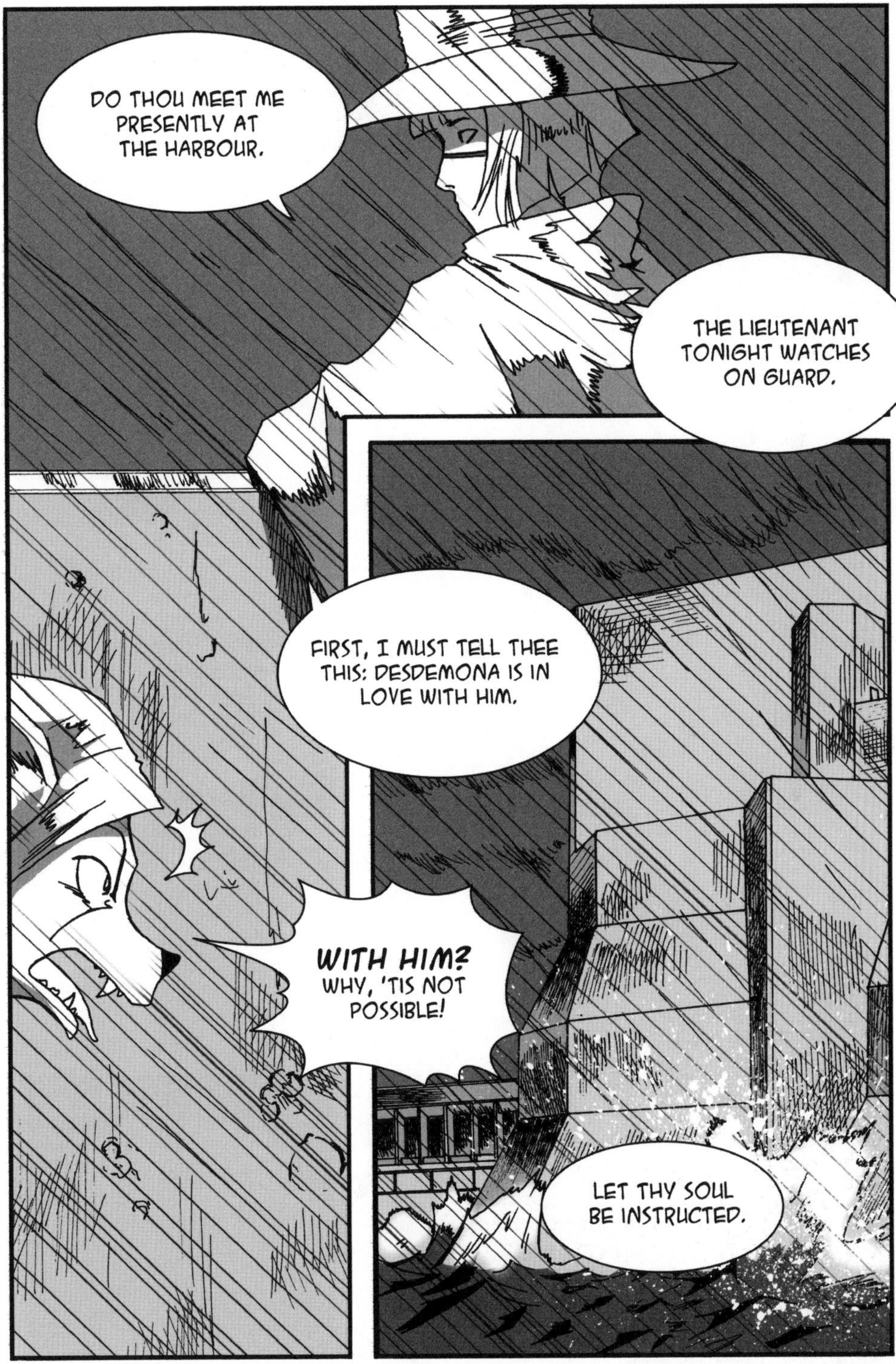
DO THOU MEET ME PRESENTLY AT THE HARBOUR.
THE LIEUTENANT TONIGHT WATCHES ON GUARD.
FIRST, I MUST TELL THEE THIS: DESDEMONA IS IN LOVE WITH HIM.
WITH HIM? WHY, 'TIS NOT POSSIBLE!
LET THY SOUL BE INSTRUCTED.

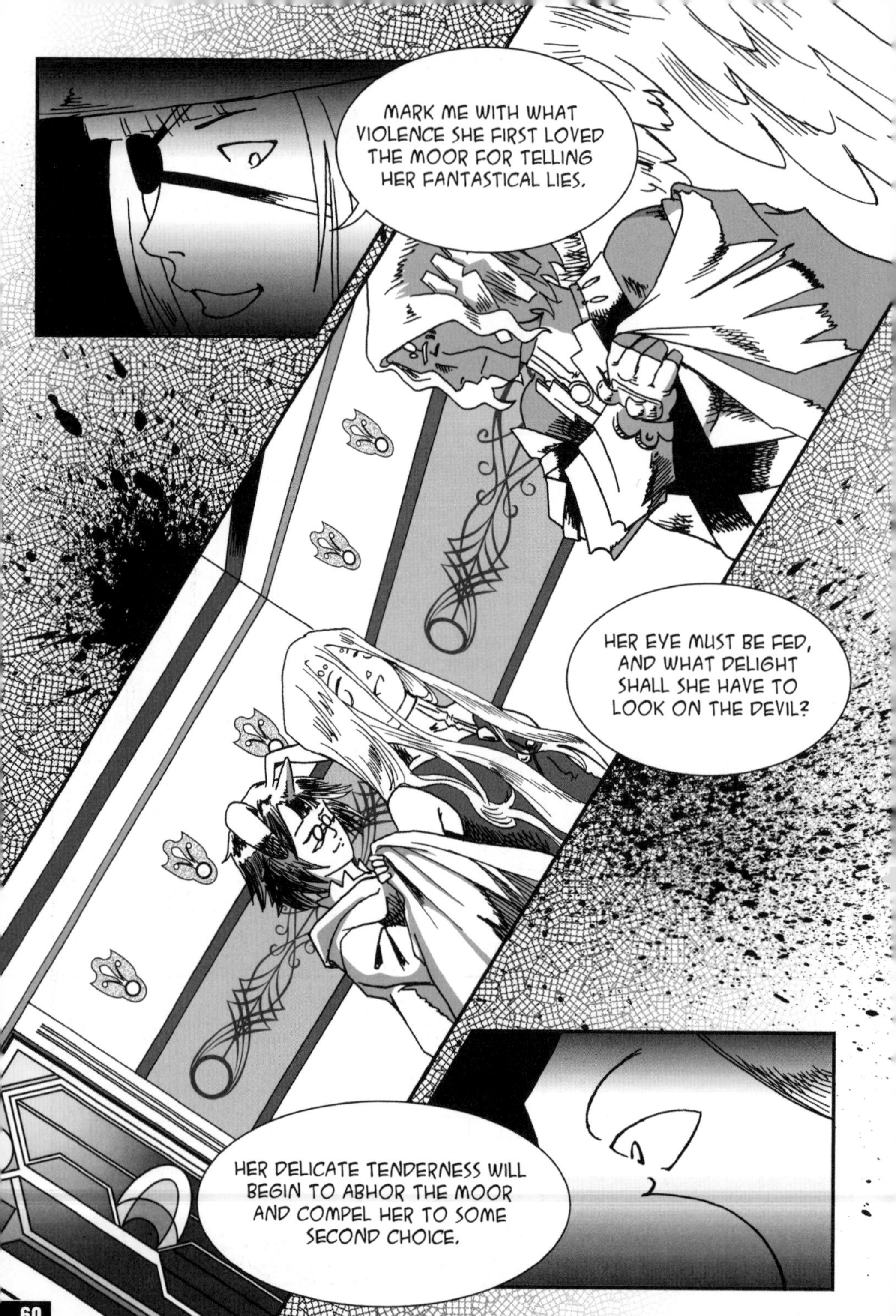
MARK ME WITH WHAT VIOLENCE SHE FIRST LOVED THE MOOR FOR TELLING HER FANTASTICAL LIES.
HER EYE MUST BE FED, AND WHAT DELIGHT SHALL SHE HAVE TO LOOK ON THE DEVIL?
HER DELICATE TENDERNESS WILL BEGIN TO ABHOR THE MOOR AND COMPEL HER TO SOME SECOND CHOICE.

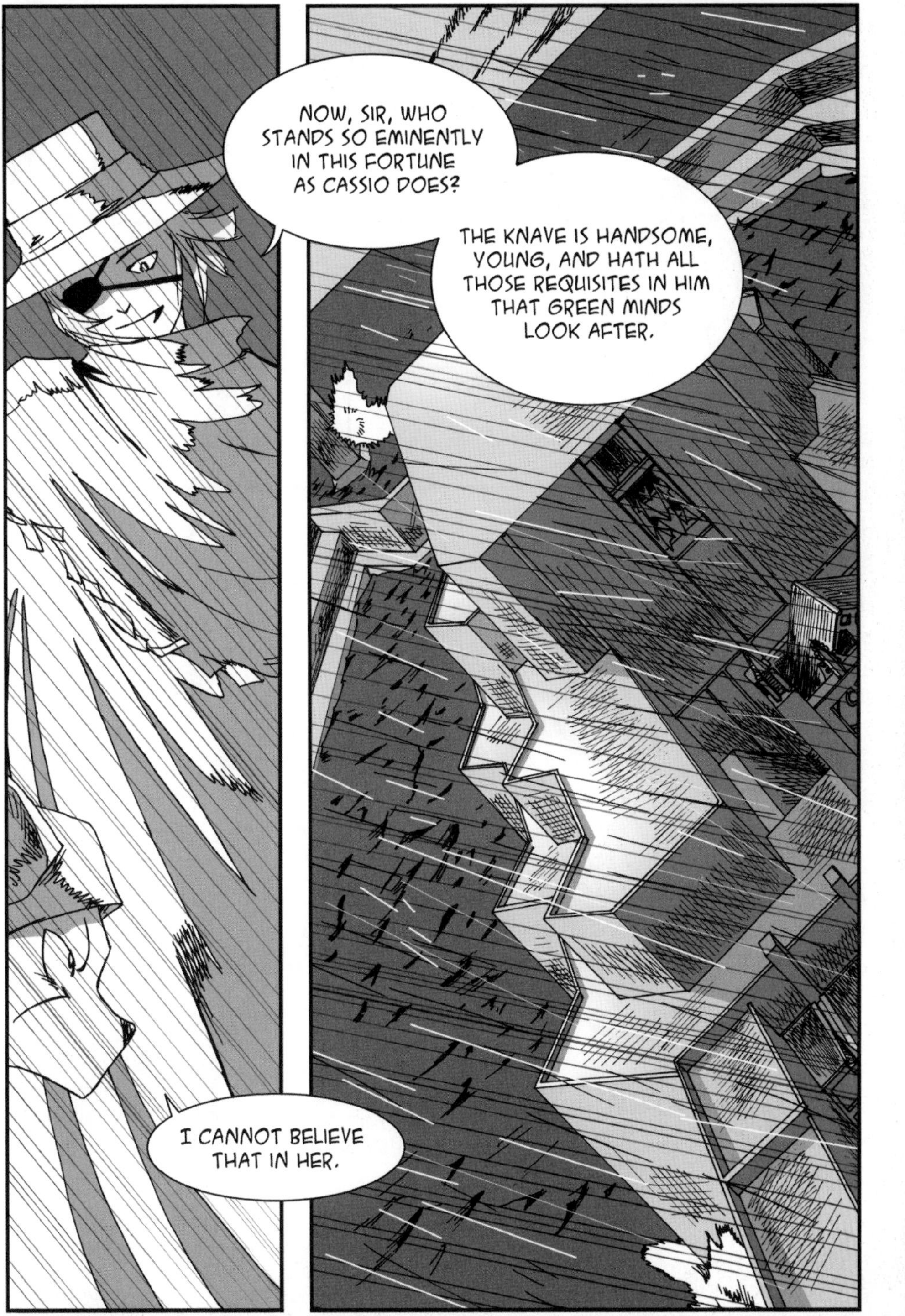
NOW, SIR, WHO STANDS SO EMINENTLY IN THIS FORTUNE AS CASSIO DOES?
THE KNAVE IS HANDSOME, YOUNG, AND HATH ALL THOSE REQUISITES IN HIM THAT GREEN MINDS LOOK AFTER.
I CANNOT BELIEVE THAT IN HER.

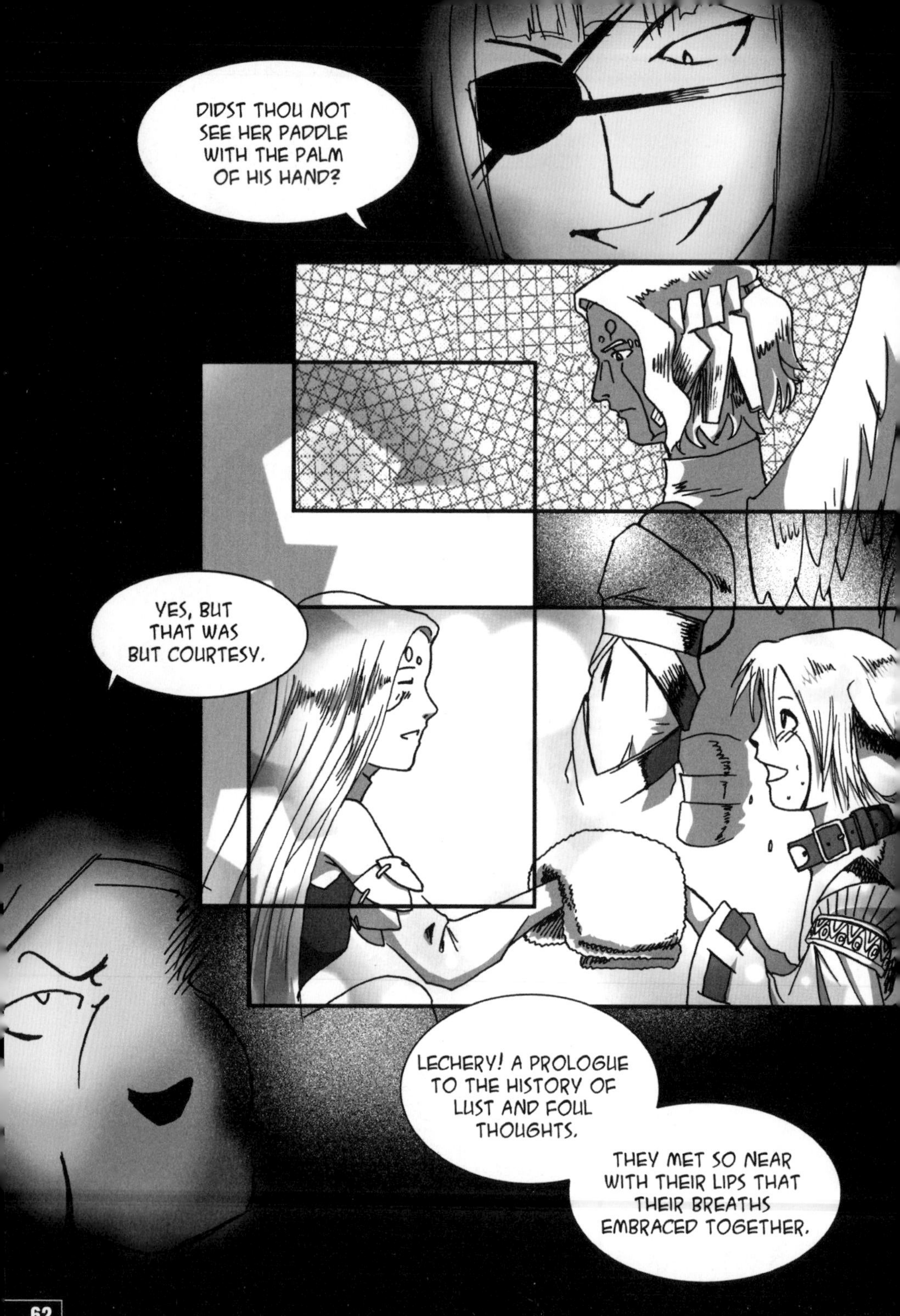
DIDST THOU NOT SEE HER PADDLE WITH THE PALM OF HIS HAND?
YES, BUT THAT WAS BUT COURTESY.
LECHERY! A PROLOGUE TO THE HISTORY OF LUST AND FOUL THOUGHTS.
THEY MET SO NEAR WITH THEIR LIPS THAT THEIR BREATHS EMBRACED TOGETHER.

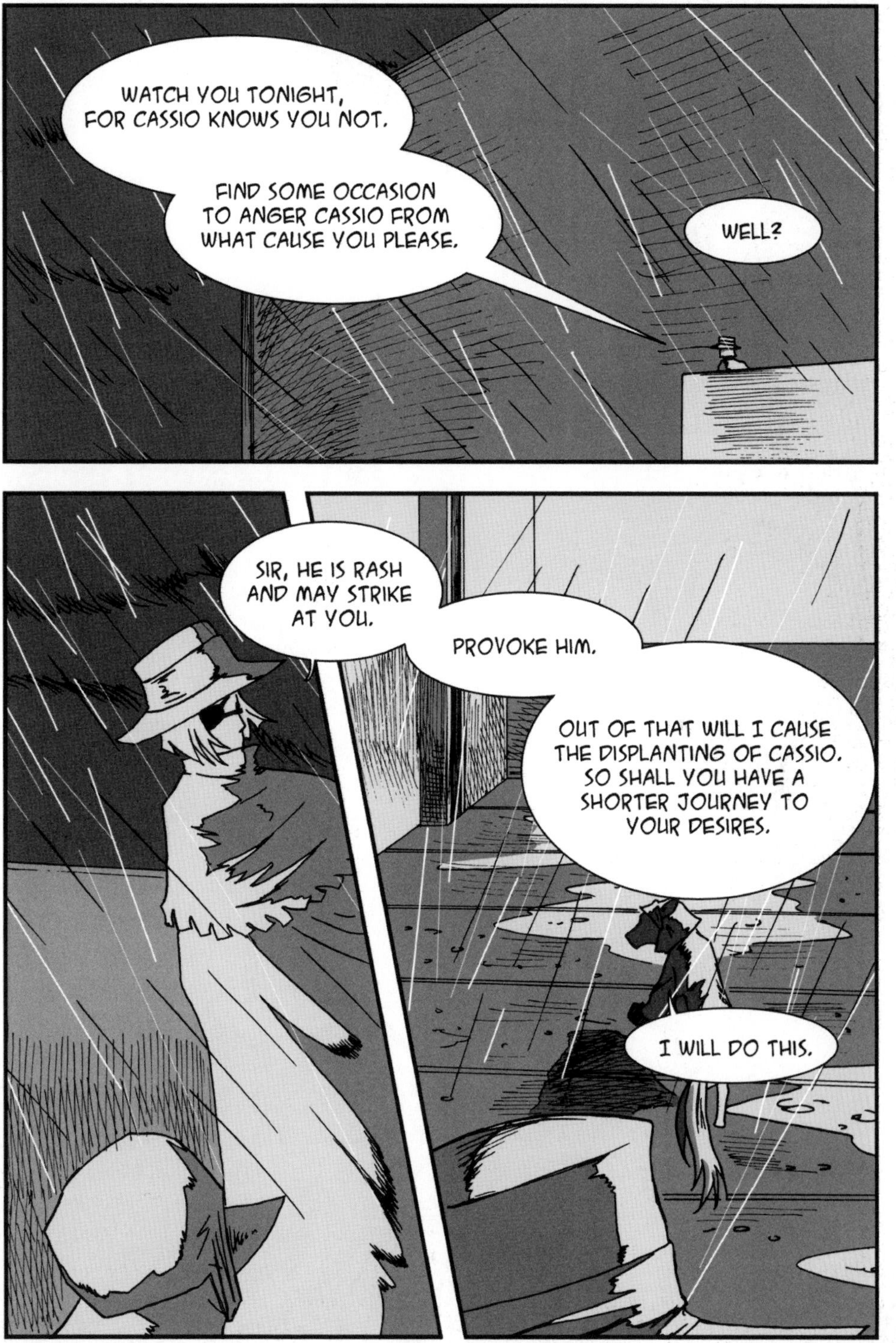
WATCH YOU TONIGHT, FOR CASSIO KNOWS YOU NOT.
FIND SOME OCCASION TO ANGER CASSIO FROM WHAT CAUSE YOU PLEASE.
WELL?
SIR, HE IS RASH AND MAY STRIKE AT YOU.
PROVOKE HIM.
OUT OF THAT WILL I CAUSE THE DISPLANTING OF CASSIO. SO SHALL YOU HAVE A SHORTER JOURNEY TO YOUR DESIRES.
I WILL DO THIS.

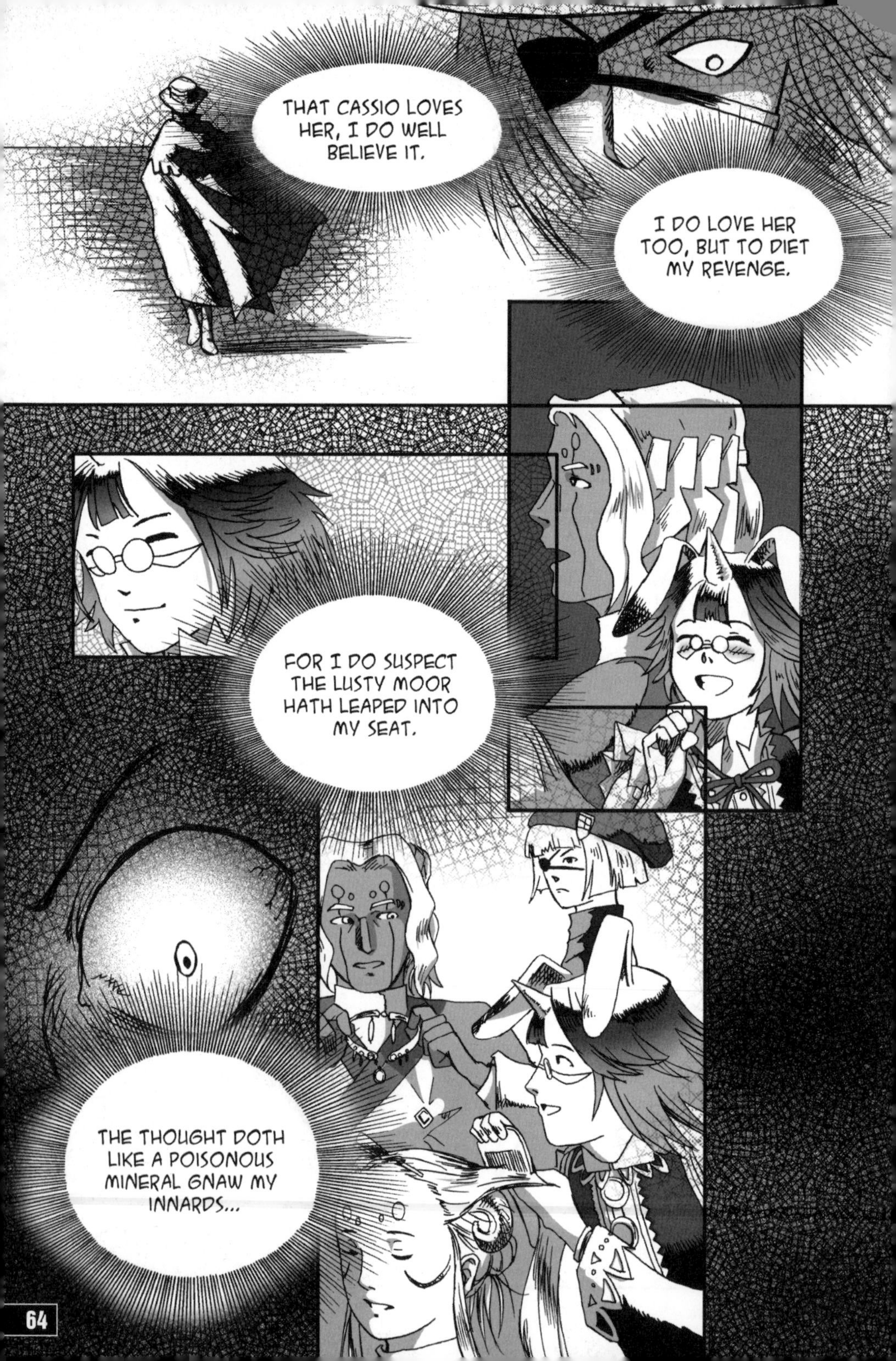
THAT CASSIO LOVES HER, I DO WELL BELIEVE IT.
I DO LOVE HER TOO, BUT TO DIET MY REVENGE.
FOR I DO SUSPECT THE LUSTY MOOR HATH LEAPED INTO MY SEAT.
THE THOUGHT DOTH LIKE A POISONOUS MINERAL GNAW MY INNARDS...

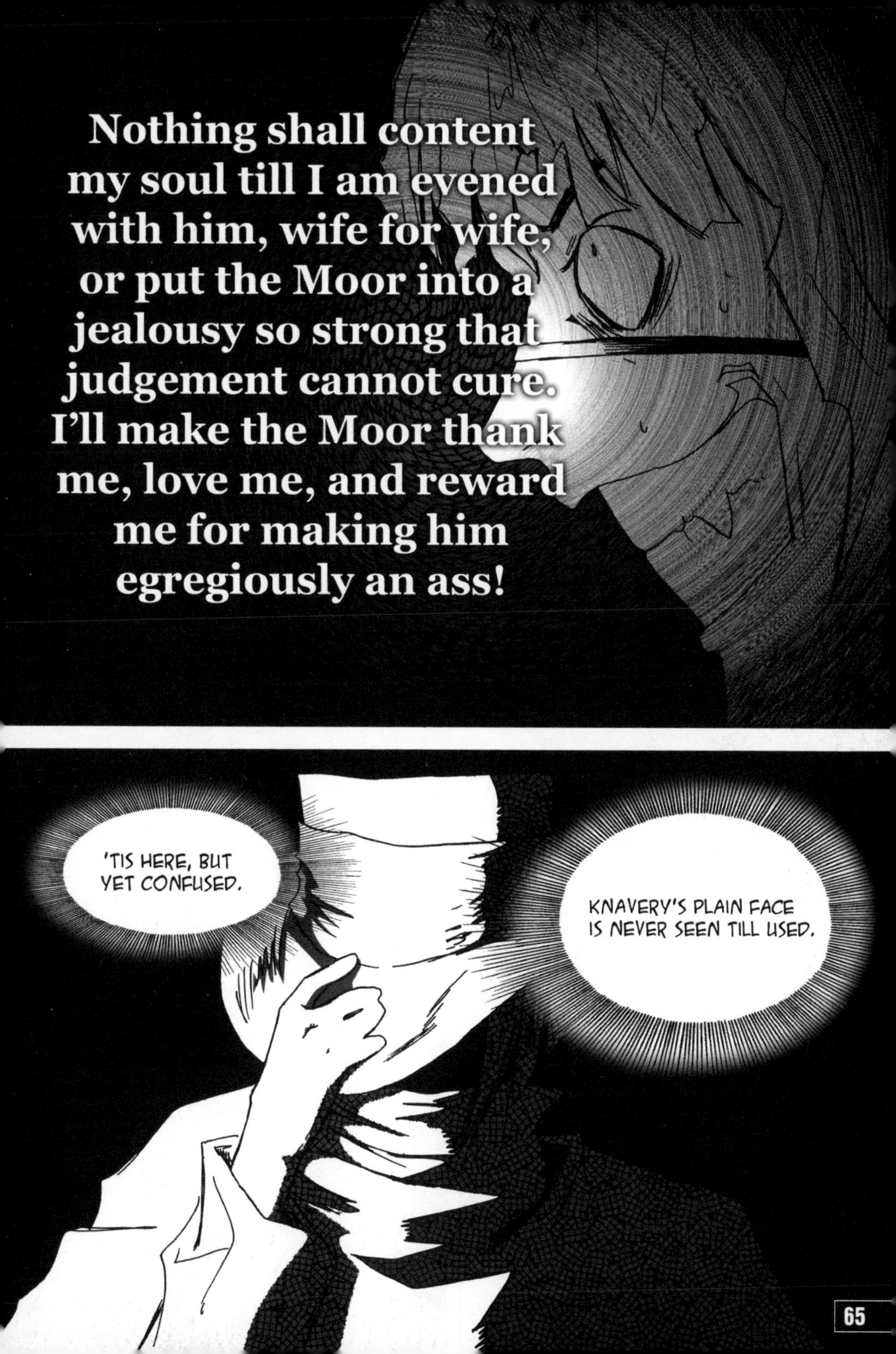
Nothing shall content my soul till I am evened with him, wife for wife, or put the Moor into a jealousy so strong that judgement cannot cure. I'll make the Moor thank me, love me, and reward me for making him egregiously an ass!
'TIS HERE, BUT YET CONFUSED.
KNAVERY'S PLAIN FACE IS NEVER SEEN TILL USED.

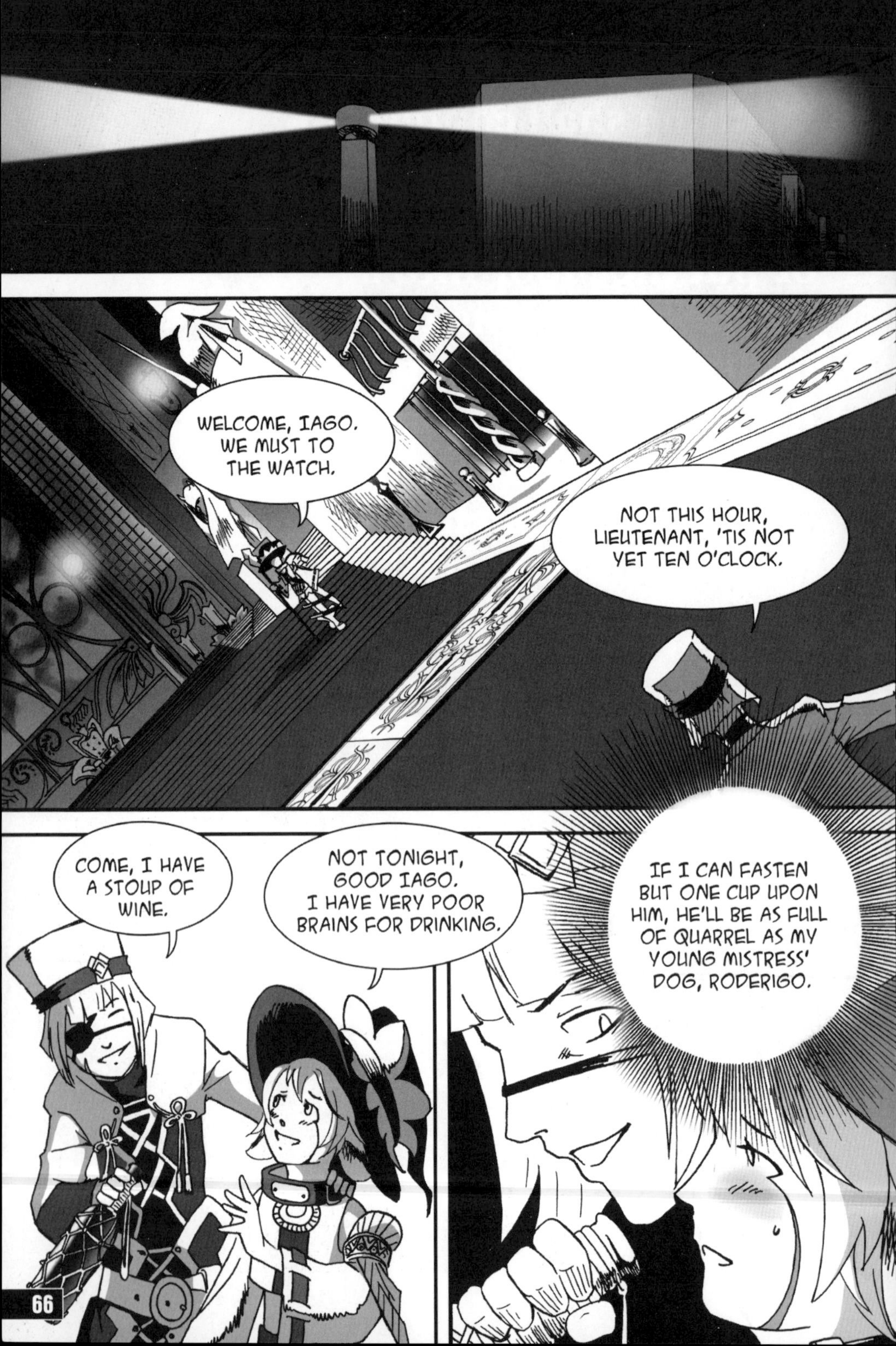
WELCOME, IAGO. WE MUST TO THE WATCH.
NOT THIS HOUR, LIEUTENANT, 'TIS NOT YET TEN O'CLOCK.
COME, I HAVE A STOUP OF WINE.
NOT TONIGHT, GOOD IAGO. I HAVE VERY POOR BRAINS FOR DRINKING.
IF I CAN FASTEN BUT ONE CUP UPON HIM, HE'LL BE AS FULL OF QUARREL AS MY YOUNG MISTRESS' DOG, RODERIGO.

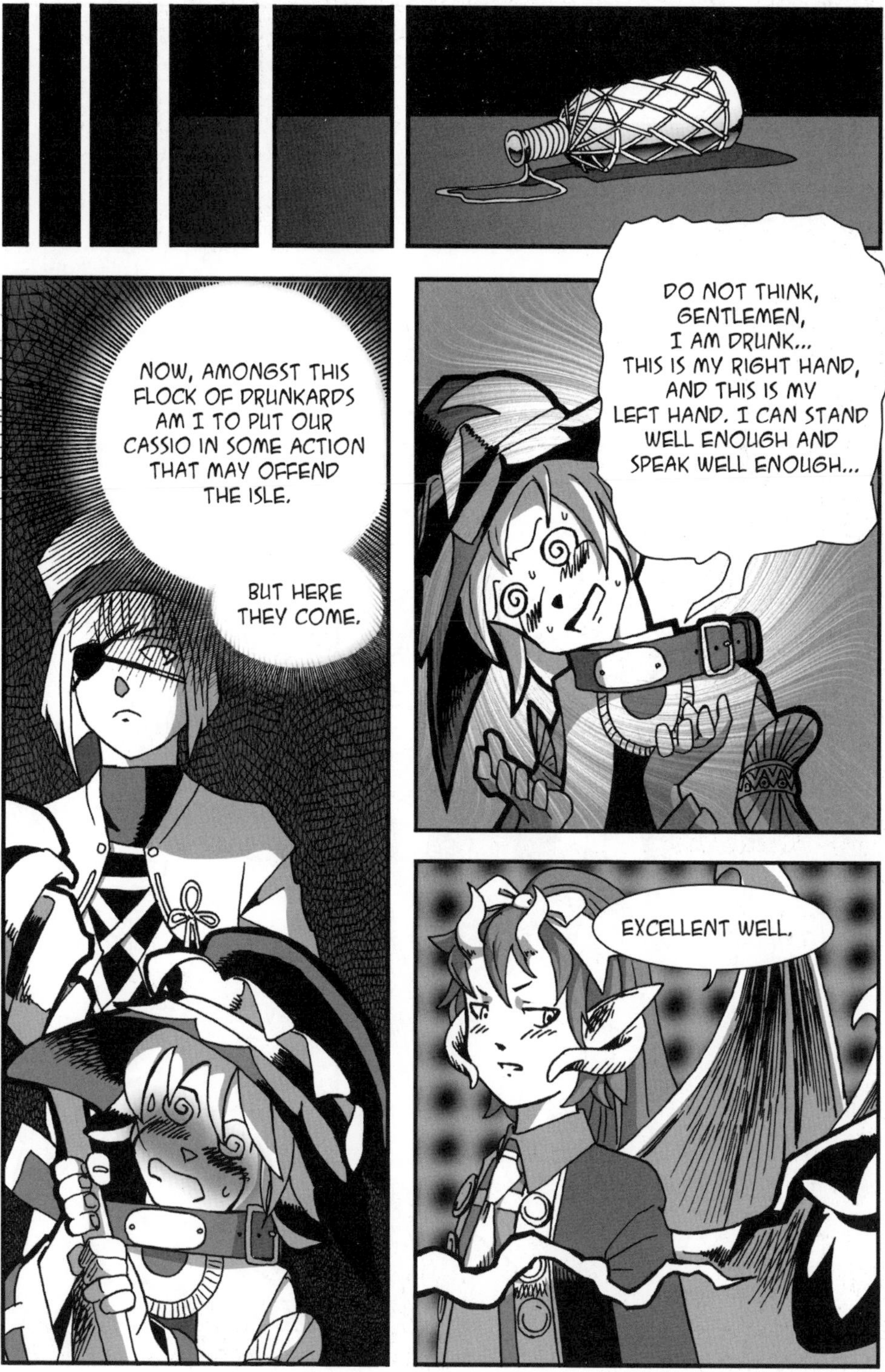
NOW, AMONGST THIS FLOCK OF DRUNKARDS AM I TO PUT OUR CASSIO IN SOME ACTION THAT MAY OFFEND THE ISLE.
BUT HERE THEY COME.
DO NOT THINK, GENTLEMEN, I AM DRUNK... THIS IS MY RIGHT HAND, AND THIS IS MY LEFT HAND. I CAN STAND WELL ENOUGH AND SPEAK WELL ENOUGH...
EXCELLENT WELL.

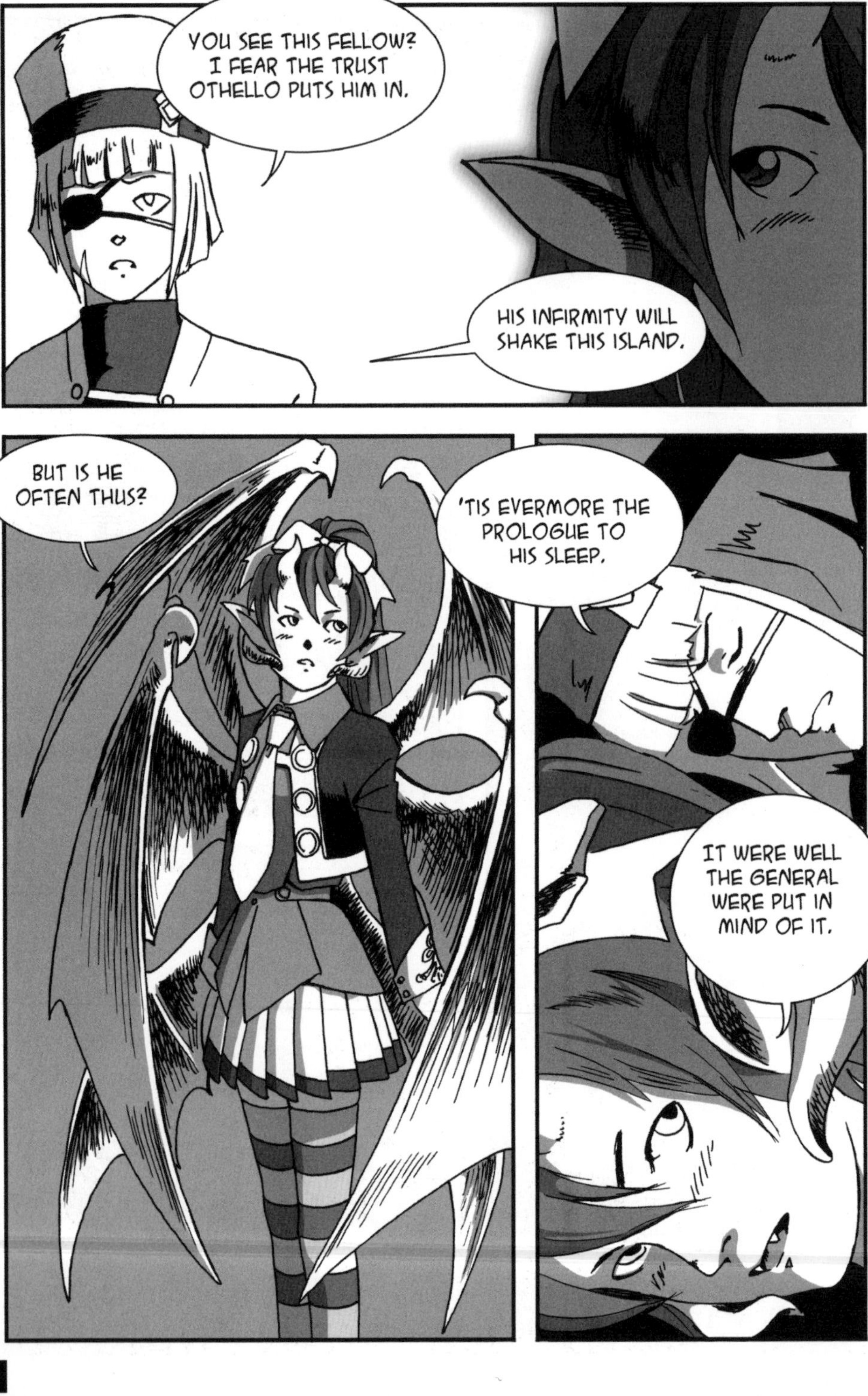
YOU SEE THIS FELLOW? I FEAR THE TRUST OTHELLO PUTS HIM IN.
HIS INFIRMITY WILL SHAKE THIS ISLAND.
BUT IS HE OFTEN THUS?
'TIS EVERMORE THE PROLOGUE TO HIS SLEEP.
IT WERE WELL THE GENERAL WERE PUT IN MIND OF IT.

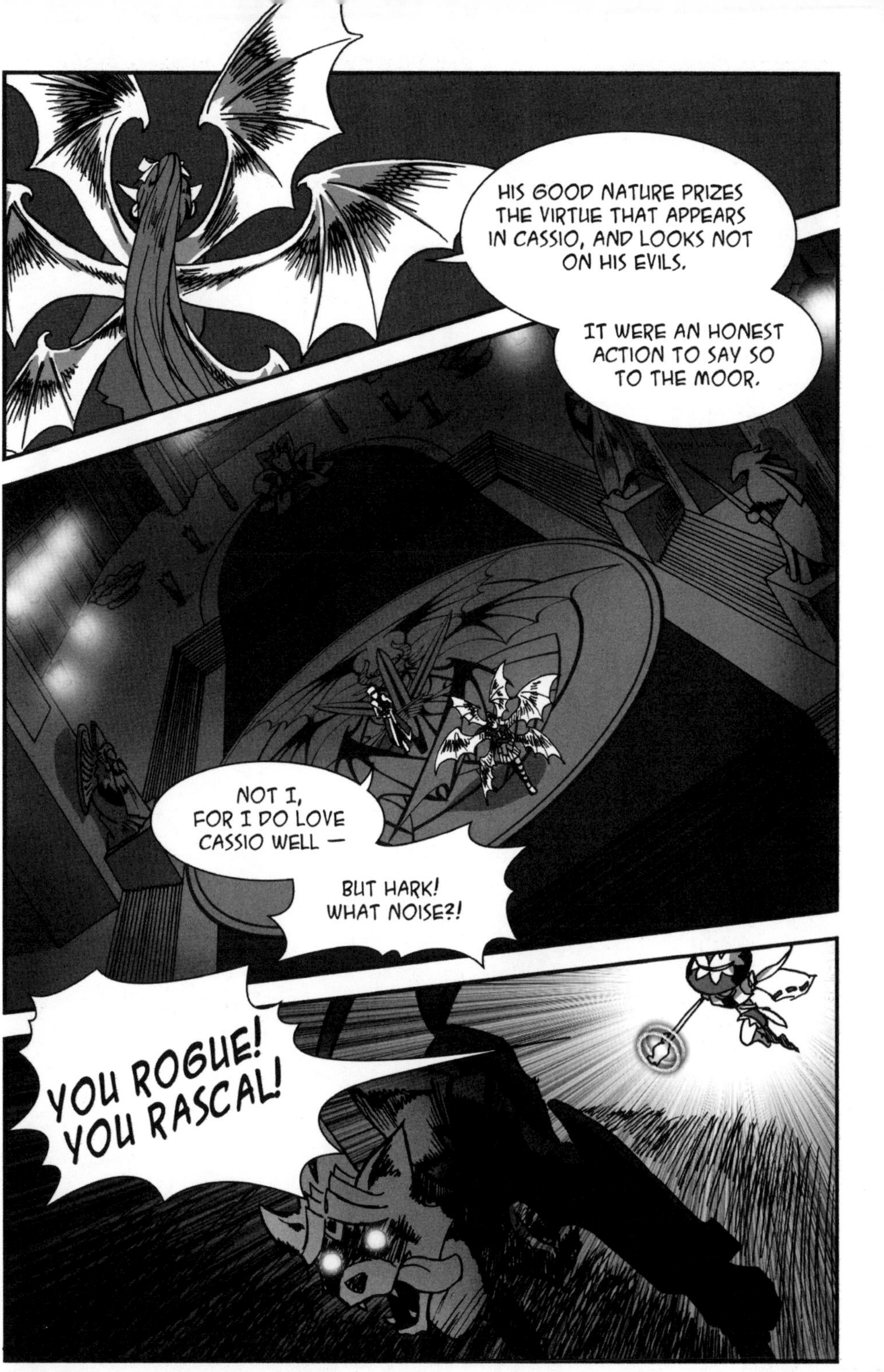
HIS GOOD NATURE PRIZES THE VIRTUE THAT APPEARS IN CASSIO, AND LOOKS NOT ON HIS EVILS.
IT WERE AN HONEST ACTION TO SAY SO TO THE MOOR.
NOT I, FOR I DO LOVE CASSIO WELL —
BUT HARK! WHAT NOISE?!
YOU ROGUE! YOU RASCAL!

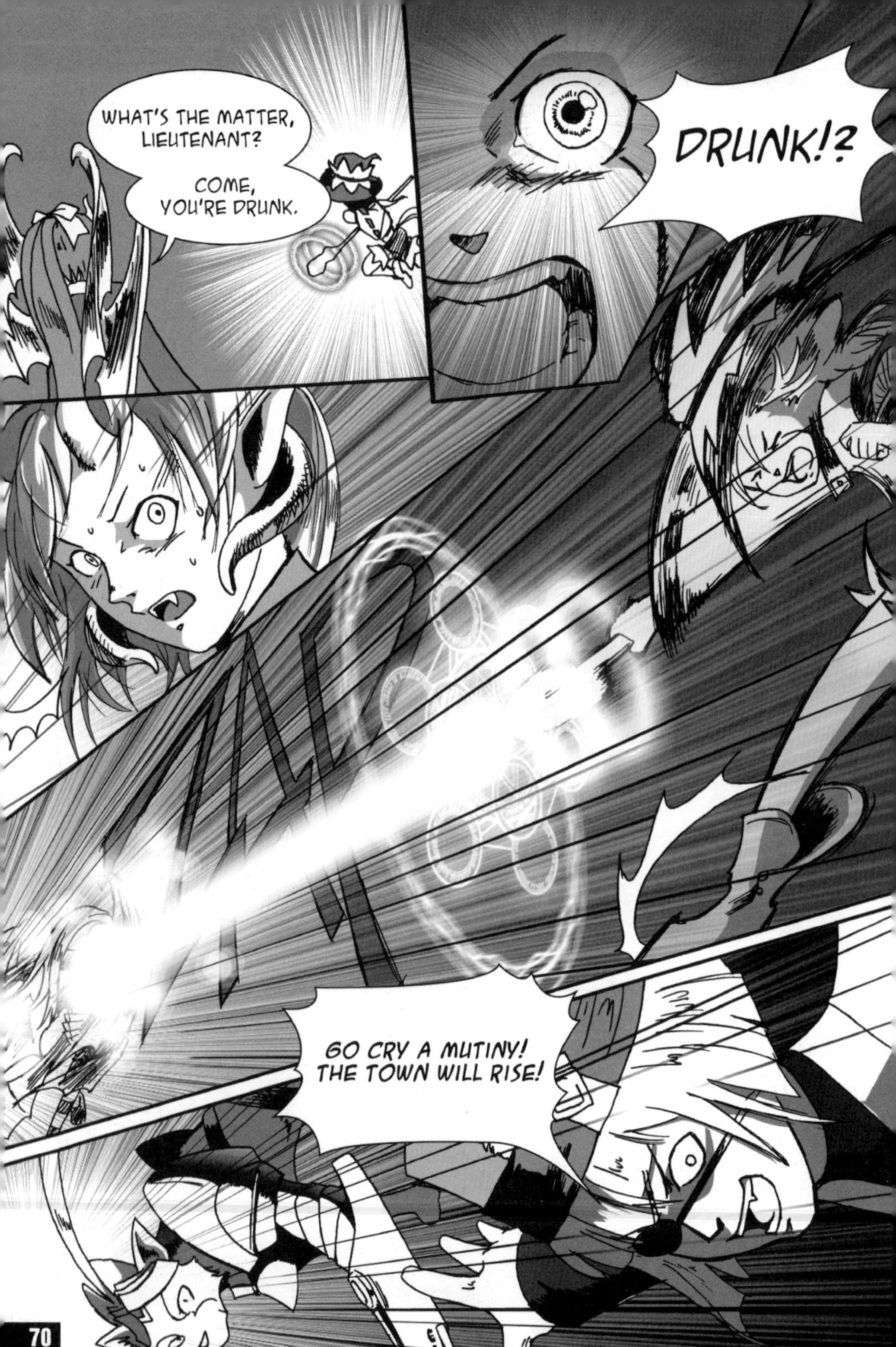

WHAT'S THE MATTER, LIEUTENANT?
COME, YOU'RE DRUNK.
DRUNK!?
GO CRY A MUTINY! THE TOWN WILL RISE!

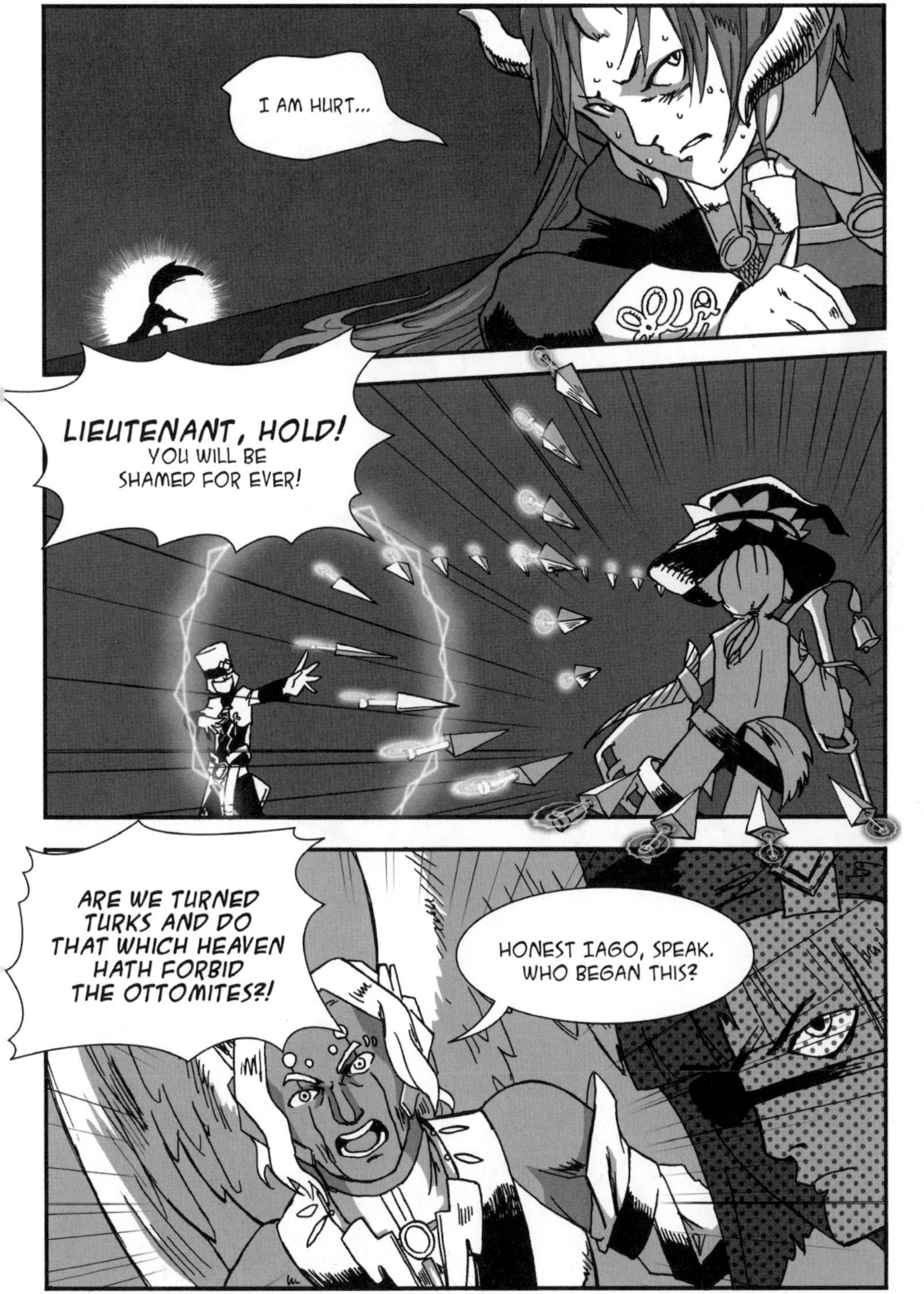
I AM HURT...
LIEUTENANT, HOLD! YOU WILL BE SHAMED FOR EVER!
ARE WE TURNED TURKS AND DO THAT WHICH HEAVEN HATH FORBID THE OTTOMITES?!
HONEST IAGO, SPEAK. WHO BEGAN THIS?

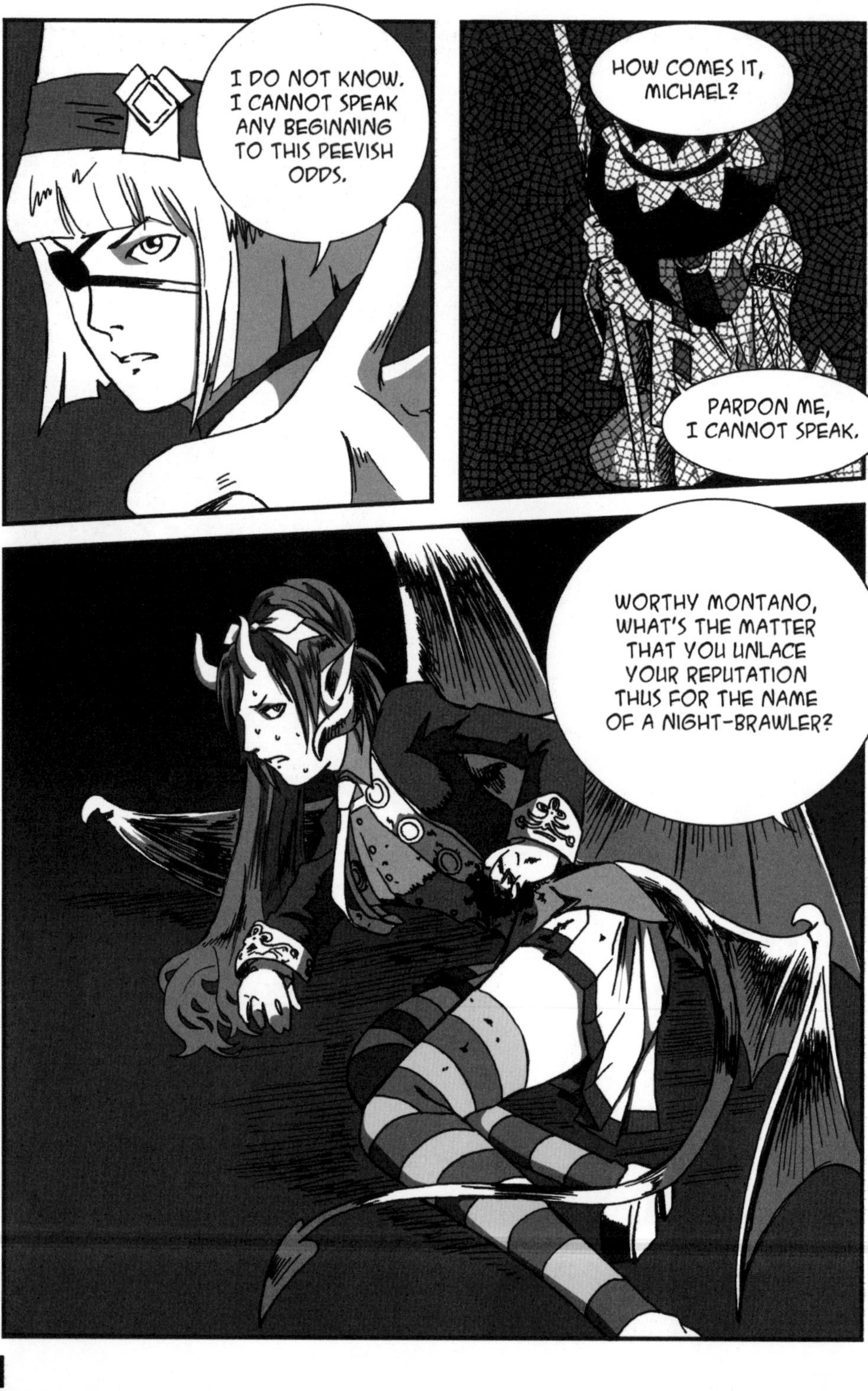
I DO NOT KNOW. I CANNOT SPEAK ANY BEGINNING TO THIS PEEVISH ODDS.
HOW COMES IT, MICHAEL?
PARDON ME, I CANNOT SPEAK.
WORTHY MONTANO, WHAT'S THE MATTER THAT YOU UNLACE YOUR REPUTATION THUS FOR THE NAME OF A NIGHT-BRAWLER?

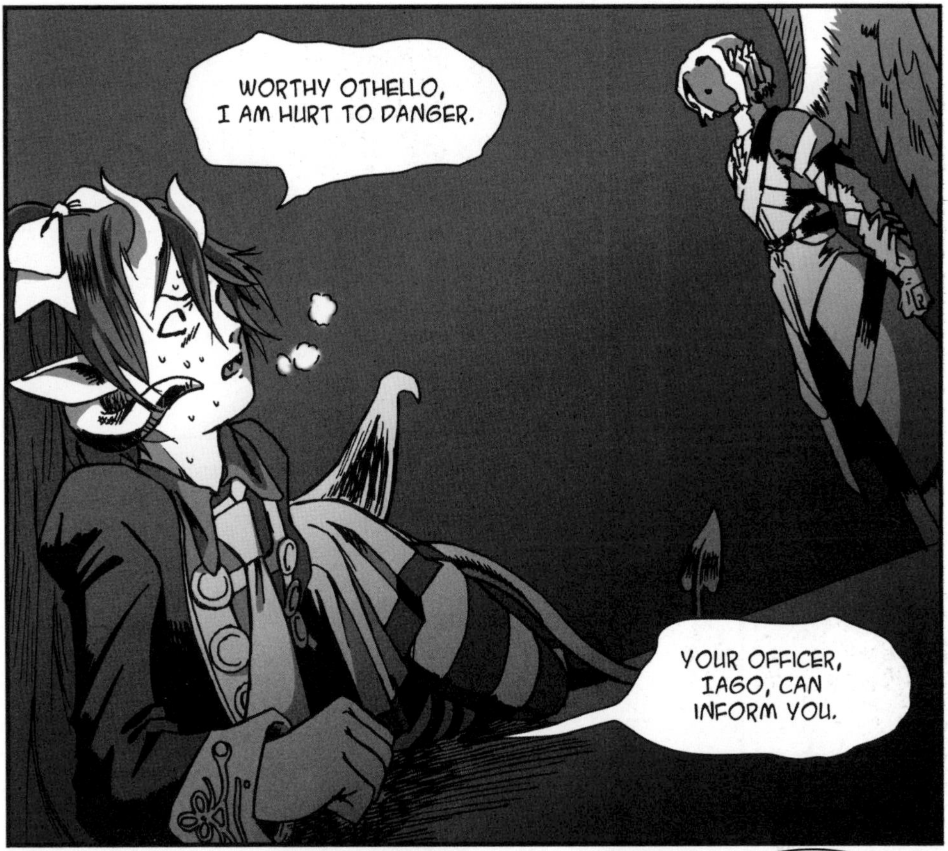
WORTHY OTHELLO, I AM HURT TO DANGER.
YOUR OFFICER, IAGO, CAN INFORM YOU.

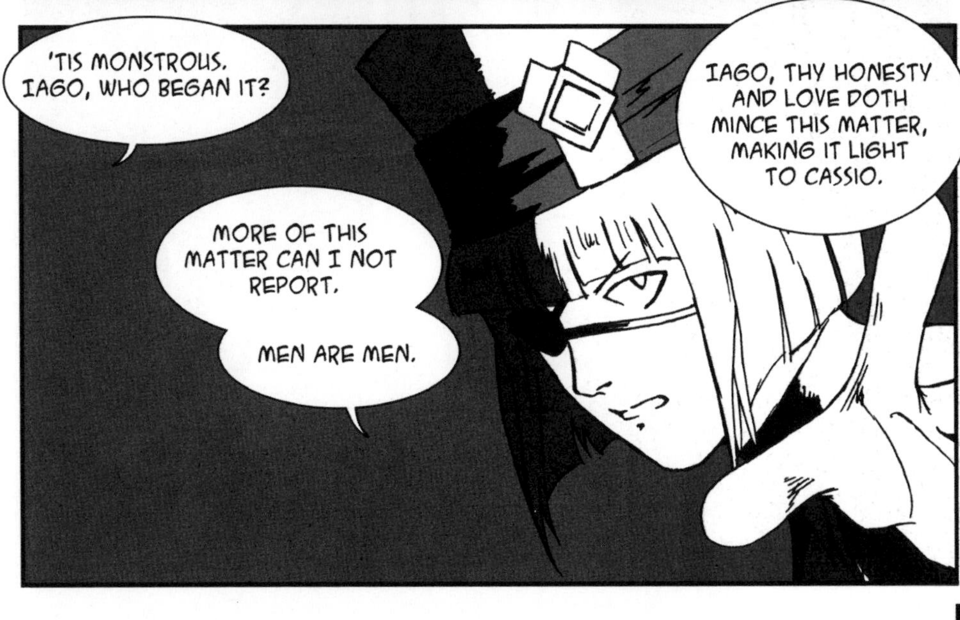
'TIS MONSTROUS. IAGO, WHO BEGAN IT?
MORE OF THIS MATTER CAN I NOT REPORT.
MEN ARE MEN.
IAGO, THY HONESTY AND LOVE DOTH MINCE THIS MATTER, MAKING IT LIGHT TO CASSIO.

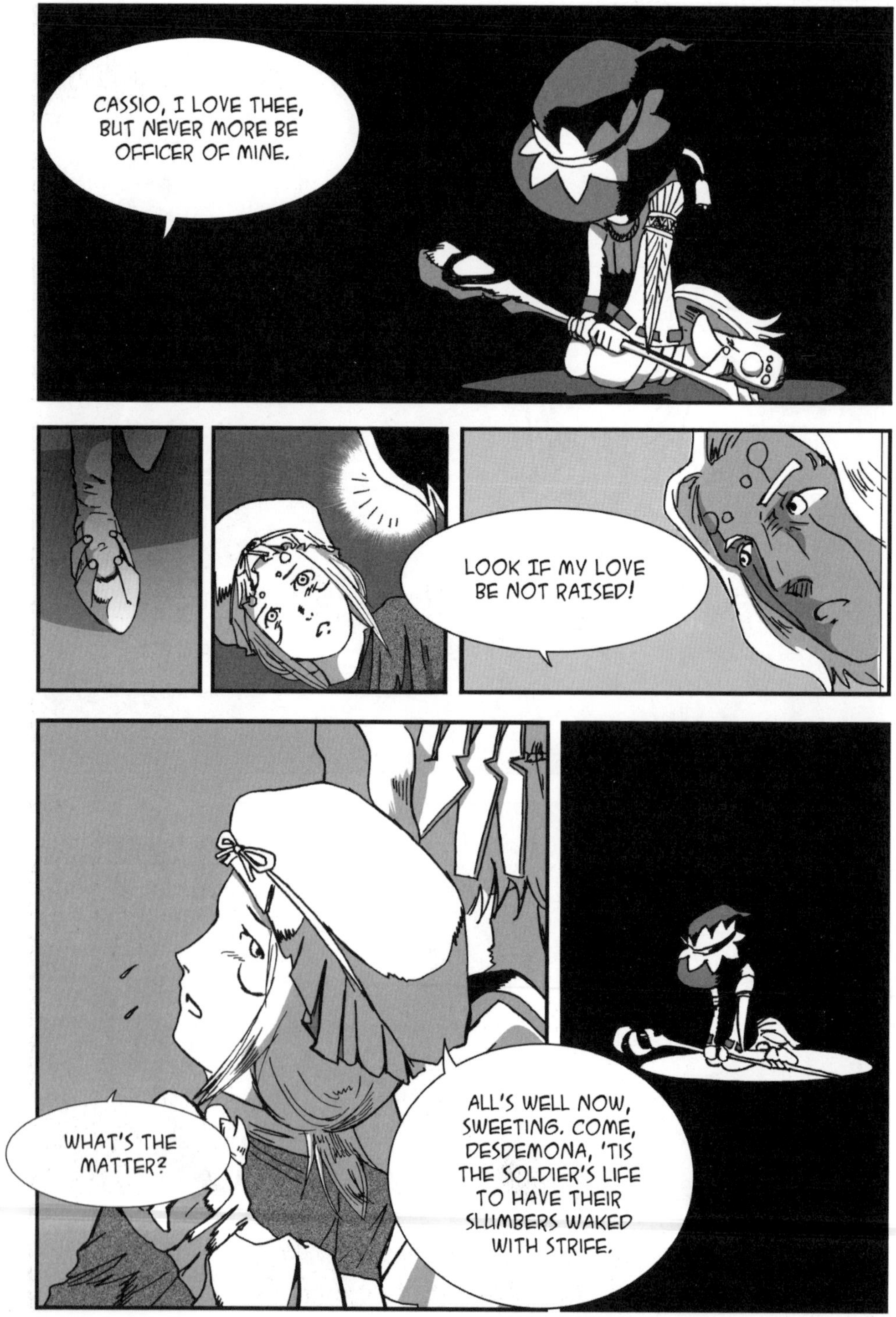
CASSIO, I LOVE THEE, BUT NEVER MORE BE OFFICER OF MINE.
LOOK IF MY LOVE BE NOT RAISED!
WHAT'S THE MATTER?
ALL'S WELL NOW, SWEETING. COME, DESDEMONA, 'TIS THE SOLDIER'S LIFE TO HAVE THEIR SLUMBERS WAKED WITH STRIFE.

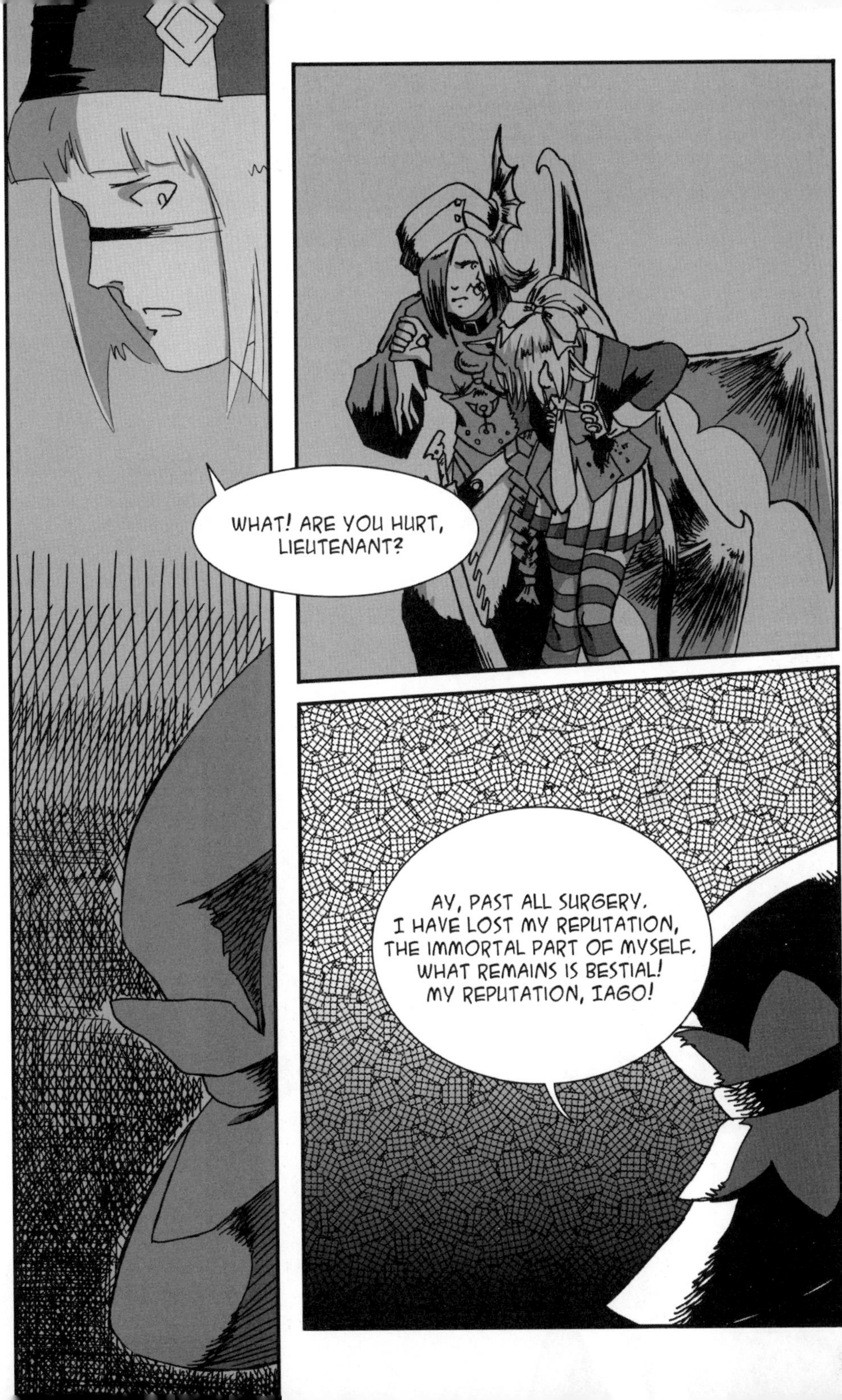
WHAT! ARE YOU HURT, LIEUTENANT?
AY, PAST ALL SURGERY. I HAVE LOST MY REPUTATION, THE IMMORTAL PART OF MYSELF. WHAT REMAINS IS BESTIAL! MY REPUTATION, IAGO!

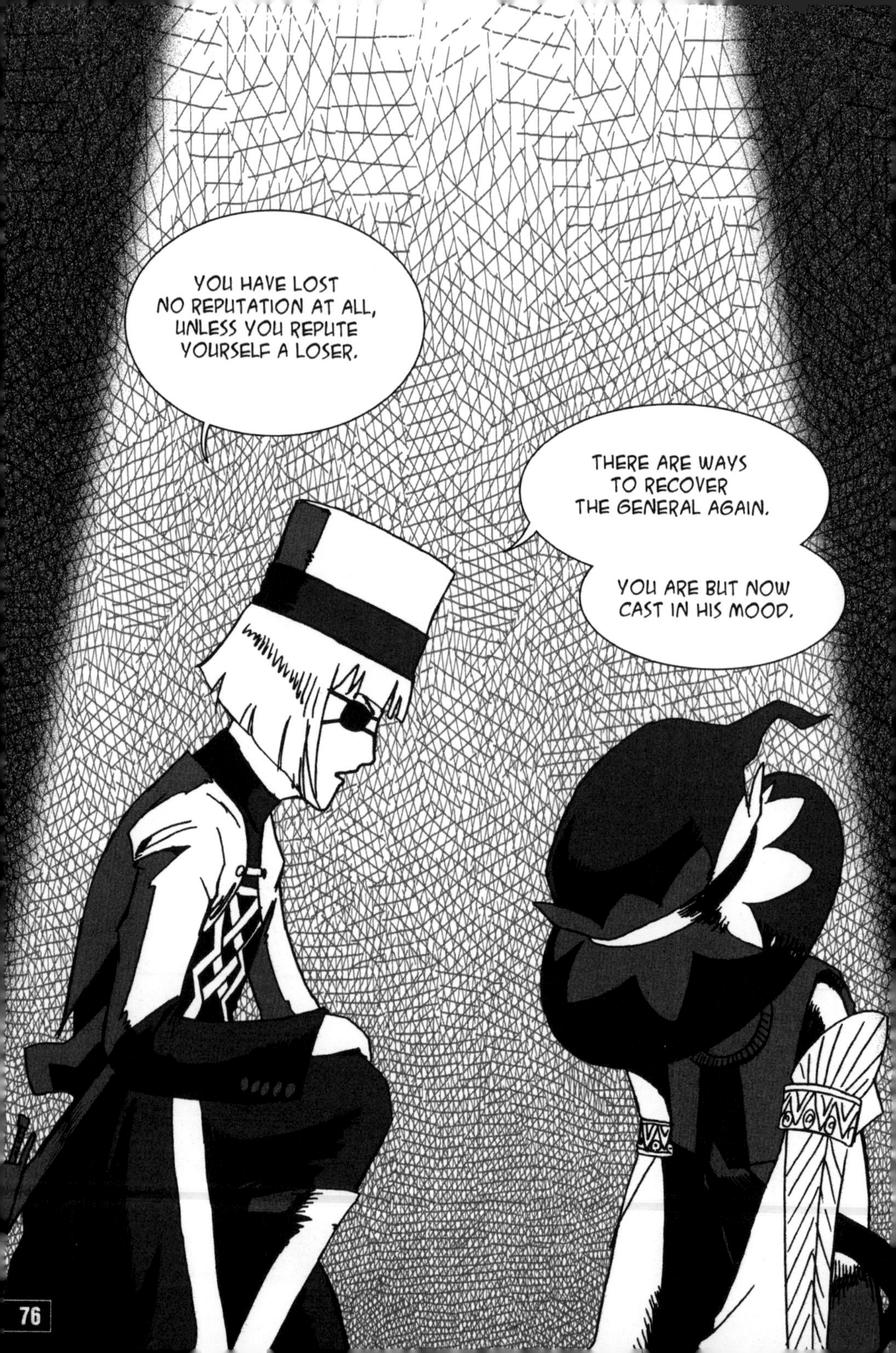
YOU HAVE LOST NO REPUTATION AT ALL, UNLESS YOU REPUTE YOURSELF A LOSER.
THERE ARE WAYS TO RECOVER THE GENERAL AGAIN.
YOU ARE BUT NOW CAST IN HIS MOOD.

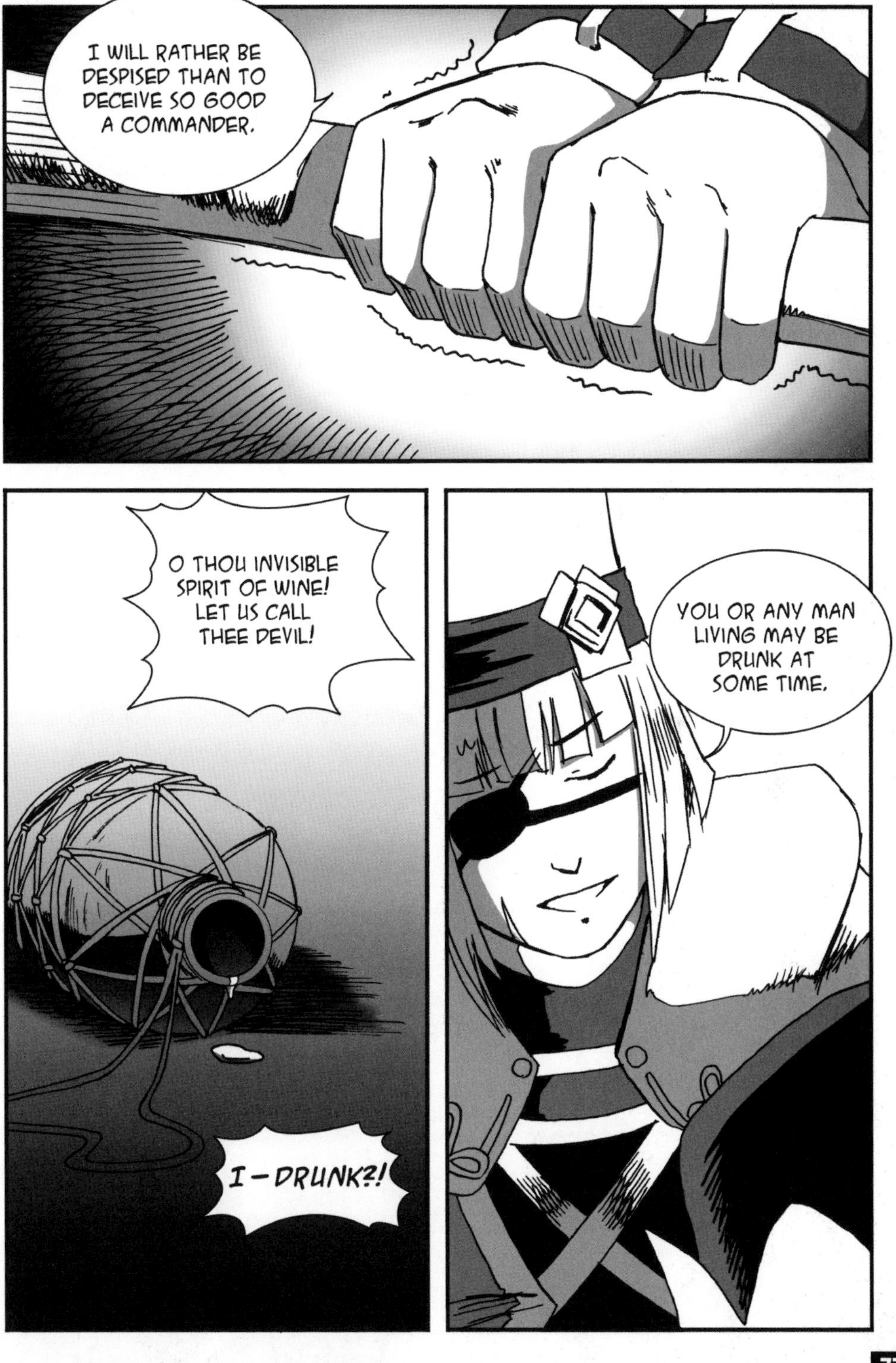
I WILL RATHER BE DESPISED THAN TO DECEIVE SO GOOD A COMMANDER.
O THOU INVISIBLE SPIRIT OF WINE! LET US CALL THEE DEVIL!
I-DRUNK?!
YOU OR ANY MAN LIVING MAY BE DRUNK AT SOME TIME.

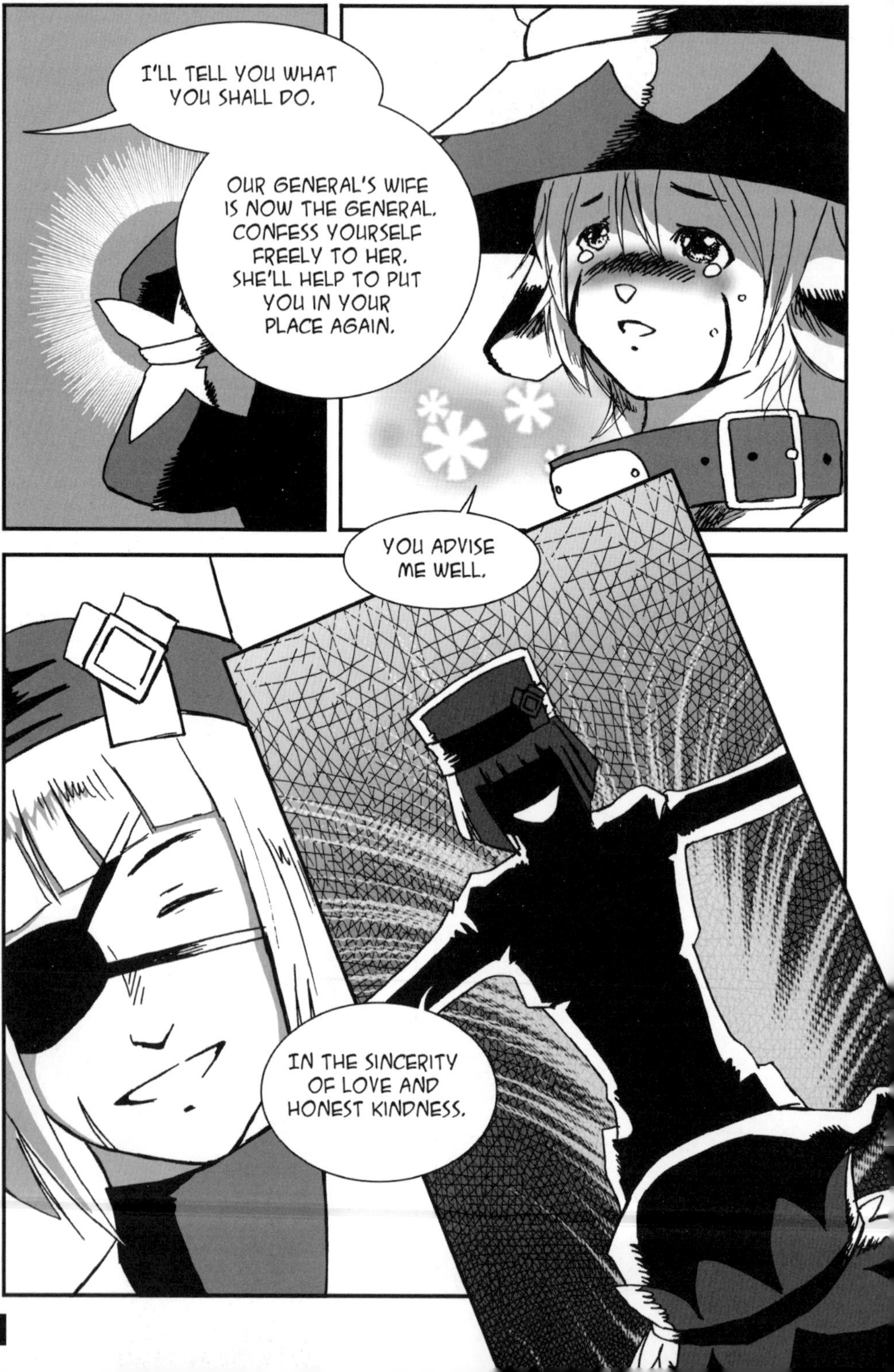
I'LL TELL YOU WHAT YOU SHALL DO.
OUR GENERAL'S WIFE IS NOW THE GENERAL. CONFESS YOURSELF FREELY TO HER. SHE'LL HELP TO PUT YOU IN YOUR PLACE AGAIN.
YOU ADVISE ME WELL.
IN THE SINCERITY OF LOVE AND HONEST KINDNESS.

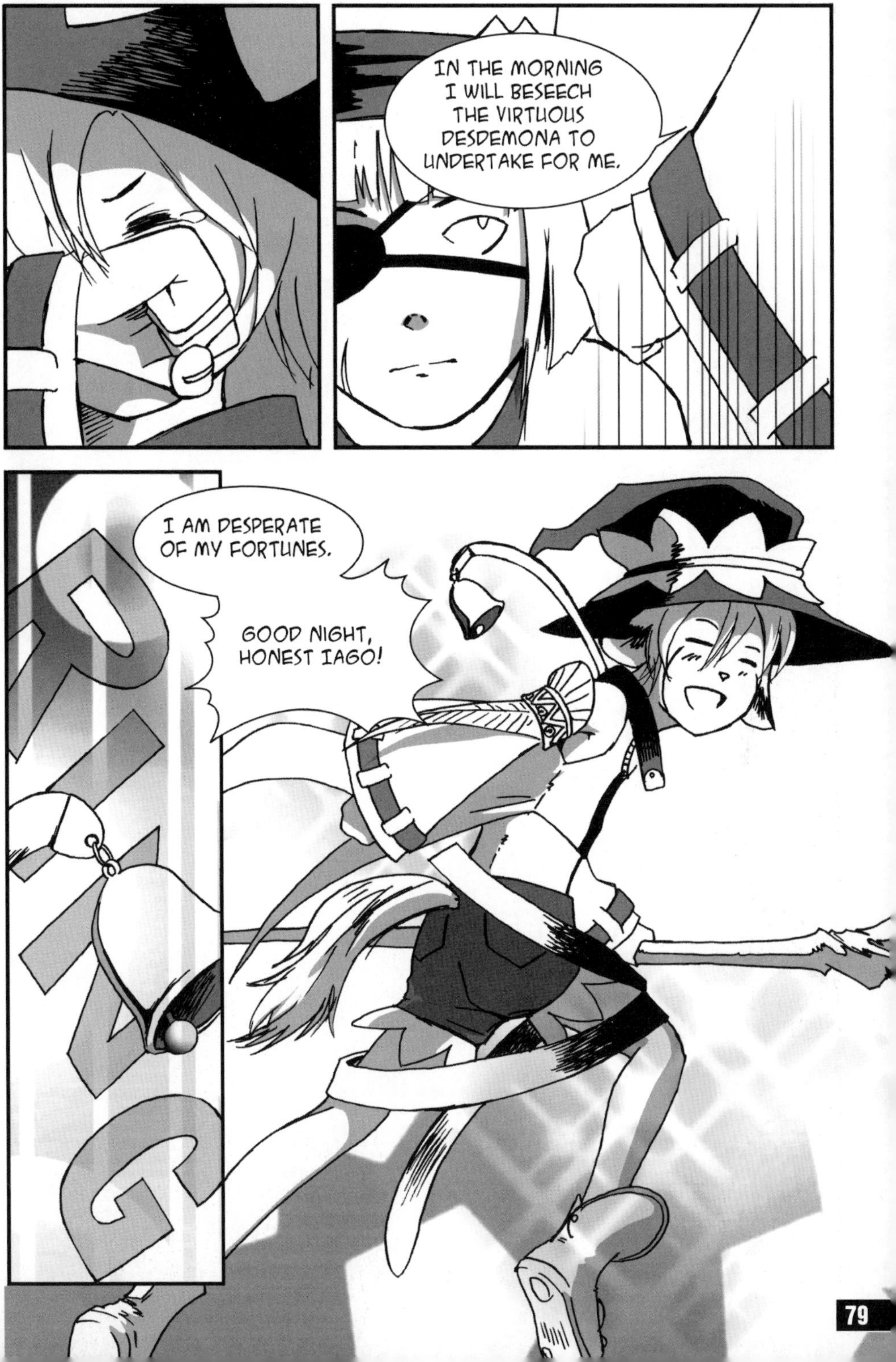
IN THE MORNING I WILL BESEECH THE VIRTUOUS DESDEMONA TO UNDERTAKE FOR ME.
I AM DESPERATE OF MY FORTUNES.
GOOD NIGHT, HONEST IAGO!

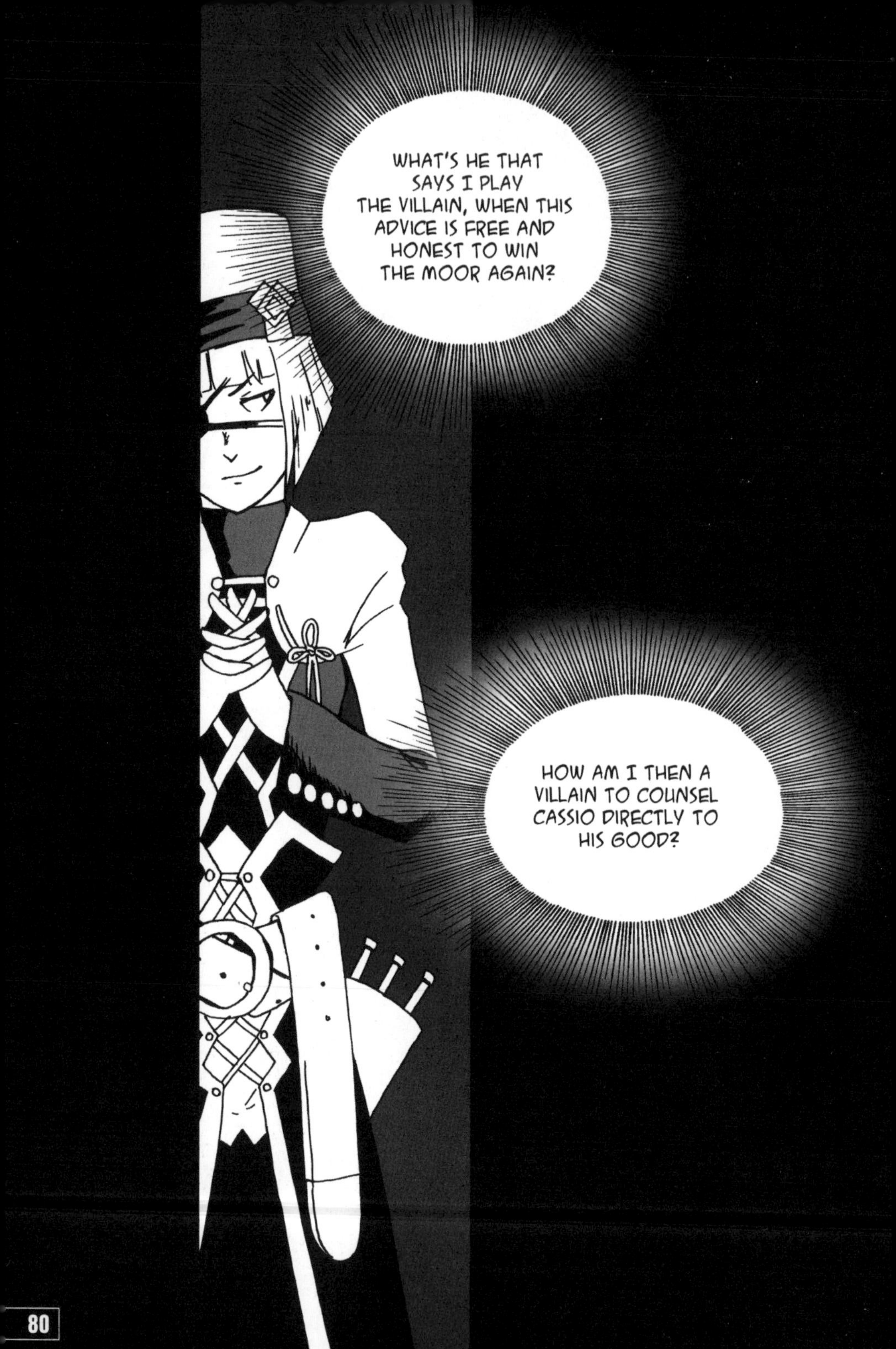
WHAT'S HE THAT SAYS I PLAY THE VILLAIN, WHEN THIS ADVICE IS FREE AND HONEST TO WIN THE MOOR AGAIN?
HOW AM I THEN A VILLAIN TO COUNSEL CASSIO DIRECTLY TO HIS GOOD?

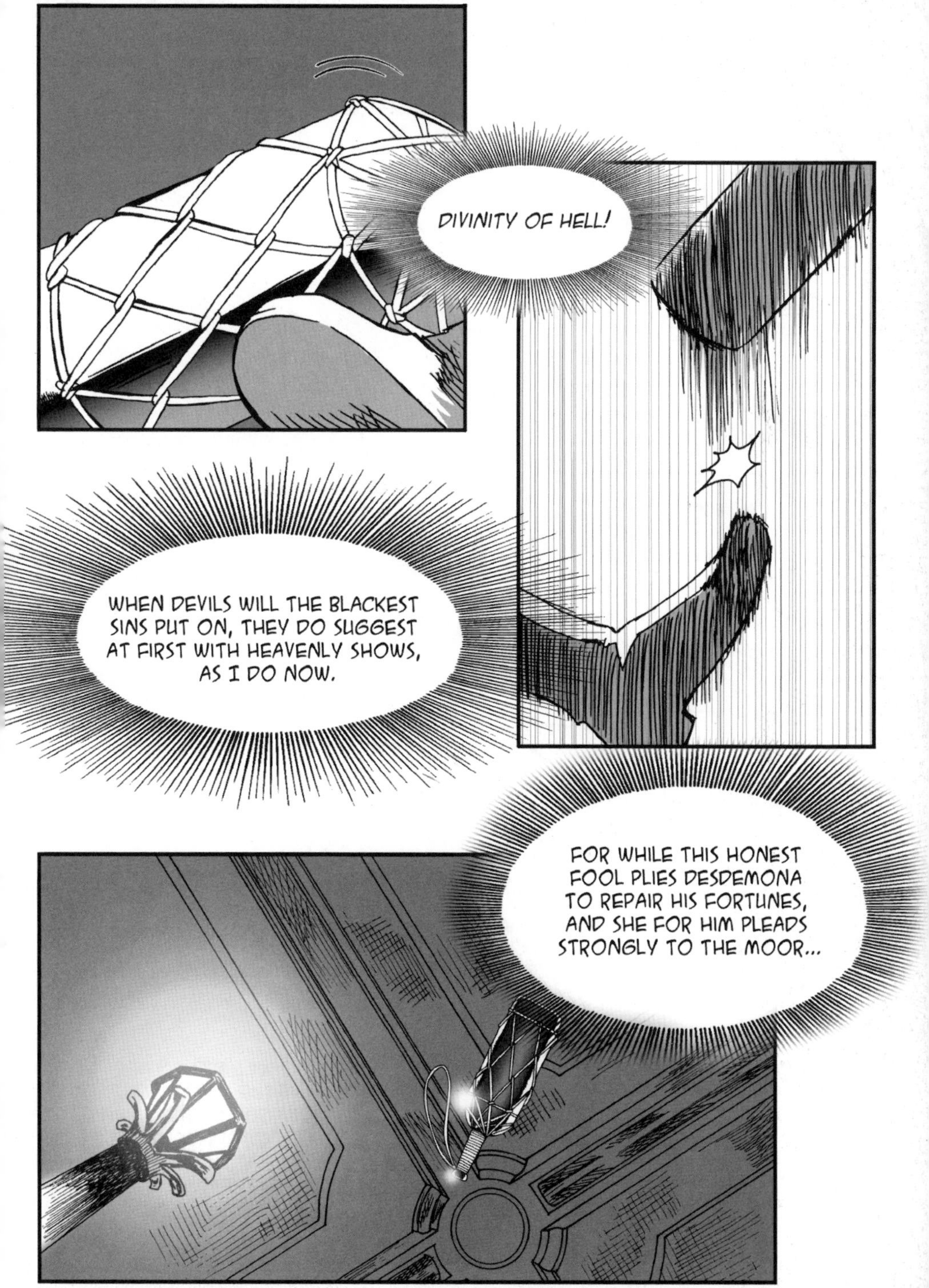
DIVINITY OF HELL!
WHEN DEVILS WILL THE BLACKEST SINS PUT ON, THEY DO SUGGEST AT FIRST WITH HEAVENLY SHOWS, AS I DO NOW.
FOR WHILE THIS HONEST FOOL PLIES DESDEMONA TO REPAIR HIS FORTUNES, AND SHE FOR HIM PLEADS STRONGLY TO THE MOOR...

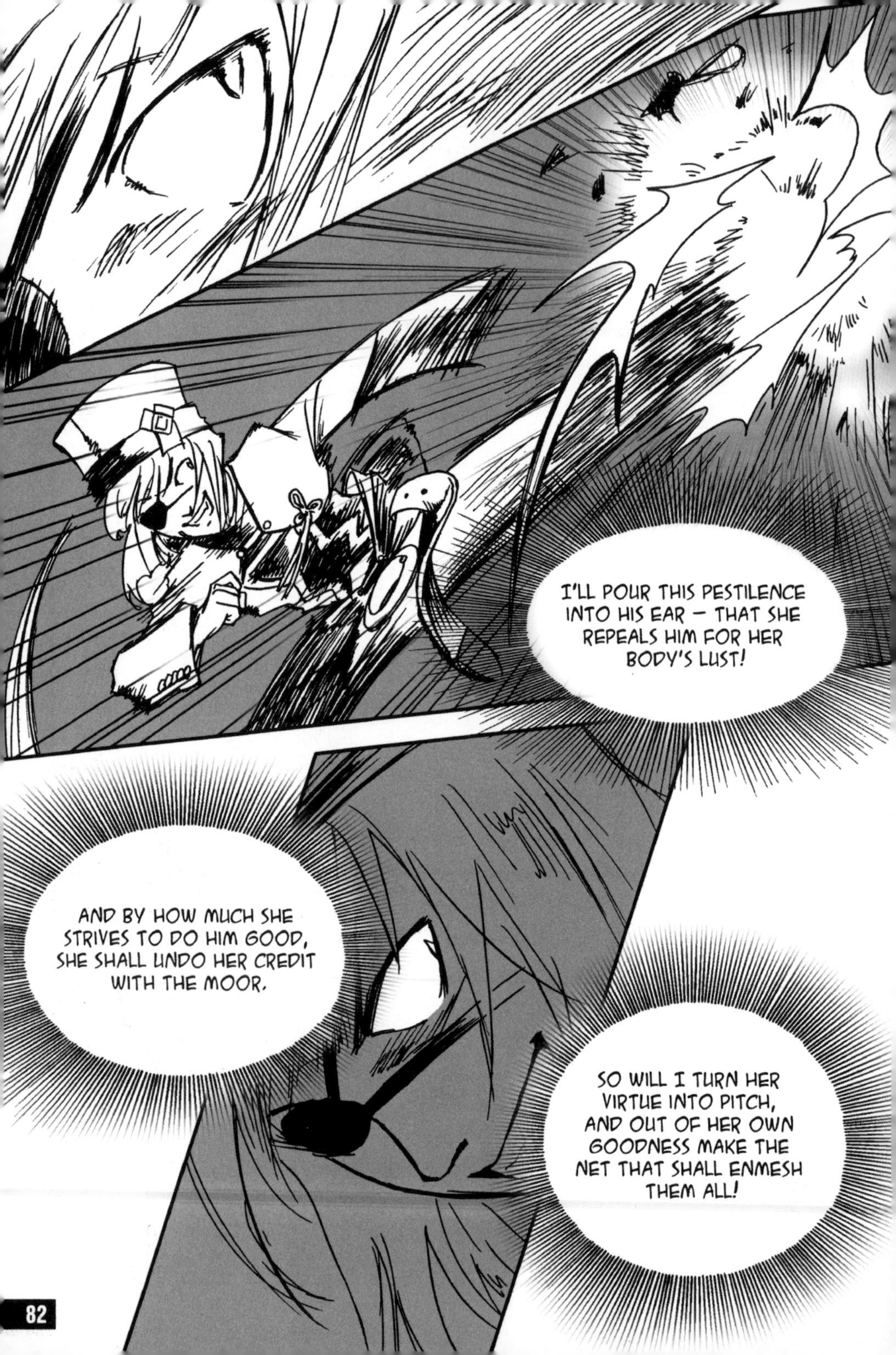
I'LL POUR THIS PESTILENCE INTO HIS EAR – THAT SHE REPEALS HIM FOR HER BODY'S LUST!
AND BY HOW MUCH SHE STRIVES TO DO HIM GOOD, SHE SHALL UNDO HER CREDIT WITH THE MOOR.
SO WILL I TURN HER VIRTUE INTO PITCH, AND OUT OF HER OWN GOODNESS MAKE THE NET THAT SHALL ENMESH THEM ALL!

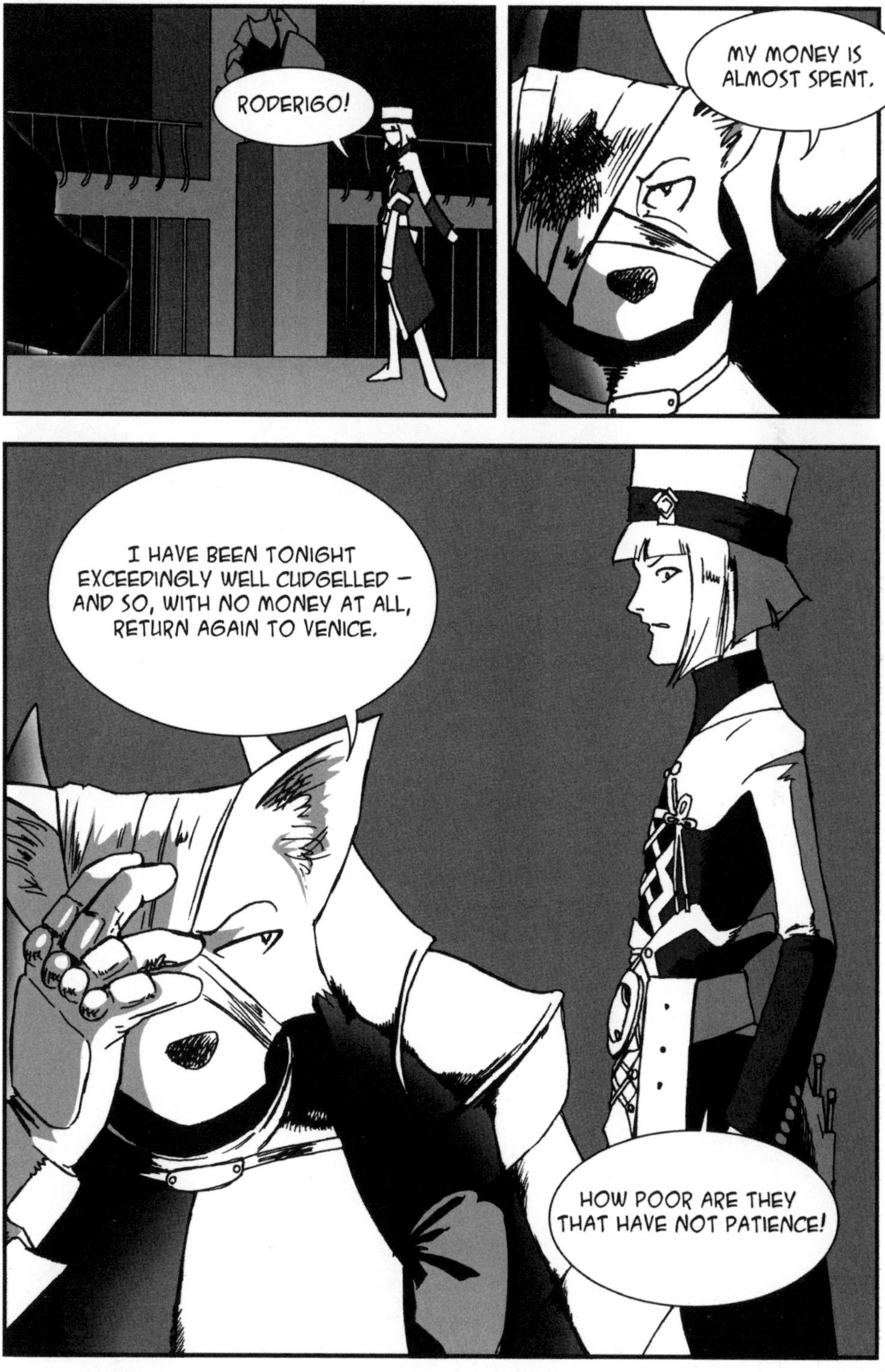
RODERIGO!
MY MONEY IS ALMOST SPENT.
I HAVE BEEN TONIGHT EXCEEDINGLY WELL CUDGELLED – AND SO, WITH NO MONEY AT ALL, RETURN AGAIN TO VENICE.
HOW POOR ARE THEY THAT HAVE NOT PATIENCE!

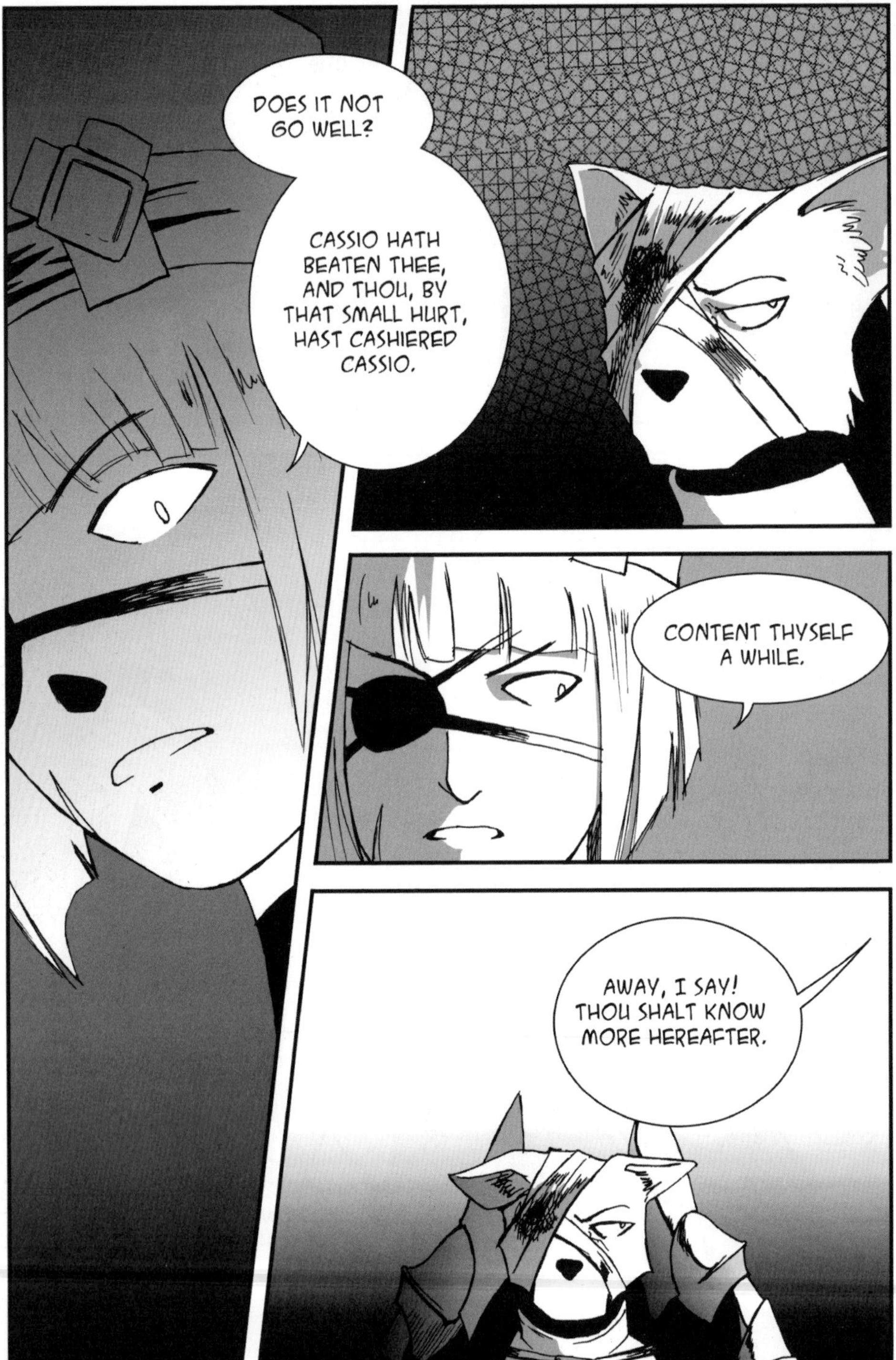
DOES IT NOT GO WELL?
CASSIO HATH BEATEN THEE, AND THOU, BY THAT SMALL HURT, HAST CASHIERED CASSIO.
CONTENT THYSELF A WHILE.
AWAY, I SAY! THOU SHALT KNOW MORE HEREAFTER.

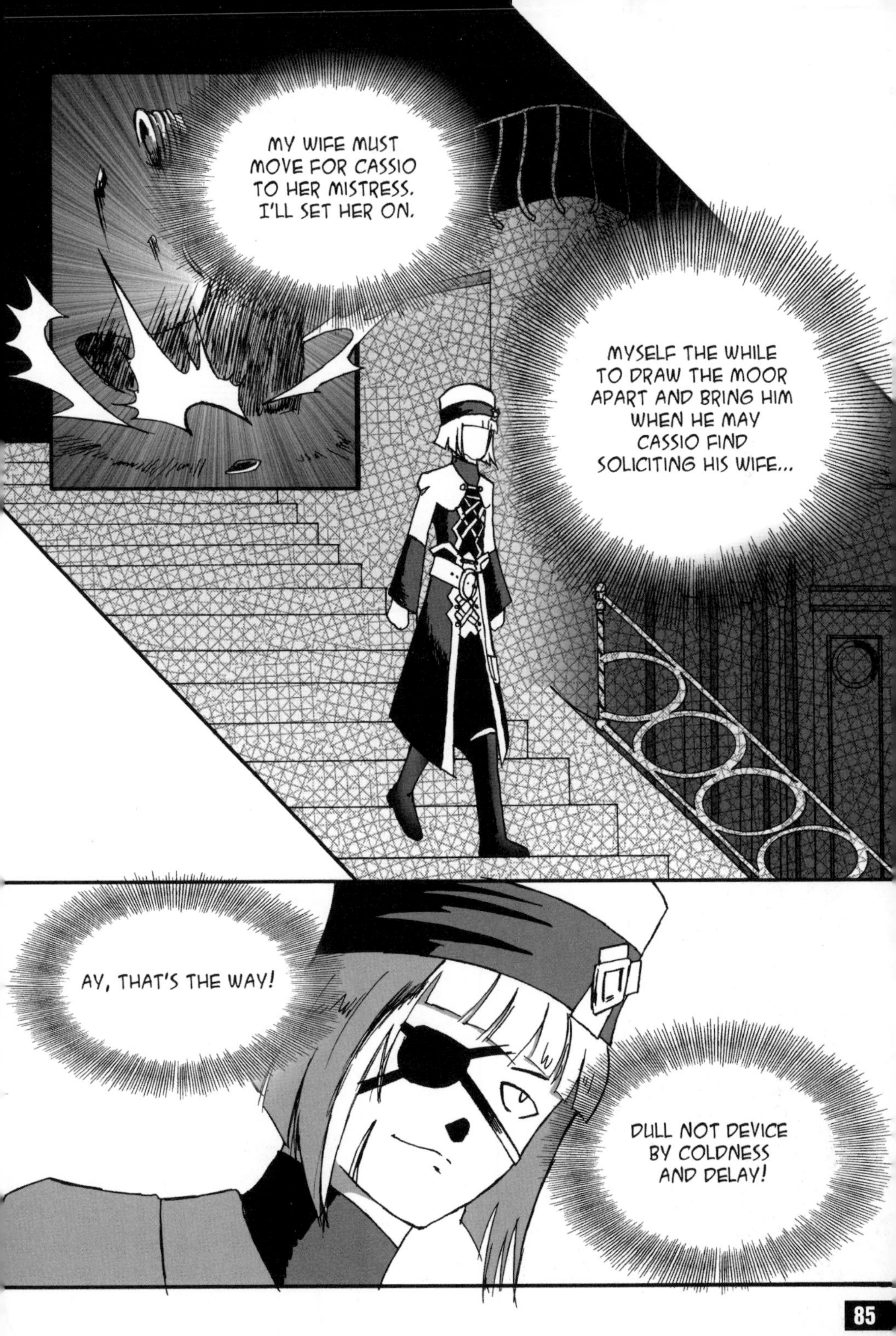
MY WIFE MUST MOVE FOR CASSIO TO HER MISTRESS. I'LL SET HER ON.
MYSELF THE WHILE TO DRAW THE MOOR APART AND BRING HIM WHEN HE MAY CASSIO FIND SOLICITING HIS WIFE...
AY, THAT'S THE WAY!
DULL NOT DEVICE BY COLDNESS AND DELAY!

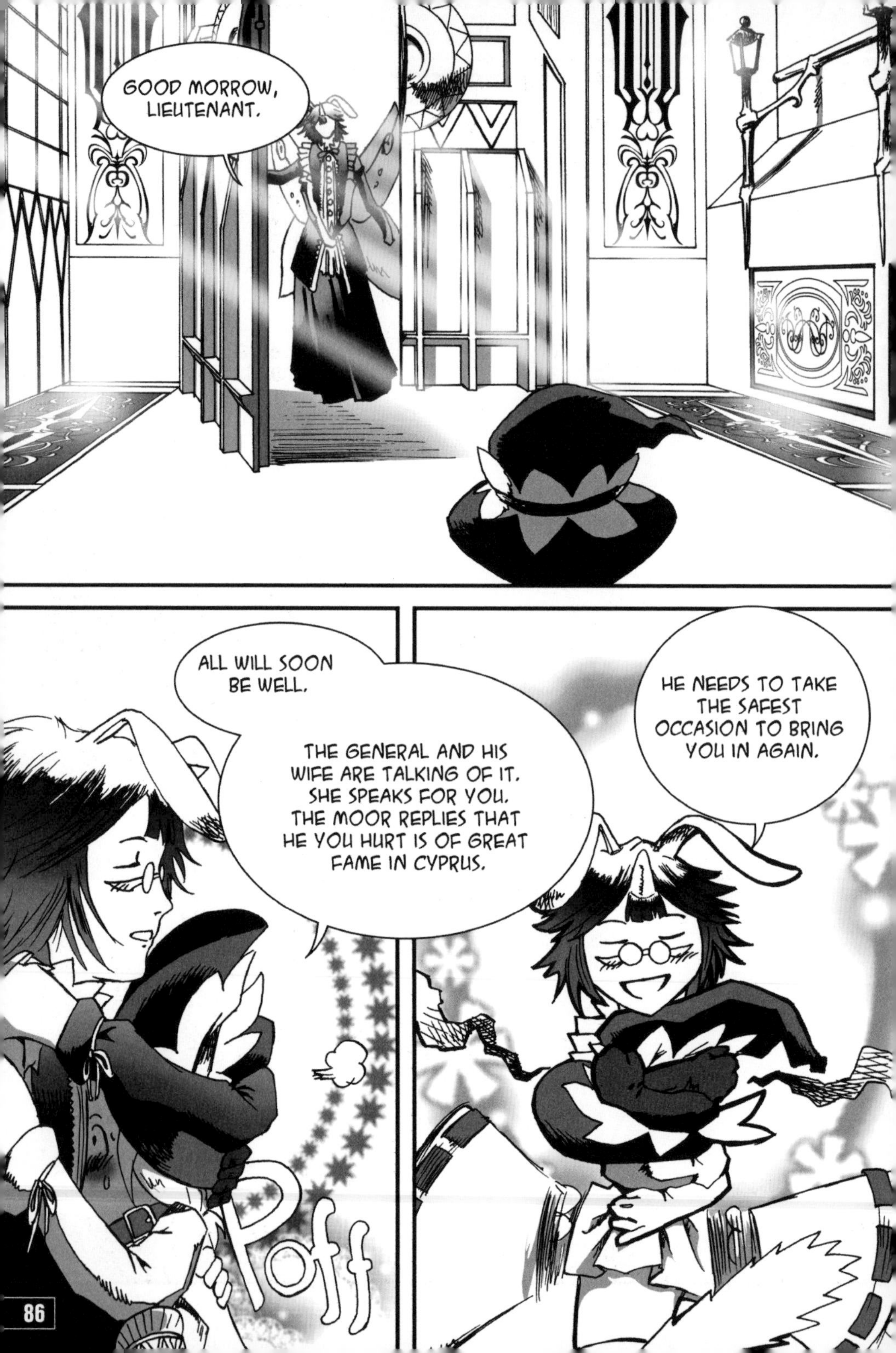
GOOD MORROW, LIEUTENANT.
ALL WILL SOON BE WELL.
THE GENERAL AND HIS WIFE ARE TALKING OF IT. SHE SPEAKS FOR YOU. THE MOOR REPLIES THAT HE YOU HURT IS OF GREAT FAME IN CYPRUS.
HE NEEDS TO TAKE THE SAFEST OCCASION TO BRING YOU IN AGAIN.
Poff

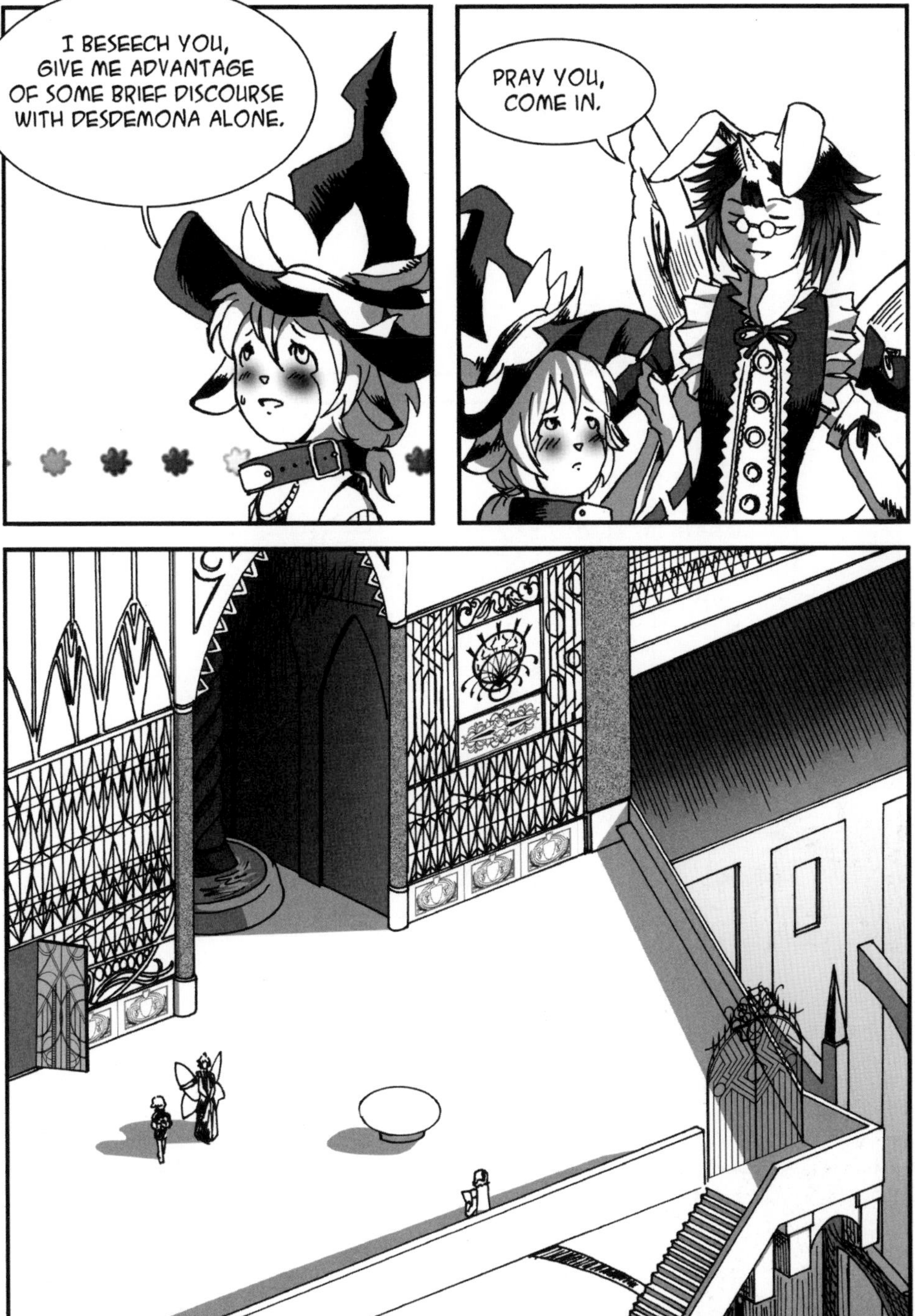
I BESEECH YOU, GIVE ME ADVANTAGE OF SOME BRIEF DISCOURSE WITH DESDEMONA ALONE.
PRAY YOU, COME IN.

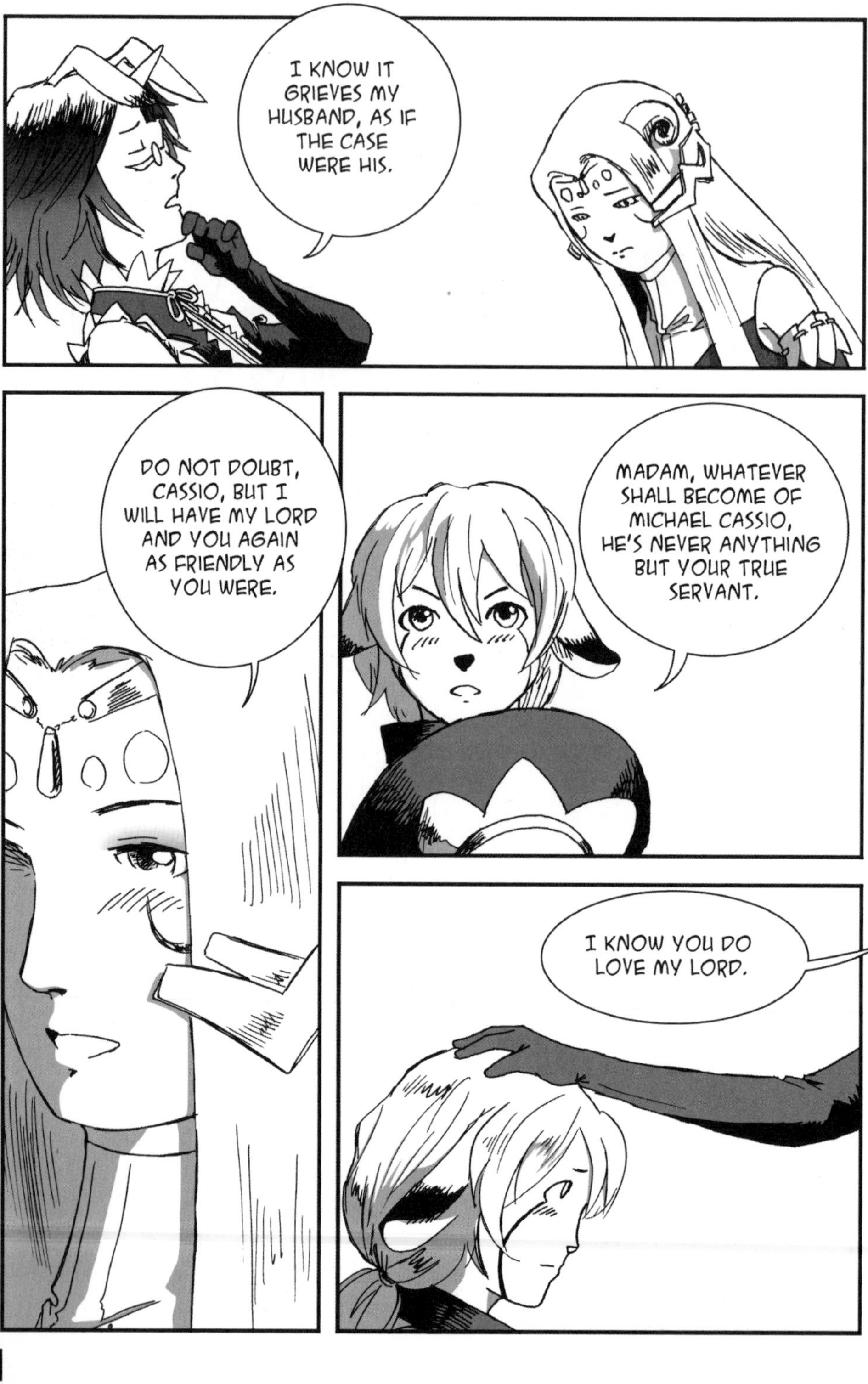
I KNOW IT GRIEVES MY HUSBAND, AS IF THE CASE WERE HIS.
DO NOT DOUBT, CASSIO, BUT I WILL HAVE MY LORD AND YOU AGAIN AS FRIENDLY AS YOU WERE.
MADAM, WHATEVER SHALL BECOME OF MICHAEL CASSIO, HE'S NEVER ANYTHING BUT YOUR TRUE SERVANT.
I KNOW YOU DO LOVE MY LORD.

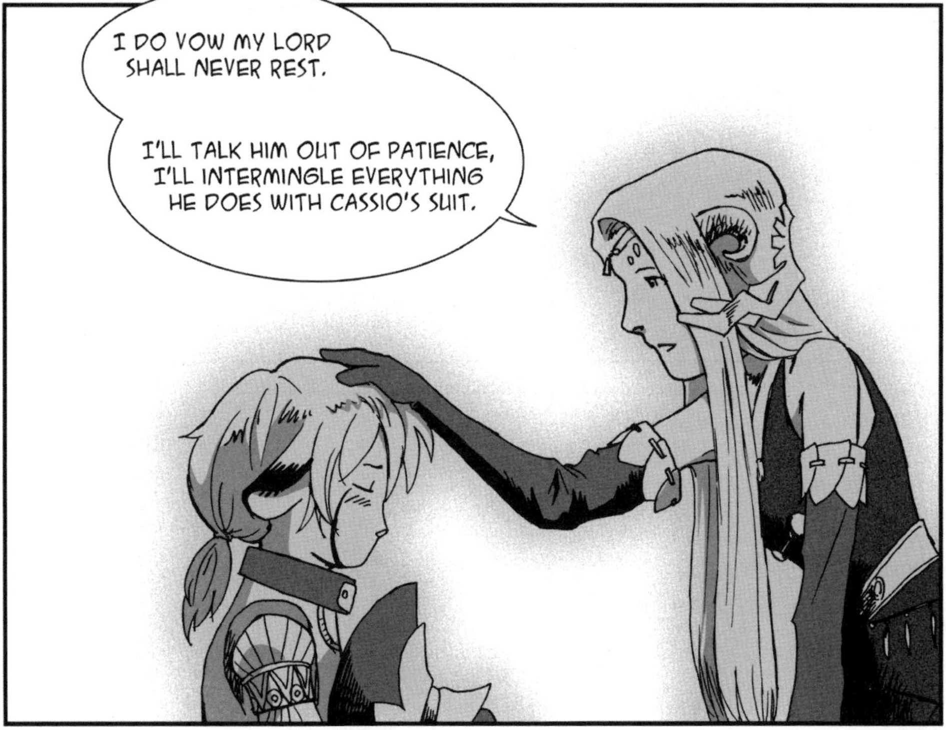
I DO VOW MY LORD SHALL NEVER REST.
I'LL TALK HIM OUT OF PATIENCE, I'LL INTERMINGLE EVERYTHING HE DOES WITH CASSIO'S SUIT.

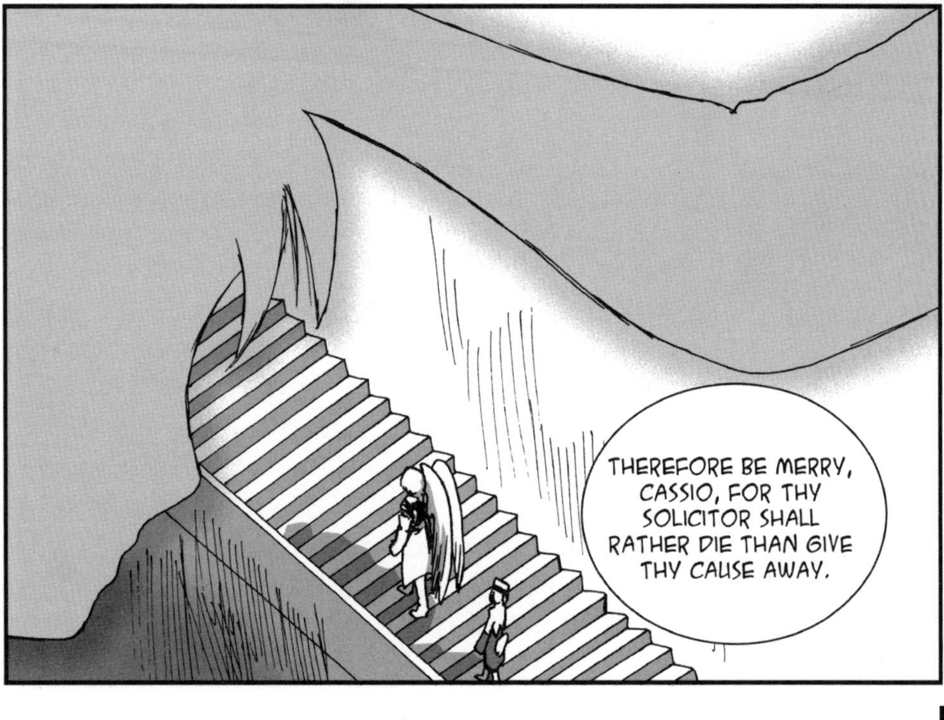
THEREFORE BE MERRY, CASSIO, FOR THY SOLICITOR SHALL RATHER DIE THAN GIVE THY CAUSE AWAY.

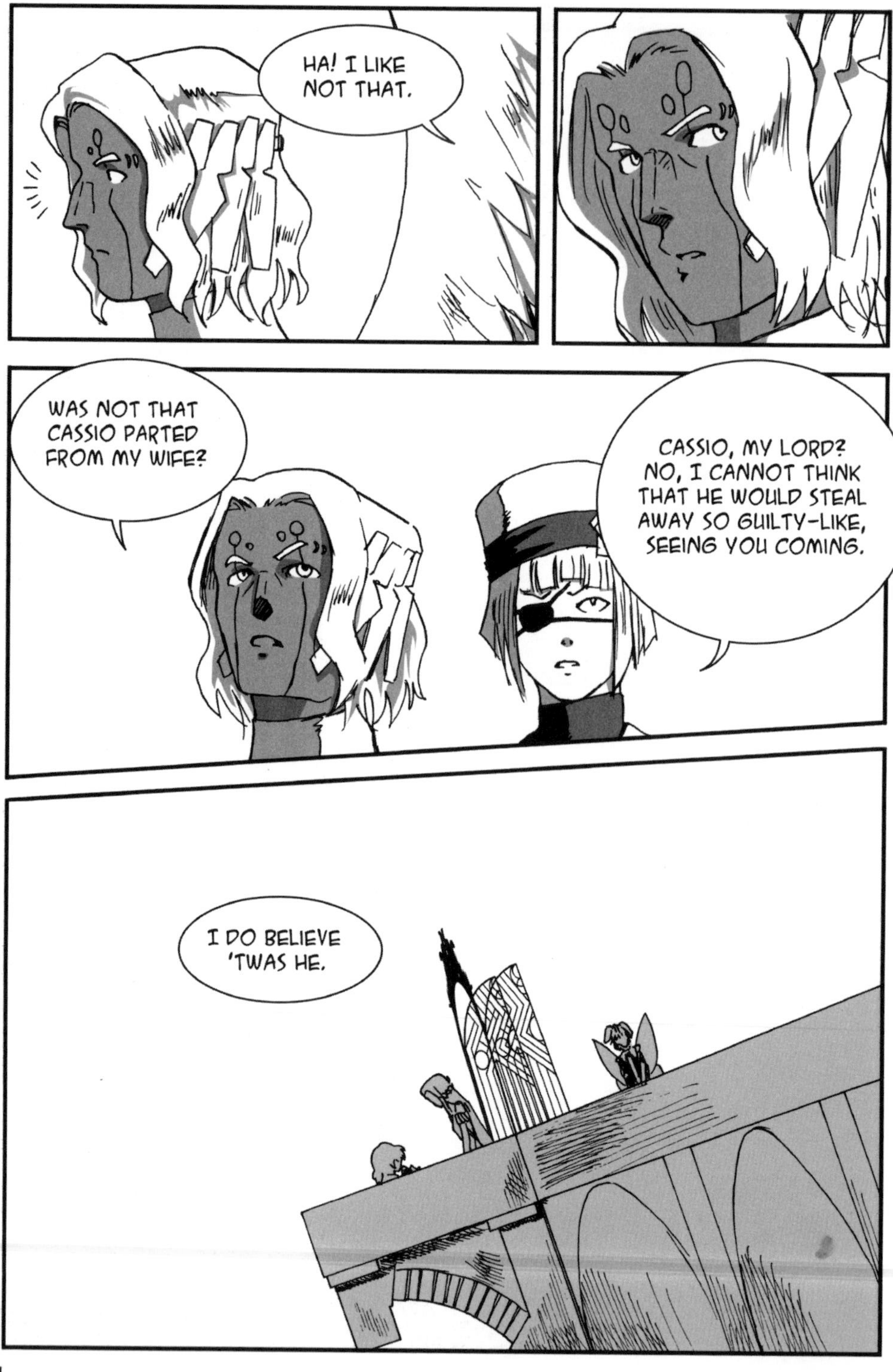
HA! I LIKE NOT THAT.
WAS NOT THAT CASSIO PARTED FROM MY WIFE?
CASSIO, MY LORD? NO, I CANNOT THINK THAT HE WOULD STEAL AWAY SO GUILTY-LIKE, SEEING YOU COMING.
I DO BELIEVE 'TWAS HE.

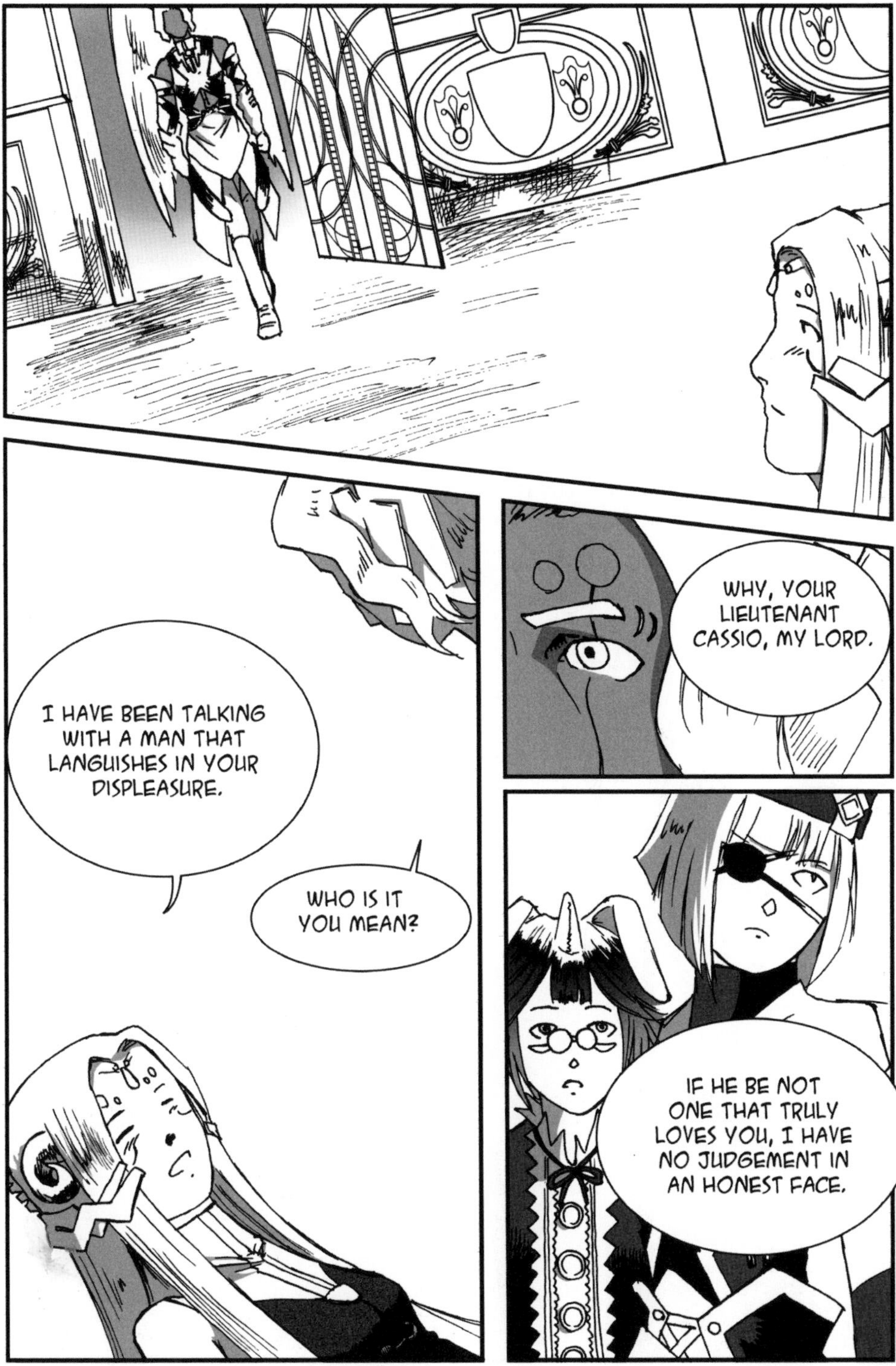
WHY, YOUR LIEUTENANT CASSIO, MY LORD.
I HAVE BEEN TALKING WITH A MAN THAT LANGUISHES IN YOUR DISPLEASURE.
WHO IS IT YOU MEAN?
IF HE BE NOT ONE THAT TRULY LOVES YOU, I HAVE NO JUDGEMENT IN AN HONEST FACE.

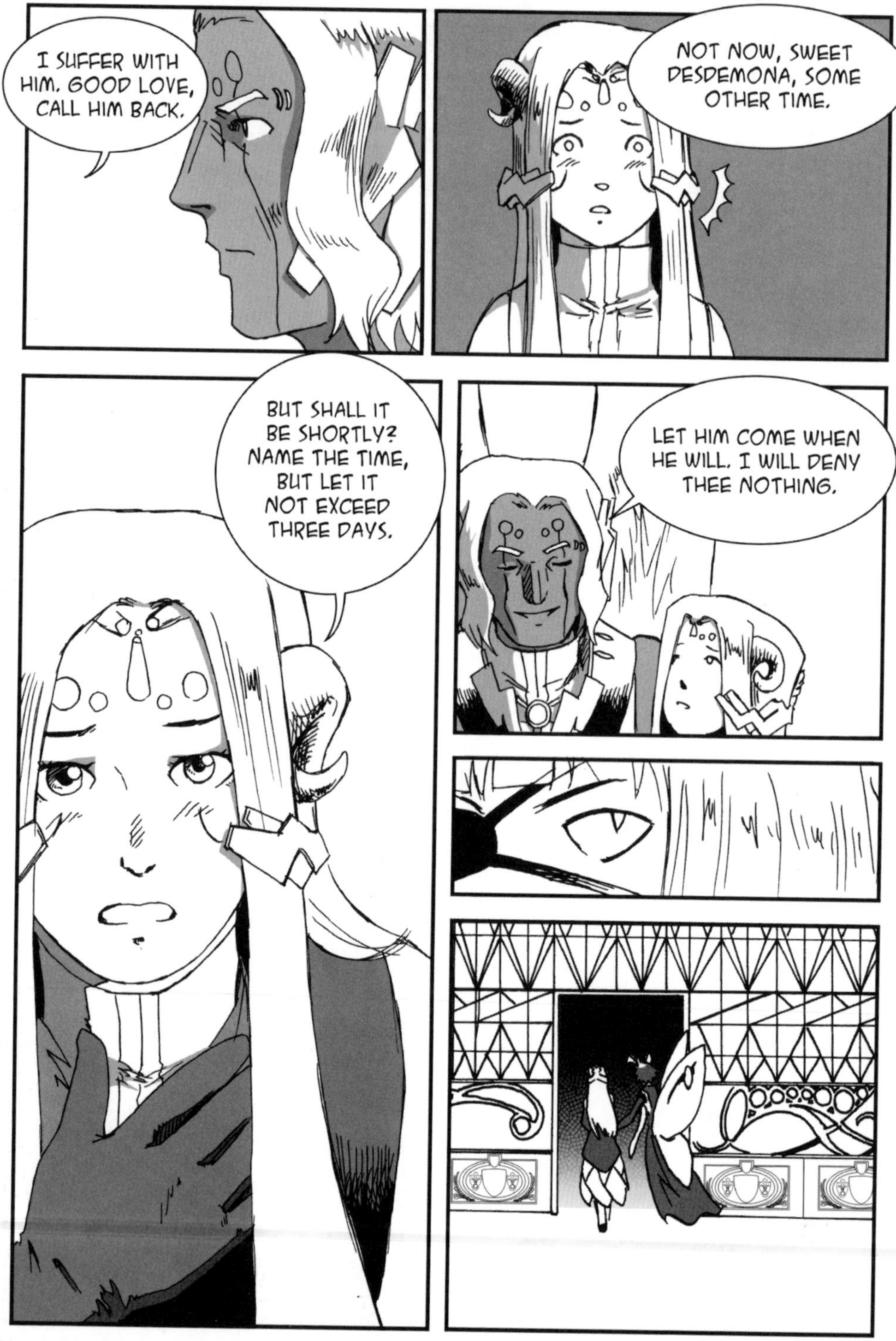
I SUFFER WITH HIM. GOOD LOVE, CALL HIM BACK.
NOT NOW, SWEET DESDEMONA, SOME OTHER TIME.
BUT SHALL IT BE SHORTLY? NAME THE TIME, BUT LET IT NOT EXCEED THREE DAYS.
LET HIM COME WHEN HE WILL. I WILL DENY THEE NOTHING.

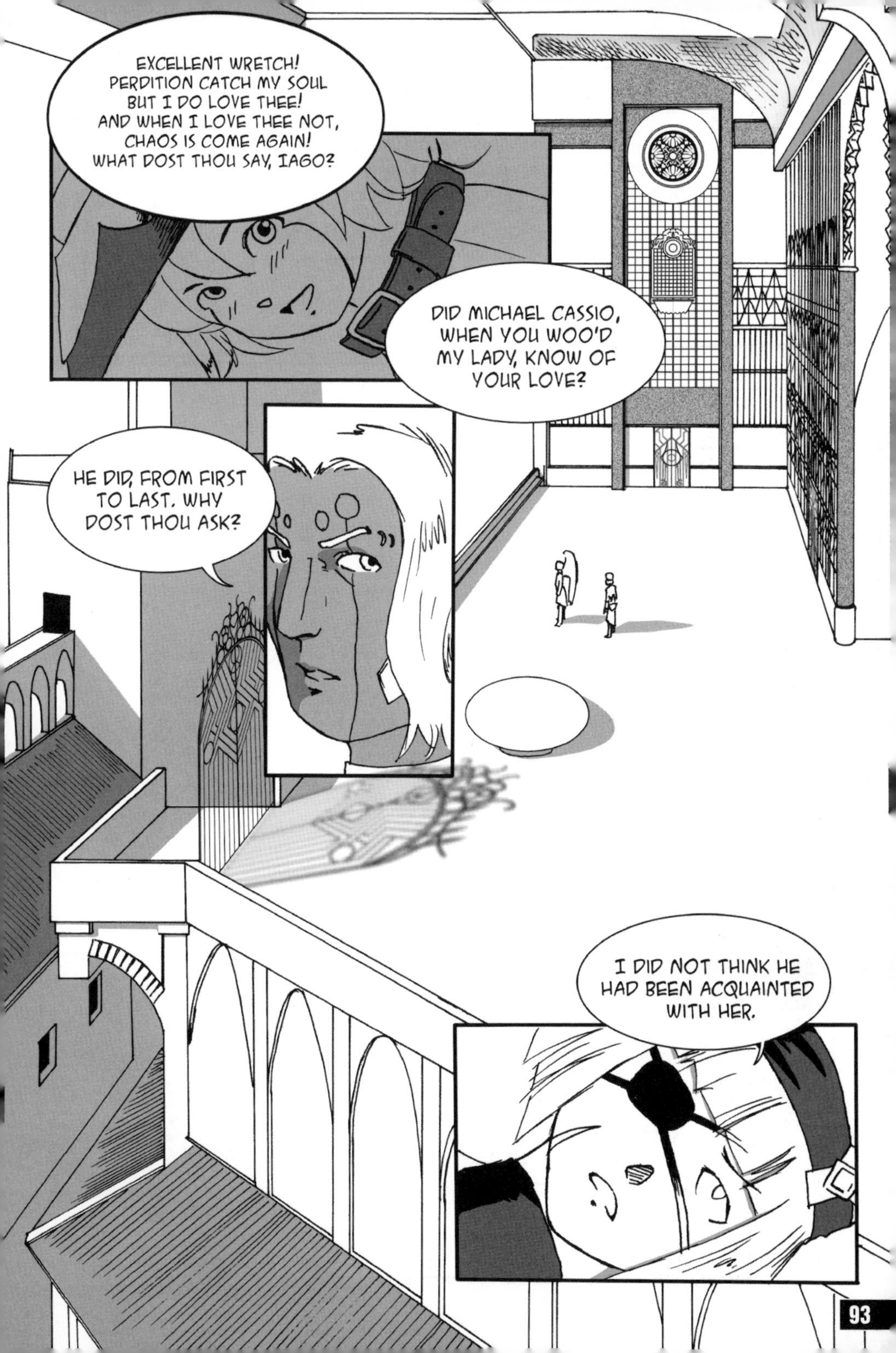

EXCELLENT WRETCH! PERDITION CATCH MY SOUL BUT I DO LOVE THEE! AND WHEN I LOVE THEE NOT, CHAOS IS COME AGAIN! WHAT DOST THOU SAY, IAGO?
DID MICHAEL CASSIO, WHEN YOU WOO'D MY LADY, KNOW OF YOUR LOVE?
HE DID, FROM FIRST TO LAST. WHY DOST THOU ASK?
I DID NOT THINK HE HAD BEEN ACQUAINTED WITH HER.

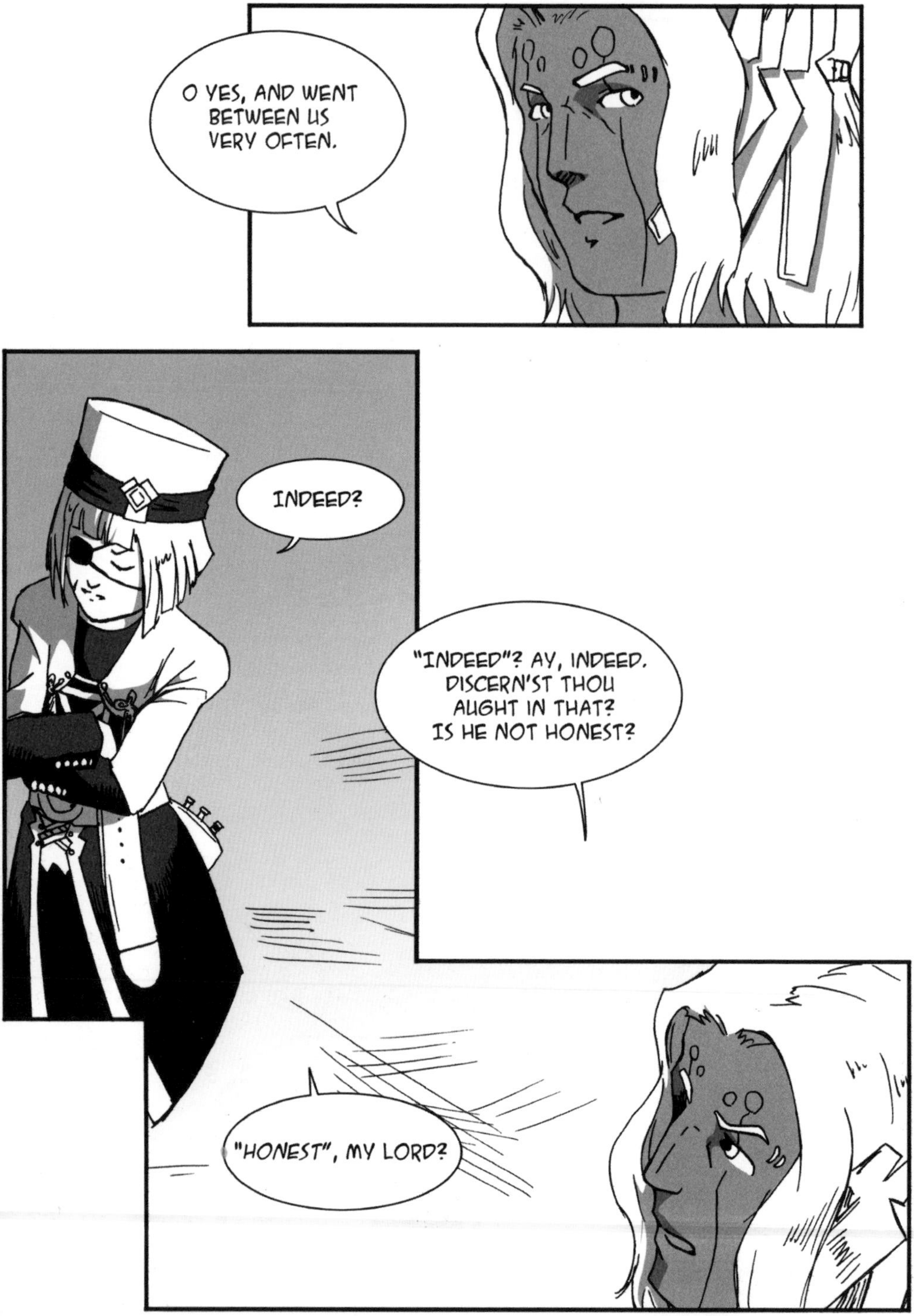
O YES, AND WENT BETWEEN US VERY OFTEN.
INDEED?
"INDEED"? AY, INDEED. DISCERN'ST THOU AUGHT IN THAT? IS HE NOT HONEST?
"HONEST", MY LORD?

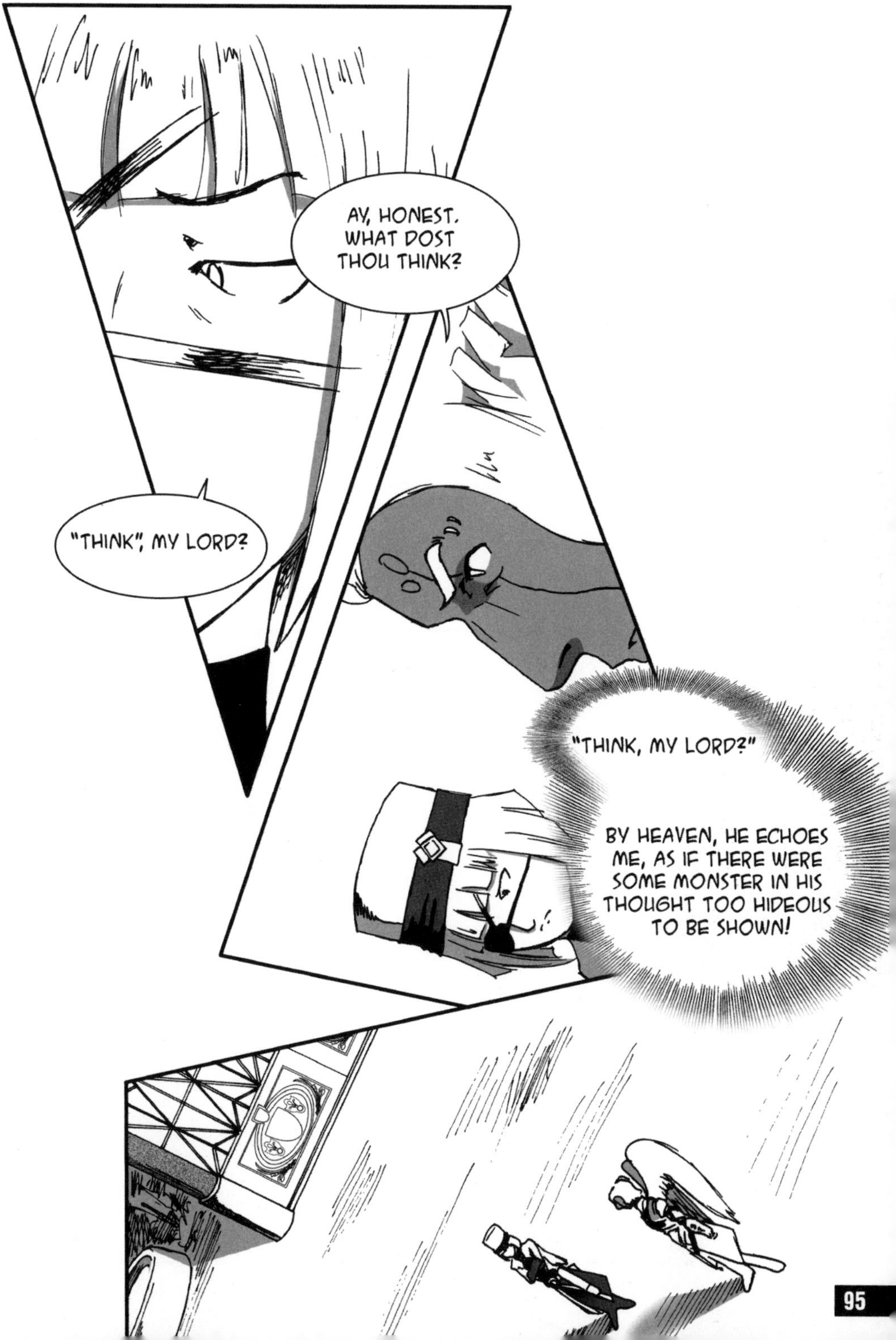
AY, HONEST. WHAT DOST THOU THINK?
"THINK", MY LORD?
"THINK, MY LORD?"
BY HEAVEN, HE ECHOES ME, AS IF THERE WERE SOME MONSTER IN HIS THOUGHT TOO HIDEOUS TO BE SHOWN!

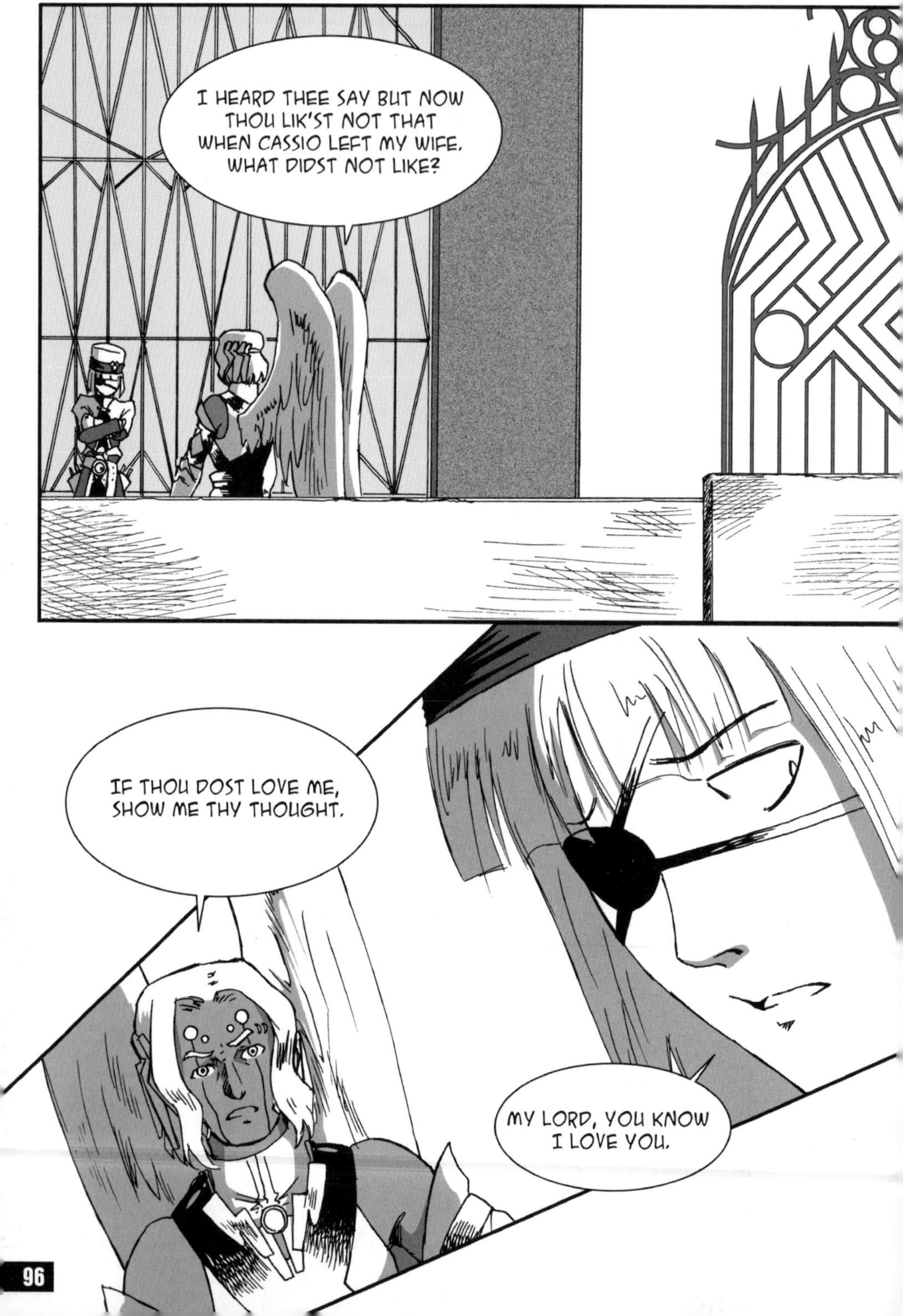
I HEARD THEE SAY BUT NOW THOU LIK'ST NOT THAT WHEN CASSIO LEFT MY WIFE. WHAT DIDST NOT LIKE?
IF THOU DOST LOVE ME, SHOW ME THY THOUGHT.
MY LORD, YOU KNOW I LOVE YOU.

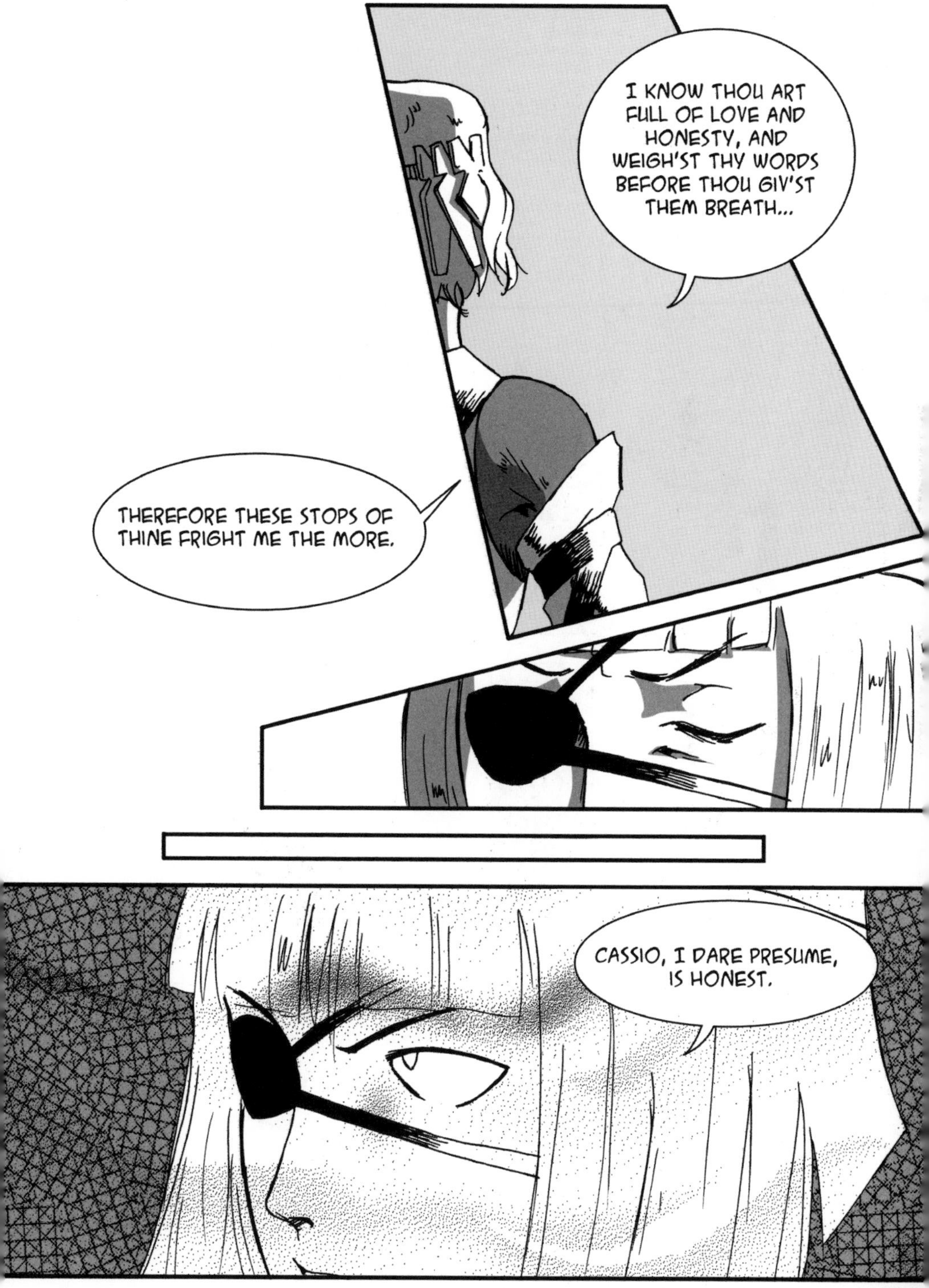
I KNOW THOU ART FULL OF LOVE AND HONESTY, AND WEIGH'ST THY WORDS BEFORE THOU GIV'ST THEM BREATH...
THEREFORE THESE STOPS OF THINE FRIGHT ME THE MORE.
CASSIO, I DARE PRESUME, IS HONEST.

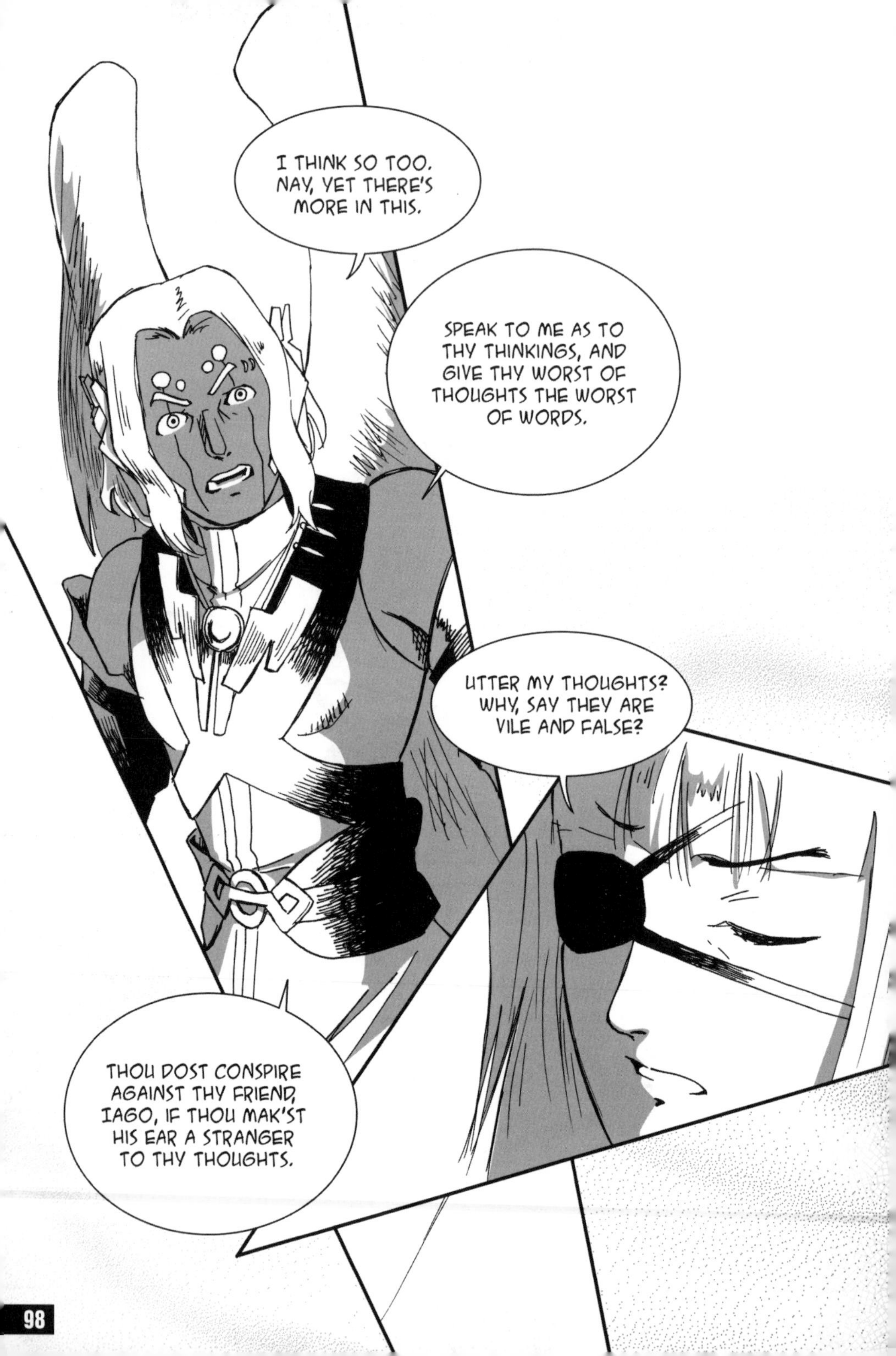
I THINK SO TOO. NAY, YET THERE'S MORE IN THIS.
SPEAK TO ME AS TO THY THINKINGS, AND GIVE THY WORST OF THOUGHTS THE WORST OF WORDS.
UTTER MY THOUGHTS? WHY, SAY THEY ARE VILE AND FALSE?
THOU DOST CONSPIRE AGAINST THY FRIEND, IAGO, IF THOU MAK'ST HIS EAR A STRANGER TO THY THOUGHTS.

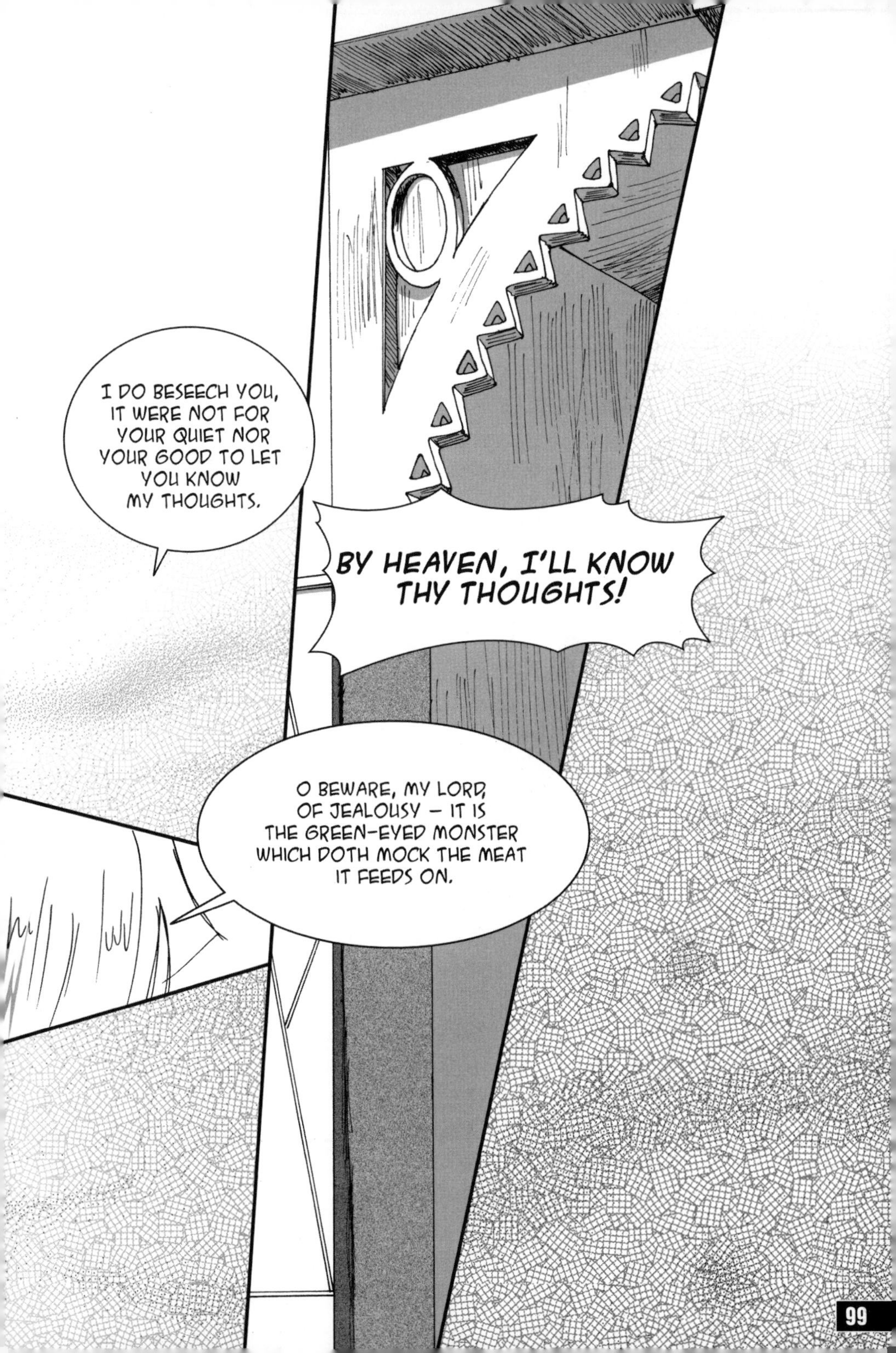
I DO BESEECH YOU, IT WERE NOT FOR YOUR QUIET NOR YOUR GOOD TO LET YOU KNOW MY THOUGHTS.
BY HEAVEN, I'LL KNOW THY THOUGHTS!
O BEWARE, MY LORD, OF JEALOUSY – IT IS THE GREEN-EYED MONSTER WHICH DOTH MOCK THE MEAT IT FEEDS ON.

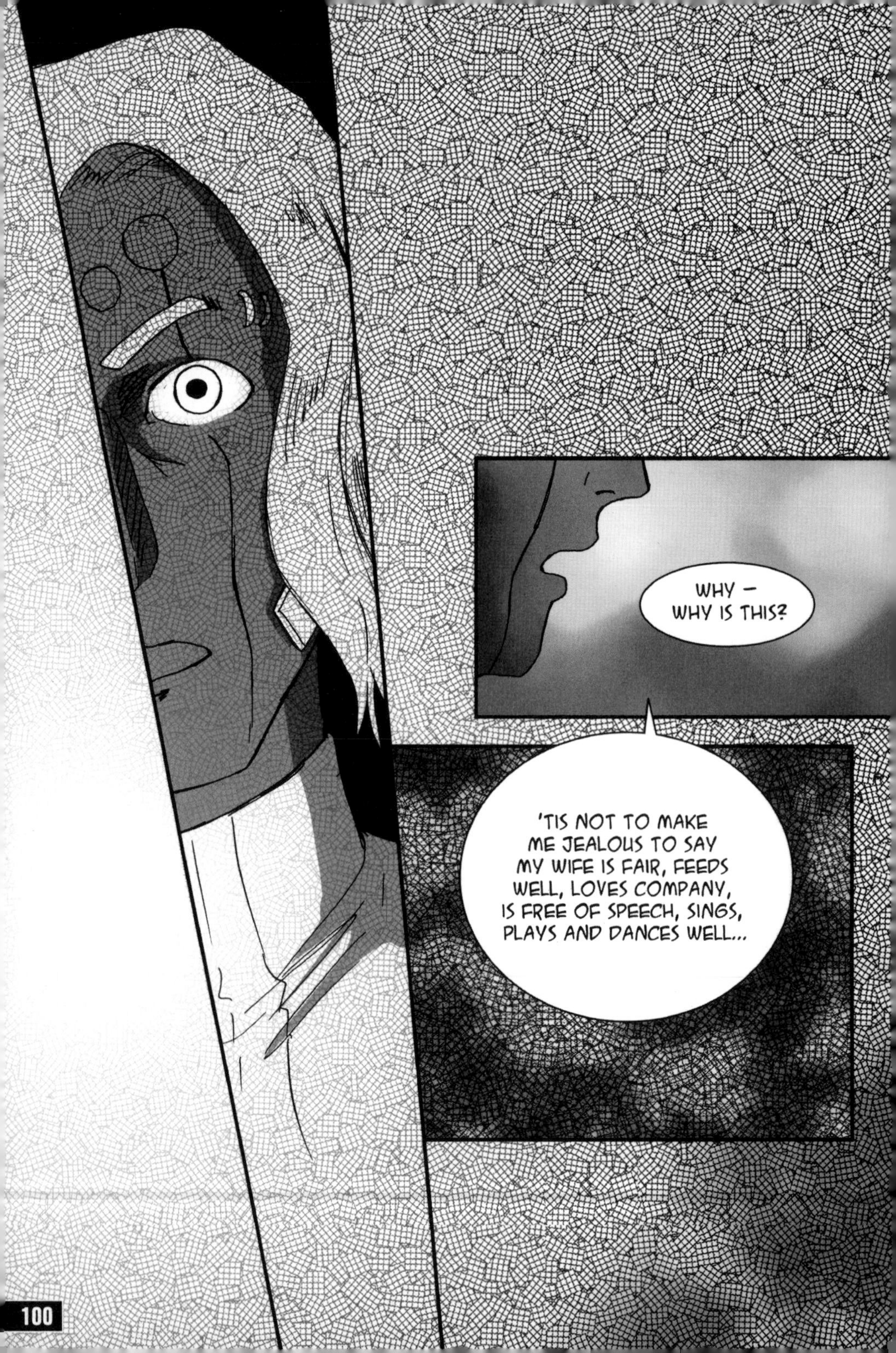
WHY —
WHY IS THIS?
'TIS NOT TO MAKE ME JEALOUS TO SAY MY WIFE IS FAIR, FEEDS WELL, LOVES COMPANY, IS FREE OF SPEECH, SINGS, PLAYS AND DANCES WELL...

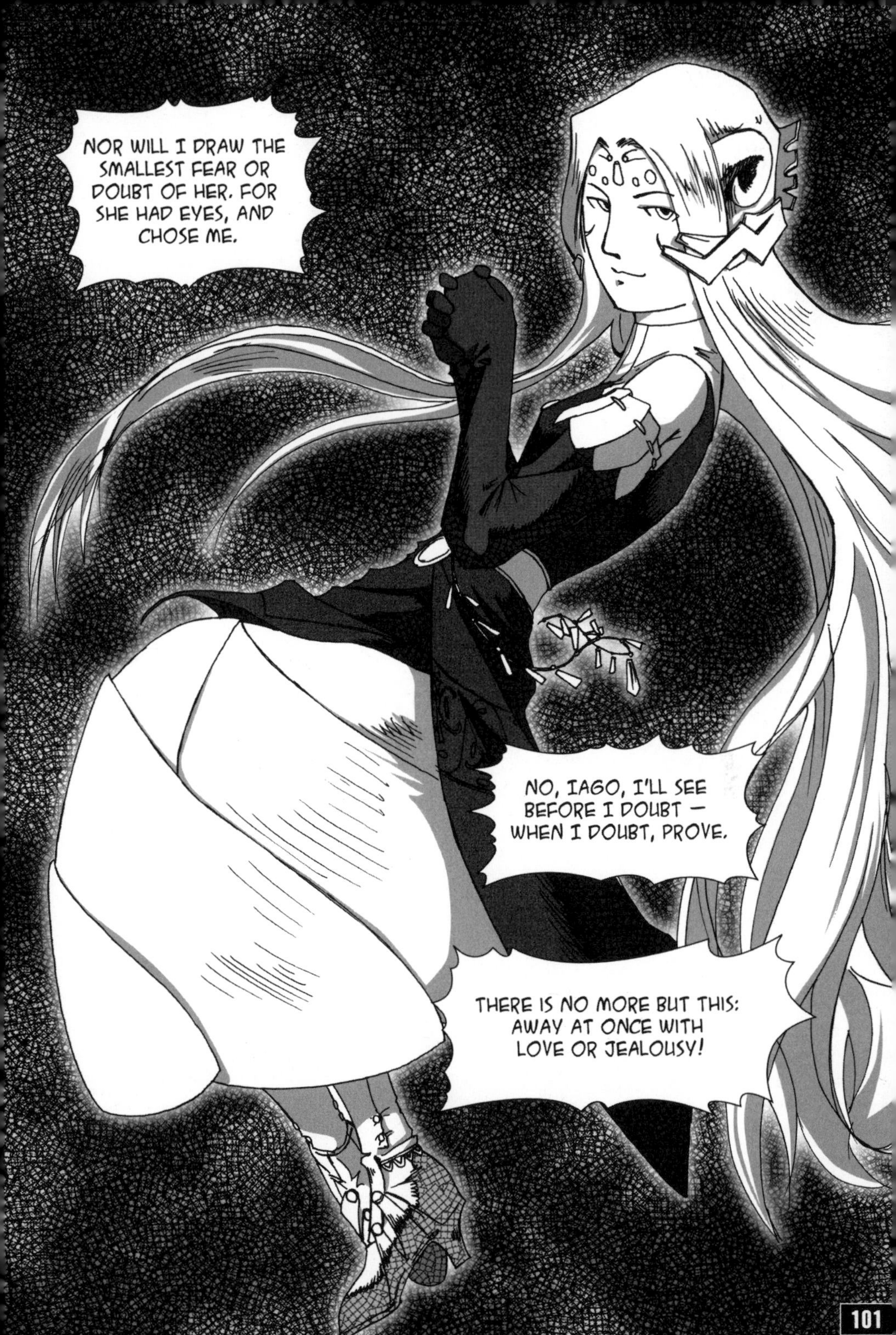
NOR WILL I DRAW THE SMALLEST FEAR OR DOUBT OF HER. FOR SHE HAD EYES, AND CHOSE ME.
NO, IAGO, I'LL SEE BEFORE I DOUBT — WHEN I DOUBT, PROVE.
THERE IS NO MORE BUT THIS: AWAY AT ONCE WITH LOVE OR JEALOUSY!

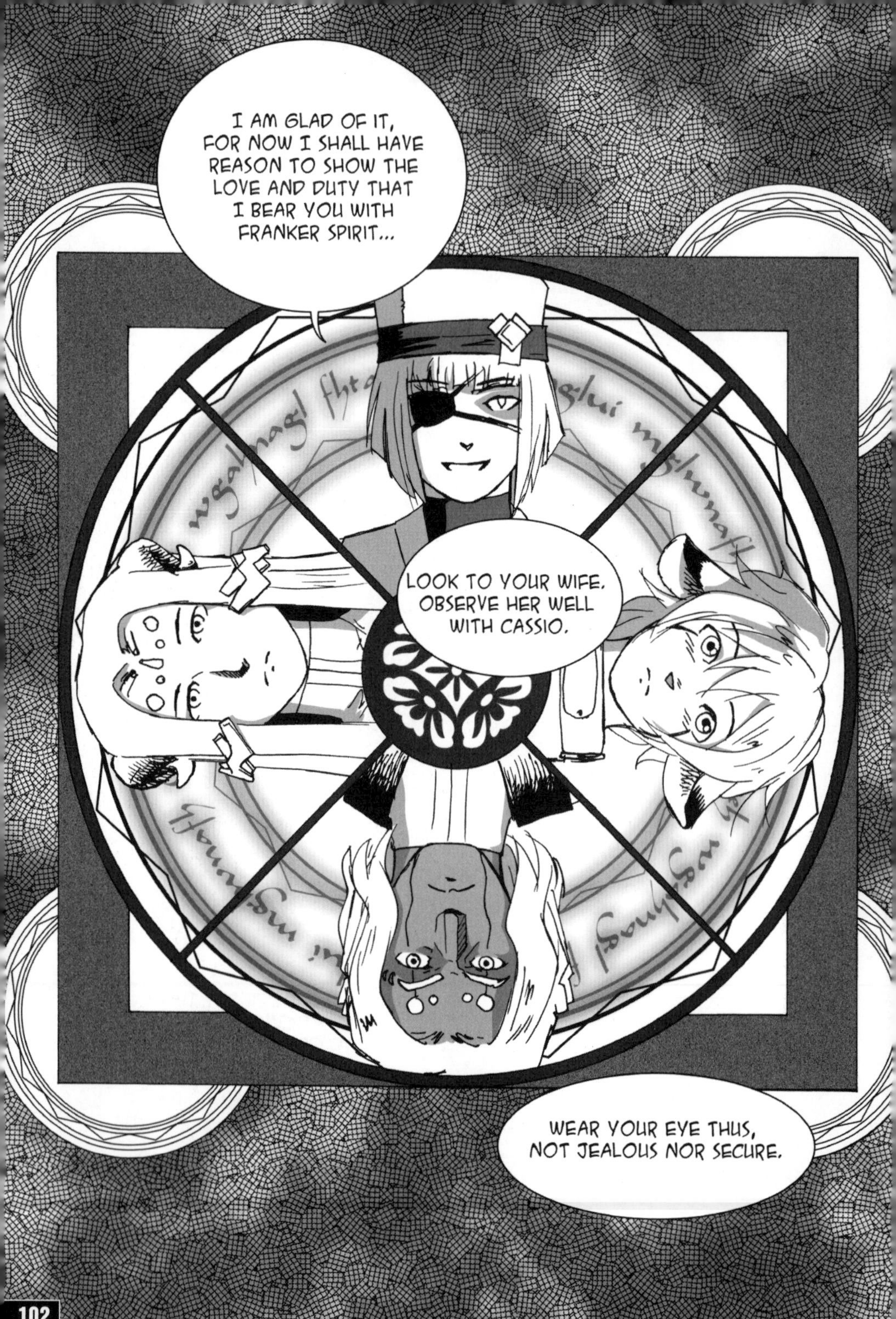
I AM GLAD OF IT, FOR NOW I SHALL HAVE REASON TO SHOW THE LOVE AND DUTY THAT I BEAR YOU WITH FRANKER SPIRIT...
LOOK TO YOUR WIFE. OBSERVE HER WELL WITH CASSIO.
WEAR YOUR EYE THUS, NOT JEALOUS NOR SECURE.

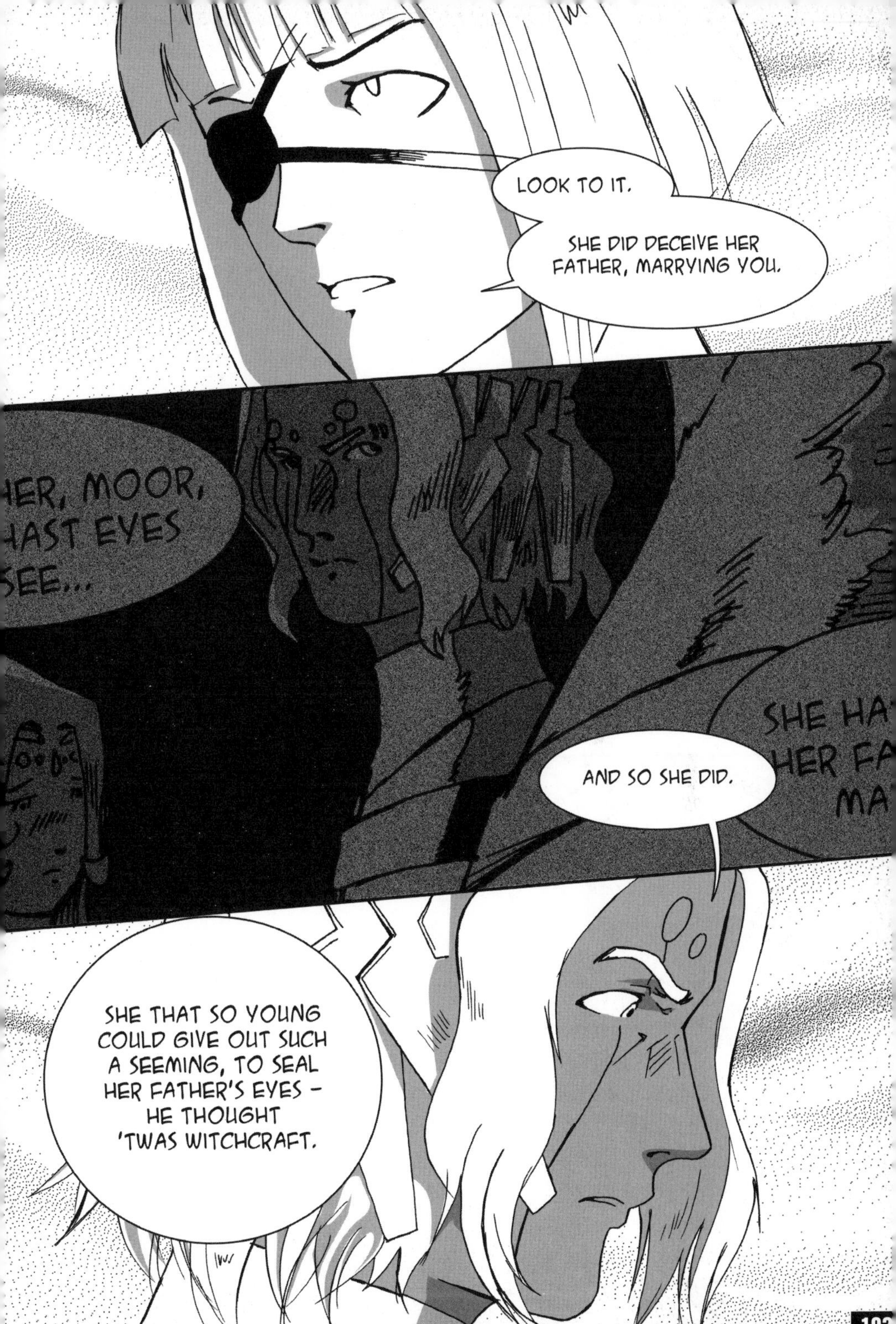
LOOK TO IT.
SHE DID DECEIVE HER FATHER, MARRYING YOU.
AND SO SHE DID.
SHE THAT SO YOUNG COULD GIVE OUT SUCH A SEEMING, TO SEAL HER FATHER'S EYES – HE THOUGHT 'TWAS WITCHCRAFT.

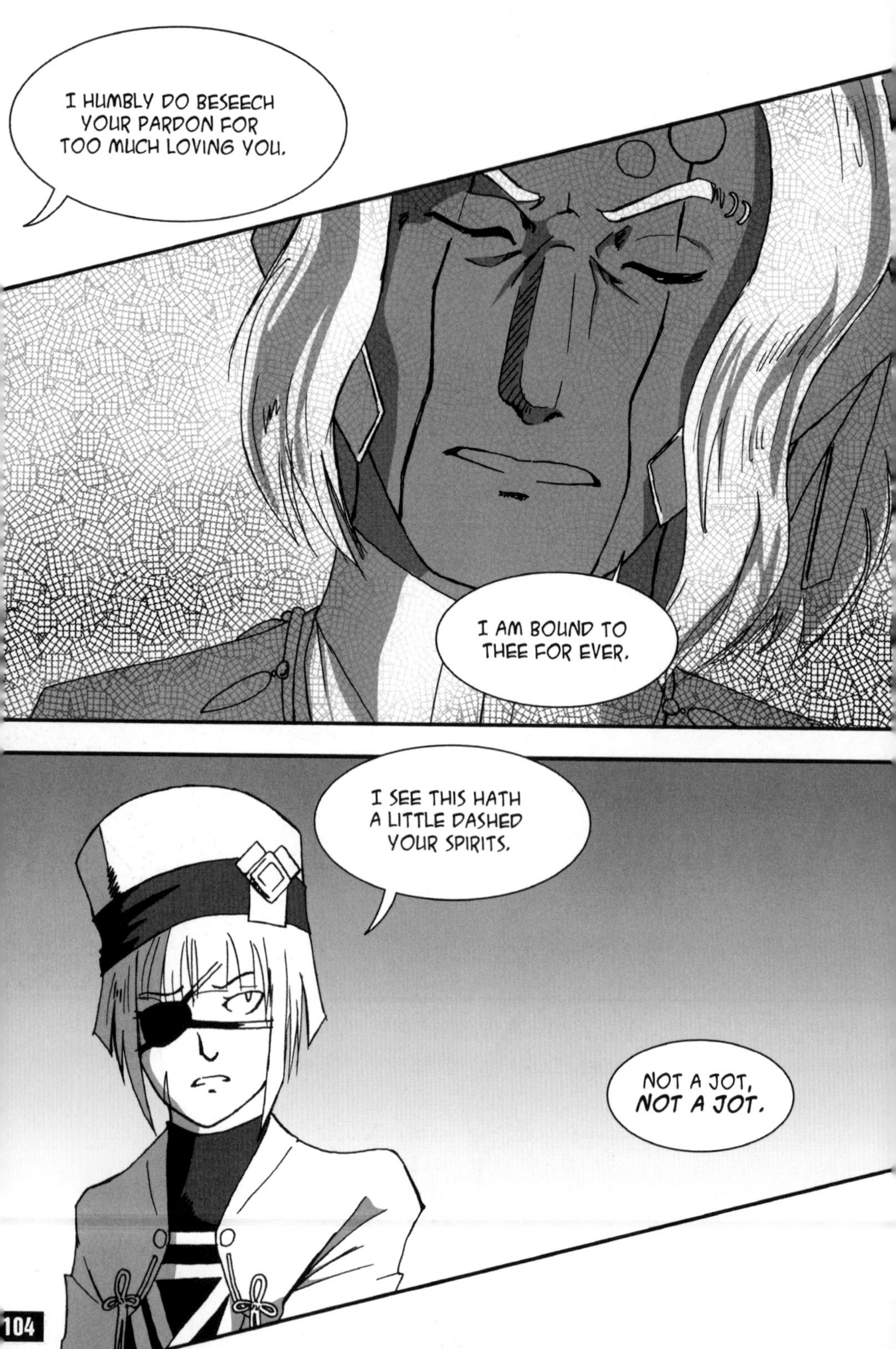
I HUMBLY DO BESEECH YOUR PARDON FOR TOO MUCH LOVING YOU.
I AM BOUND TO THEE FOR EVER.
I SEE THIS HATH A LITTLE DASHED YOUR SPIRITS.
NOT A JOT, NOT A JOT.

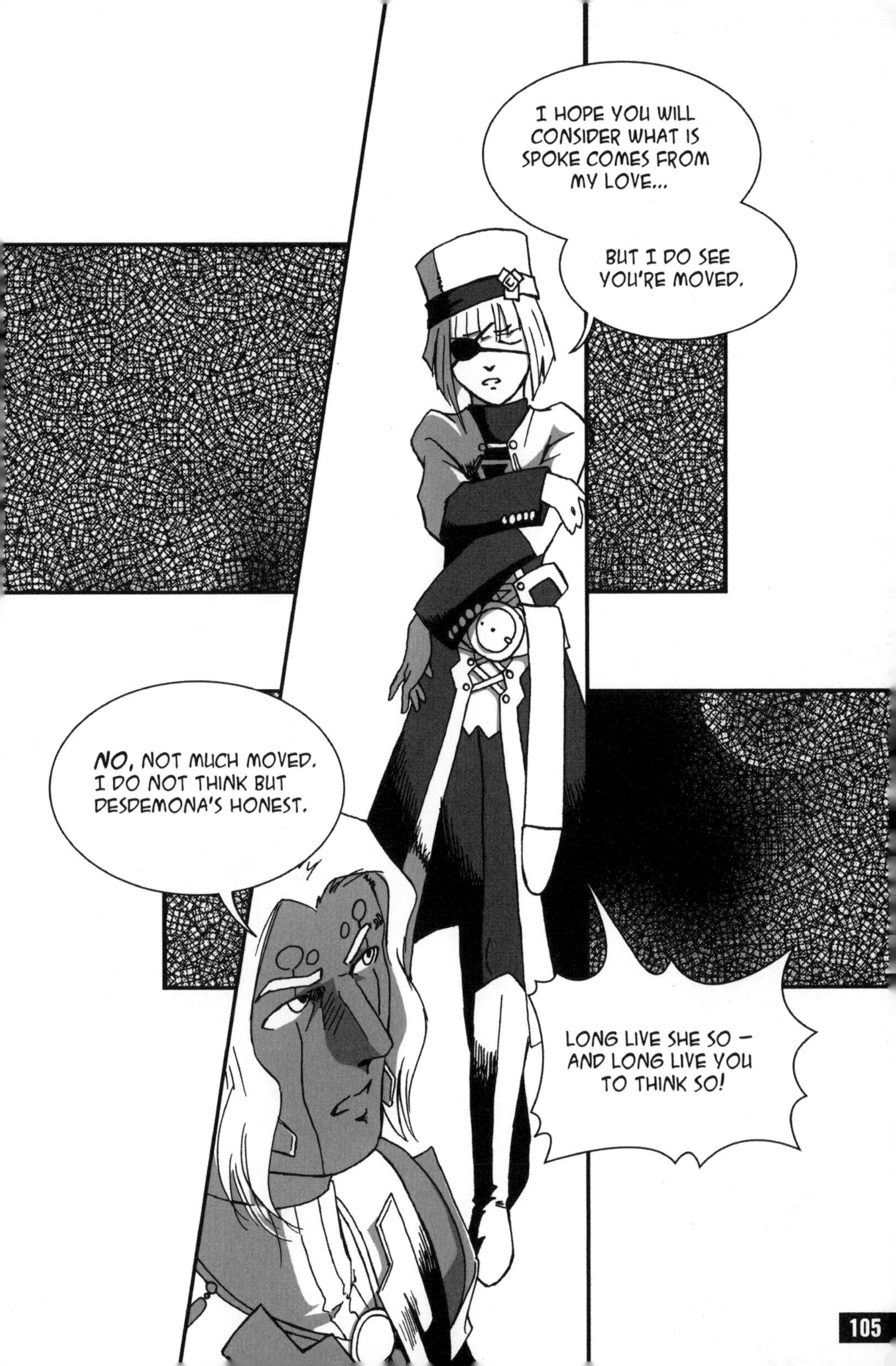
I HOPE YOU WILL CONSIDER WHAT IS SPOKE COMES FROM MY LOVE...
BUT I DO SEE YOU'RE MOVED.
NO, NOT MUCH MOVED. I DO NOT THINK BUT DESDEMONA'S HONEST.
LONG LIVE SHE SO – AND LONG LIVE YOU TO THINK SO!

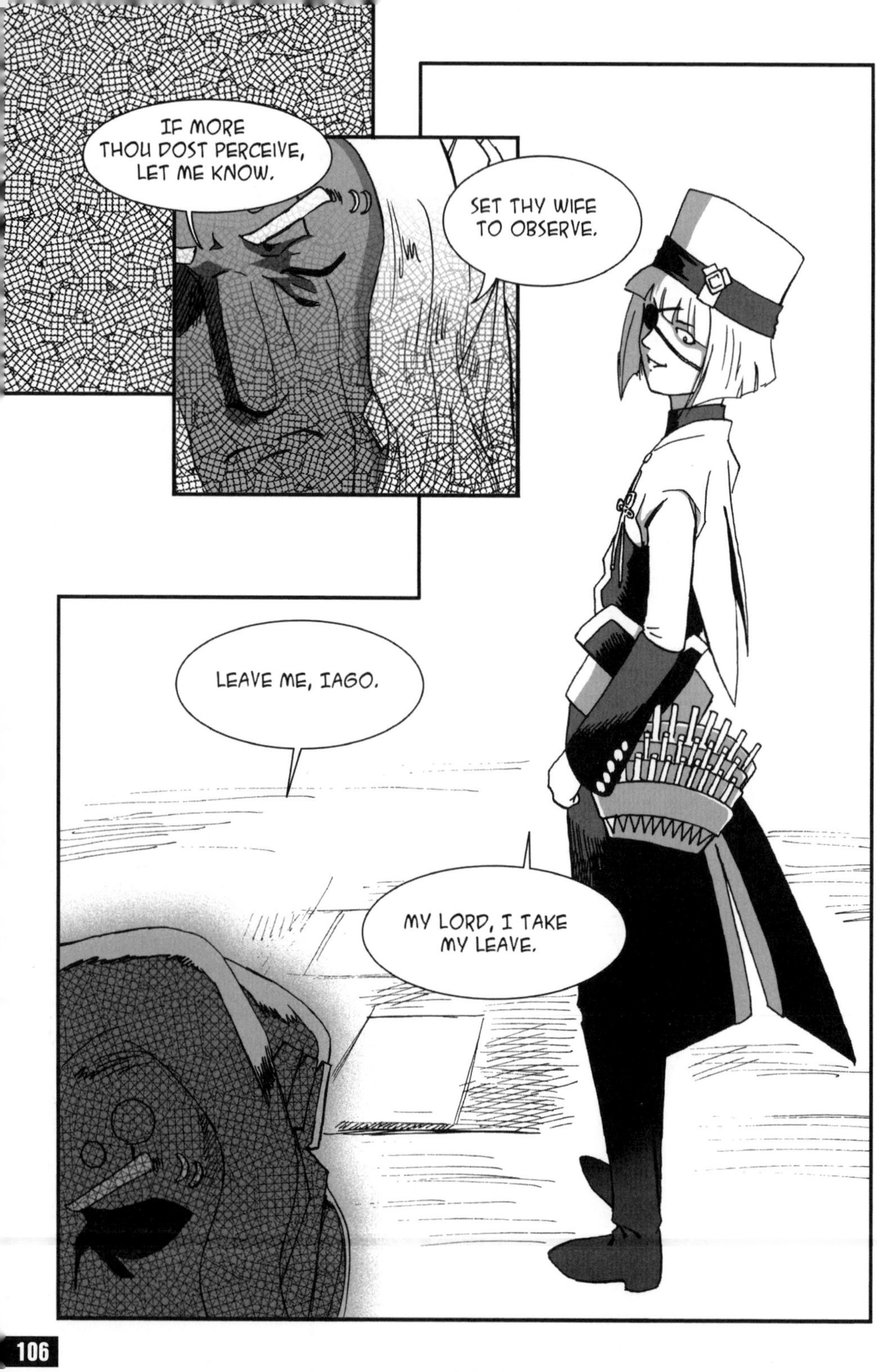
IF MORE THOU DOST PERCEIVE, LET ME KNOW.
SET THY WIFE TO OBSERVE.
LEAVE ME, IAGO.
MY LORD, I TAKE MY LEAVE.

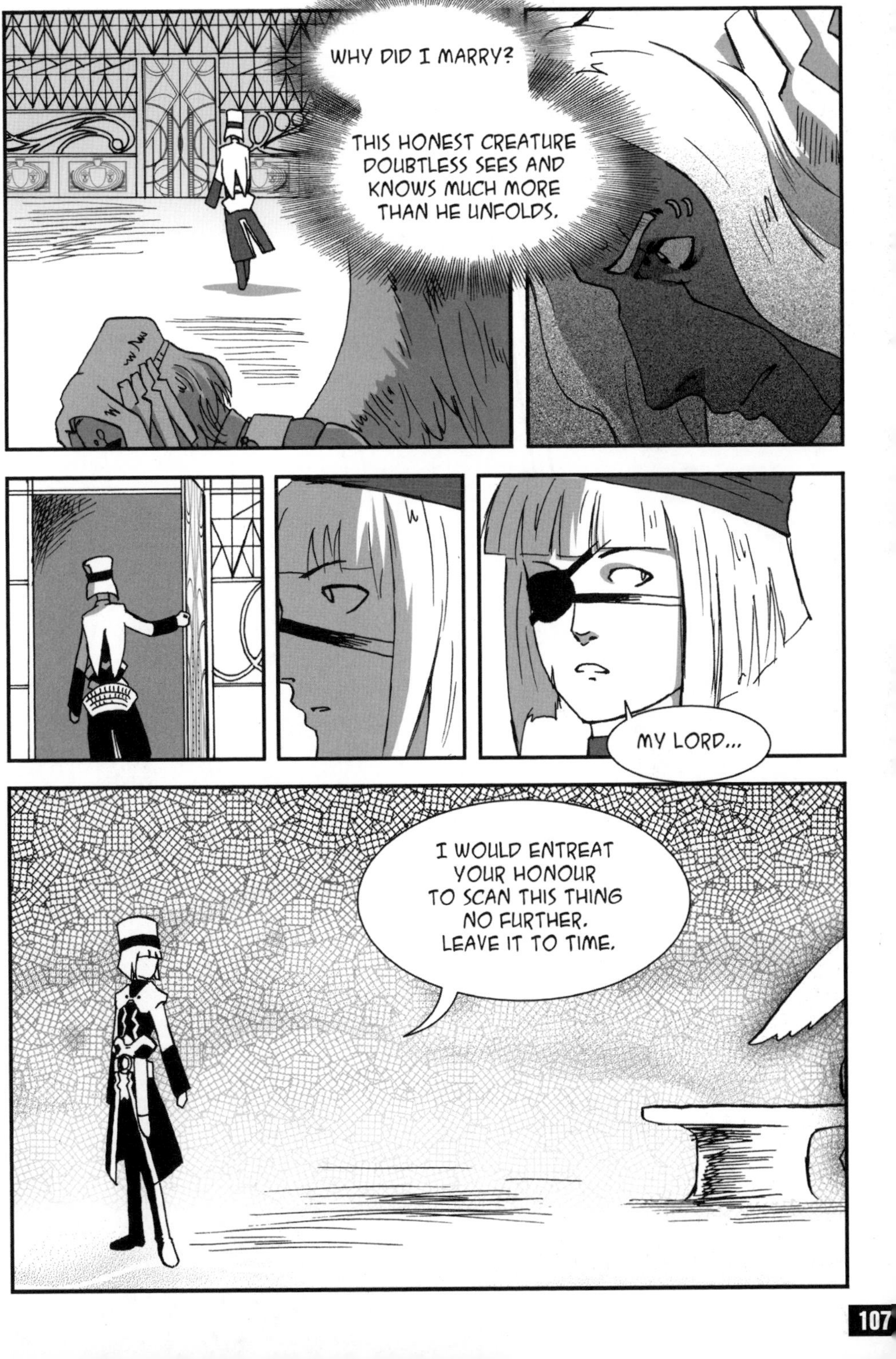
WHY DID I MARRY?
THIS HONEST CREATURE DOUBTLESS SEES AND KNOWS MUCH MORE THAN HE UNFOLDS.
MY LORD...
I WOULD ENTREAT YOUR HONOUR TO SCAN THIS THING NO FURTHER. LEAVE IT TO TIME.

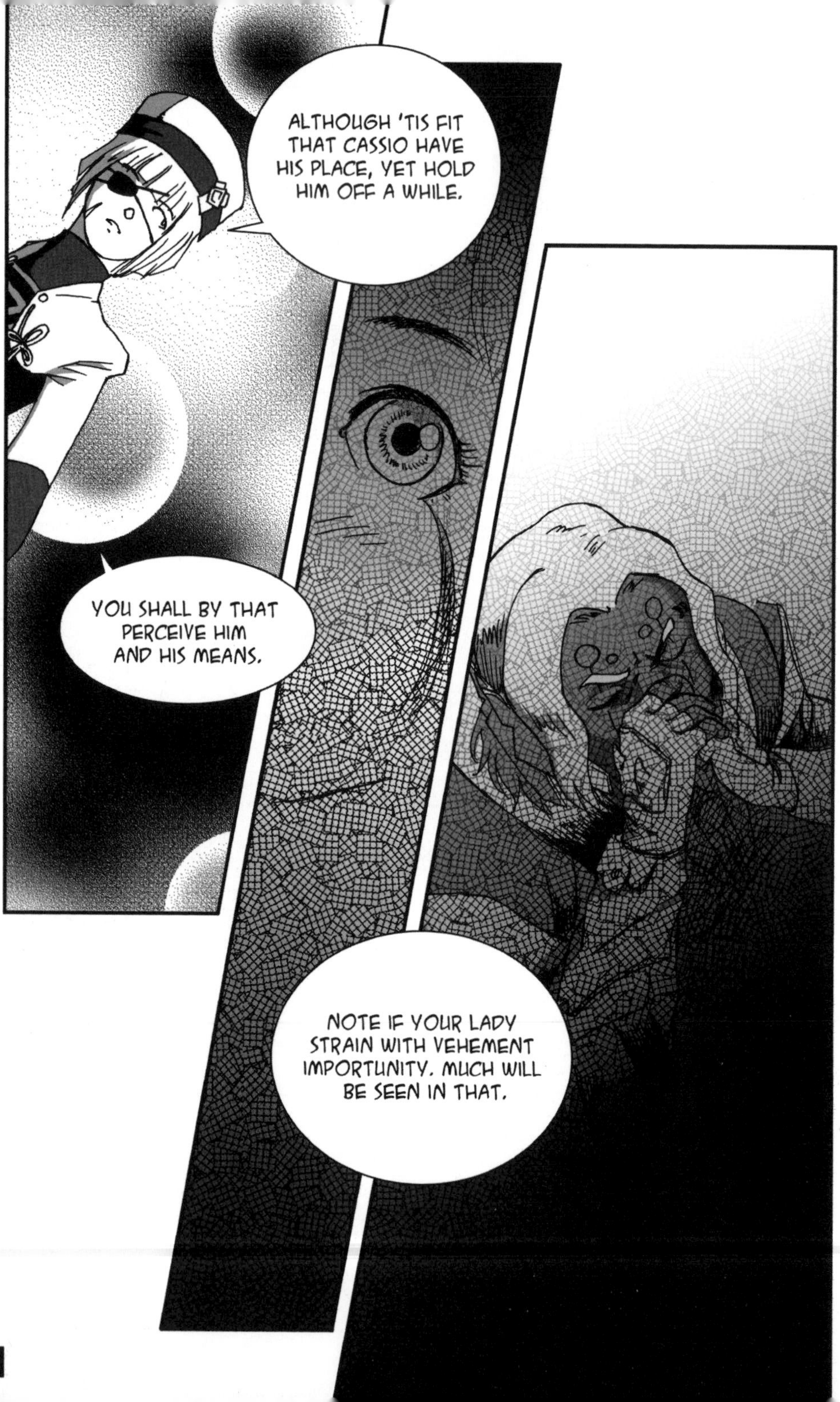
ALTHOUGH 'TIS FIT THAT CASSIO HAVE HIS PLACE, YET HOLD HIM OFF A WHILE.
YOU SHALL BY THAT PERCEIVE HIM AND HIS MEANS.
NOTE IF YOUR LADY STRAIN WITH VEHEMENT IMPORTUNITY. MUCH WILL BE SEEN IN THAT.

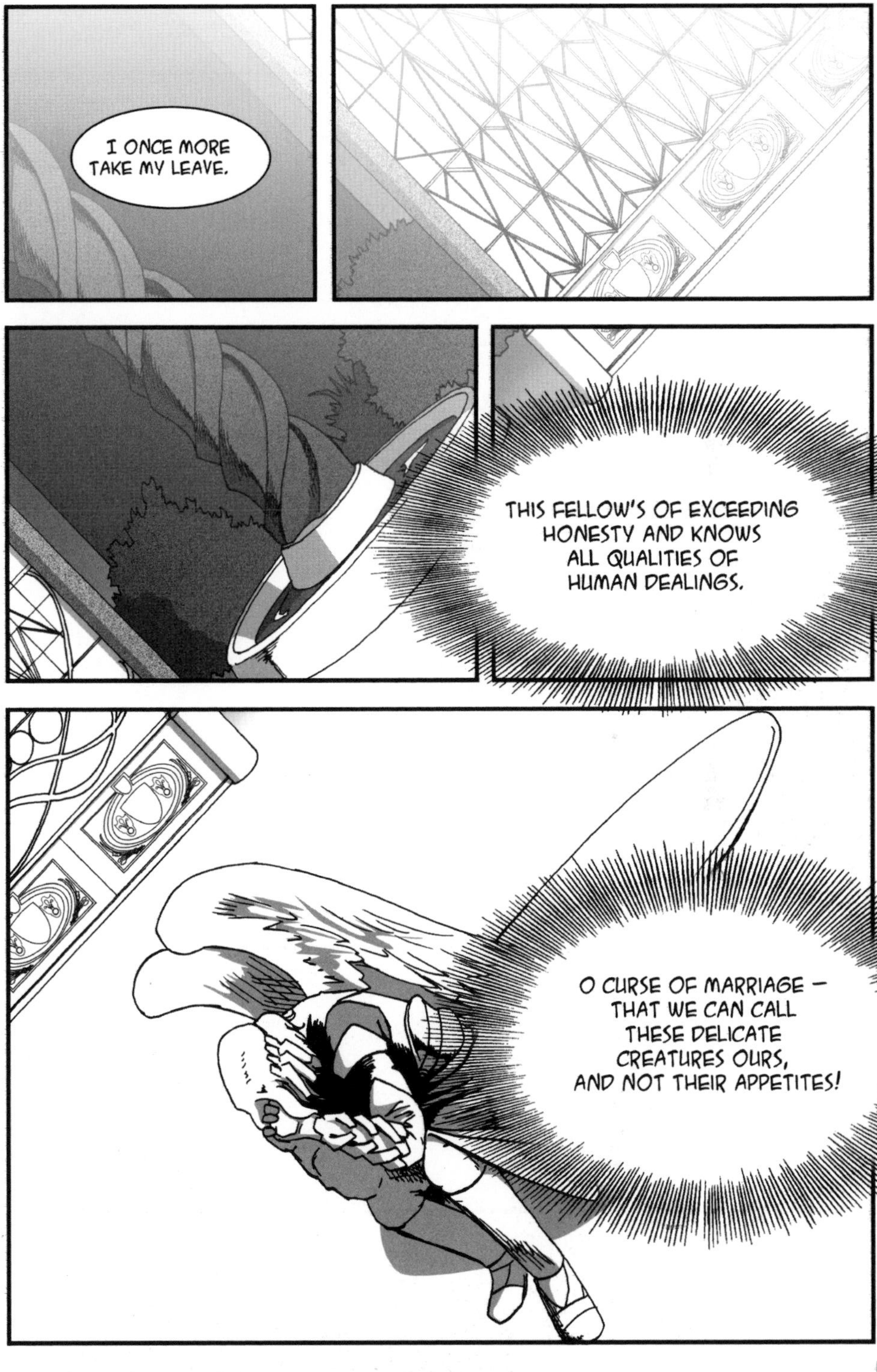
I ONCE MORE TAKE MY LEAVE.
THIS FELLOW'S OF EXCEEDING HONESTY AND KNOWS ALL QUALITIES OF HUMAN DEALINGS.
O CURSE OF MARRIAGE – THAT WE CAN CALL THESE DELICATE CREATURES OURS, AND NOT THEIR APPETITES!

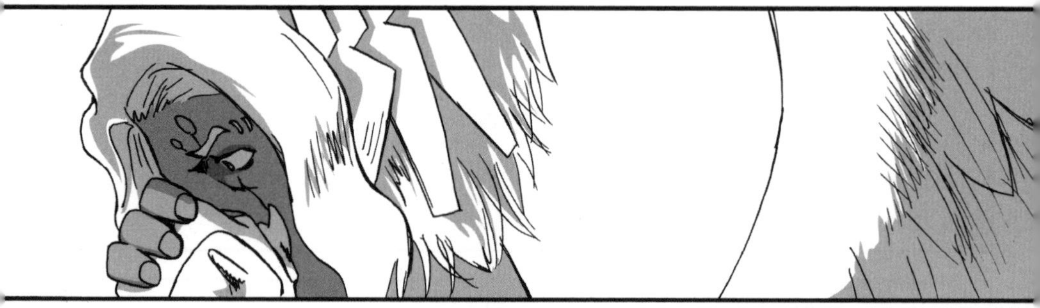

I had rather be a toad, and live upon the vapour of a dungeon,
than keep a corner in the thing I love for others' uses.

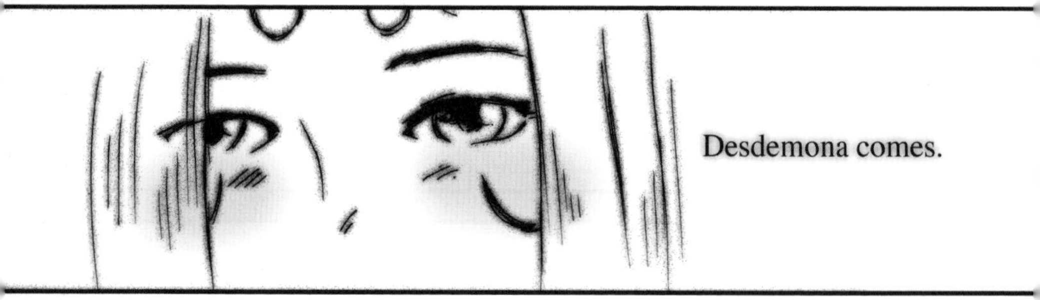
Desdemona comes.

If she be false – o, then heaven mocks itself!

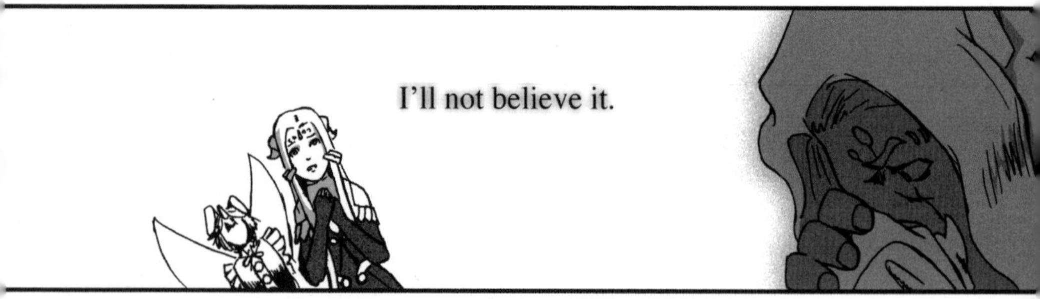
I'll not believe it.

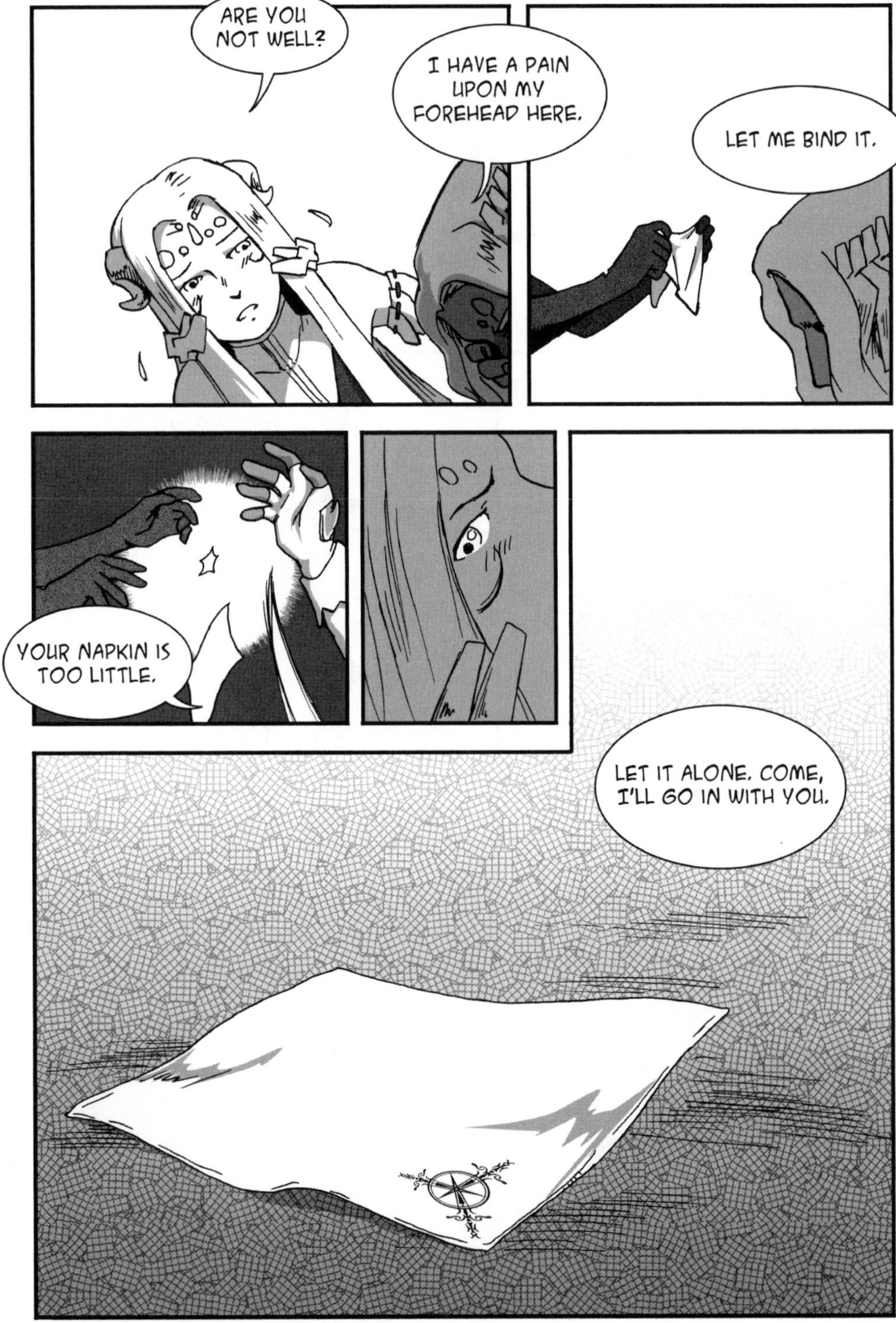
ARE YOU NOT WELL?
I HAVE A PAIN UPON MY FOREHEAD HERE.
LET ME BIND IT.
YOUR NAPKIN IS TOO LITTLE.
LET IT ALONE. COME, I'LL GO IN WITH YOU.

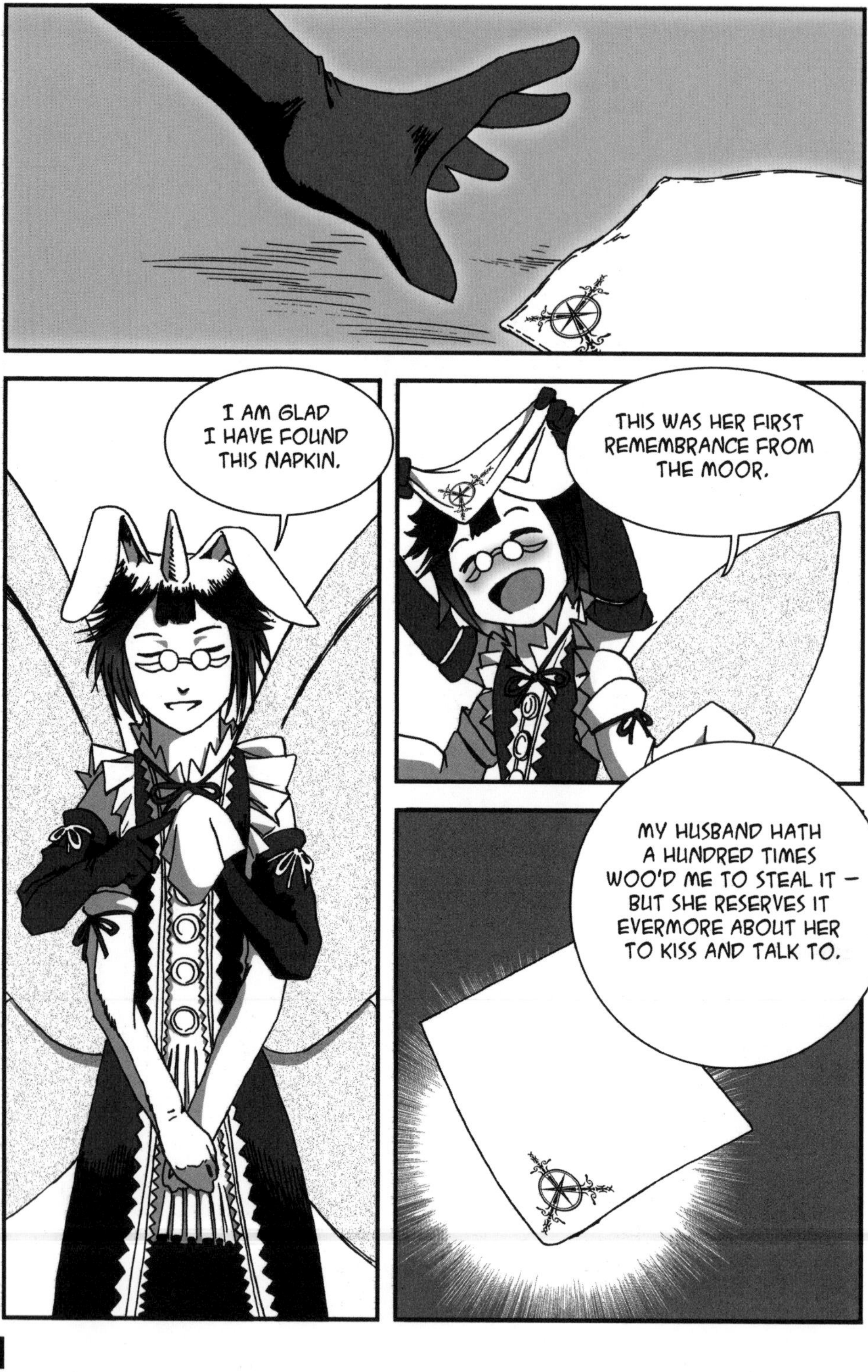
I AM GLAD I HAVE FOUND THIS NAPKIN.
THIS WAS HER FIRST REMEMBRANCE FROM THE MOOR.
MY HUSBAND HATH A HUNDRED TIMES WOO'D ME TO STEAL IT — BUT SHE RESERVES IT EVERMORE ABOUT HER TO KISS AND TALK TO.

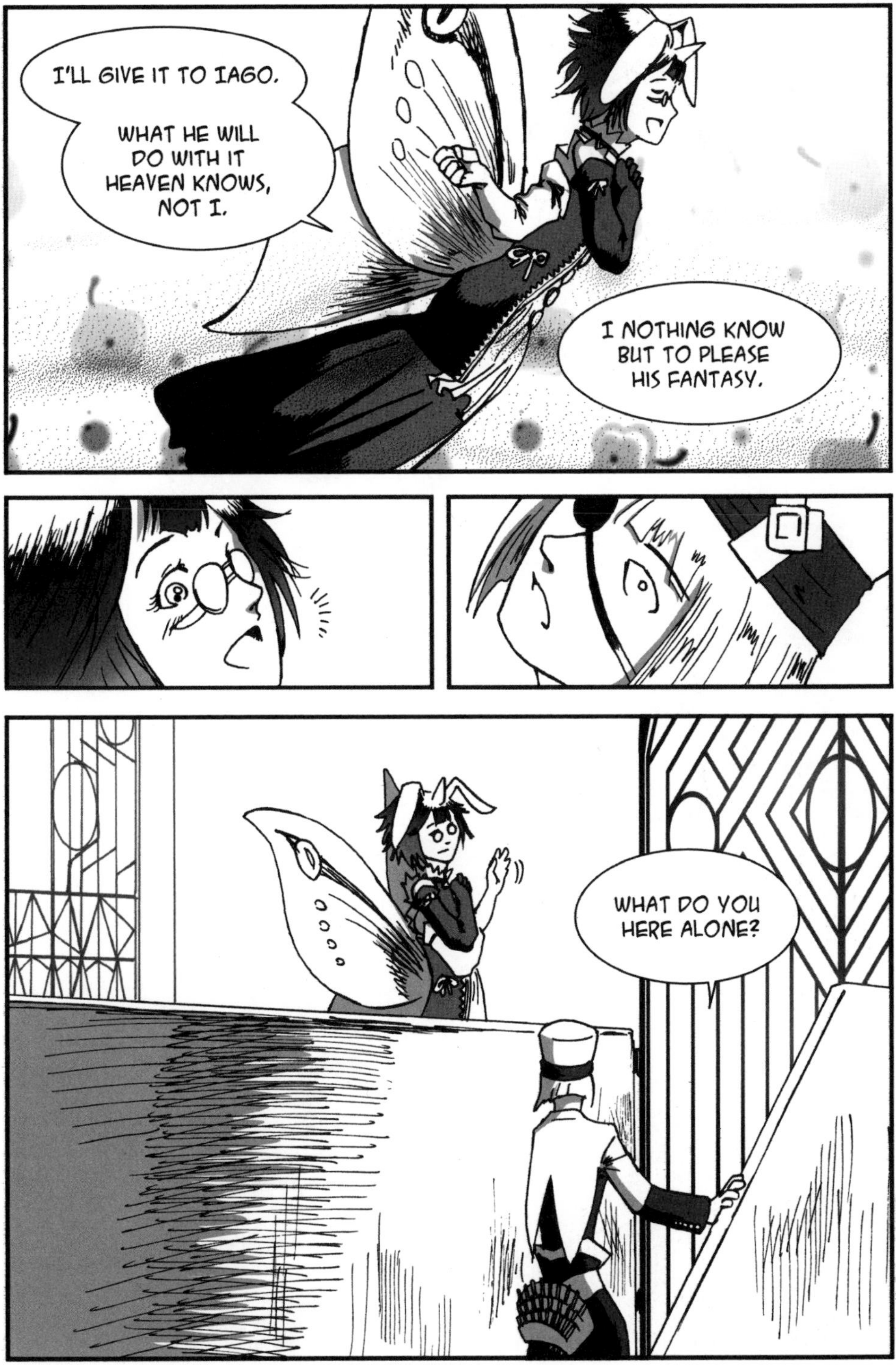

I'LL GIVE IT TO IAGO.
WHAT HE WILL DO WITH IT HEAVEN KNOWS, NOT I.
I NOTHING KNOW BUT TO PLEASE HIS FANTASY.
WHAT DO YOU HERE ALONE?

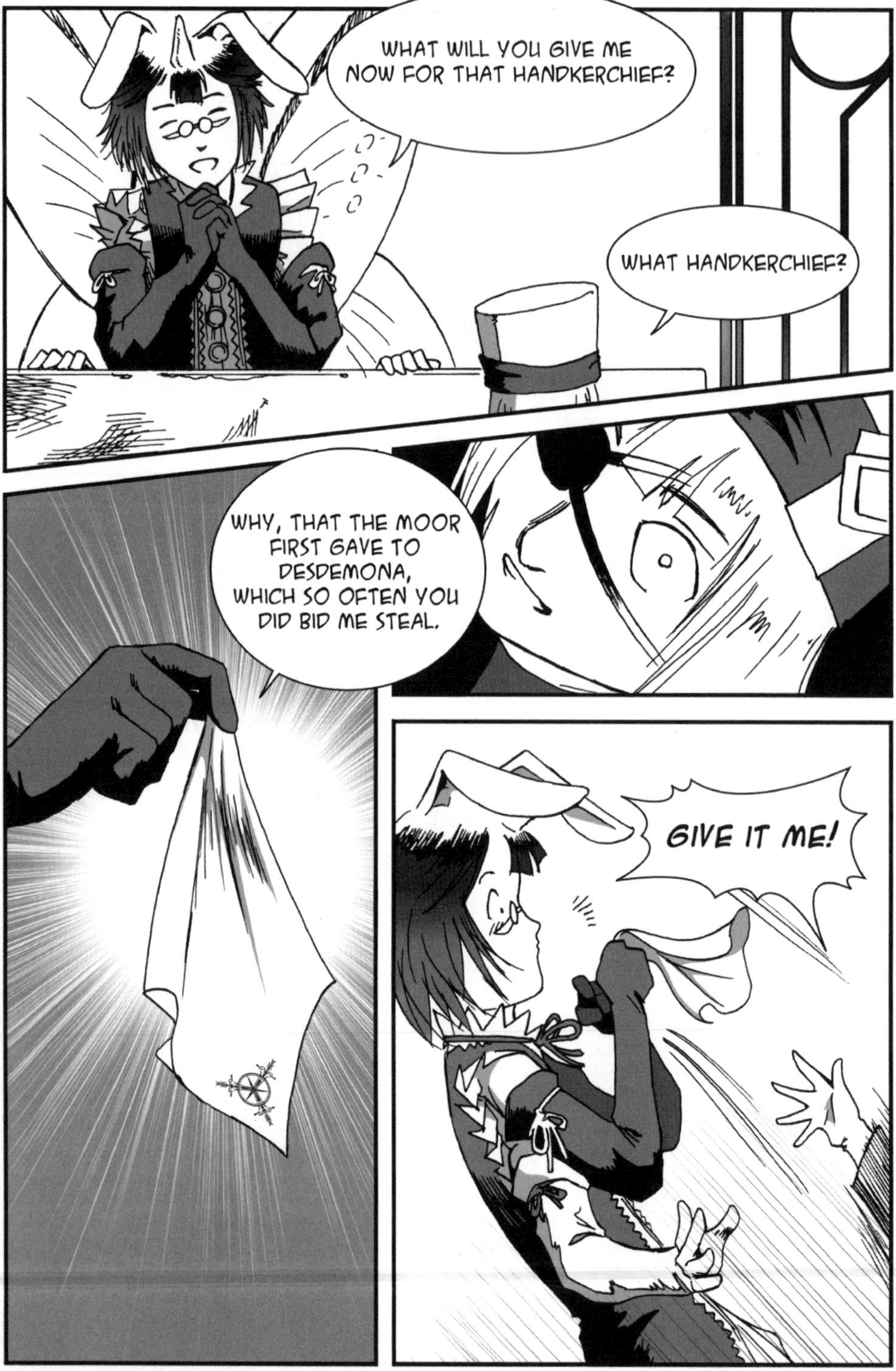
WHAT WILL YOU GIVE ME NOW FOR THAT HANDKERCHIEF?
WHAT HANDKERCHIEF?
WHY, THAT THE MOOR FIRST GAVE TO DESDEMONA, WHICH SO OFTEN YOU DID BID ME STEAL.
GIVE IT ME!

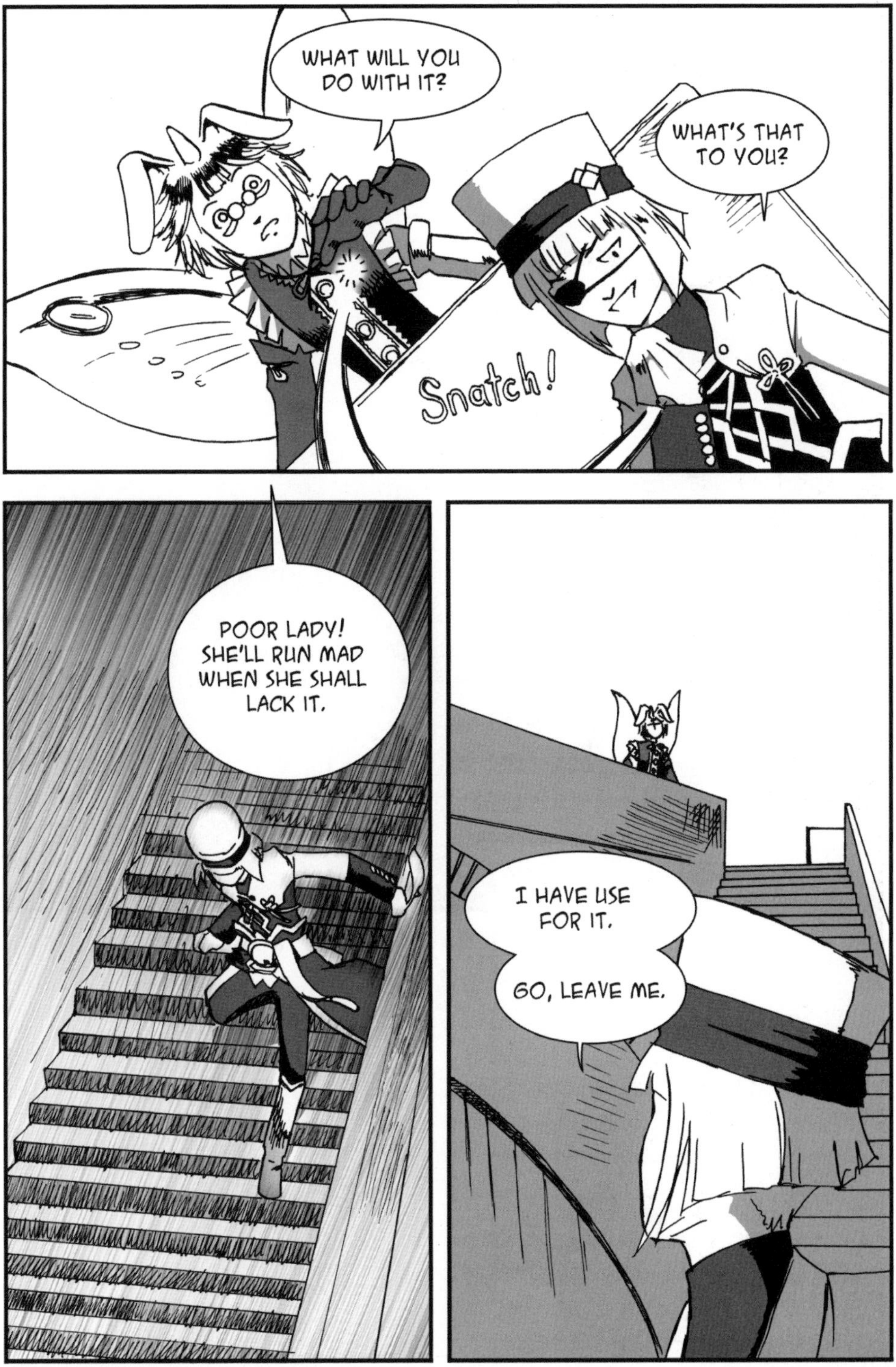
WHAT WILL YOU DO WITH IT?
WHAT'S THAT TO YOU?
Snatch!
POOR LADY! SHE'LL RUN MAD WHEN SHE SHALL LACK IT.
I HAVE USE FOR IT.
GO, LEAVE ME.

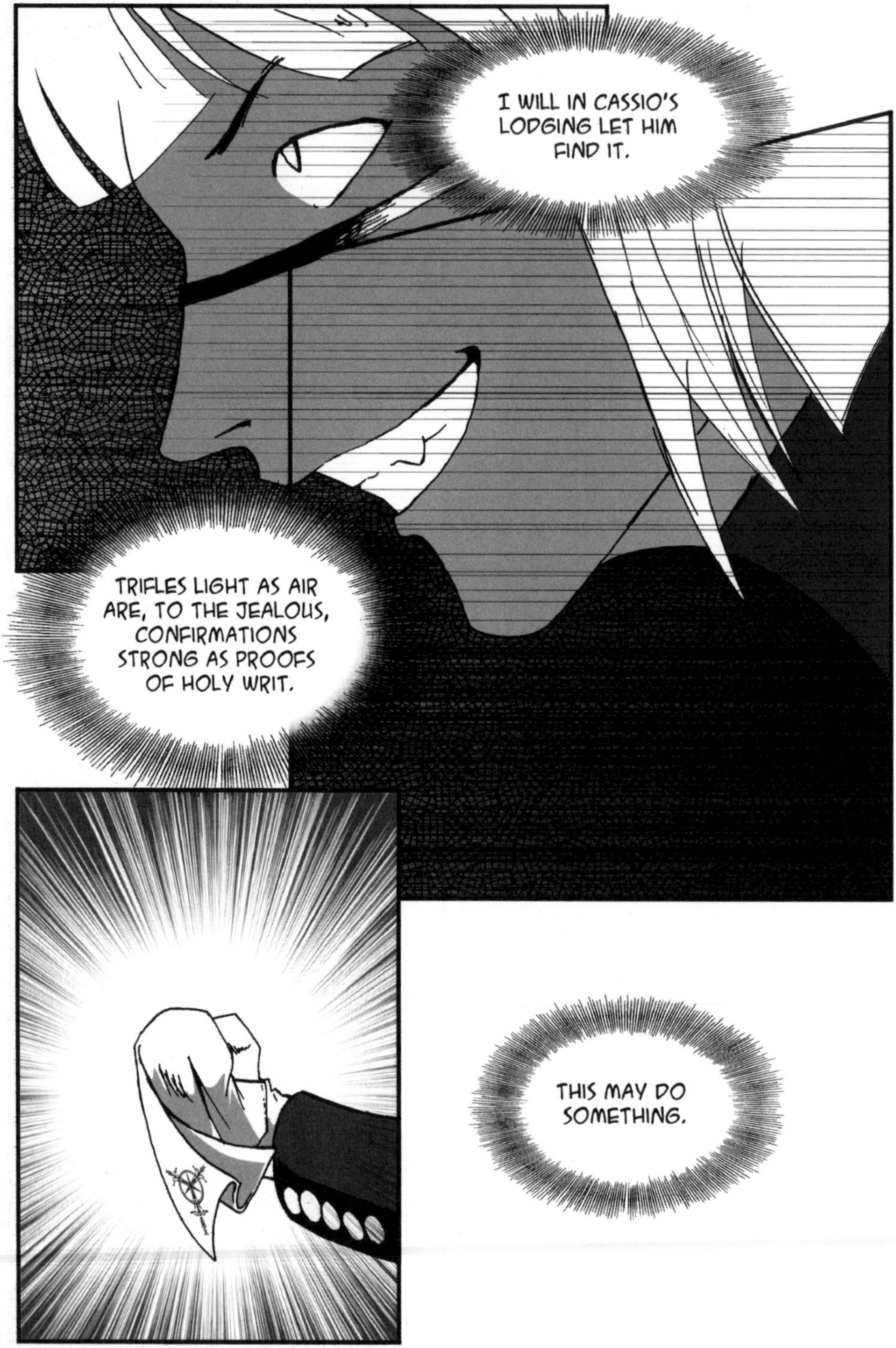
I WILL IN CASSIO'S LODGING LET HIM FIND IT.
TRIFLES LIGHT AS AIR ARE, TO THE JEALOUS, CONFIRMATIONS STRONG AS PROOFS OF HOLY WRIT.
THIS MAY DO SOMETHING.

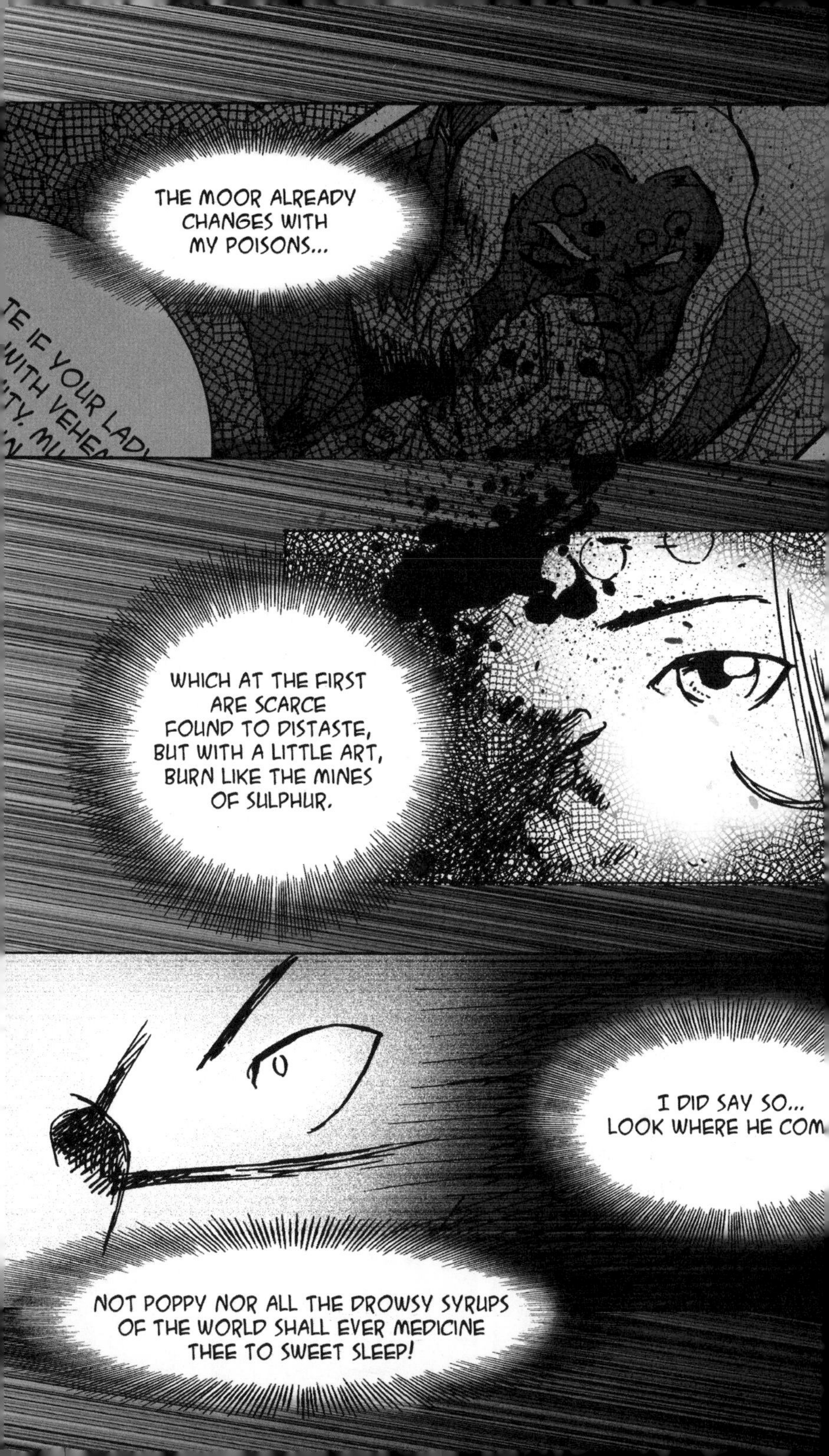
THE MOOR ALREADY CHANGES WITH MY POISONS...
WHICH AT THE FIRST ARE SCARCE FOUND TO DISTASTE, BUT WITH A LITTLE ART, BURN LIKE THE MINES OF SULPHUR.
I DID SAY SO... LOOK WHERE HE COM
NOT POPPY NOR ALL THE DROWSY SYRUPS OF THE WORLD SHALL EVER MEDICINE THEE TO SWEET SLEEP!

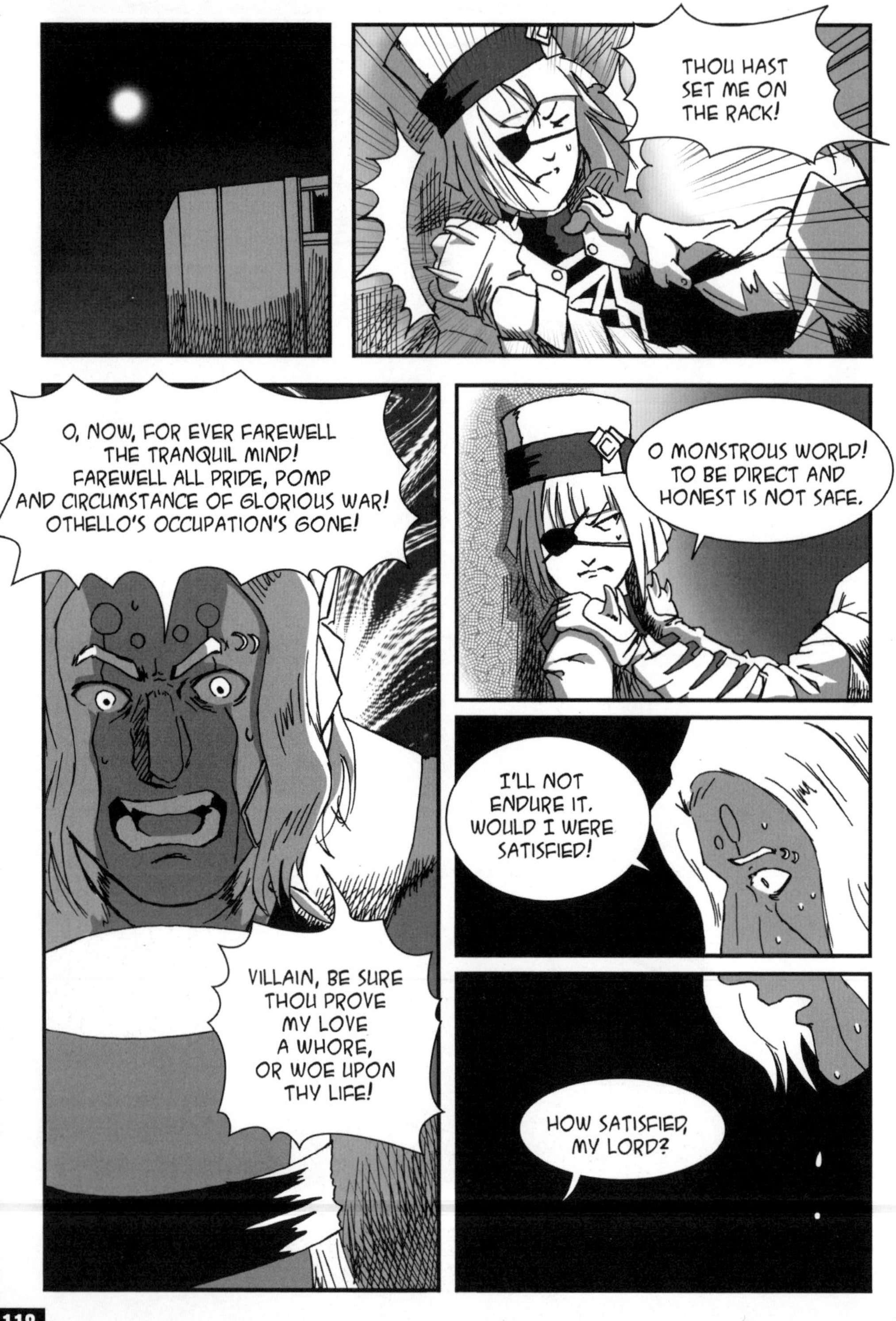
THOU HAST SET ME ON THE RACK!
O, NOW, FOR EVER FAREWELL THE TRANQUIL MIND! FAREWELL ALL PRIDE, POMP AND CIRCUMSTANCE OF GLORIOUS WAR! OTHELLO'S OCCUPATION'S GONE!
O MONSTROUS WORLD! TO BE DIRECT AND HONEST IS NOT SAFE.
VILLAIN, BE SURE THOU PROVE MY LOVE A WHORE, OR WOE UPON THY LIFE!
I'LL NOT ENDURE IT. WOULD I WERE SATISFIED!
HOW SATISFIED, MY LORD?

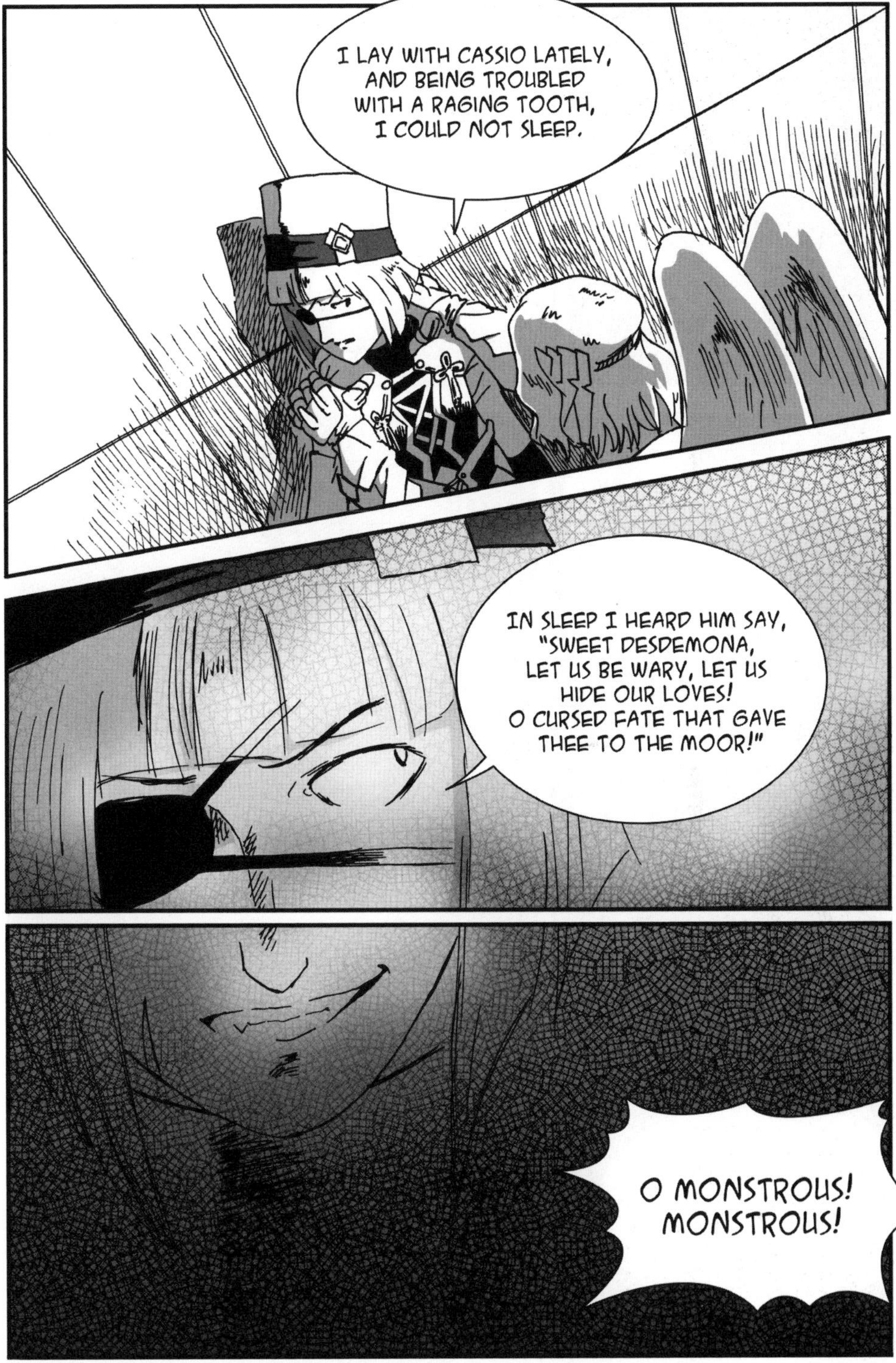
I LAY WITH CASSIO LATELY, AND BEING TROUBLED WITH A RAGING TOOTH, I COULD NOT SLEEP.
IN SLEEP I HEARD HIM SAY, "SWEET DESDEMONA, LET US BE WARY, LET US HIDE OUR LOVES! O CURSED FATE THAT GAVE THEE TO THE MOOR!"
O MONSTROUS! MONSTROUS!

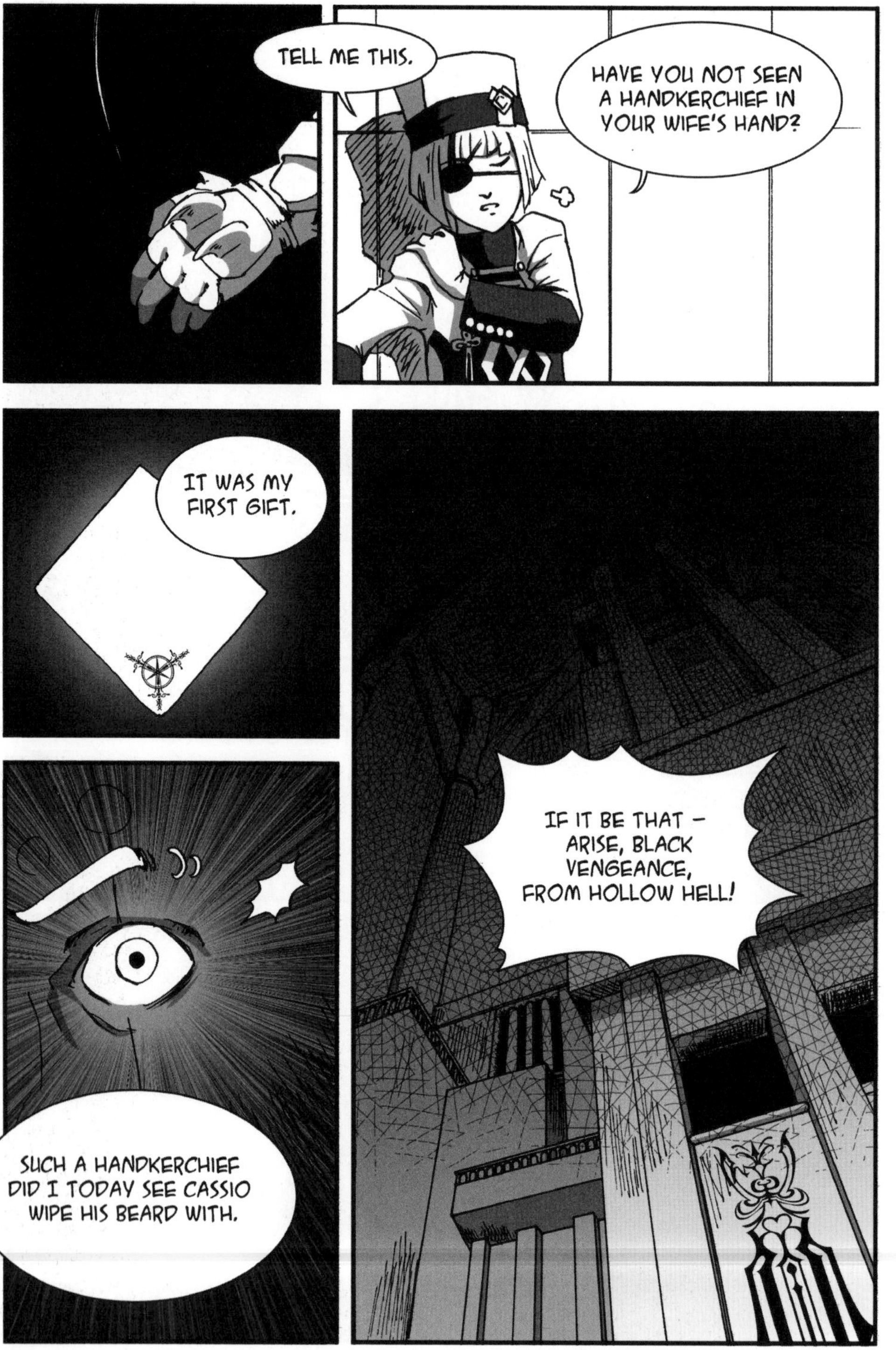
TELL ME THIS.
HAVE YOU NOT SEEN A HANDKERCHIEF IN YOUR WIFE'S HAND?
IT WAS MY FIRST GIFT.
SUCH A HANDKERCHIEF DID I TODAY SEE CASSIO WIPE HIS BEARD WITH.
IF IT BE THAT – ARISE, BLACK VENGEANCE, FROM HOLLOW HELL!

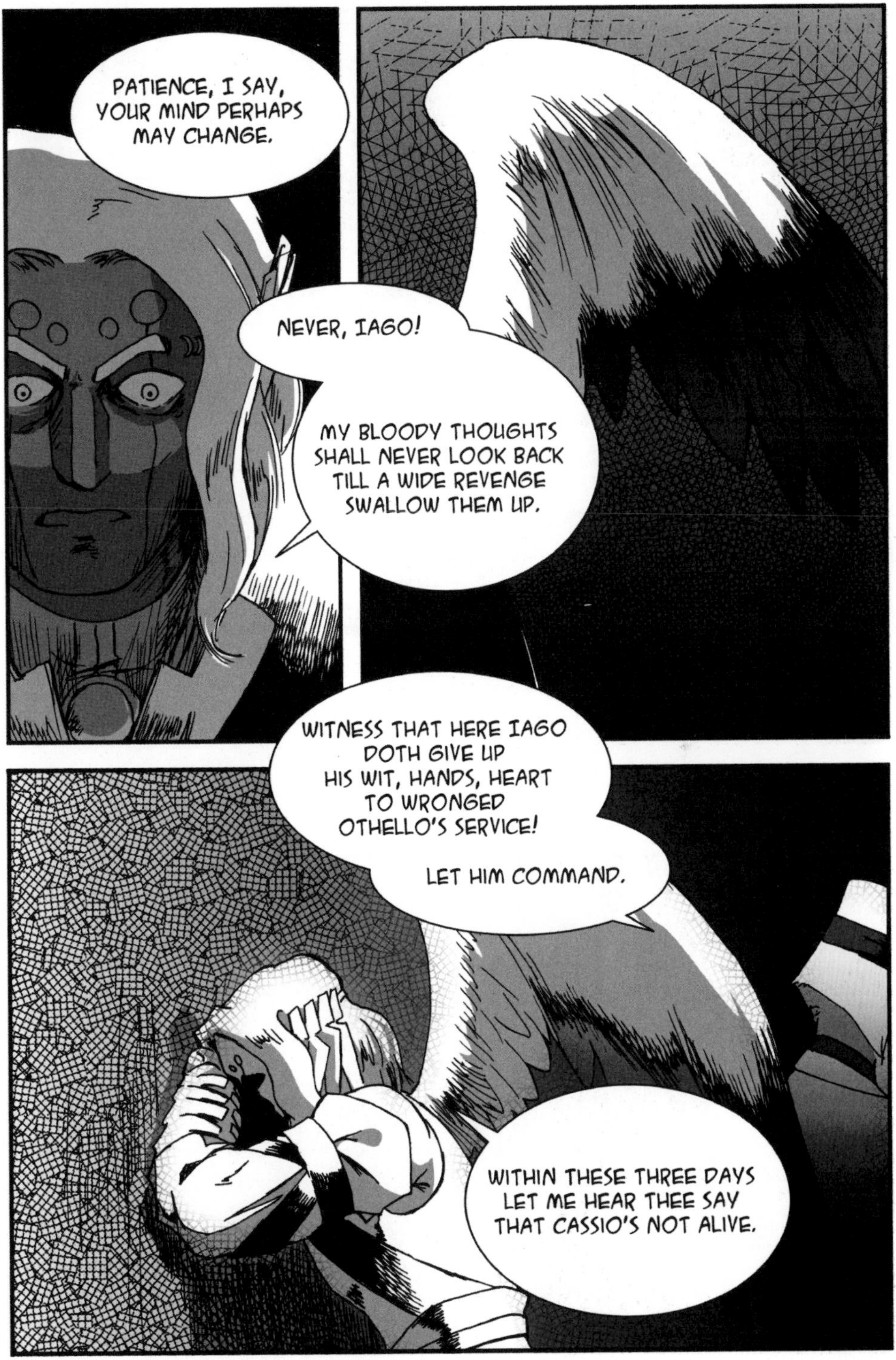
PATIENCE, I SAY, YOUR MIND PERHAPS MAY CHANGE.
NEVER, IAGO!
MY BLOODY THOUGHTS SHALL NEVER LOOK BACK TILL A WIDE REVENGE SWALLOW THEM UP.
WITNESS THAT HERE IAGO DOTH GIVE UP HIS WIT, HANDS, HEART TO WRONGED OTHELLO'S SERVICE!
LET HIM COMMAND.
WITHIN THESE THREE DAYS LET ME HEAR THEE SAY THAT CASSIO'S NOT ALIVE.

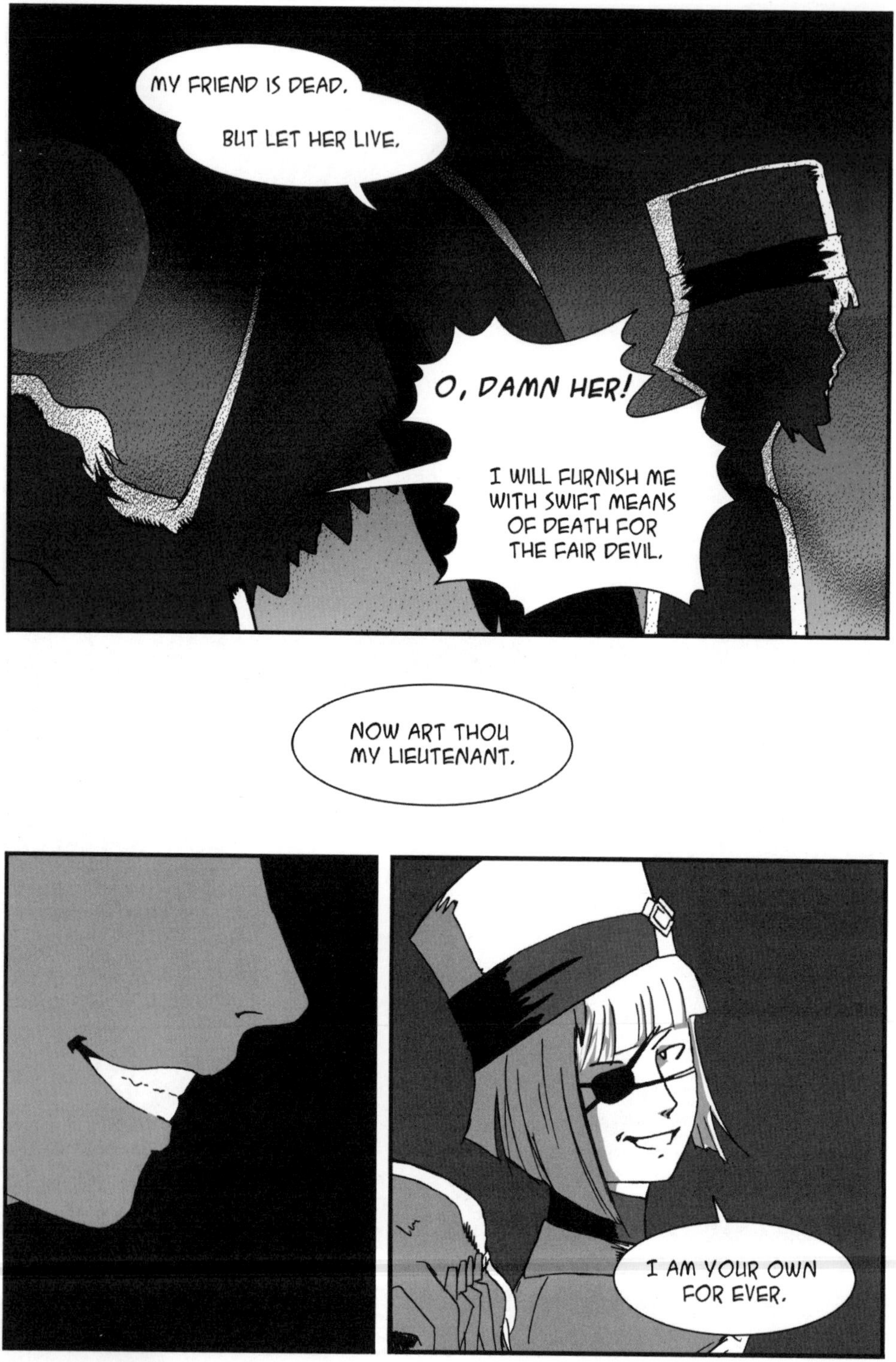
MY FRIEND IS DEAD.
BUT LET HER LIVE.
O, DAMN HER!
I WILL FURNISH ME WITH SWIFT MEANS OF DEATH FOR THE FAIR DEVIL.
NOW ART THOU MY LIEUTENANT.
I AM YOUR OWN FOR EVER.

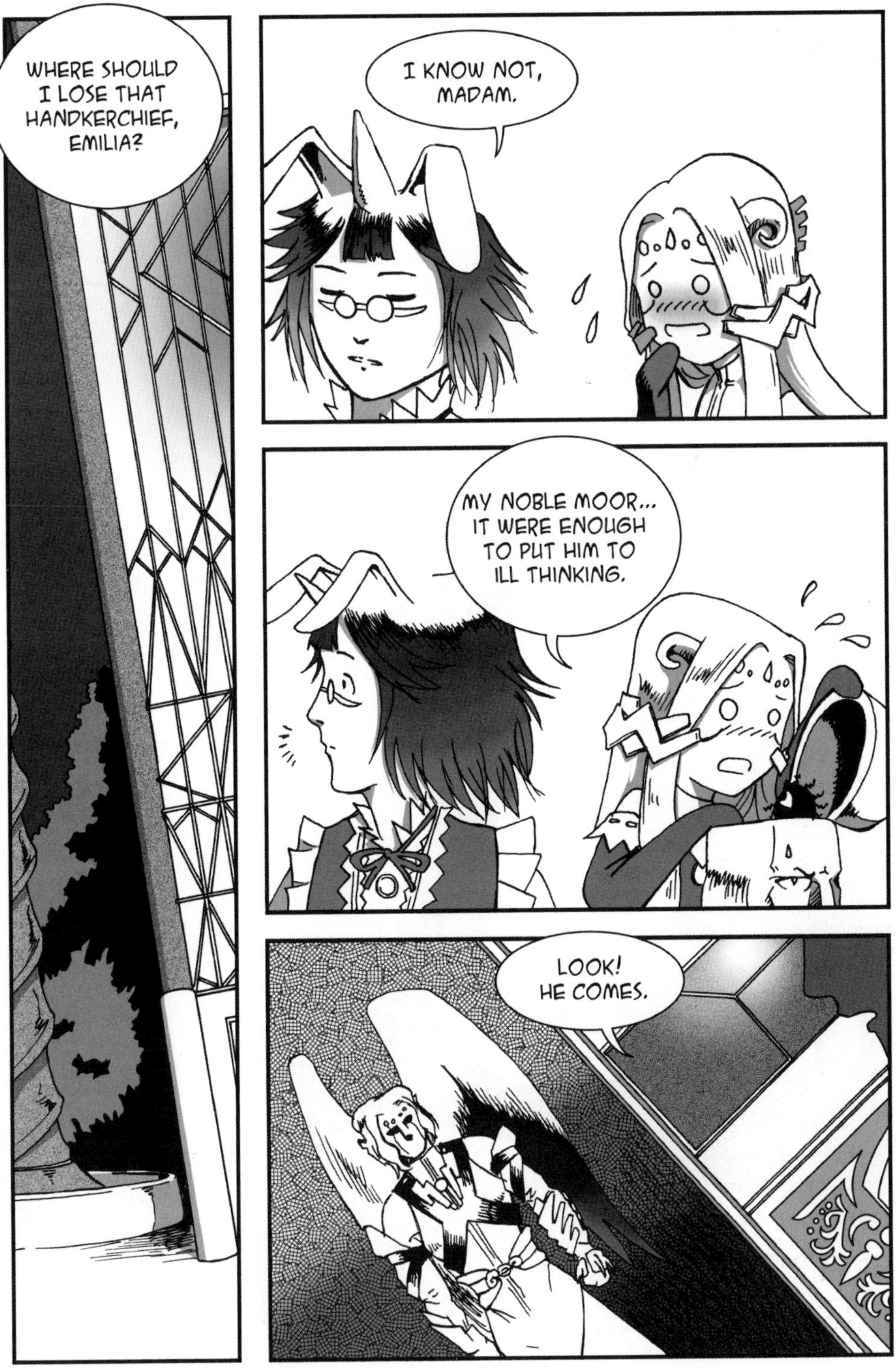
WHERE SHOULD I LOSE THAT HANDKERCHIEF, EMILIA?
I KNOW NOT, MADAM.
MY NOBLE MOOR... IT WERE ENOUGH TO PUT HIM TO ILL THINKING.
LOOK! HE COMES.

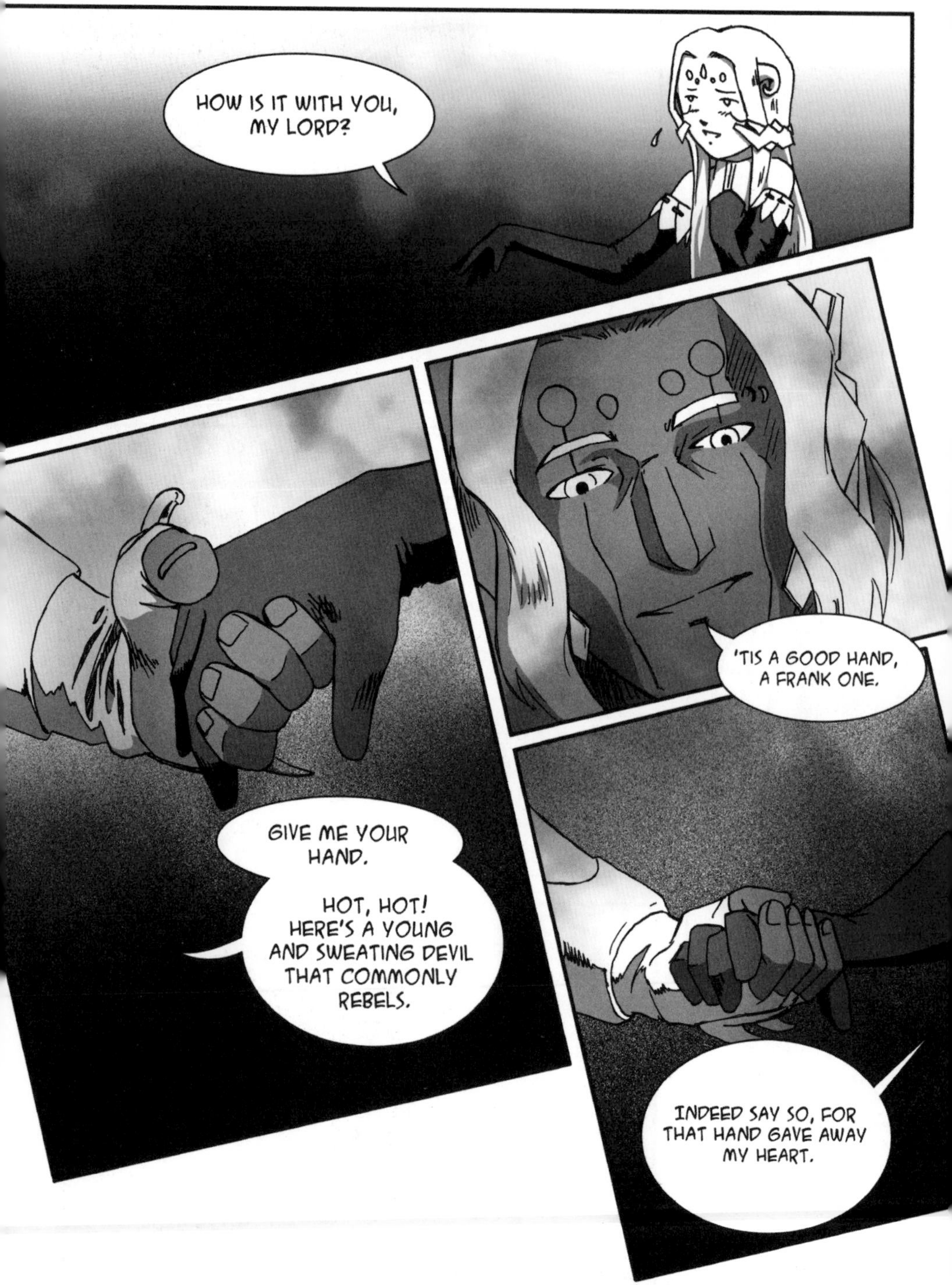
HOW IS IT WITH YOU, MY LORD?
'TIS A GOOD HAND, A FRANK ONE.
GIVE ME YOUR HAND.
HOT, HOT! HERE'S A YOUNG AND SWEATING DEVIL THAT COMMONLY REBELS.
INDEED SAY SO, FOR THAT HAND GAVE AWAY MY HEART.

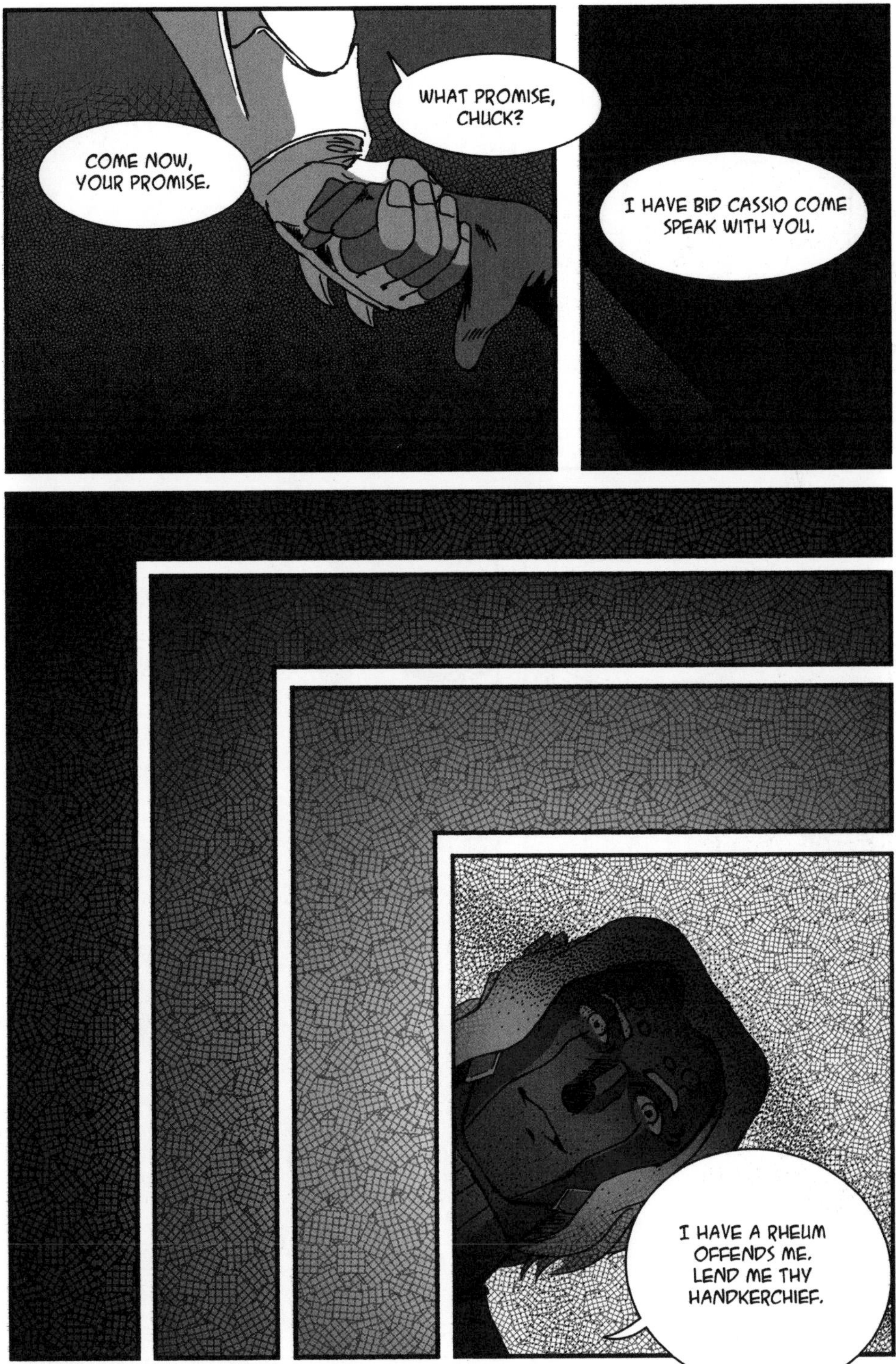
COME NOW, YOUR PROMISE.
WHAT PROMISE, CHUCK?
I HAVE BID CASSIO COME SPEAK WITH YOU.
I HAVE A RHEUM OFFENDS ME. LEND ME THY HANDKERCHIEF.

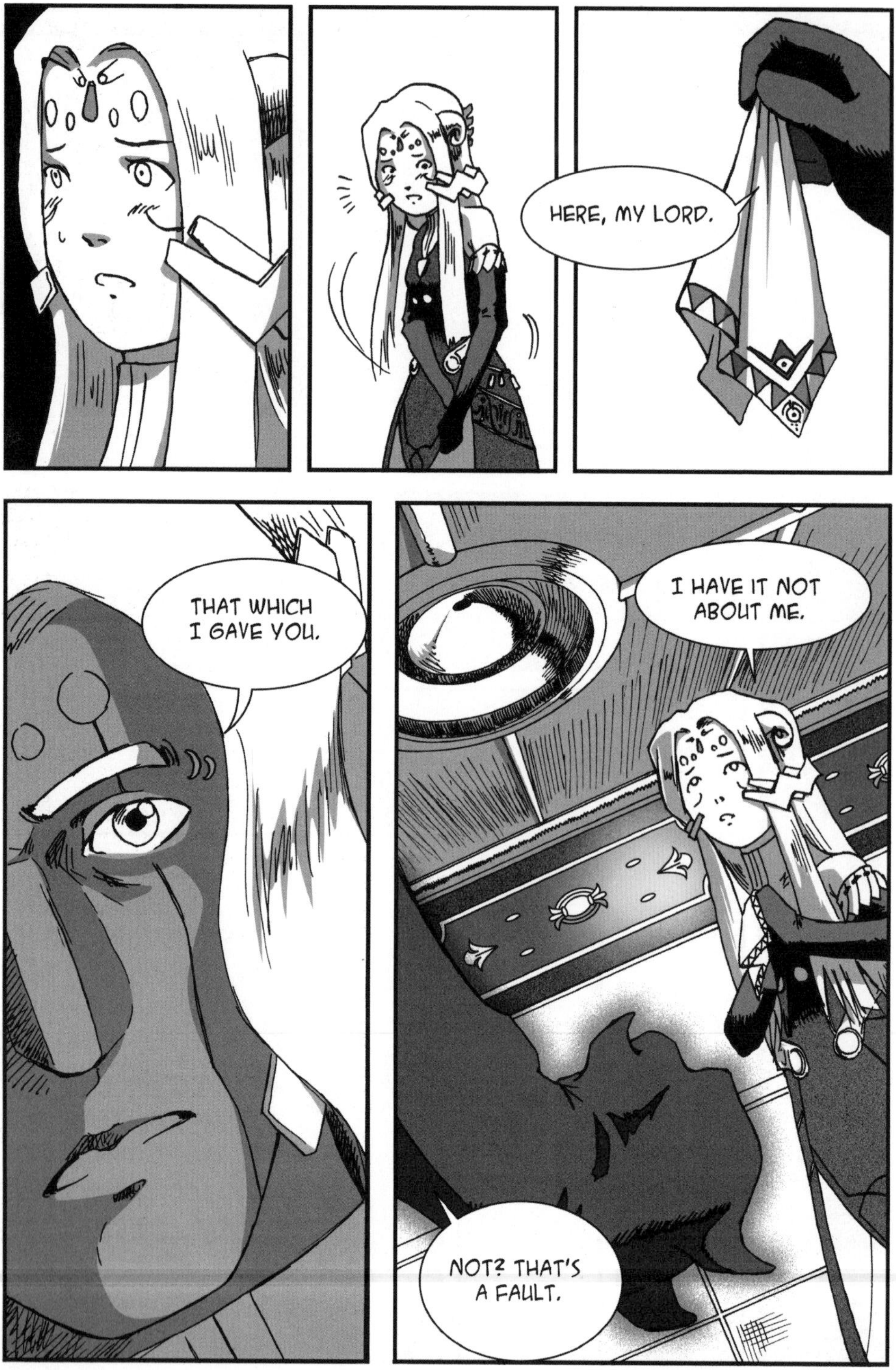
HERE, MY LORD.
THAT WHICH I GAVE YOU.
I HAVE IT NOT ABOUT ME.
NOT? THAT'S A FAULT.

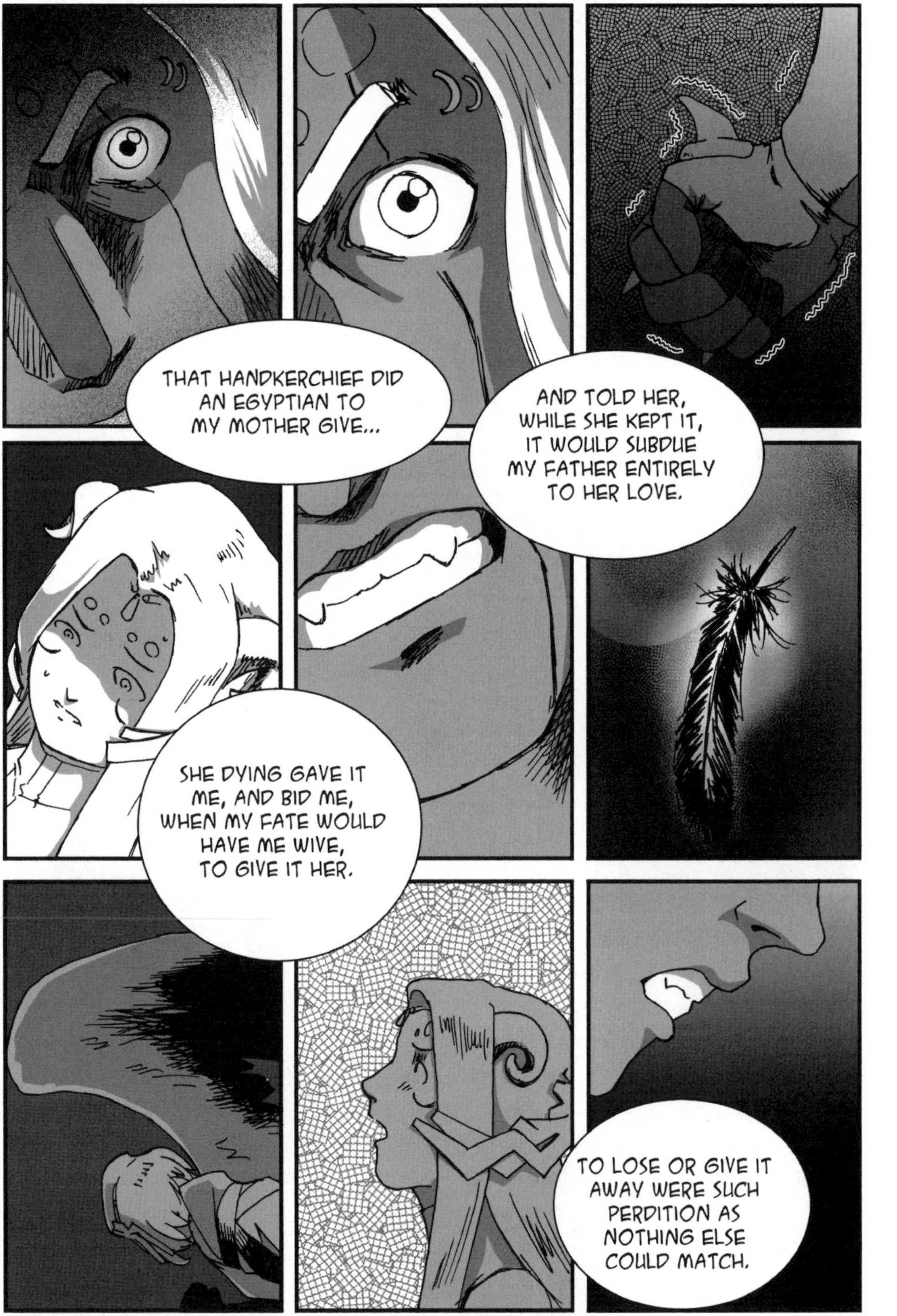
THAT HANDKERCHIEF DID AN EGYPTIAN TO MY MOTHER GIVE...
AND TOLD HER, WHILE SHE KEPT IT, IT WOULD SUBDUE MY FATHER ENTIRELY TO HER LOVE.
SHE DYING GAVE IT ME, AND BID ME, WHEN MY FATE WOULD HAVE ME WIVE, TO GIVE IT HER.
TO LOSE OR GIVE IT AWAY WERE SUCH PERDITION AS NOTHING ELSE COULD MATCH.

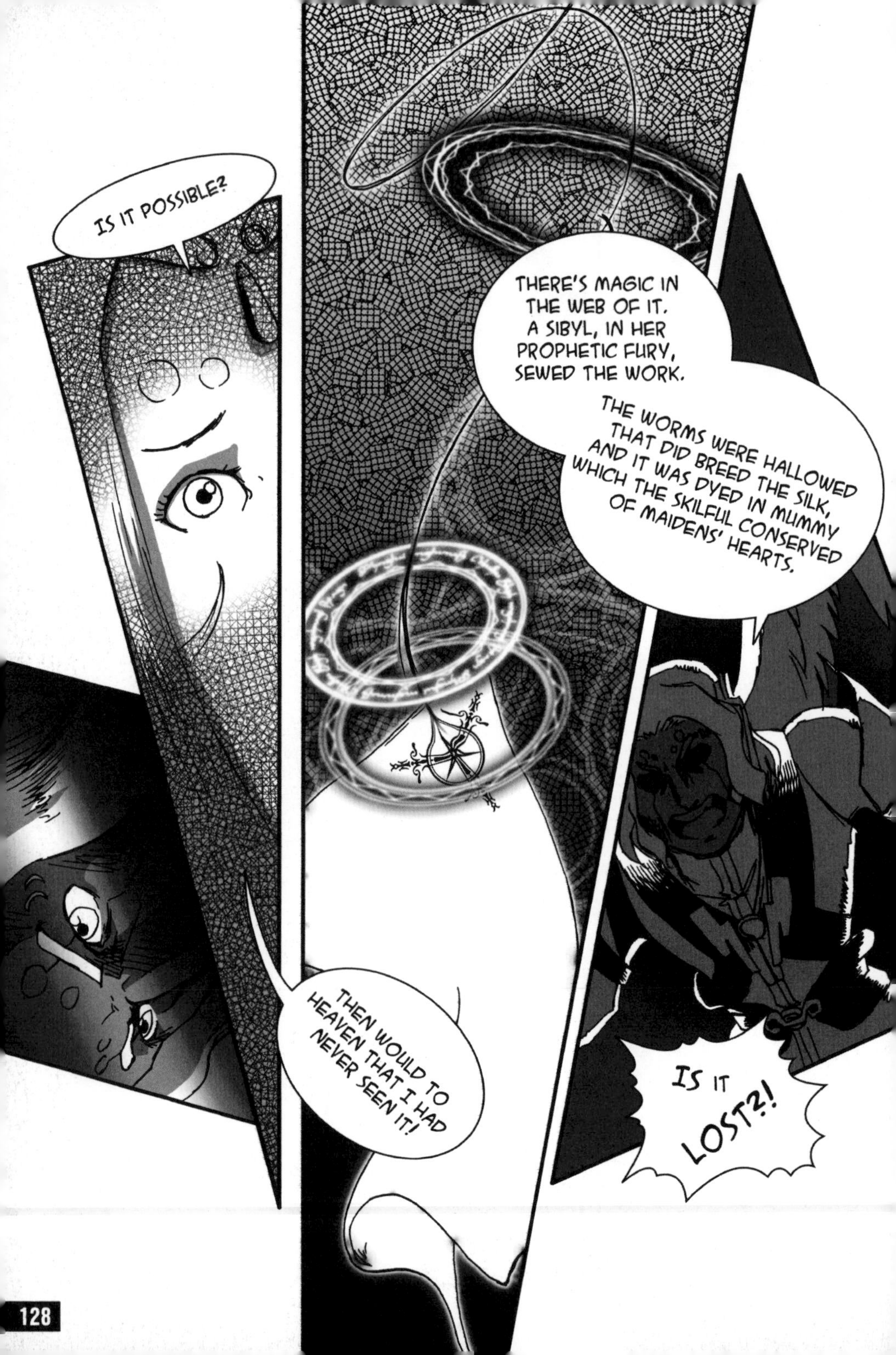

IS IT POSSIBLE?
THERE'S MAGIC IN THE WEB OF IT. A SIBYL, IN HER PROPHETIC FURY, SEWED THE WORK.
THE WORMS WERE HALLOWED THAT DID BREED THE SILK, AND IT WAS DYED IN MUMMY WHICH THE SKILFUL CONSERVED OF MAIDENS' HEARTS.
THEN WOULD TO HEAVEN THAT I HAD NEVER SEEN IT!
IS IT LOST?!

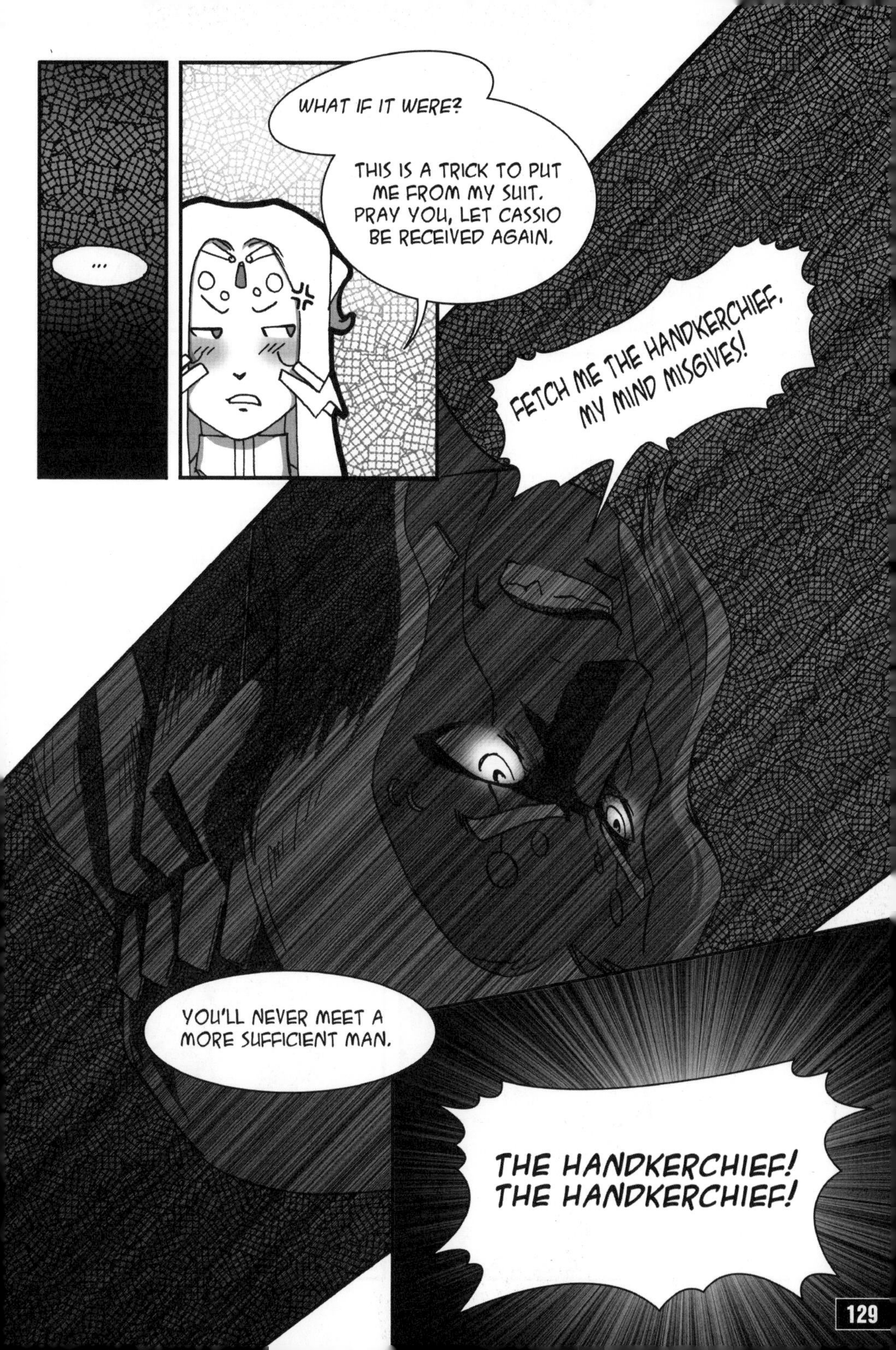
...
WHAT IF IT WERE?
THIS IS A TRICK TO PUT ME FROM MY SUIT. PRAY YOU, LET CASSIO BE RECEIVED AGAIN.
FETCH ME THE HANDKERCHIEF. MY MIND MISGIVES!
YOU'LL NEVER MEET A MORE SUFFICIENT MAN.
THE HANDKERCHIEF! THE HANDKERCHIEF!

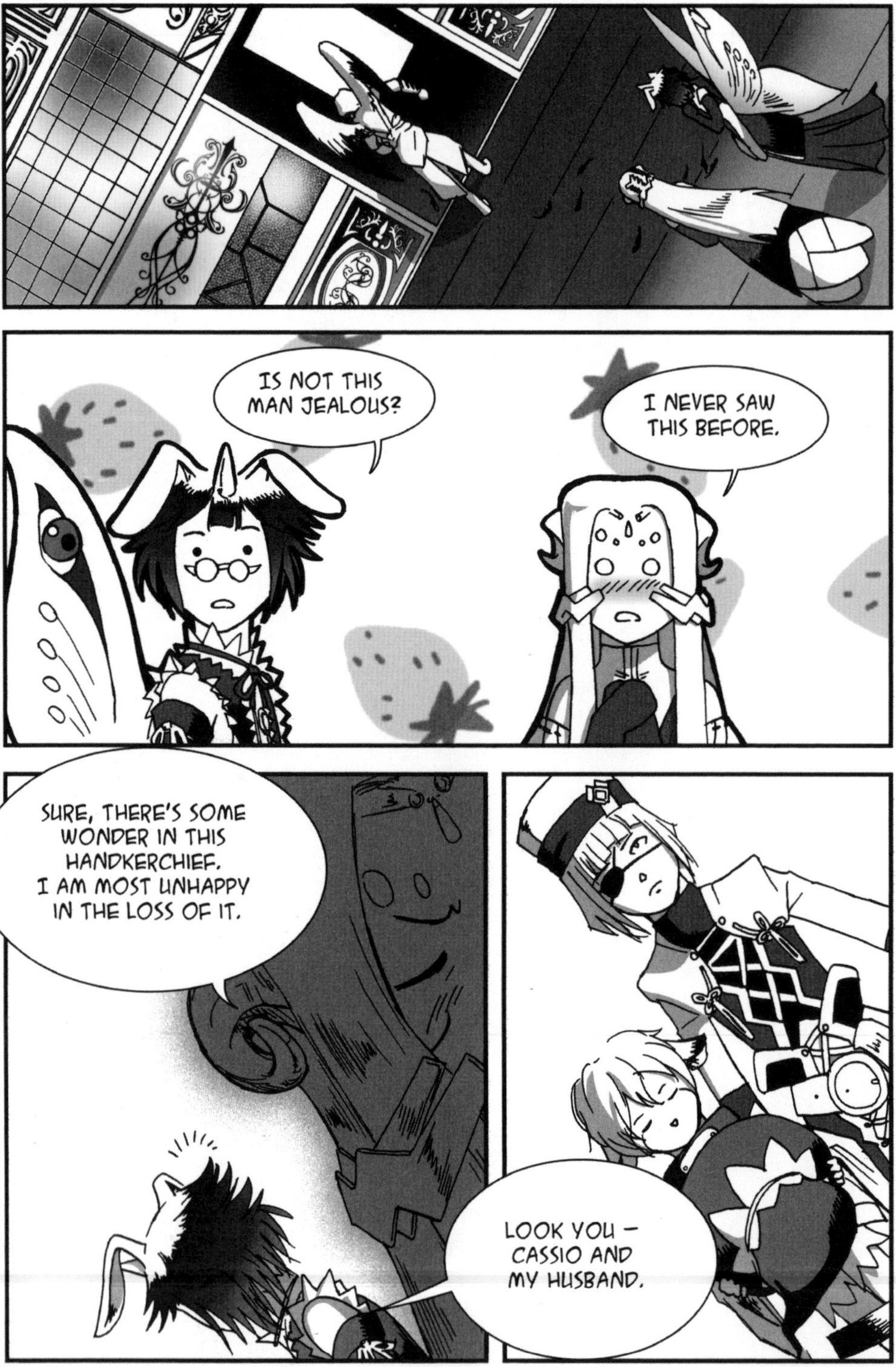
IS NOT THIS MAN JEALOUS?
I NEVER SAW THIS BEFORE.
SURE, THERE'S SOME WONDER IN THIS HANDKERCHIEF. I AM MOST UNHAPPY IN THE LOSS OF IT.
LOOK YOU – CASSIO AND MY HUSBAND.

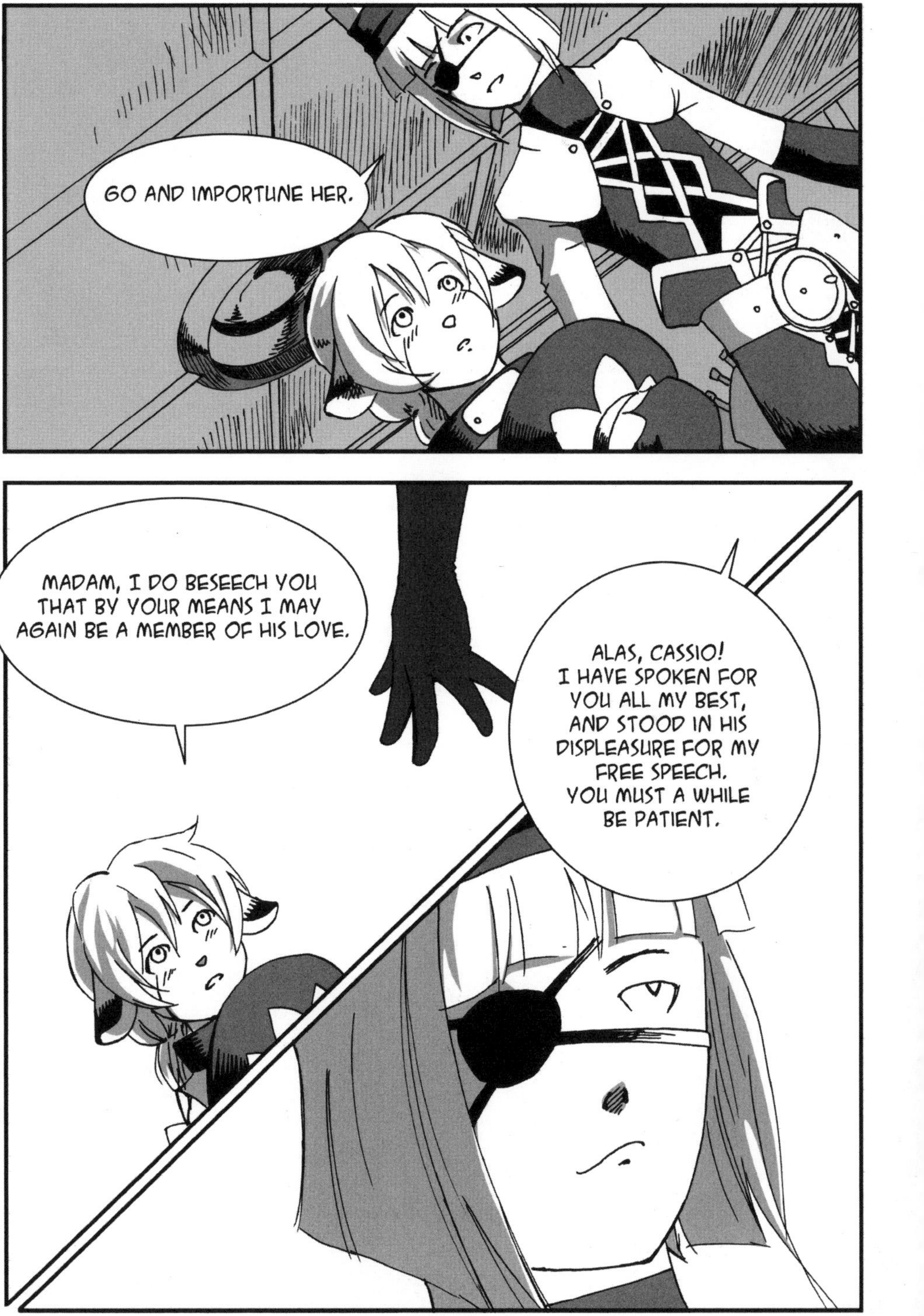
GO AND IMPORTUNE HER.
MADAM, I DO BESEECH YOU THAT BY YOUR MEANS I MAY AGAIN BE A MEMBER OF HIS LOVE.
ALAS, CASSIO! I HAVE SPOKEN FOR YOU ALL MY BEST, AND STOOD IN HIS DISPLEASURE FOR MY FREE SPEECH. YOU MUST A WHILE BE PATIENT.

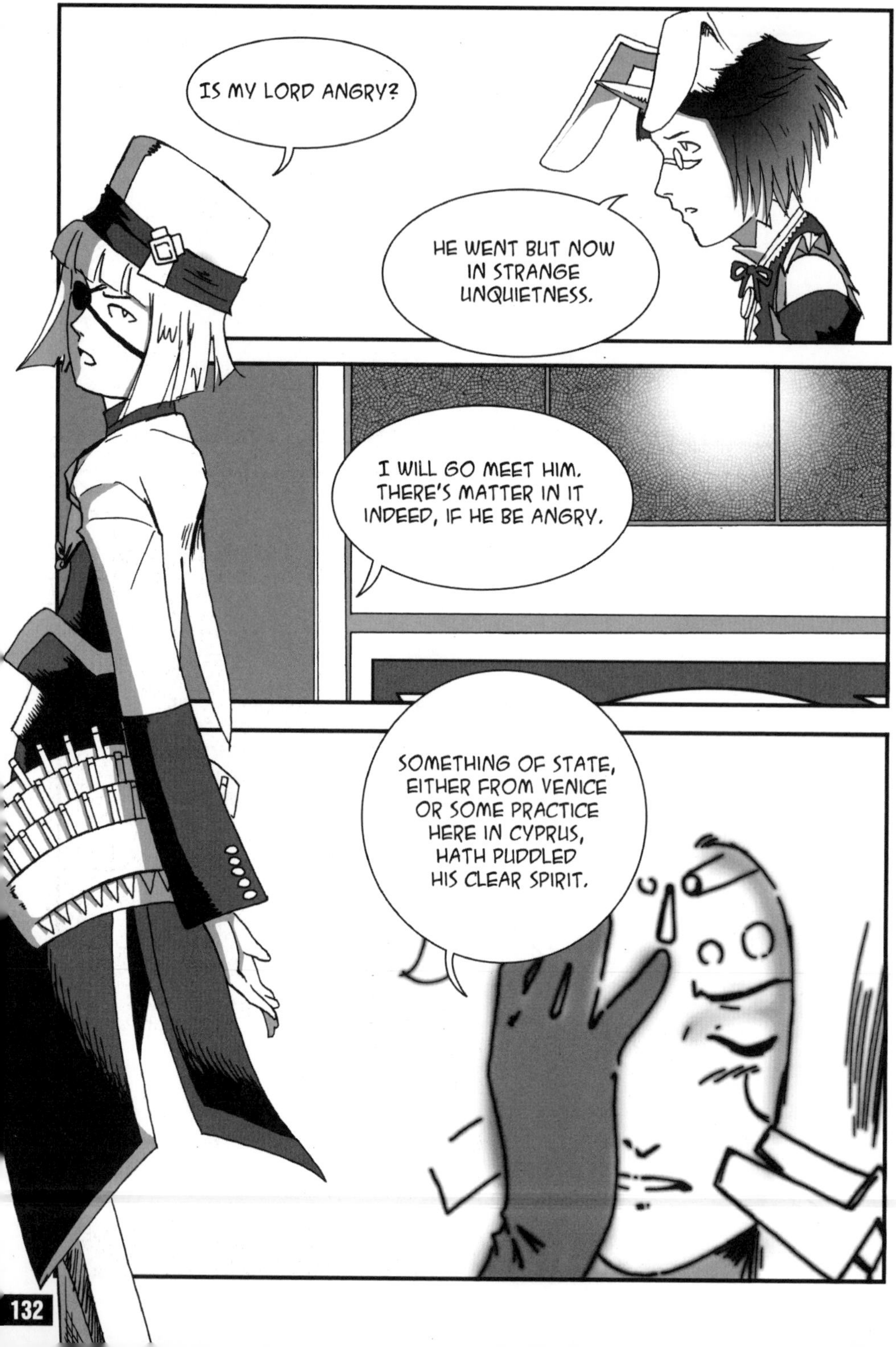
IS MY LORD ANGRY?
HE WENT BUT NOW IN STRANGE UNQUIETNESS.
I WILL GO MEET HIM. THERE'S MATTER IN IT INDEED, IF HE BE ANGRY.
SOMETHING OF STATE, EITHER FROM VENICE OR SOME PRACTICE HERE IN CYPRUS, HATH PUDDLED HIS CLEAR SPIRIT.

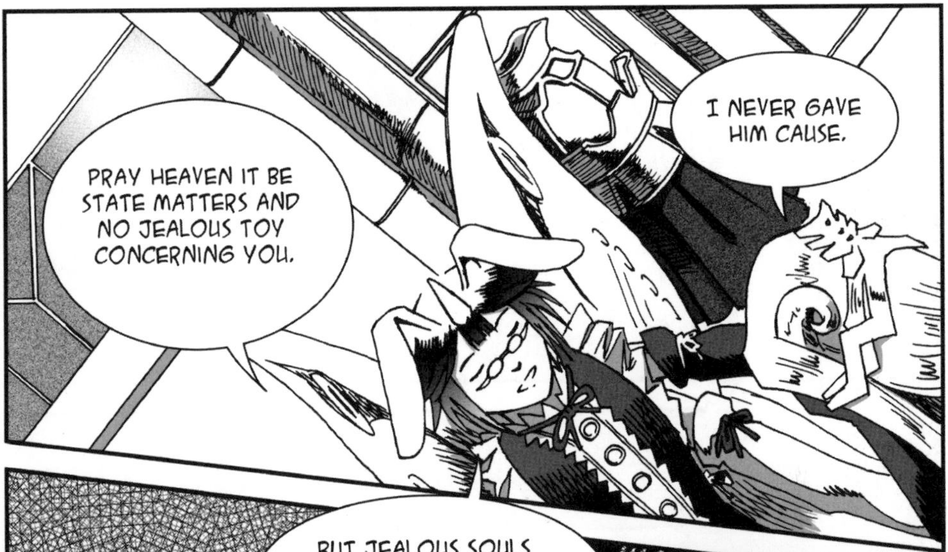
PRAY HEAVEN IT BE STATE MATTERS AND NO JEALOUS TOY CONCERNING YOU.
I NEVER GAVE HIM CAUSE.

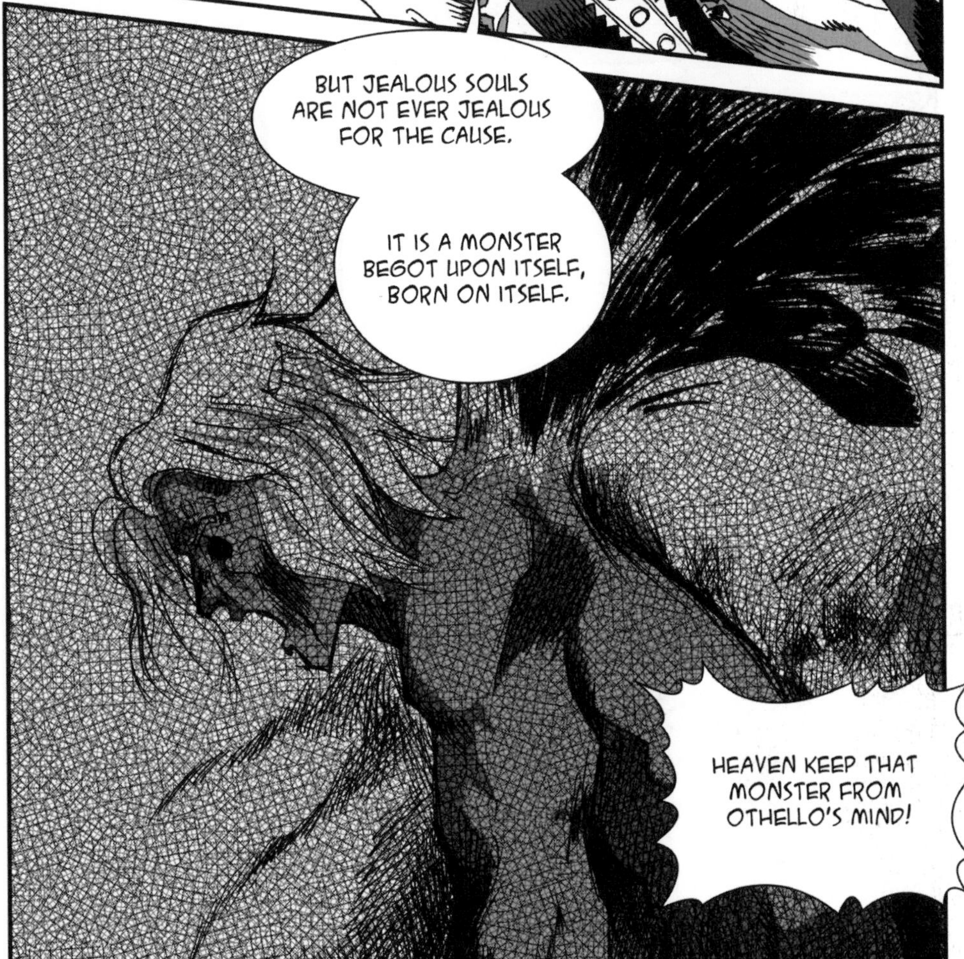
BUT JEALOUS SOULS ARE NOT EVER JEALOUS FOR THE CAUSE.
IT IS A MONSTER BEGOT UPON ITSELF, BORN ON ITSELF.
HEAVEN KEEP THAT MONSTER FROM OTHELLO'S MIND!

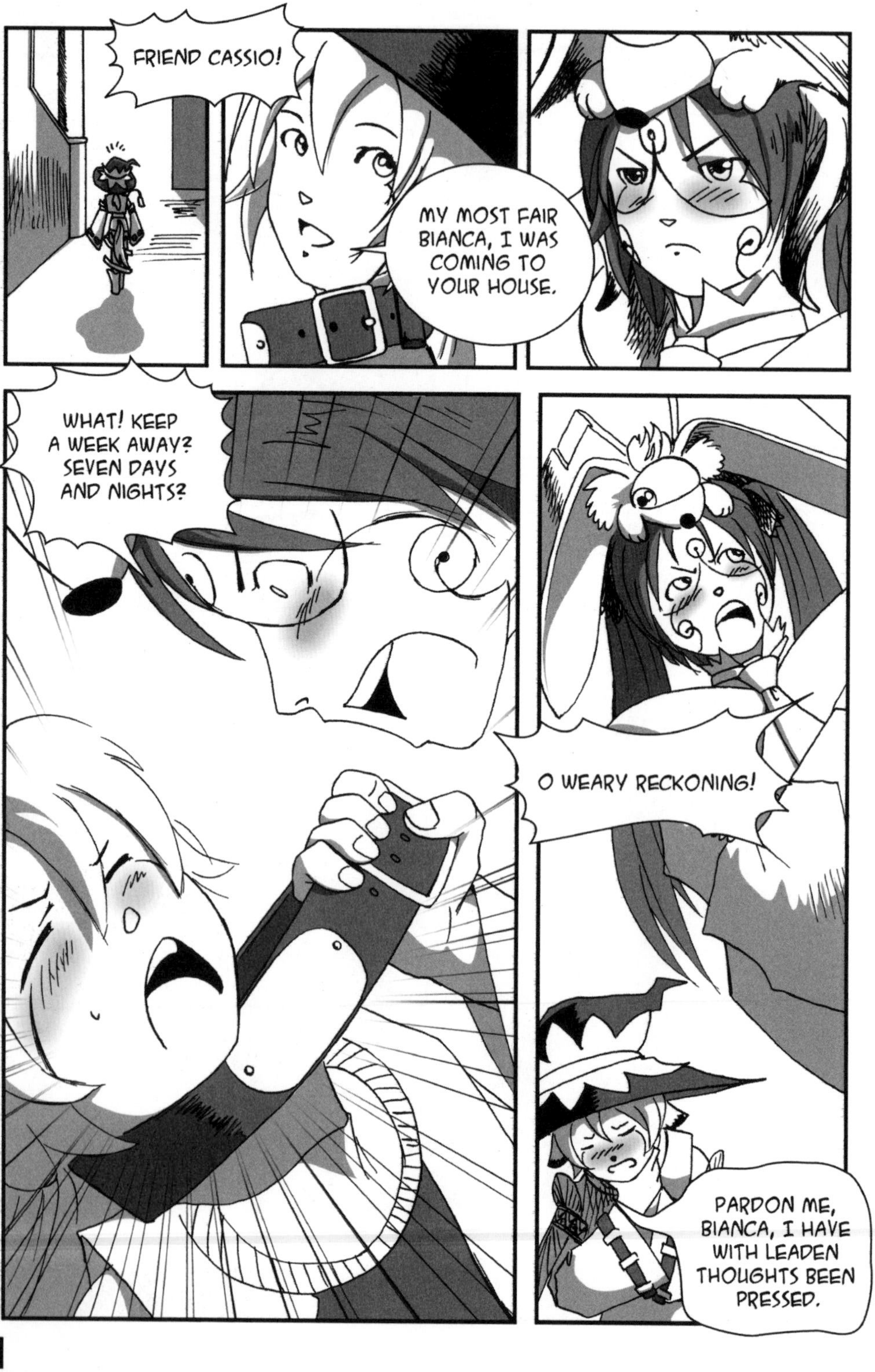
FRIEND CASSIO!
MY MOST FAIR BIANCA, I WAS COMING TO YOUR HOUSE.
WHAT! KEEP A WEEK AWAY? SEVEN DAYS AND NIGHTS?
O WEARY RECKONING!
PARDON ME, BIANCA, I HAVE WITH LEADEN THOUGHTS BEEN PRESSED.

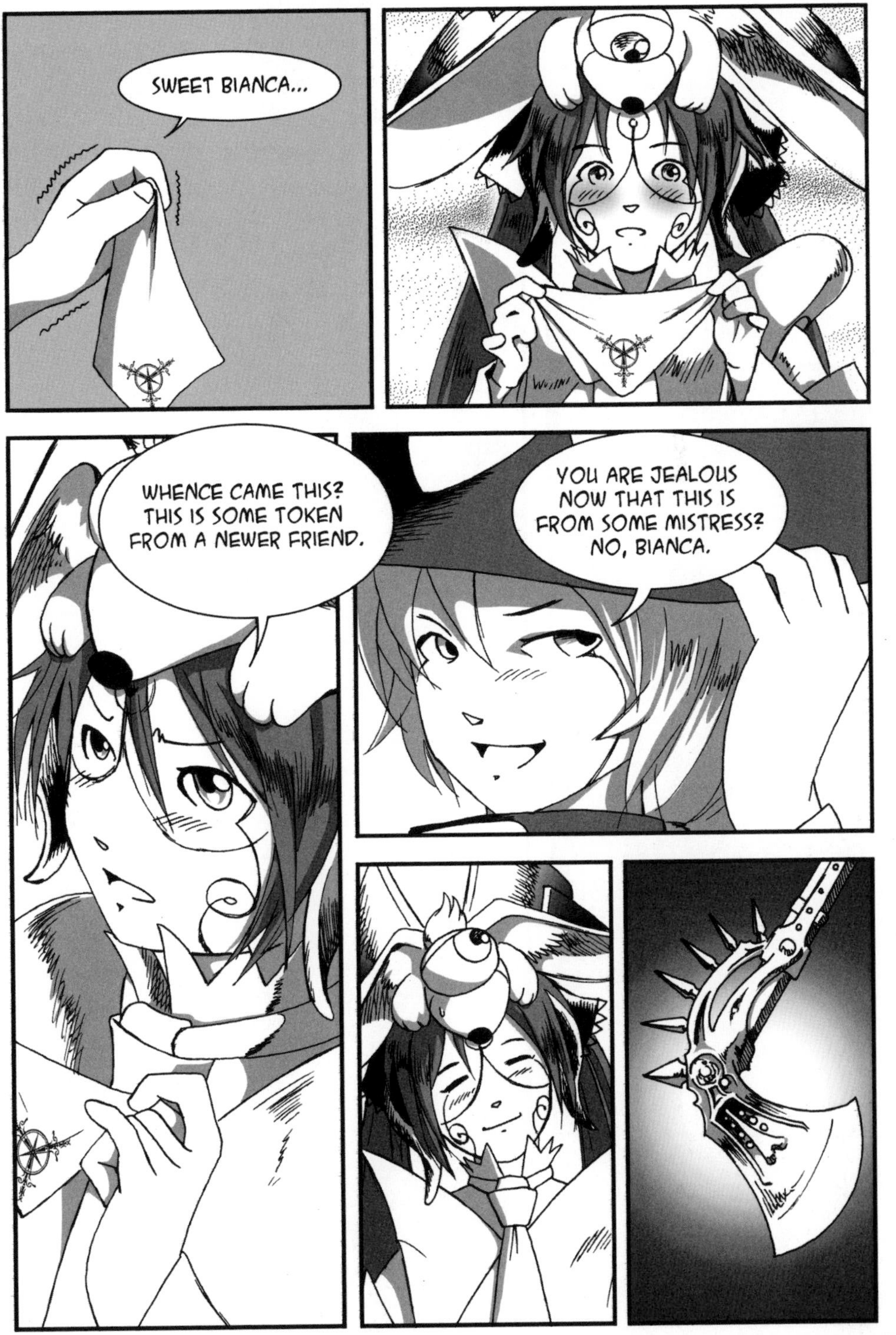
SWEET BIANCA...
WHENCE CAME THIS? THIS IS SOME TOKEN FROM A NEWER FRIEND.
YOU ARE JEALOUS NOW THAT THIS IS FROM SOME MISTRESS? NO, BIANCA.

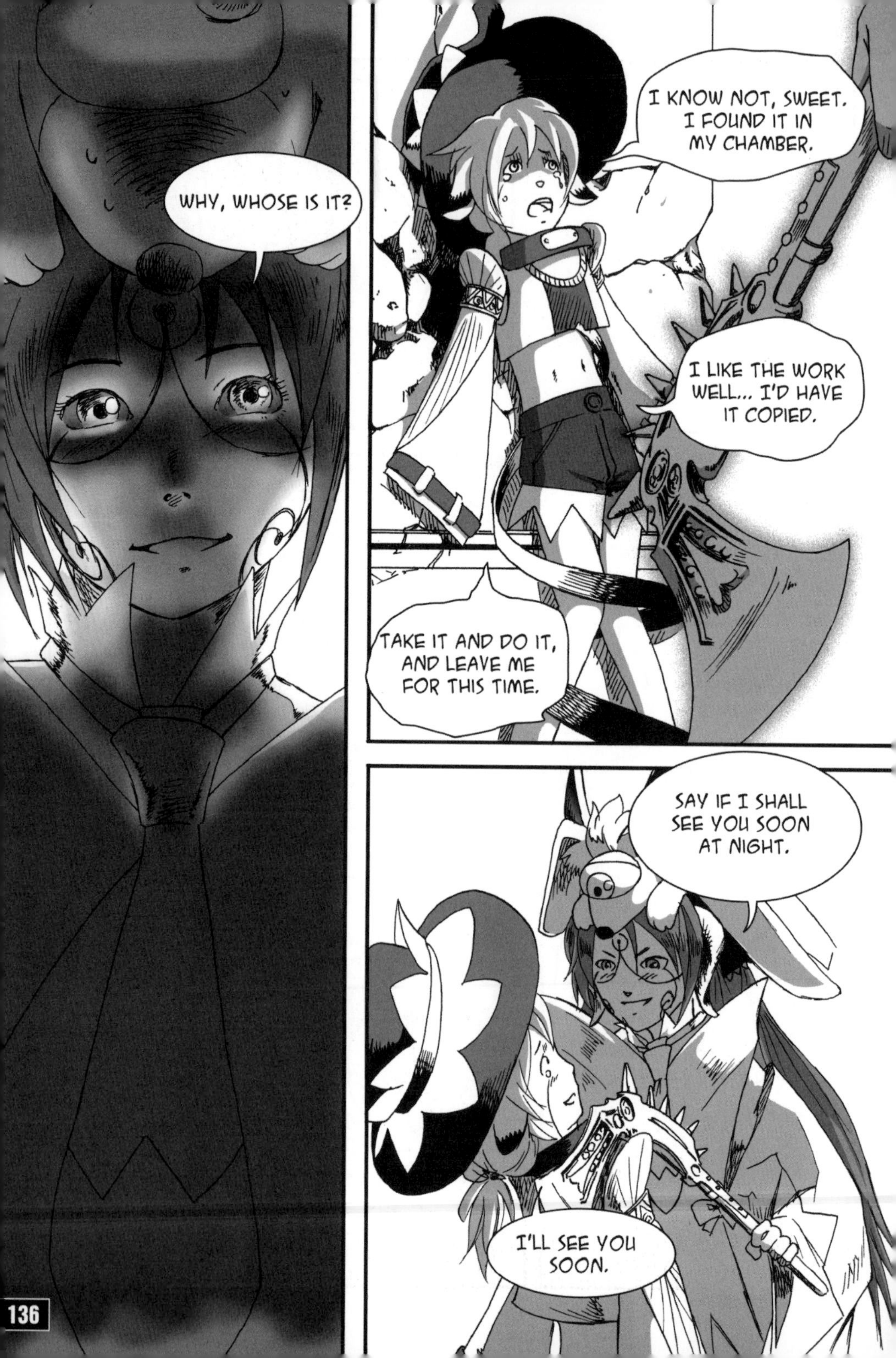
WHY, WHOSE IS IT?
I KNOW NOT, SWEET. I FOUND IT IN MY CHAMBER.
I LIKE THE WORK WELL... I'D HAVE IT COPIED.
TAKE IT AND DO IT, AND LEAVE ME FOR THIS TIME.
SAY IF I SHALL SEE YOU SOON AT NIGHT.
I'LL SEE YOU SOON.

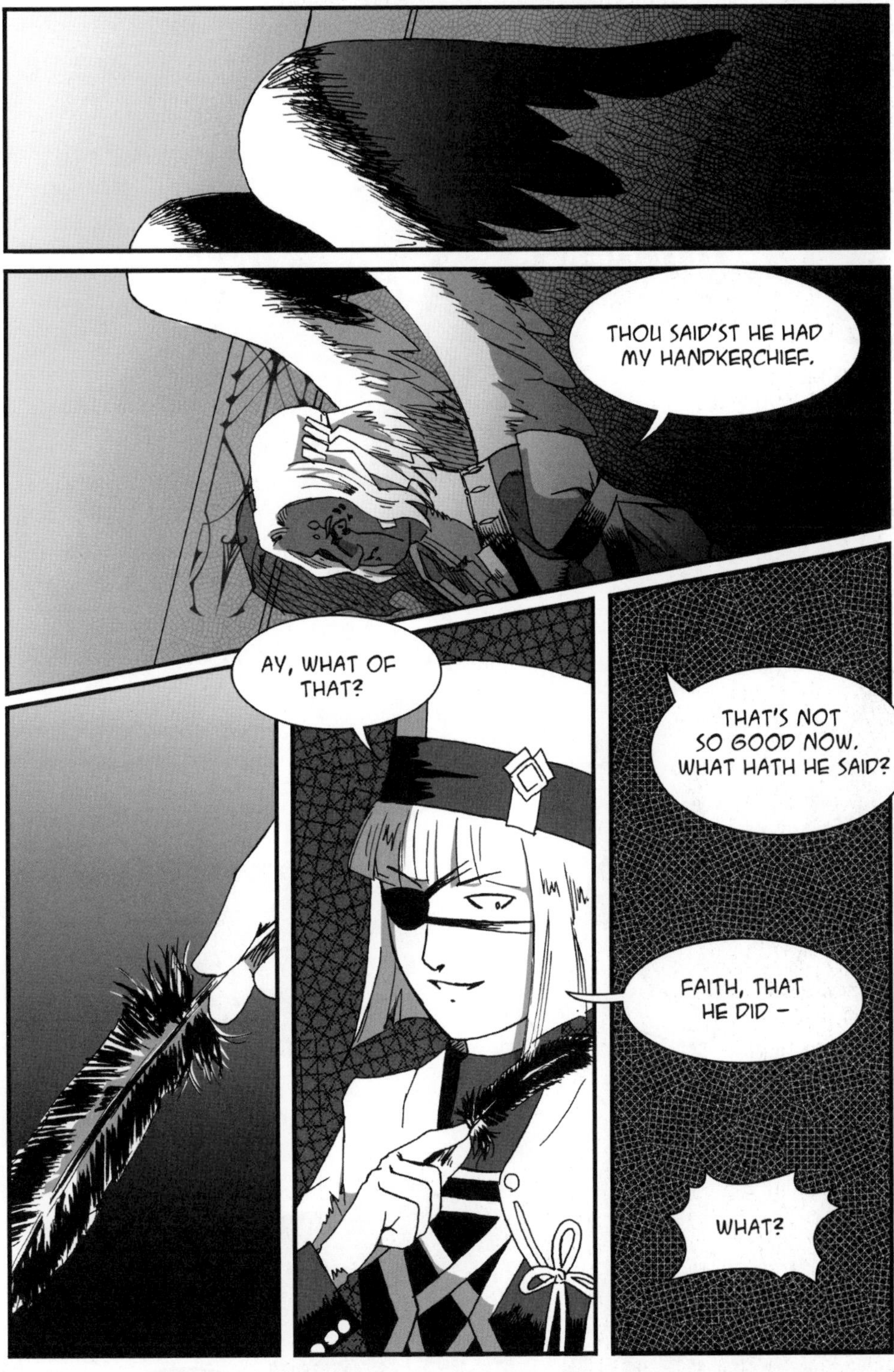
THOU SAID'ST HE HAD MY HANDKERCHIEF.
AY, WHAT OF THAT?
THAT'S NOT SO GOOD NOW. WHAT HATH HE SAID?
FAITH, THAT HE DID –
WHAT?

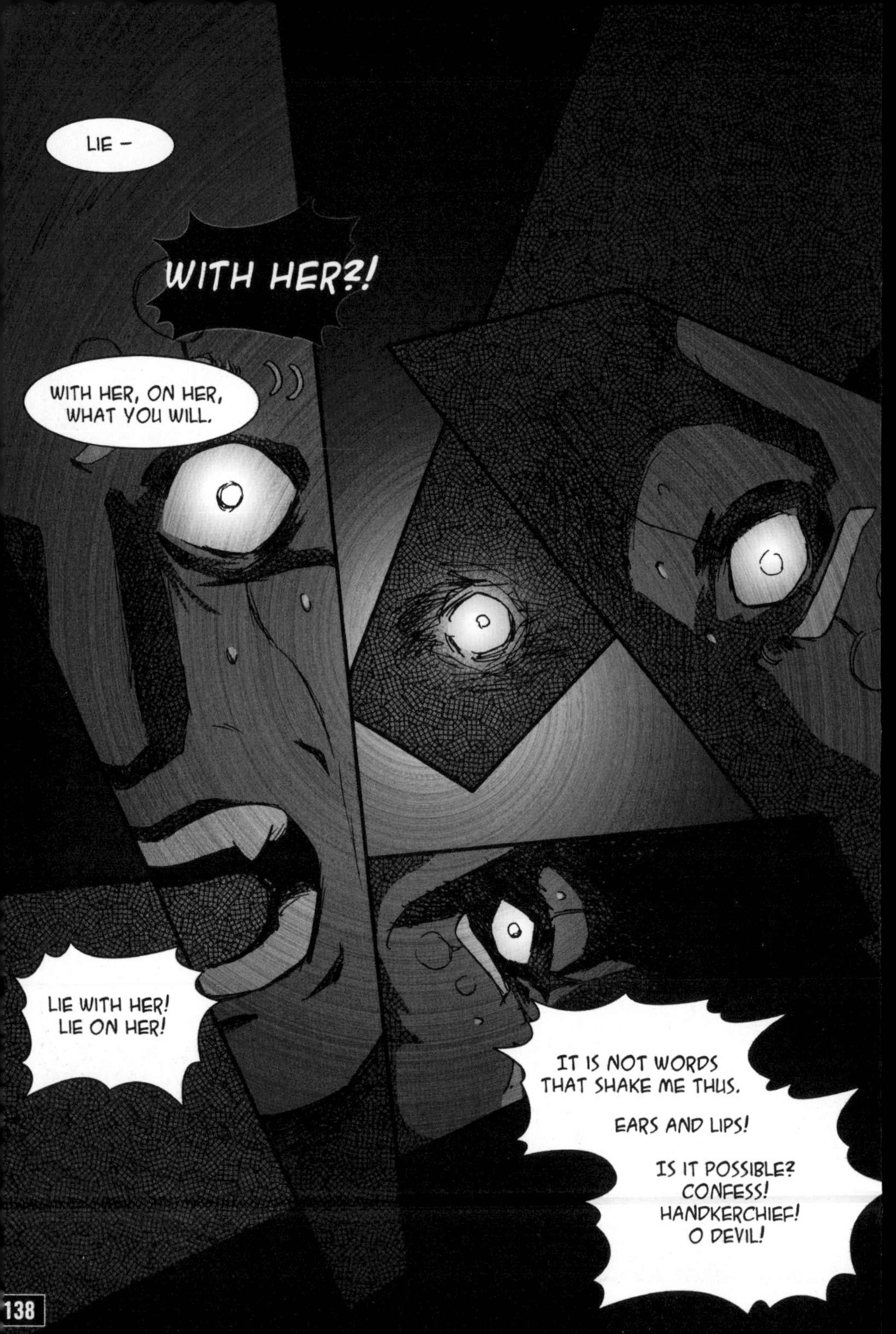
LIE –
WITH HER?!
WITH HER, ON HER, WHAT YOU WILL.
LIE WITH HER! LIE ON HER!
IT IS NOT WORDS THAT SHAKE ME THUS.
EARS AND LIPS!
IS IT POSSIBLE? CONFESS! HANDKERCHIEF! O DEVIL!

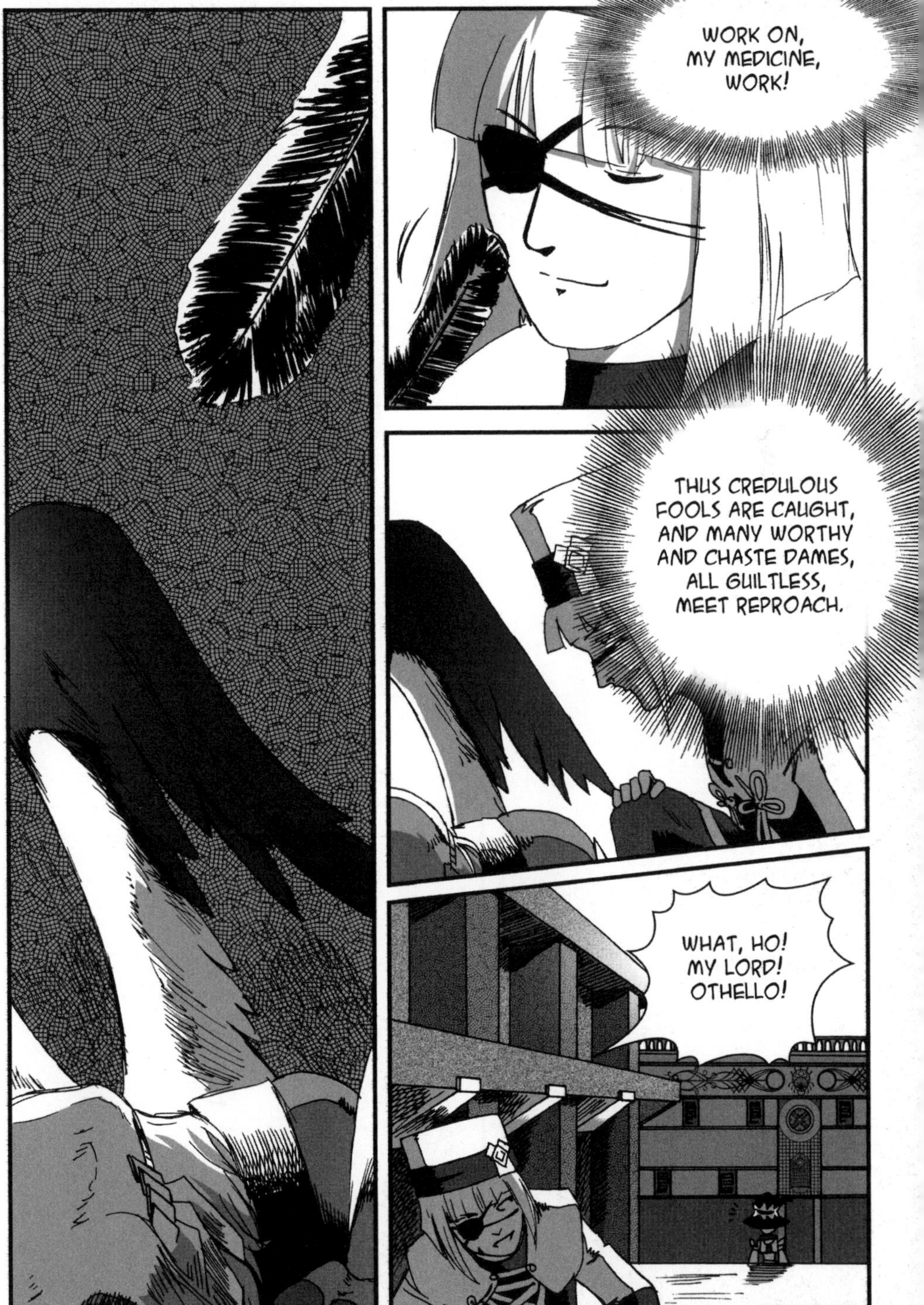
WORK ON, MY MEDICINE, WORK!
THUS CREDULOUS FOOLS ARE CAUGHT, AND MANY WORTHY AND CHASTE DAMES, ALL GUILTLESS, MEET REPROACH.
WHAT, HO! MY LORD! OTHELLO!

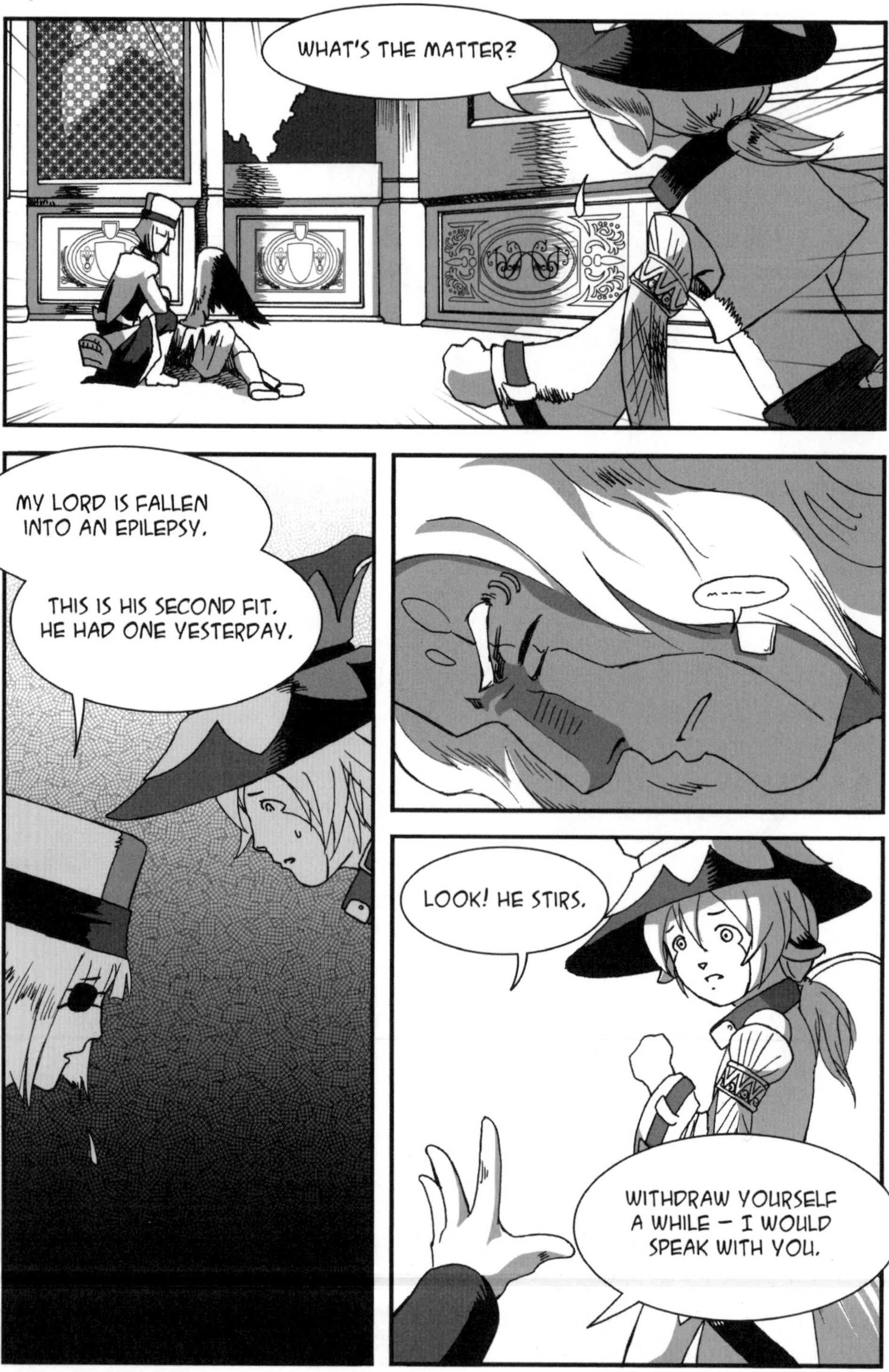
WHAT'S THE MATTER?
MY LORD IS FALLEN INTO AN EPILEPSY.
THIS IS HIS SECOND FIT. HE HAD ONE YESTERDAY.
—— — —
LOOK! HE STIRS.
WITHDRAW YOURSELF A WHILE — I WOULD SPEAK WITH YOU.

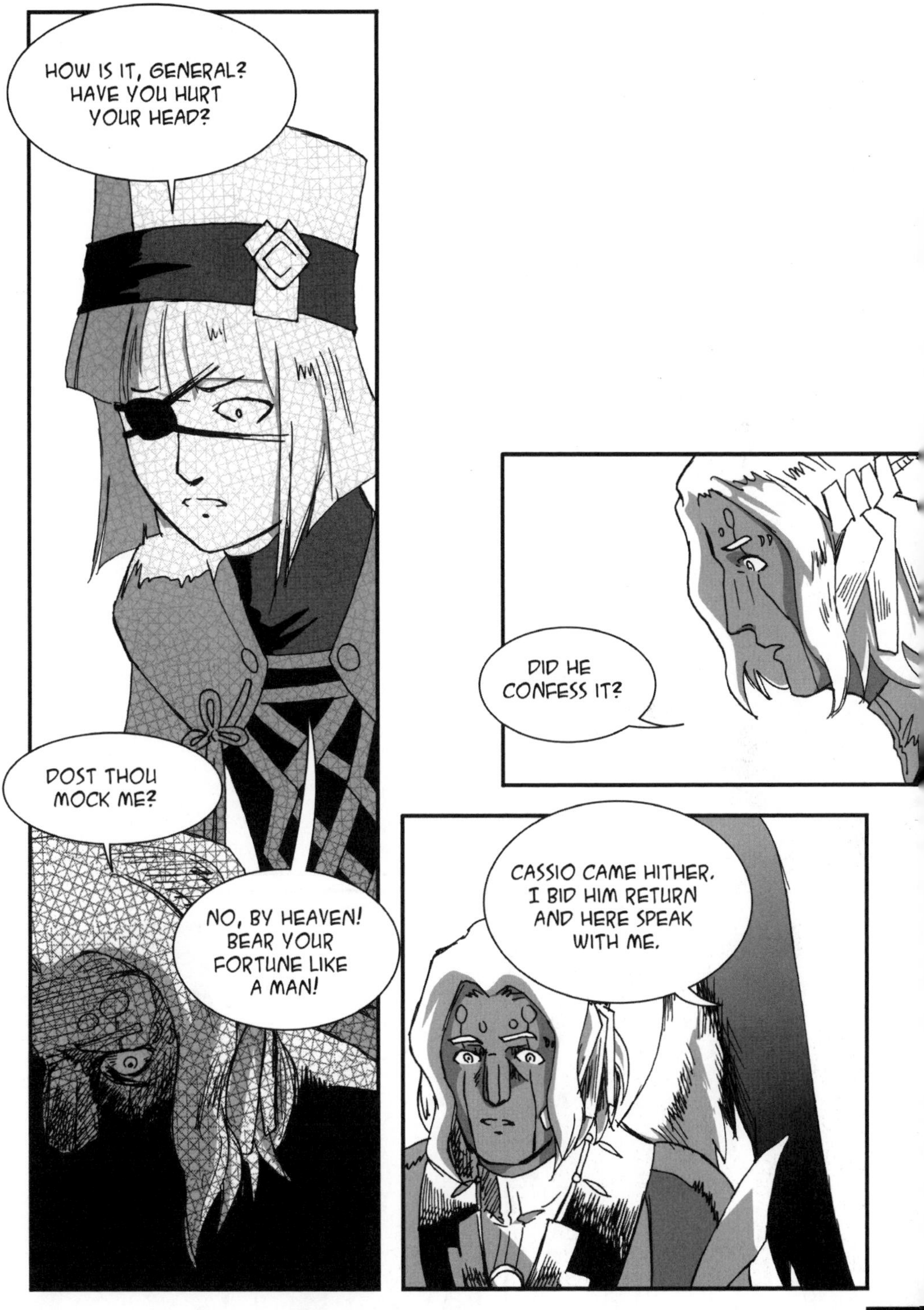
HOW IS IT, GENERAL? HAVE YOU HURT YOUR HEAD?
DOST THOU MOCK ME?
NO, BY HEAVEN! BEAR YOUR FORTUNE LIKE A MAN!
DID HE CONFESS IT?
CASSIO CAME HITHER. I BID HIM RETURN AND HERE SPEAK WITH ME.

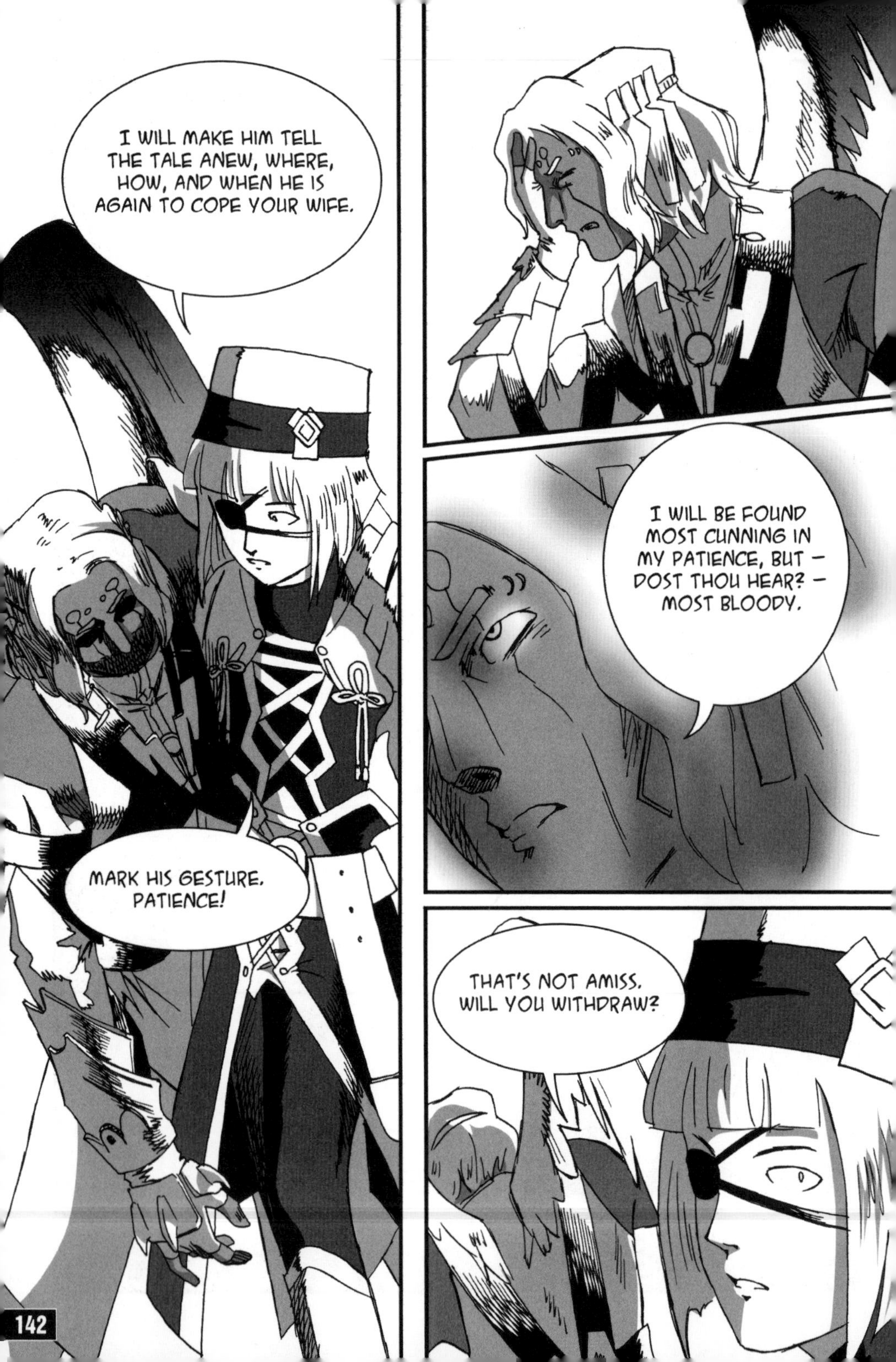
I WILL MAKE HIM TELL THE TALE ANEW, WHERE, HOW, AND WHEN HE IS AGAIN TO COPE YOUR WIFE.
MARK HIS GESTURE. PATIENCE!
I WILL BE FOUND MOST CUNNING IN MY PATIENCE, BUT – DOST THOU HEAR? – MOST BLOODY.
THAT'S NOT AMISS. WILL YOU WITHDRAW?

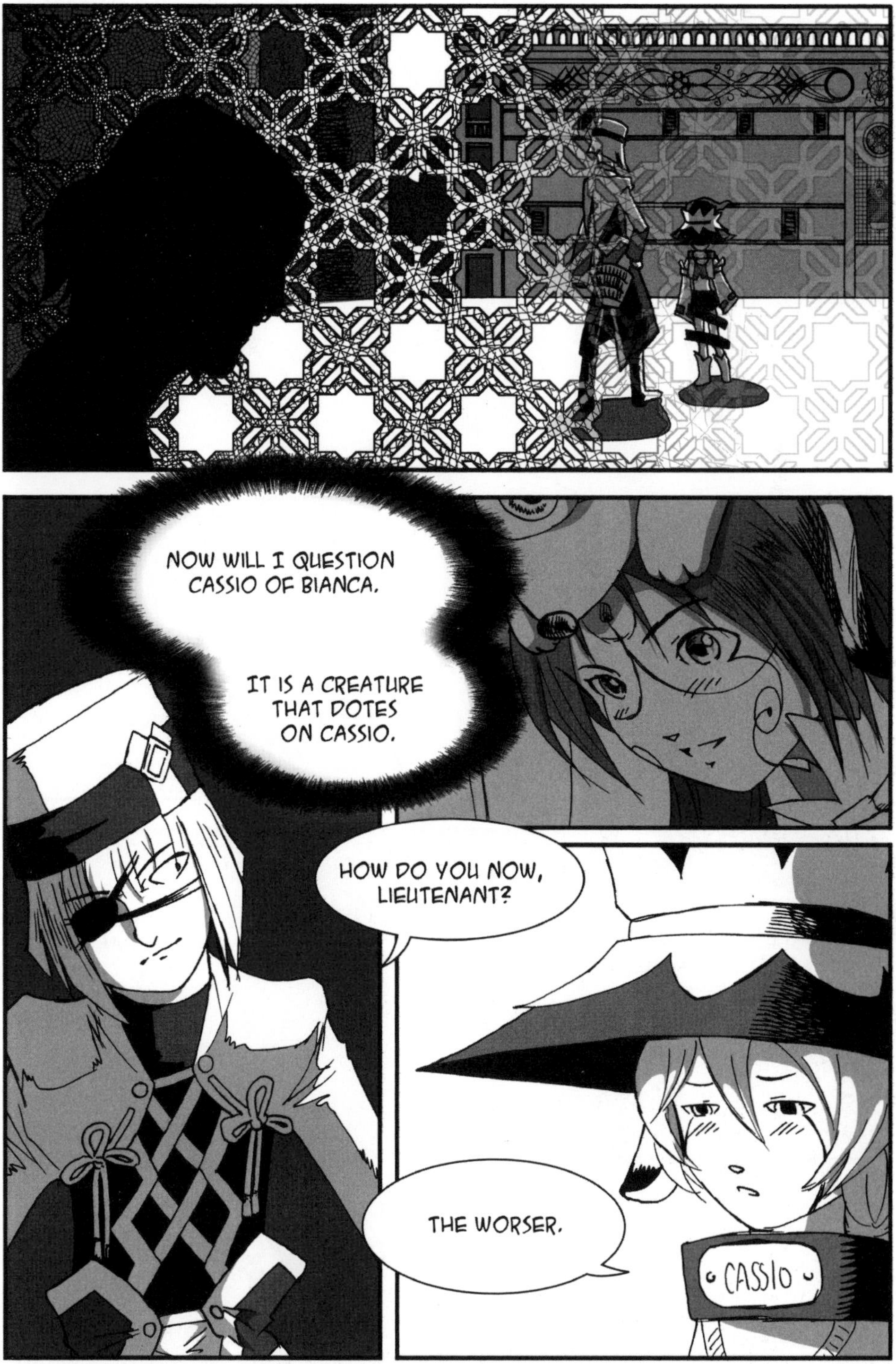
NOW WILL I QUESTION CASSIO OF BIANCA.
IT IS A CREATURE THAT DOTES ON CASSIO.
HOW DO YOU NOW, LIEUTENANT?
THE WORSER.
CASSIO

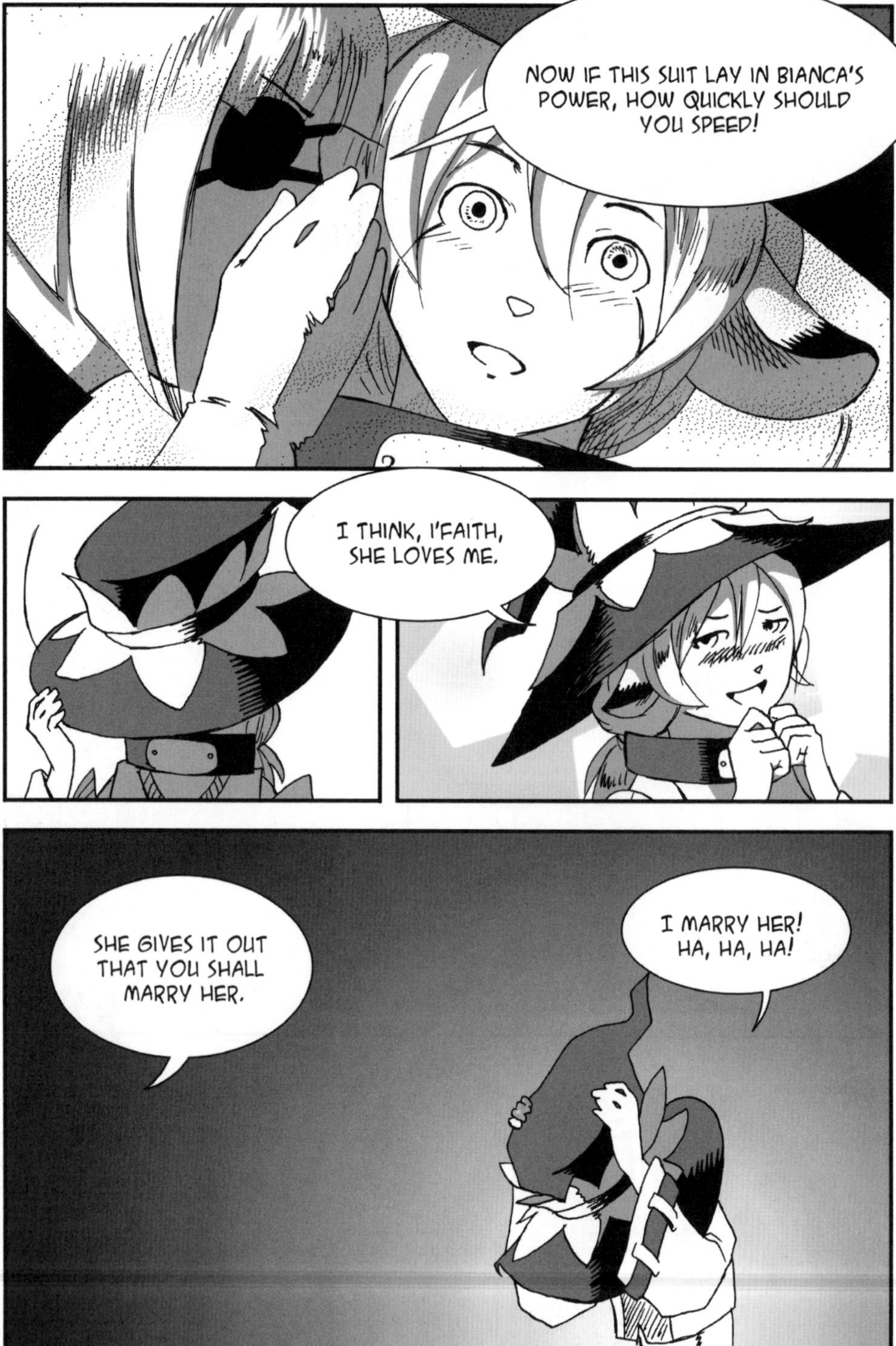

NOW IF THIS SUIT LAY IN BIANCA'S POWER, HOW QUICKLY SHOULD YOU SPEED!
I THINK, I'FAITH, SHE LOVES ME.
SHE GIVES IT OUT THAT YOU SHALL MARRY HER.
I MARRY HER! HA, HA, HA!

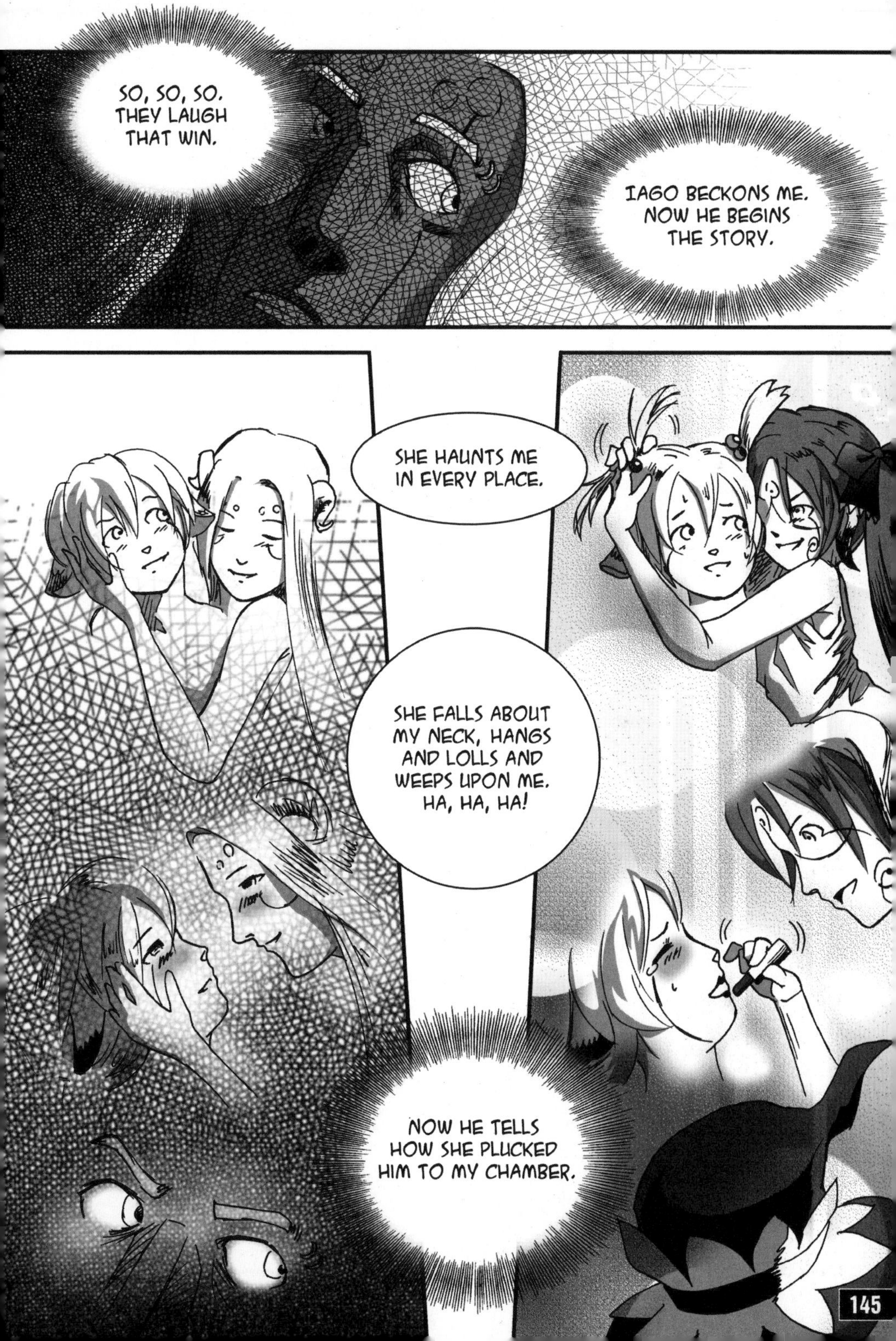

SO, SO, SO. THEY LAUGH THAT WIN.
IAGO BECKONS ME. NOW HE BEGINS THE STORY.
SHE HAUNTS ME IN EVERY PLACE.
SHE FALLS ABOUT MY NECK, HANGS AND LOLLS AND WEEPS UPON ME. HA, HA, HA!
NOW HE TELLS HOW SHE PLUCKED HIM TO MY CHAMBER.

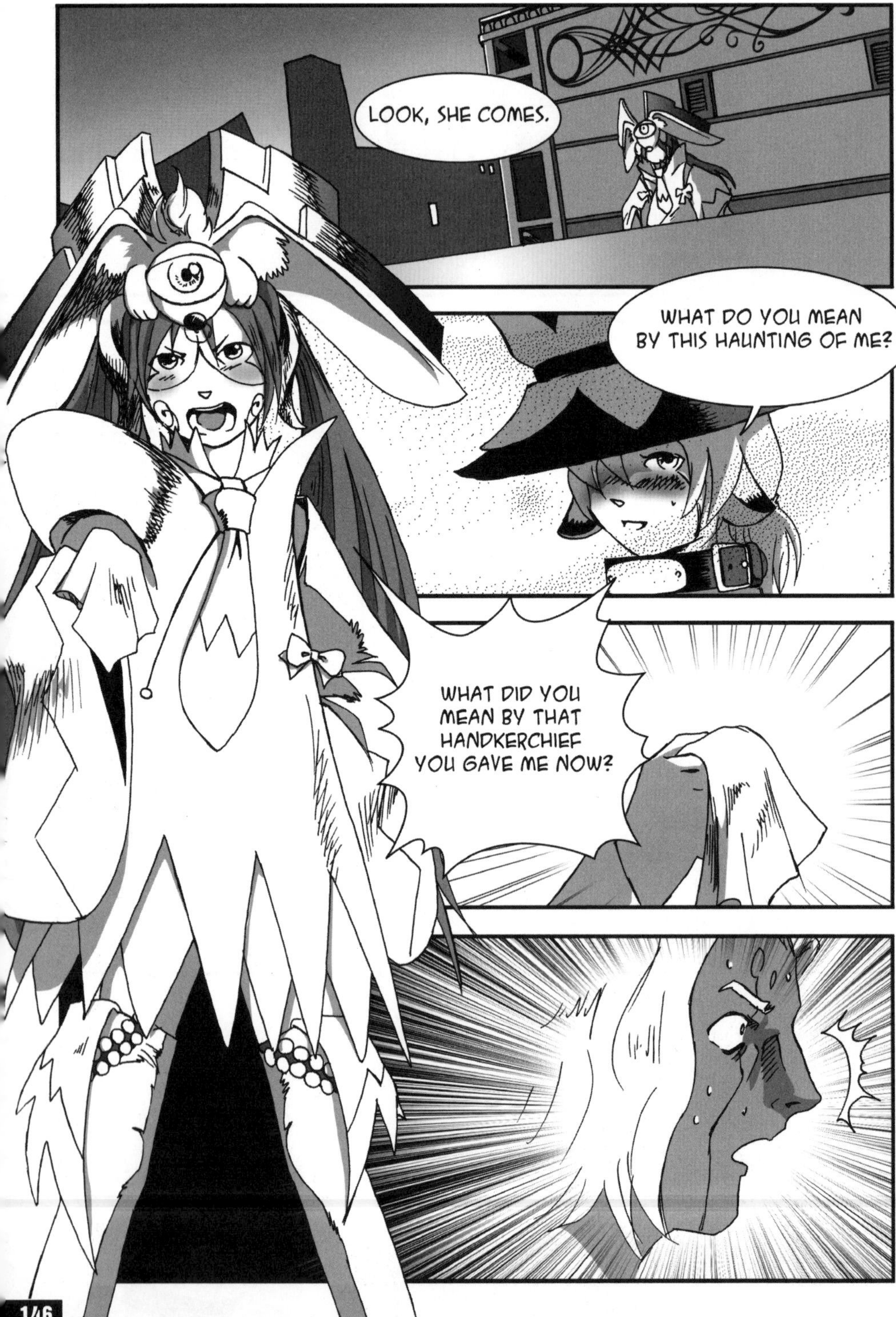
LOOK, SHE COMES.
WHAT DO YOU MEAN BY THIS HAUNTING OF ME?
WHAT DID YOU MEAN BY THAT HANDKERCHIEF YOU GAVE ME NOW?

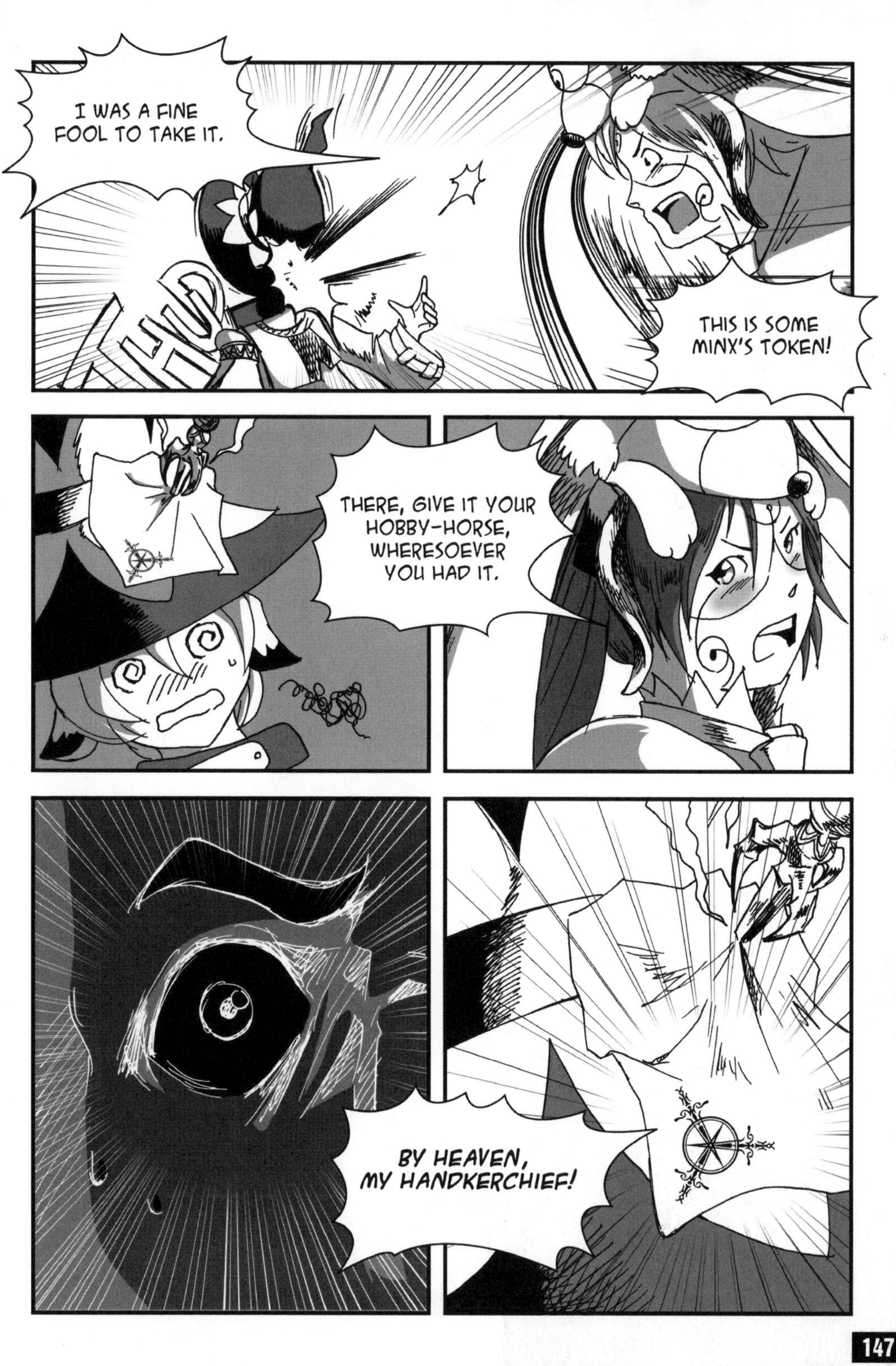
I WAS A FINE FOOL TO TAKE IT.
THUD
THIS IS SOME MINX'S TOKEN!
THERE, GIVE IT YOUR HOBBY-HORSE, WHERESOEVER YOU HAD IT.
BY HEAVEN, MY HANDKERCHIEF!

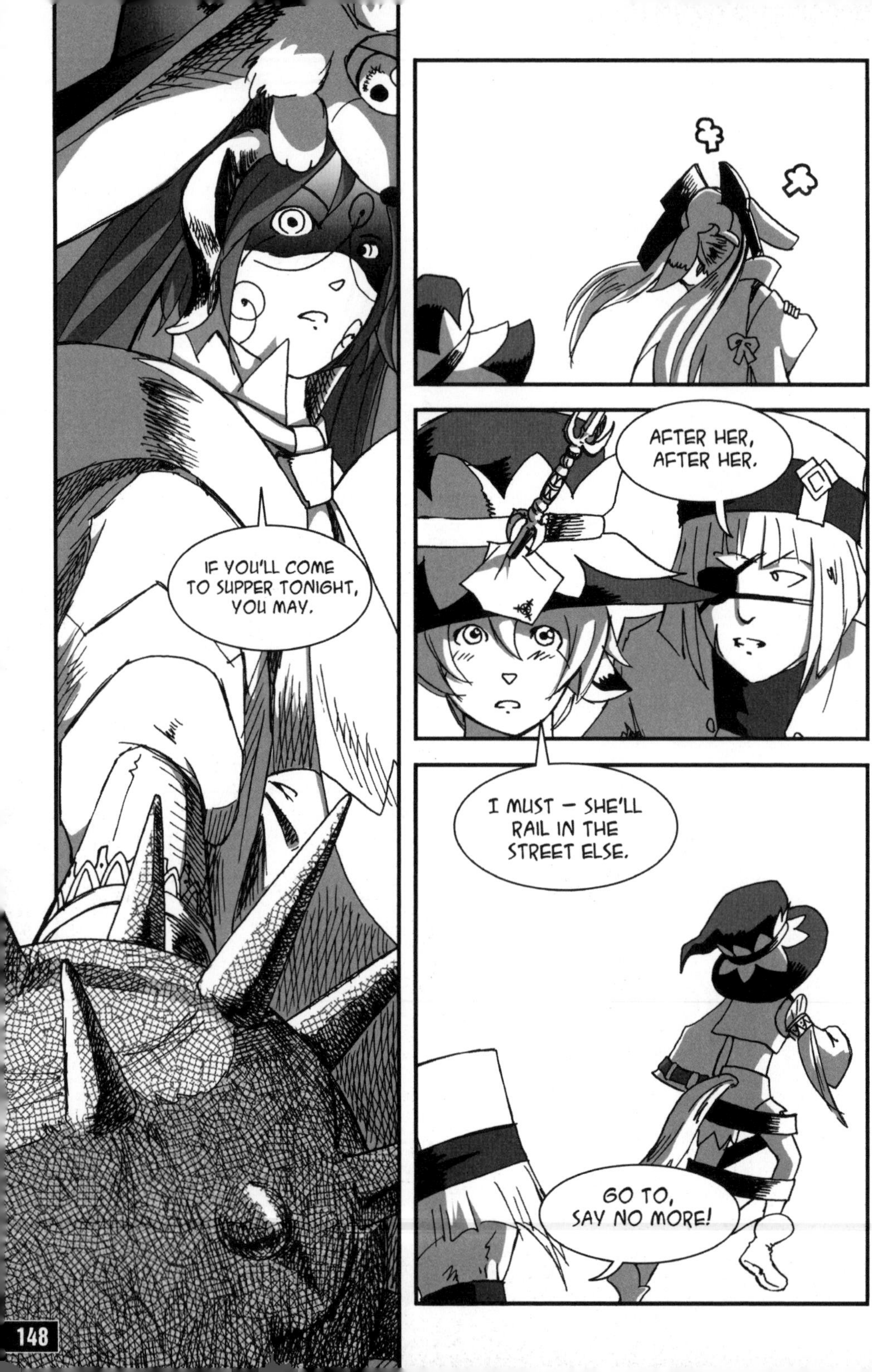
IF YOU'LL COME TO SUPPER TONIGHT, YOU MAY.
AFTER HER, AFTER HER.
I MUST — SHE'LL RAIL IN THE STREET ELSE.
GO TO, SAY NO MORE!

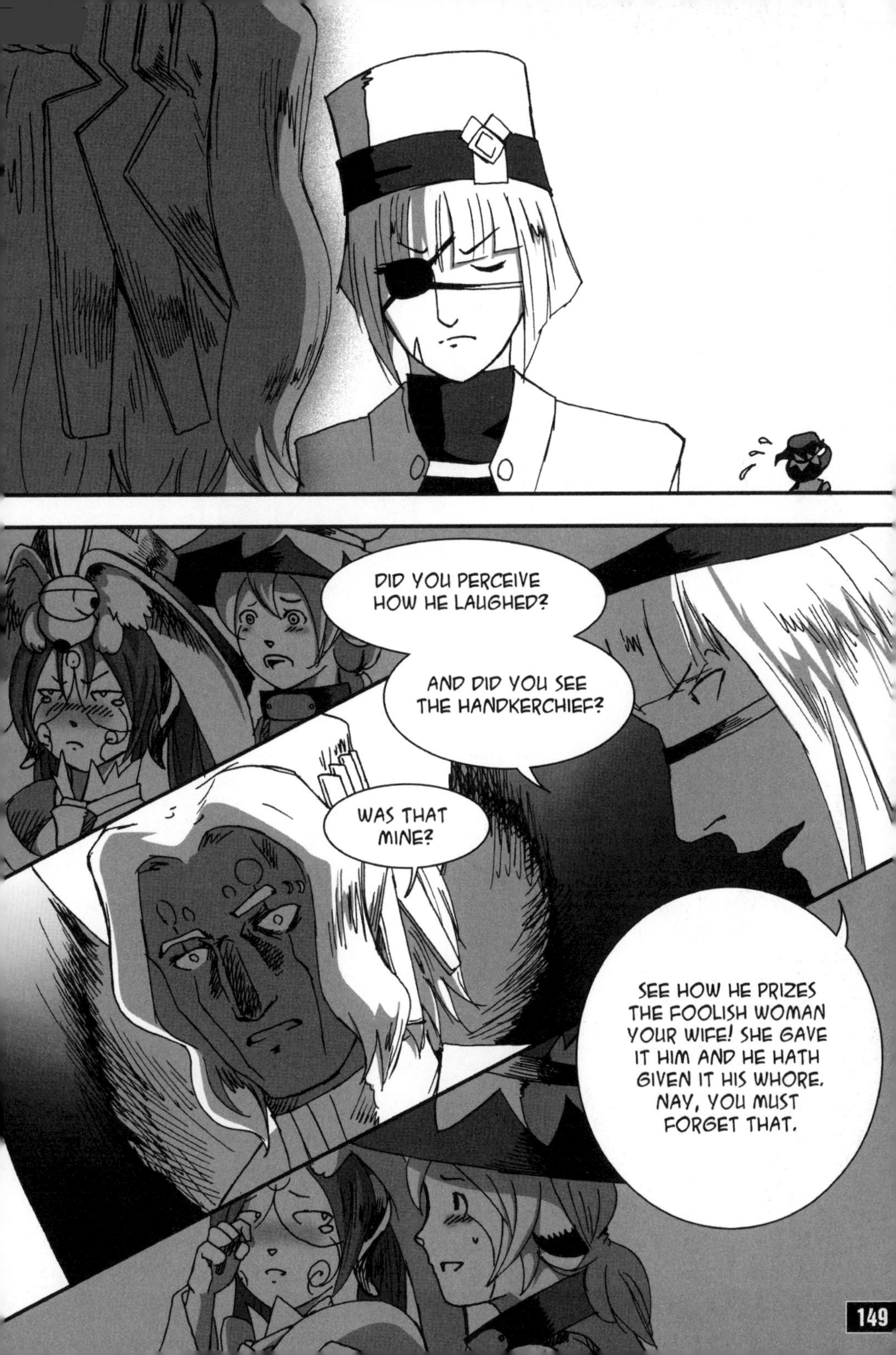
DID YOU PERCEIVE HOW HE LAUGHED?
AND DID YOU SEE THE HANDKERCHIEF?
WAS THAT MINE?
SEE HOW HE PRIZES THE FOOLISH WOMAN YOUR WIFE! SHE GAVE IT HIM AND HE HATH GIVEN IT HIS WHORE. NAY, YOU MUST FORGET THAT.

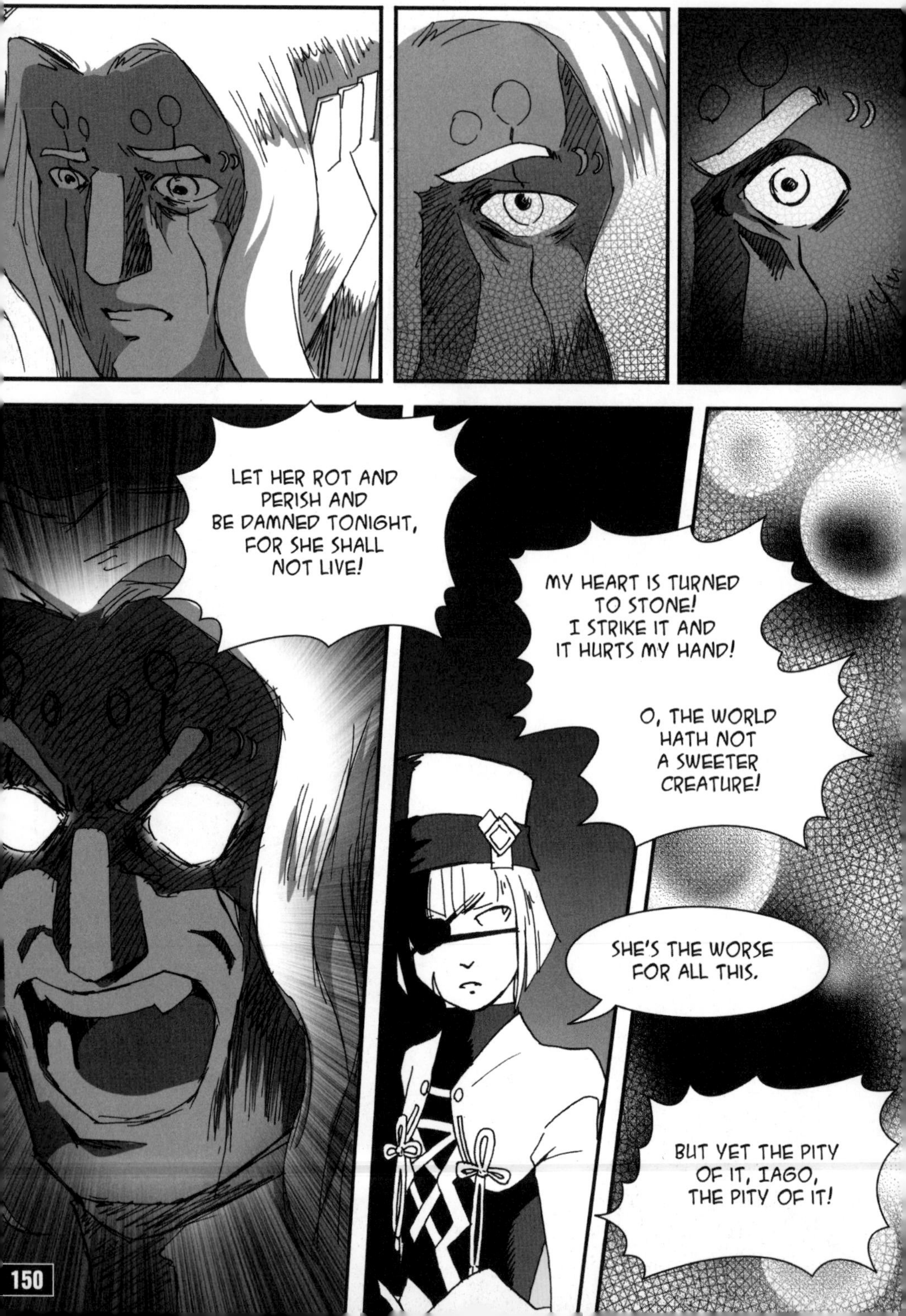
LET HER ROT AND PERISH AND BE DAMNED TONIGHT, FOR SHE SHALL NOT LIVE!
MY HEART IS TURNED TO STONE! I STRIKE IT AND IT HURTS MY HAND!
O, THE WORLD HATH NOT A SWEETER CREATURE!
SHE'S THE WORSE FOR ALL THIS.
BUT YET THE PITY OF IT, IAGO, THE PITY OF IT!

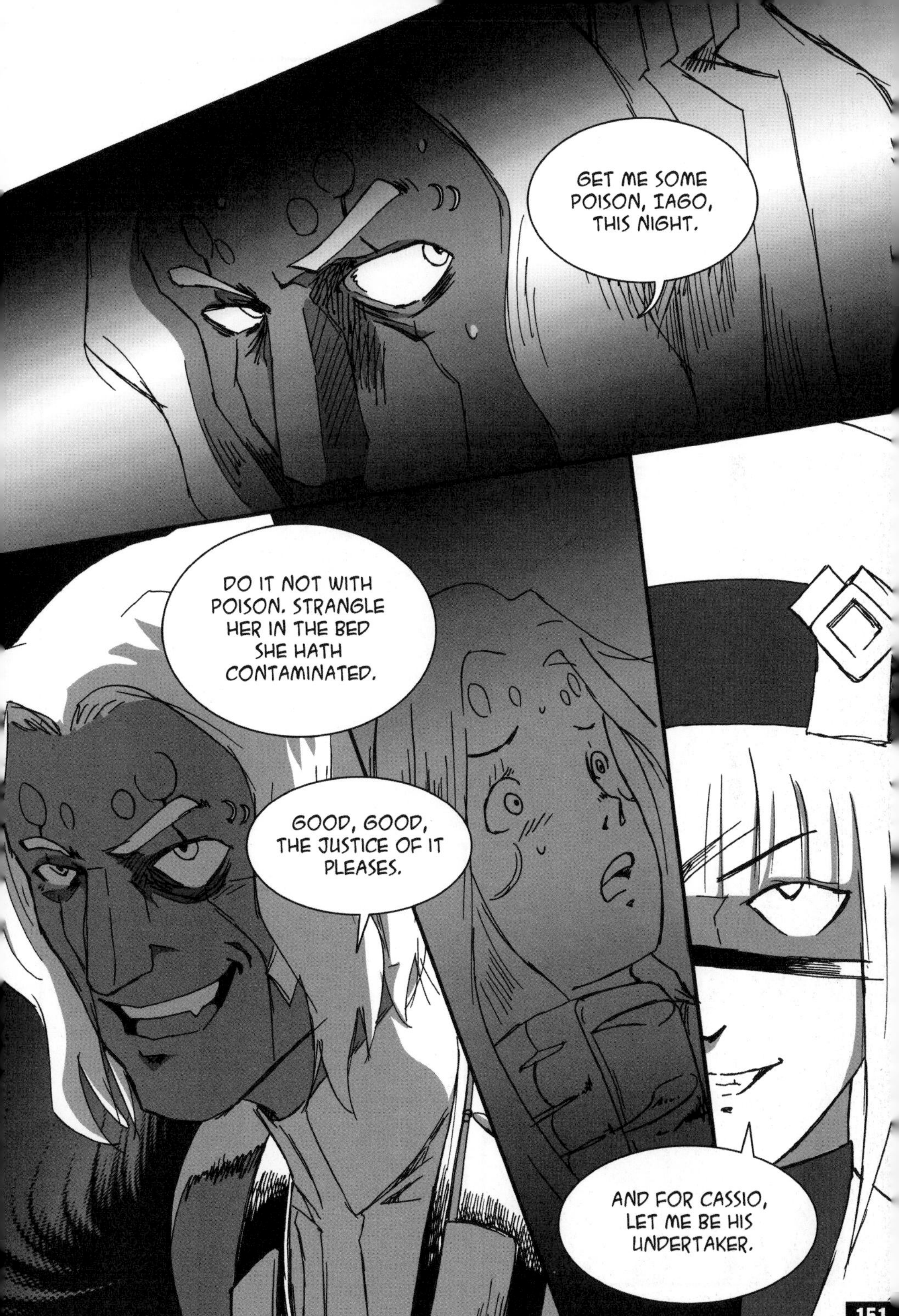
GET ME SOME POISON, IAGO, THIS NIGHT.
DO IT NOT WITH POISON. STRANGLE HER IN THE BED SHE HATH CONTAMINATED.
GOOD, GOOD, THE JUSTICE OF IT PLEASES.
AND FOR CASSIO, LET ME BE HIS UNDERTAKER.

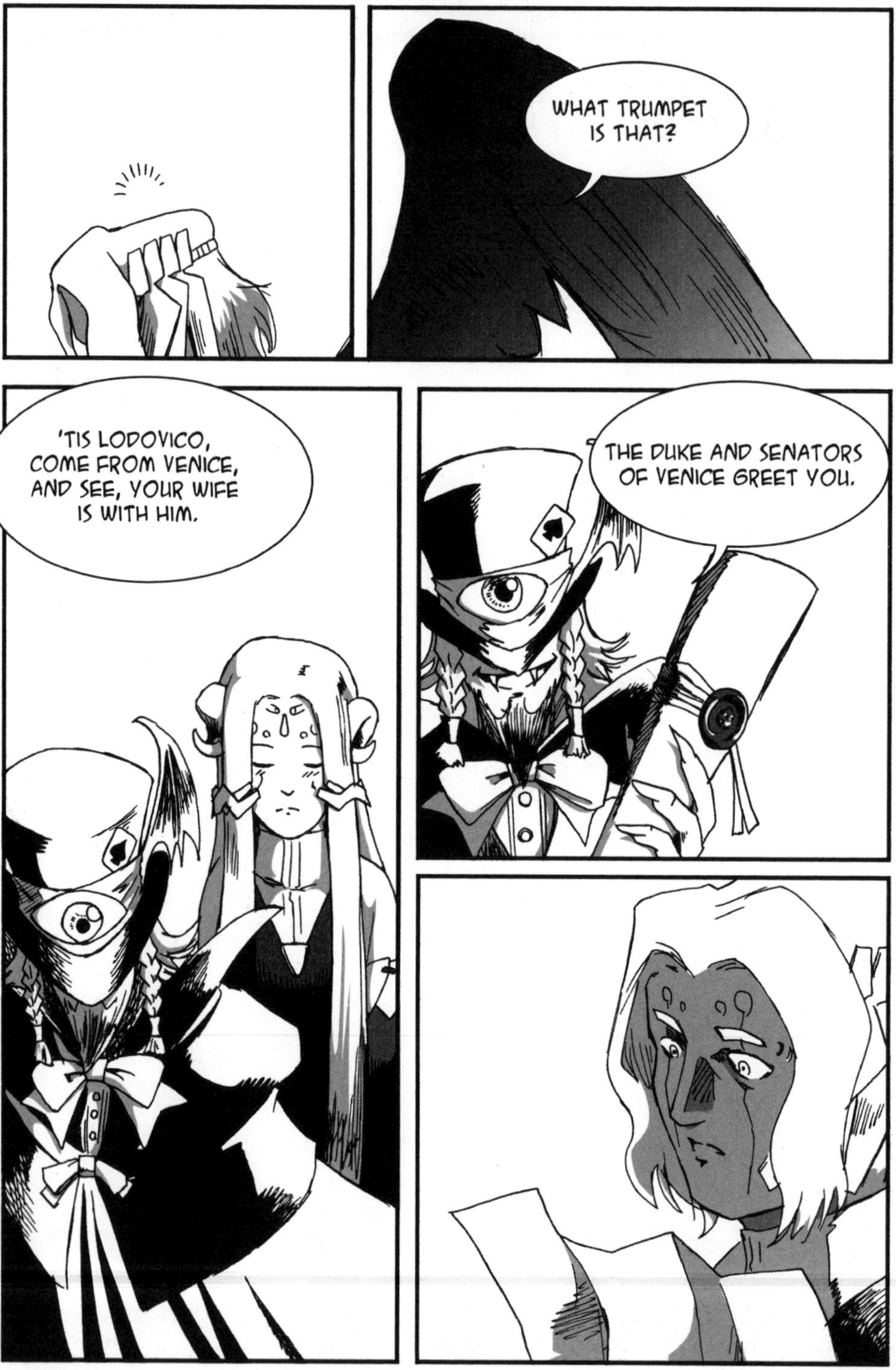
WHAT TRUMPET IS THAT?
'TIS LODOVICO, COME FROM VENICE, AND SEE, YOUR WIFE IS WITH HIM.
THE DUKE AND SENATORS OF VENICE GREET YOU.

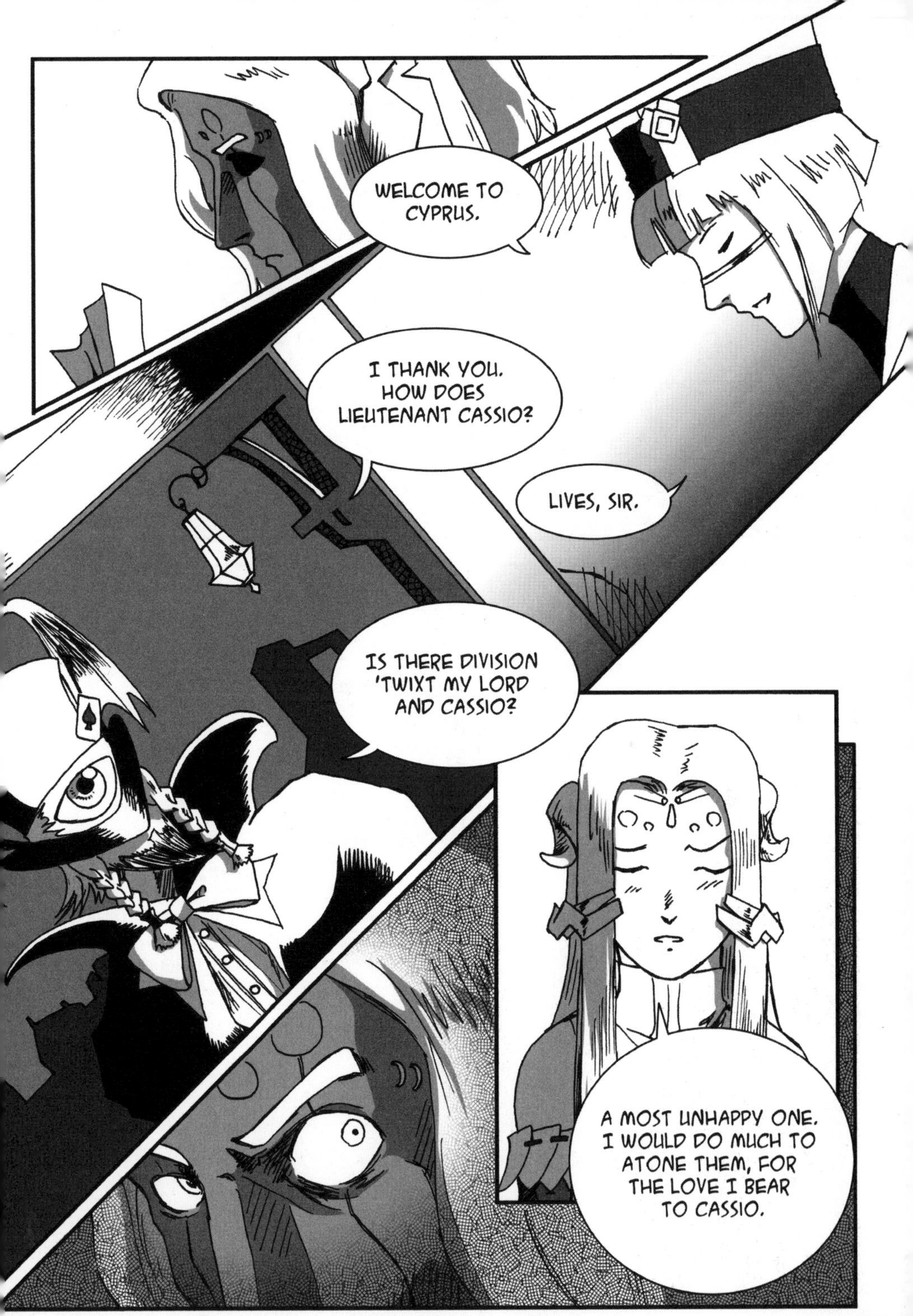
WELCOME TO CYPRUS.
I THANK YOU. HOW DOES LIEUTENANT CASSIO?
LIVES, SIR.
IS THERE DIVISION 'TWIXT MY LORD AND CASSIO?
A MOST UNHAPPY ONE. I WOULD DO MUCH TO ATONE THEM, FOR THE LOVE I BEAR TO CASSIO.

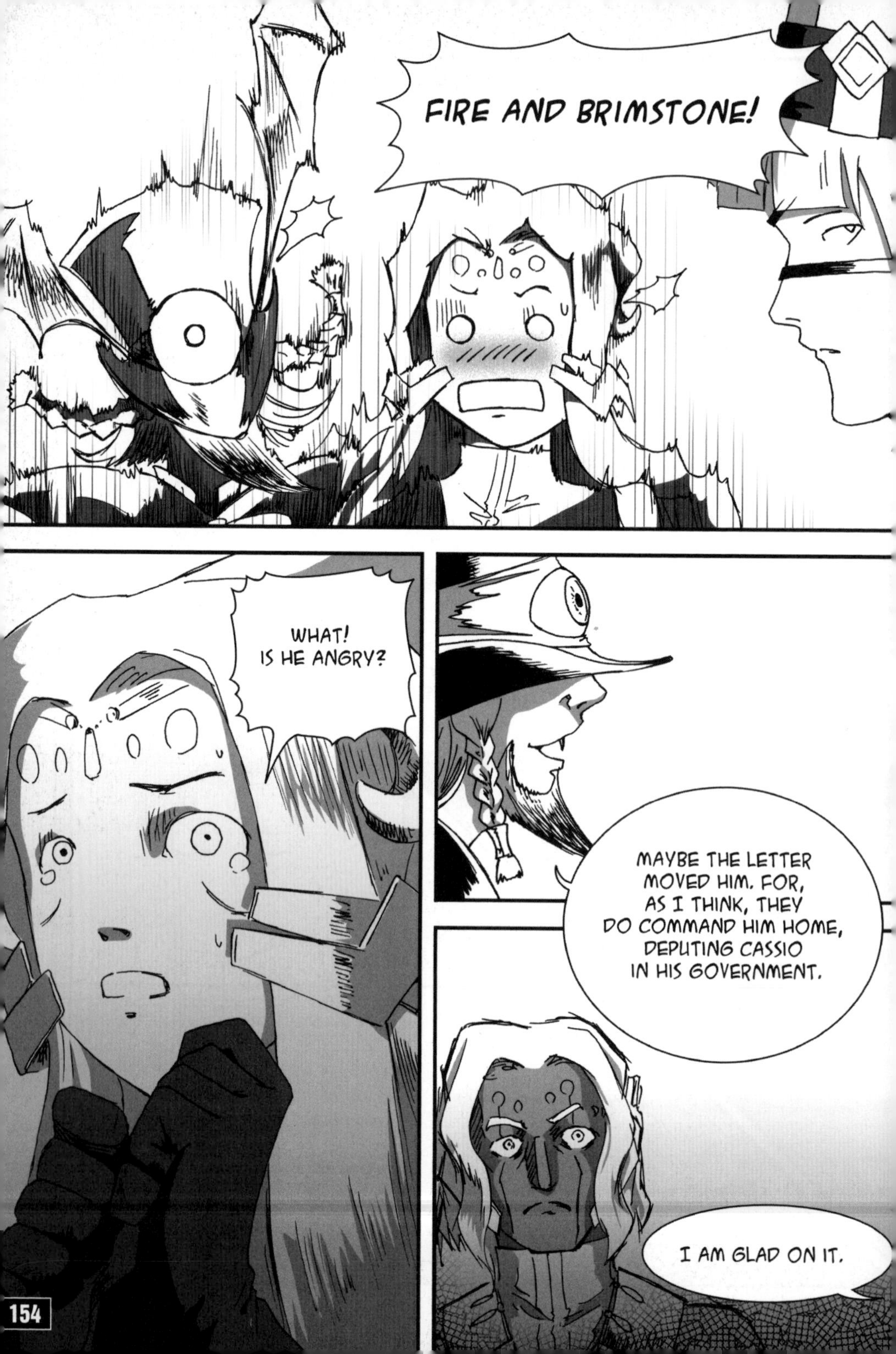
FIRE AND BRIMSTONE!
WHAT! IS HE ANGRY?
MAYBE THE LETTER MOVED HIM. FOR, AS I THINK, THEY DO COMMAND HIM HOME, DEPUTING CASSIO IN HIS GOVERNMENT.
I AM GLAD ON IT.

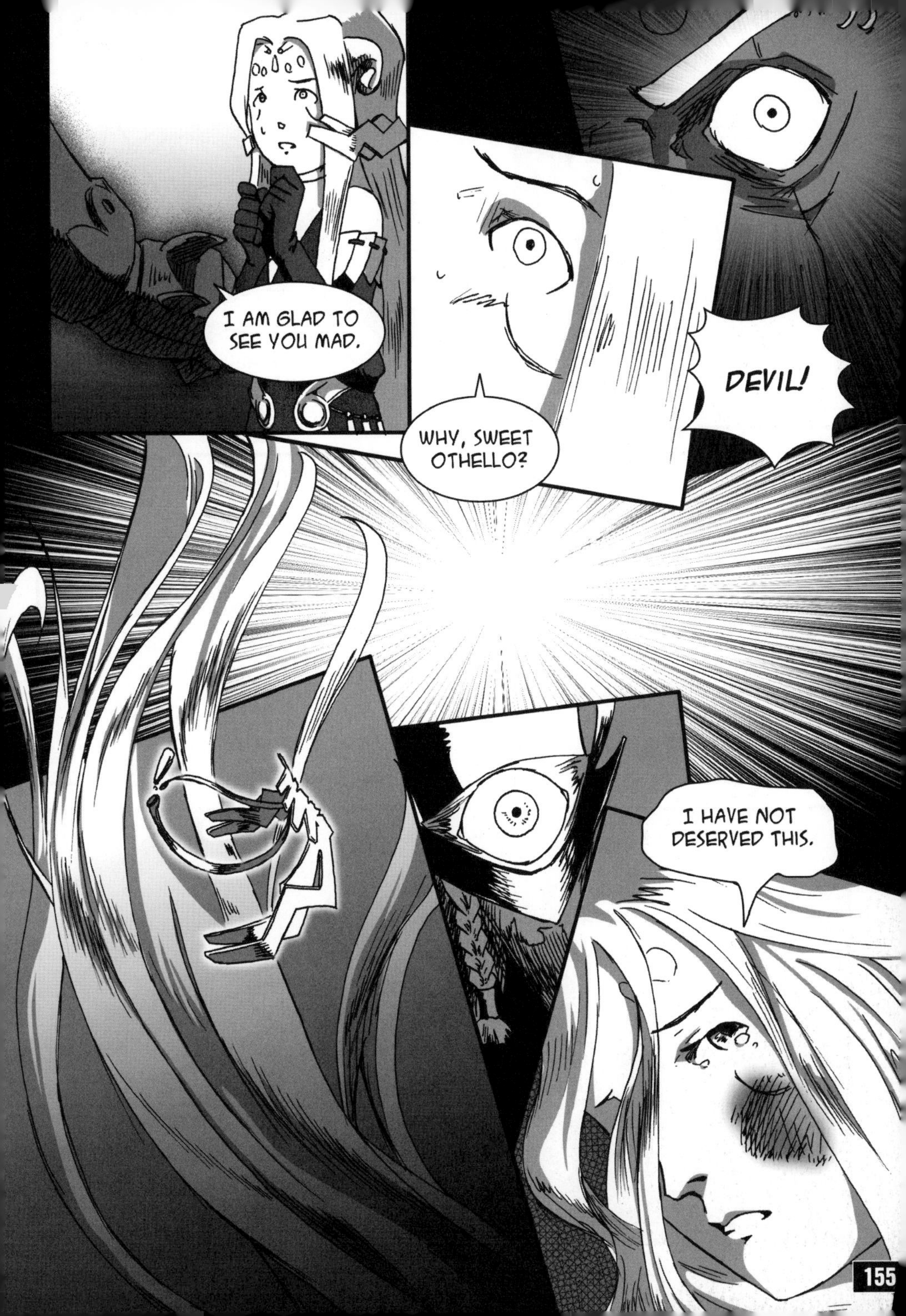
I AM GLAD TO SEE YOU MAD.
WHY, SWEET OTHELLO?
DEVIL!
I HAVE NOT DESERVED THIS.

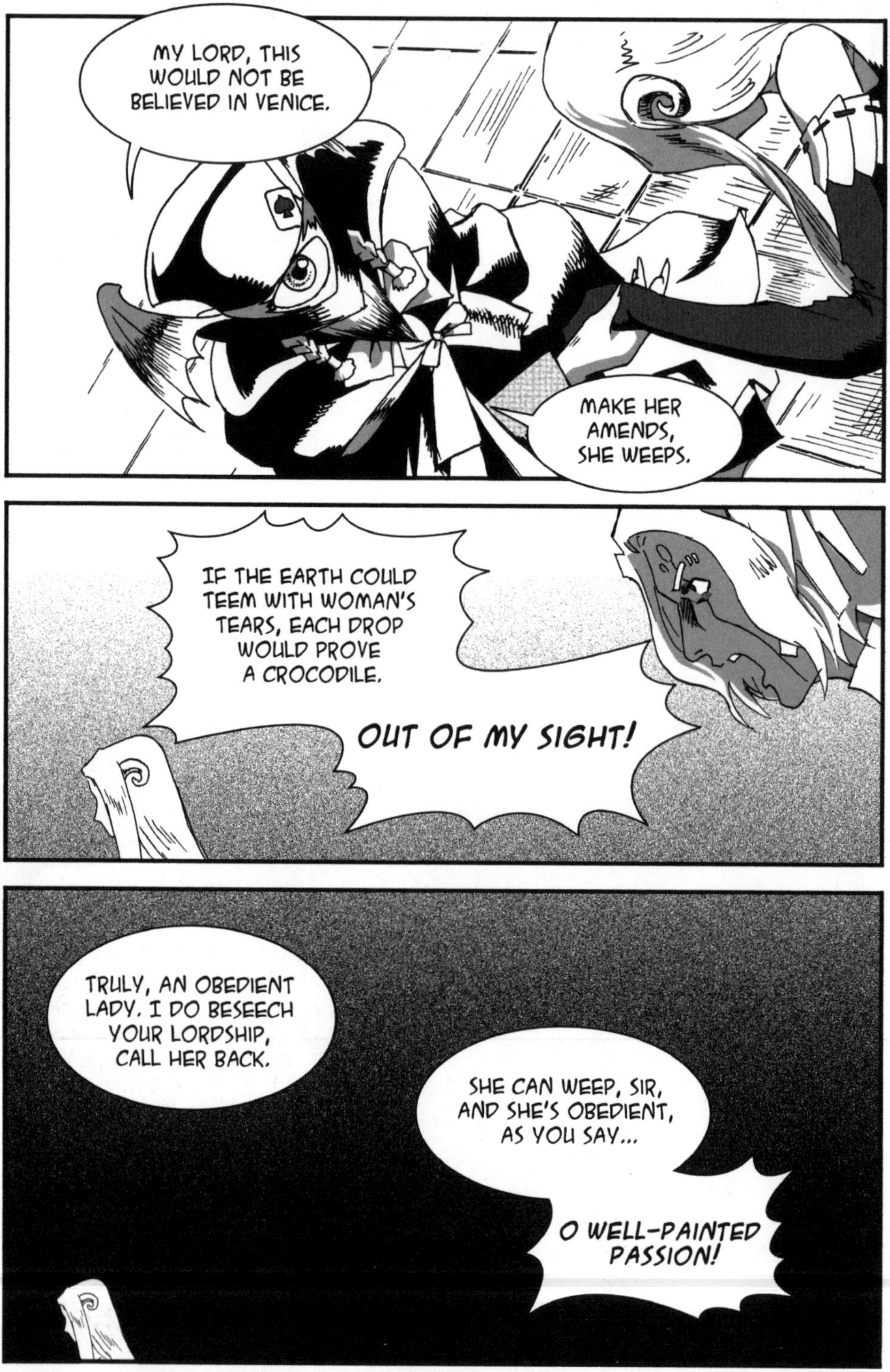

MY LORD, THIS WOULD NOT BE BELIEVED IN VENICE.
MAKE HER AMENDS, SHE WEEPS.
IF THE EARTH COULD TEEM WITH WOMAN'S TEARS, EACH DROP WOULD PROVE A CROCODILE.
OUT OF MY SIGHT!
TRULY, AN OBEDIENT LADY. I DO BESEECH YOUR LORDSHIP, CALL HER BACK.
SHE CAN WEEP, SIR, AND SHE'S OBEDIENT, AS YOU SAY...
O WELL-PAINTED PASSION!

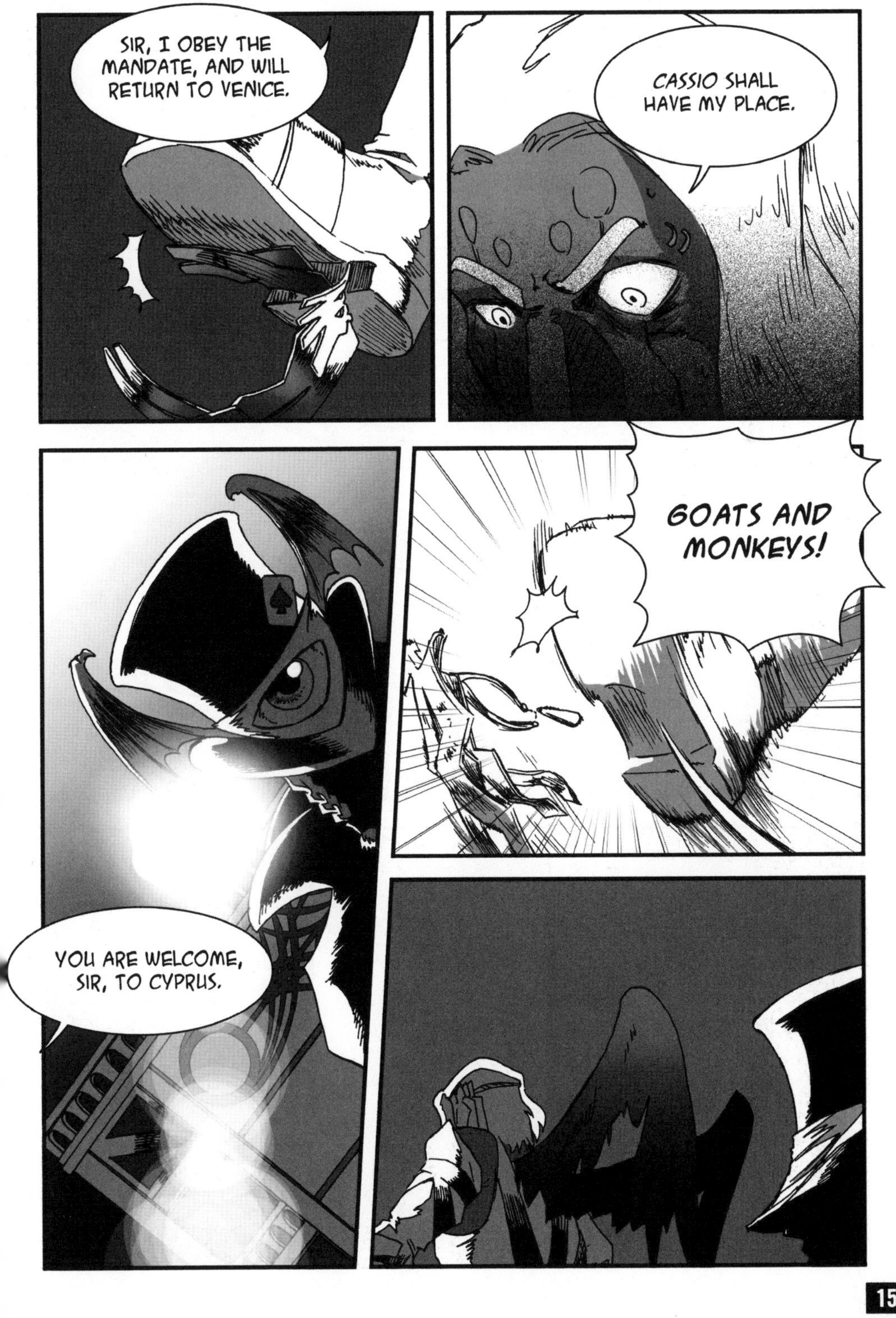
SIR, I OBEY THE MANDATE, AND WILL RETURN TO VENICE.
CASSIO SHALL HAVE MY PLACE.
GOATS AND MONKEYS!
YOU ARE WELCOME, SIR, TO CYPRUS.

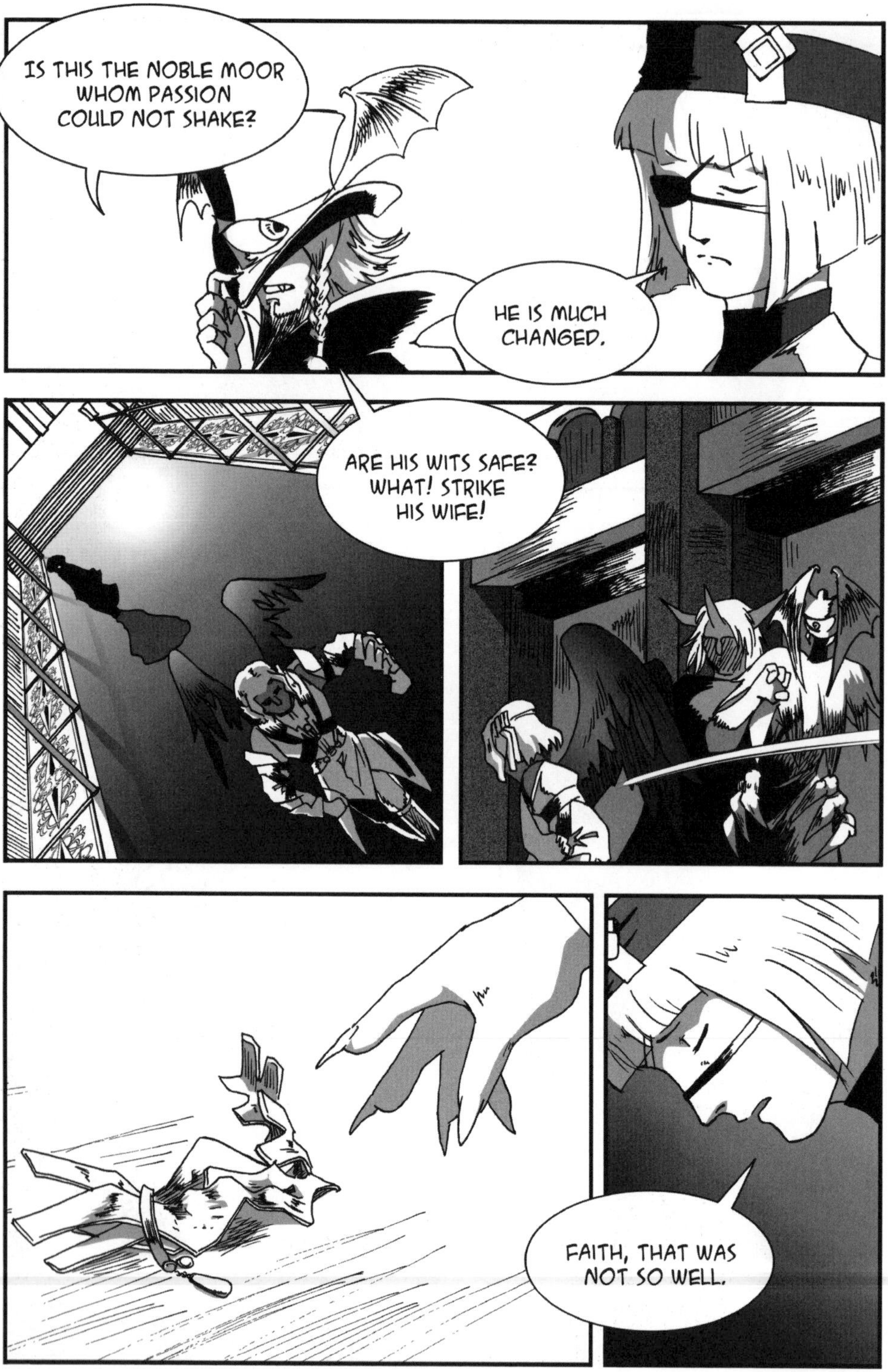
IS THIS THE NOBLE MOOR WHOM PASSION COULD NOT SHAKE?
HE IS MUCH CHANGED.
ARE HIS WITS SAFE? WHAT! STRIKE HIS WIFE!
FAITH, THAT WAS NOT SO WELL.

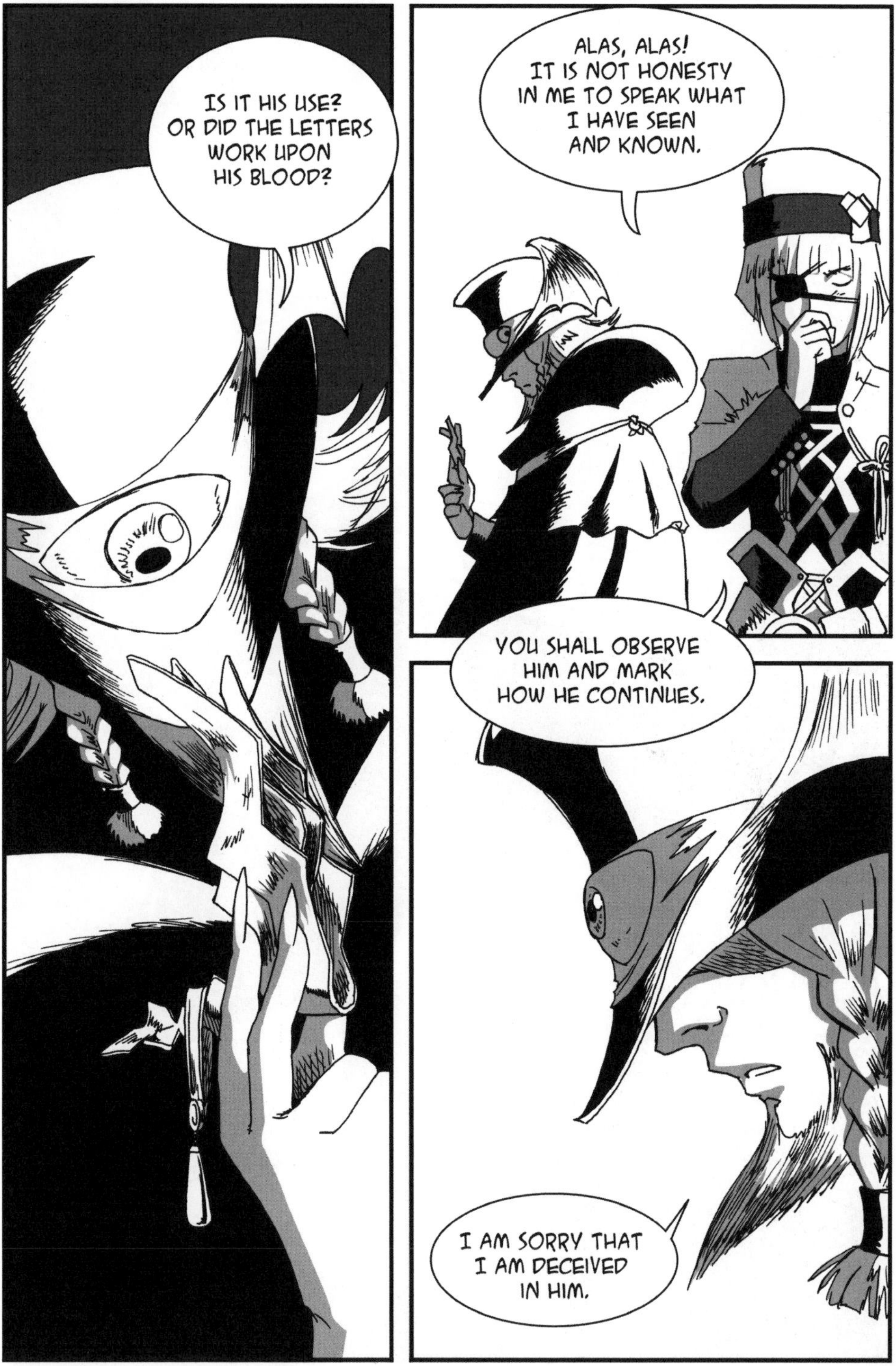
IS IT HIS USE? OR DID THE LETTERS WORK UPON HIS BLOOD?
ALAS, ALAS! IT IS NOT HONESTY IN ME TO SPEAK WHAT I HAVE SEEN AND KNOWN.
YOU SHALL OBSERVE HIM AND MARK HOW HE CONTINUES.
I AM SORRY THAT I AM DECEIVED IN HIM.

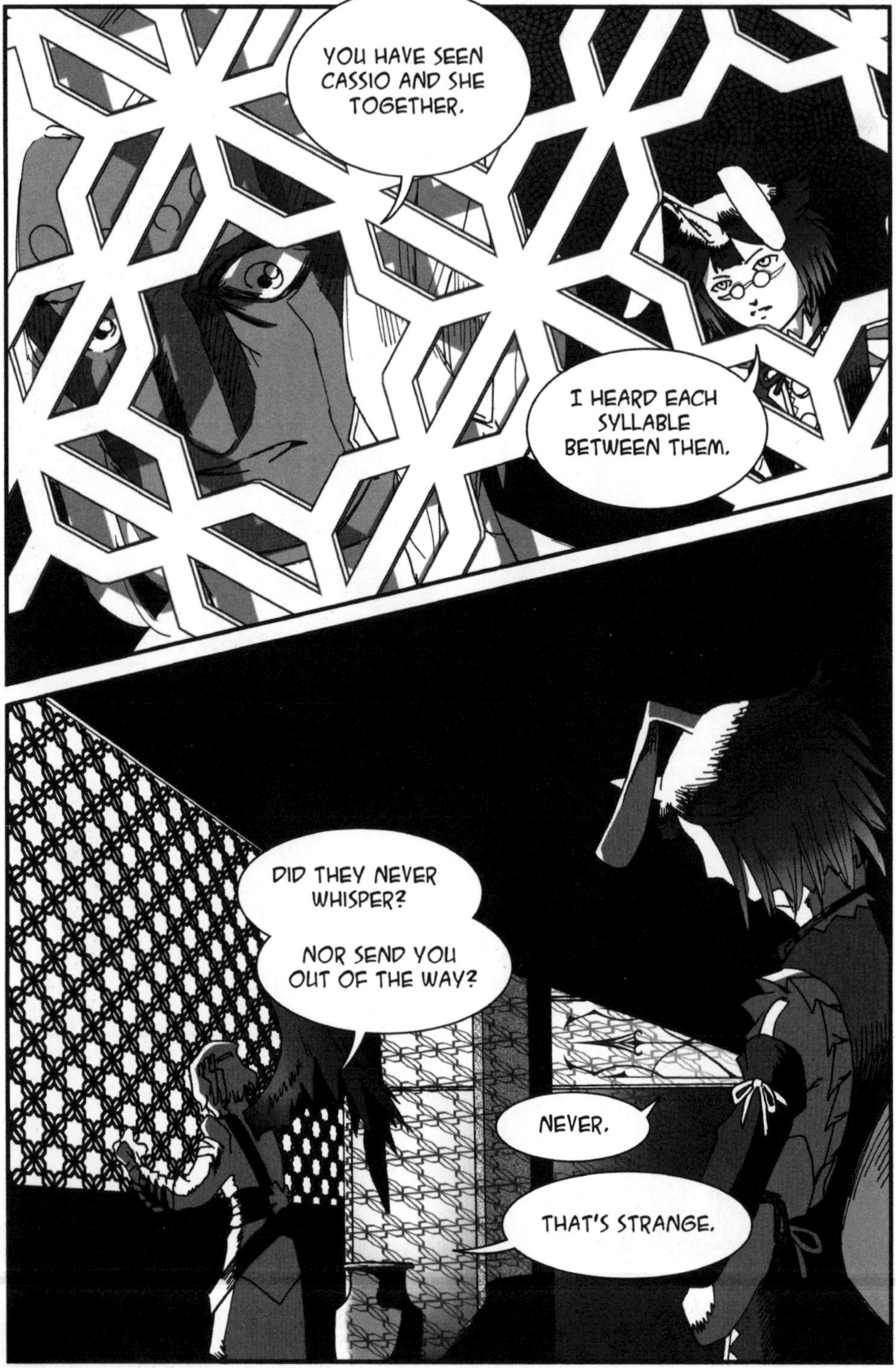
YOU HAVE SEEN CASSIO AND SHE TOGETHER.
I HEARD EACH SYLLABLE BETWEEN THEM.
DID THEY NEVER WHISPER?
NOR SEND YOU OUT OF THE WAY?
NEVER.
THAT'S STRANGE.

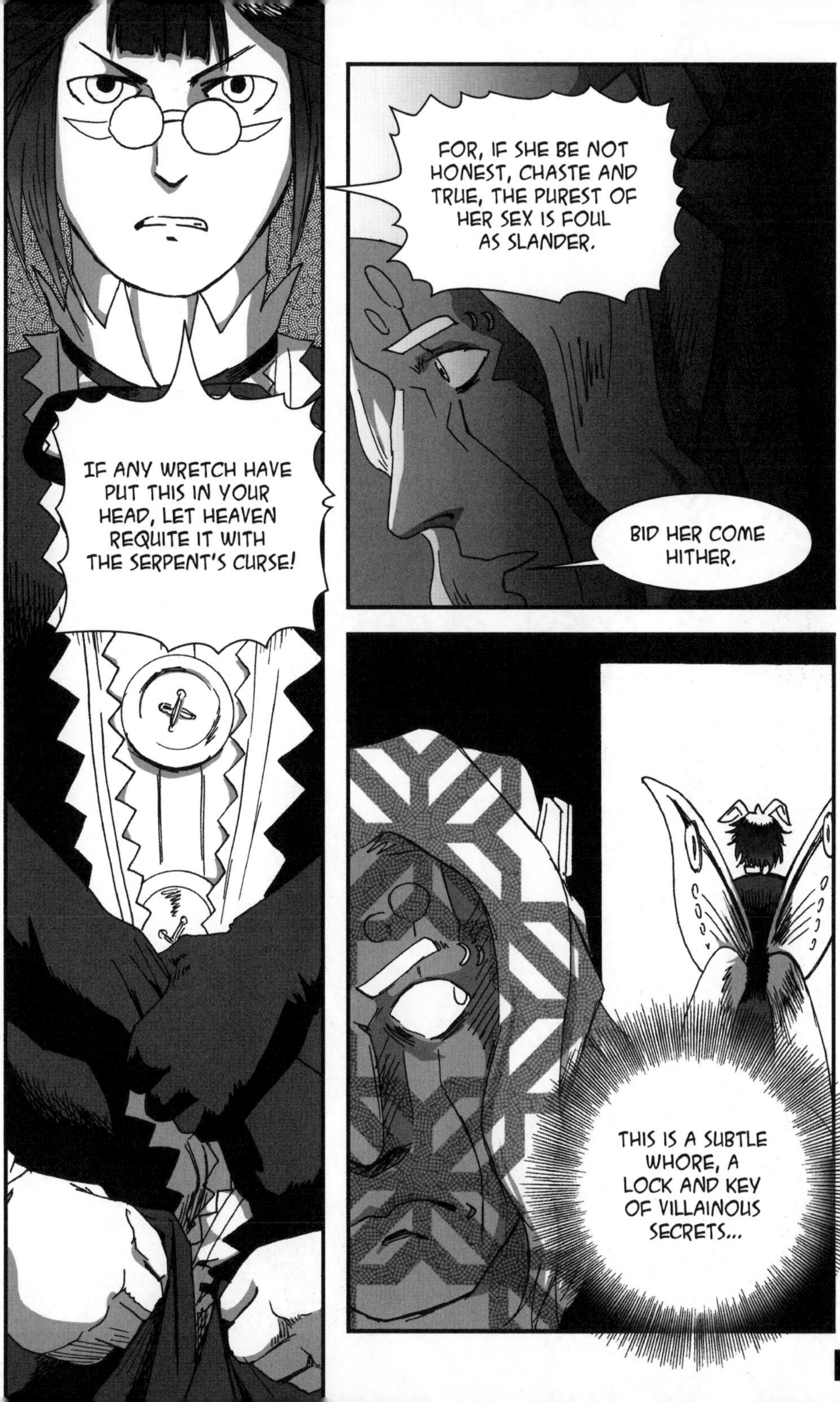

FOR, IF SHE BE NOT HONEST, CHASTE AND TRUE, THE PUREST OF HER SEX IS FOUL AS SLANDER.
IF ANY WRETCH HAVE PUT THIS IN YOUR HEAD, LET HEAVEN REQUITE IT WITH THE SERPENT'S CURSE!
BID HER COME HITHER.
THIS IS A SUBTLE WHORE, A LOCK AND KEY OF VILLAINOUS SECRETS...

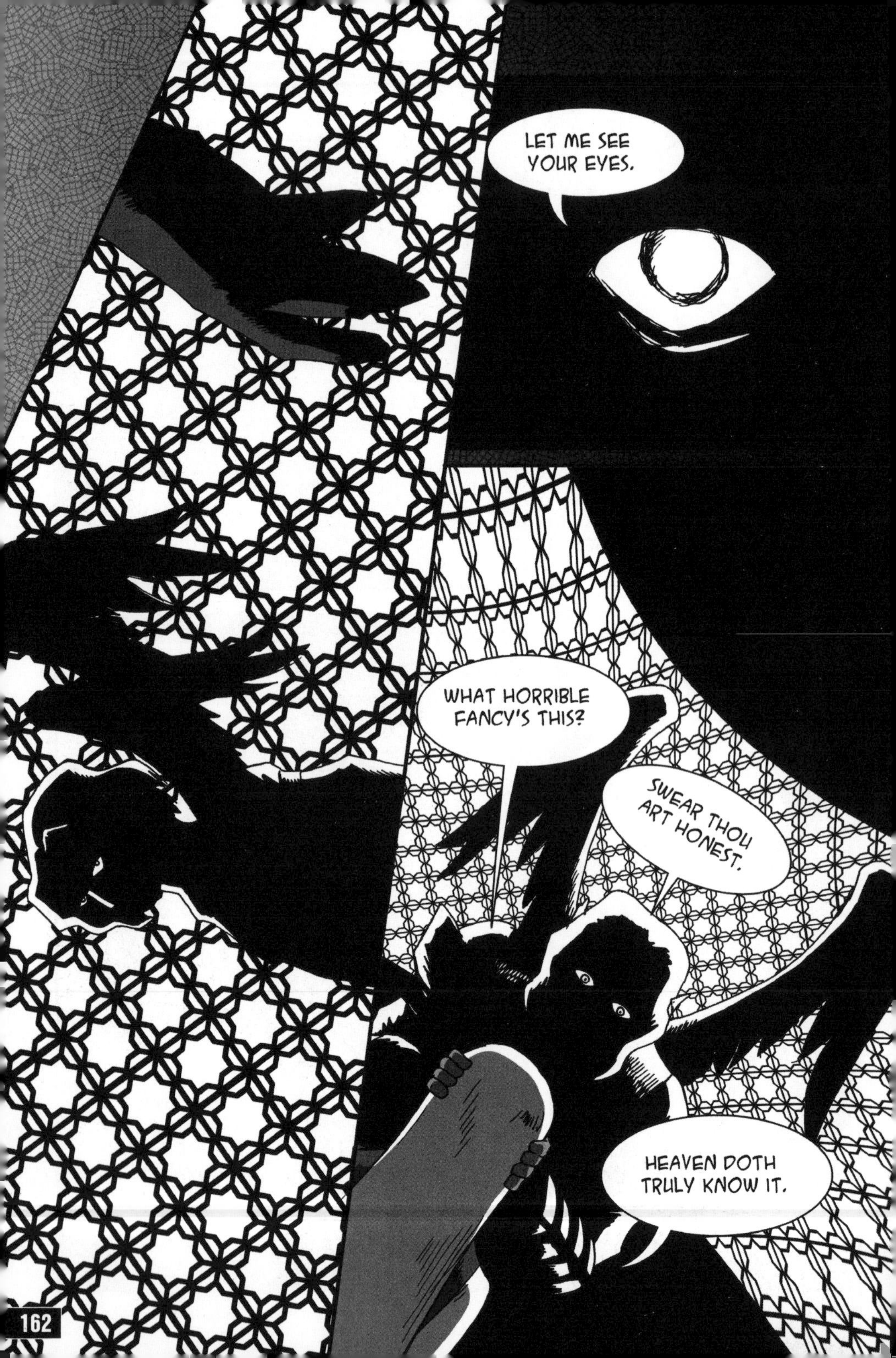
LET ME SEE YOUR EYES.
WHAT HORRIBLE FANCY'S THIS?
SWEAR THOU ART HONEST.
HEAVEN DOTH TRULY KNOW IT.

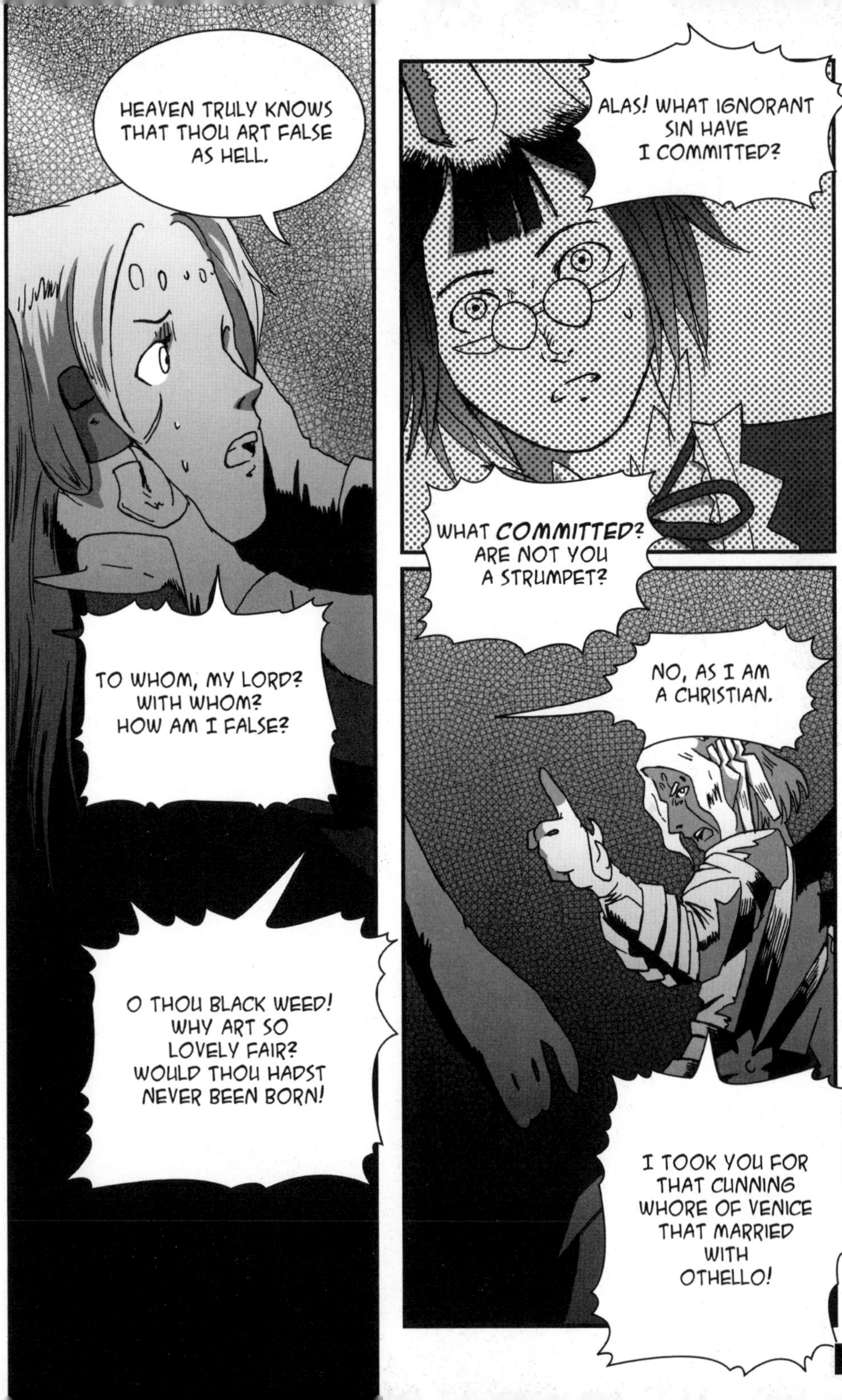
HEAVEN TRULY KNOWS THAT THOU ART FALSE AS HELL.
ALAS! WHAT IGNORANT SIN HAVE I COMMITTED?
WHAT **COMMITTED**? ARE NOT YOU A STRUMPET?
TO WHOM, MY LORD? WITH WHOM? HOW AM I FALSE?
NO, AS I AM A CHRISTIAN.
O THOU BLACK WEED! WHY ART SO LOVELY FAIR? WOULD THOU HADST NEVER BEEN BORN!
I TOOK YOU FOR THAT CUNNING WHORE OF VENICE THAT MARRIED WITH OTHELLO!

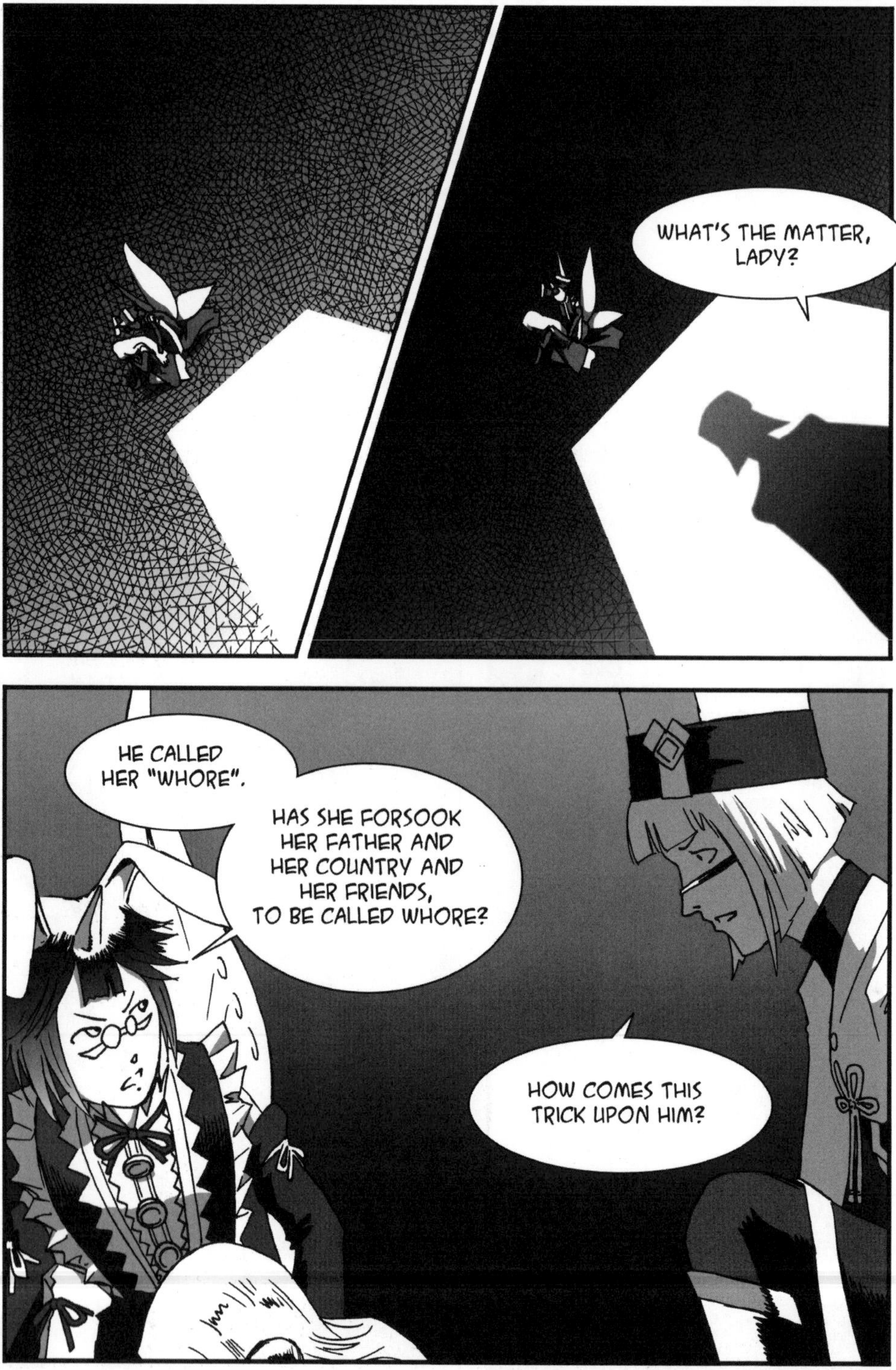
WHAT'S THE MATTER, LADY?
HE CALLED HER "WHORE".
HAS SHE FORSOOK HER FATHER AND HER COUNTRY AND HER FRIENDS, TO BE CALLED WHORE?
HOW COMES THIS TRICK UPON HIM?

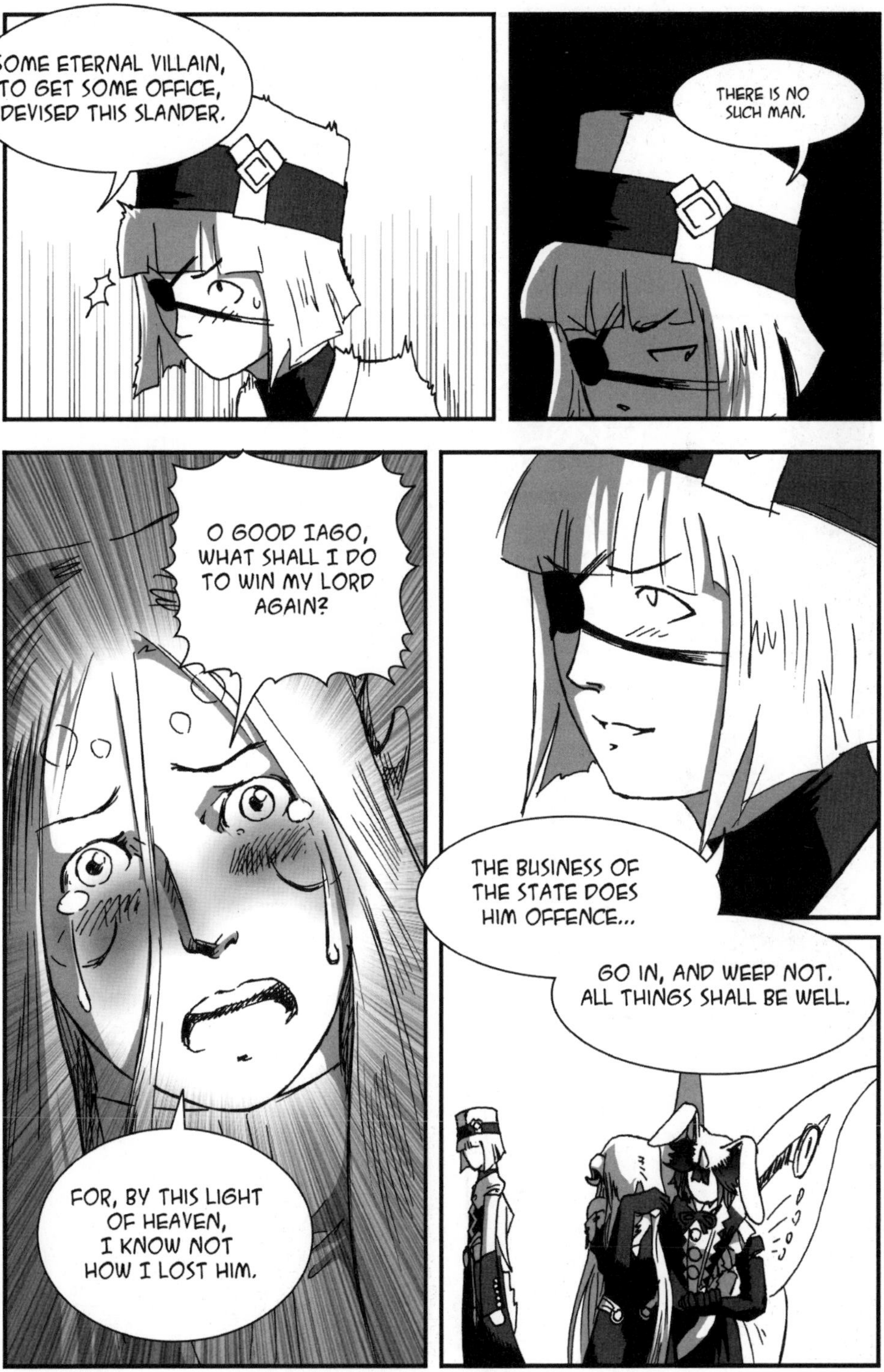
SOME ETERNAL VILLAIN, TO GET SOME OFFICE, DEVISED THIS SLANDER.
THERE IS NO SUCH MAN.
O GOOD IAGO, WHAT SHALL I DO TO WIN MY LORD AGAIN?
FOR, BY THIS LIGHT OF HEAVEN, I KNOW NOT HOW I LOST HIM.
THE BUSINESS OF THE STATE DOES HIM OFFENCE...
GO IN, AND WEEP NOT. ALL THINGS SHALL BE WELL.

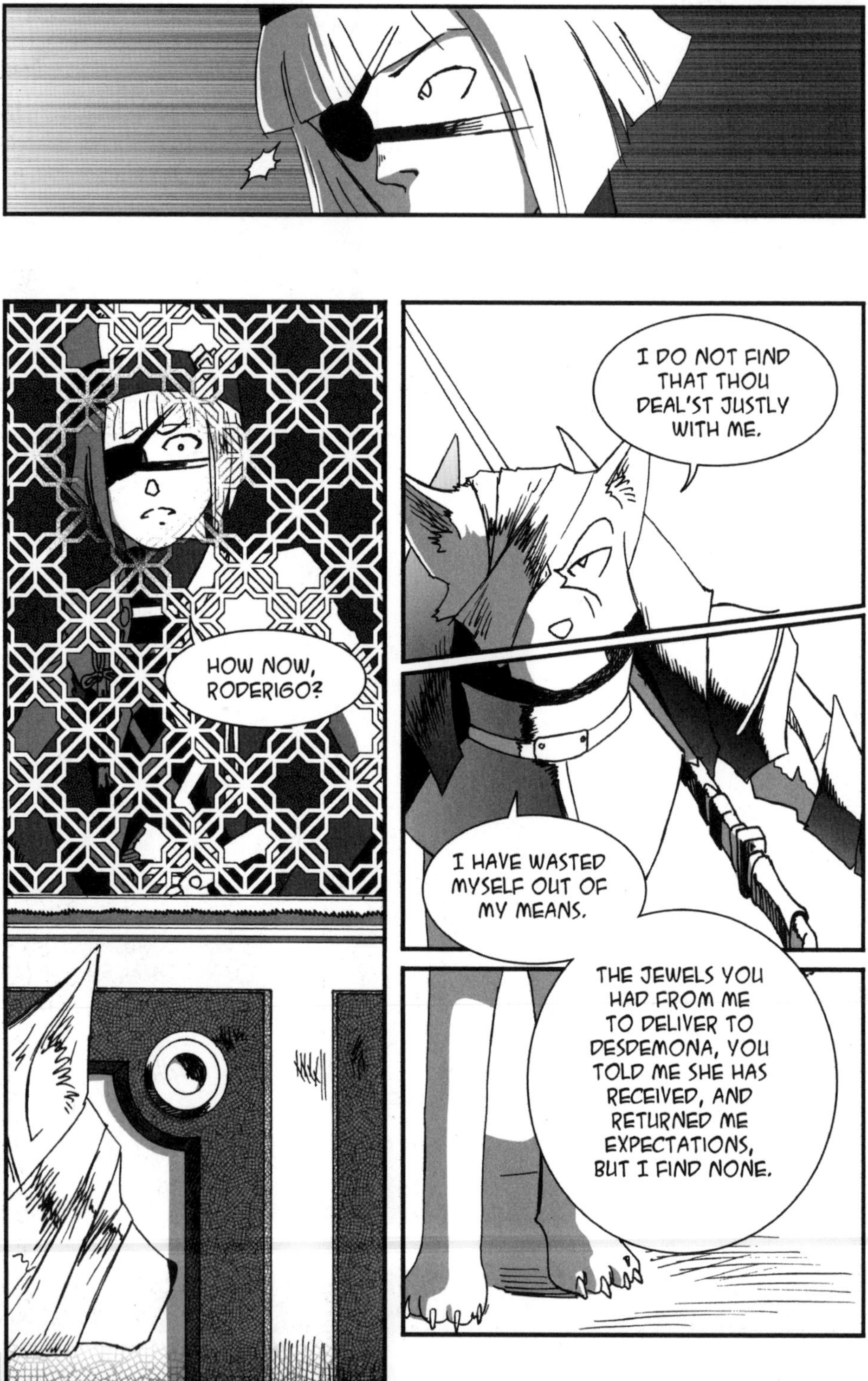
HOW NOW, RODERIGO?
I DO NOT FIND THAT THOU DEAL'ST JUSTLY WITH ME.
I HAVE WASTED MYSELF OUT OF MY MEANS.
THE JEWELS YOU HAD FROM ME TO DELIVER TO DESDEMONA, YOU TOLD ME SHE HAS RECEIVED, AND RETURNED ME EXPECTATIONS, BUT I FIND NONE.

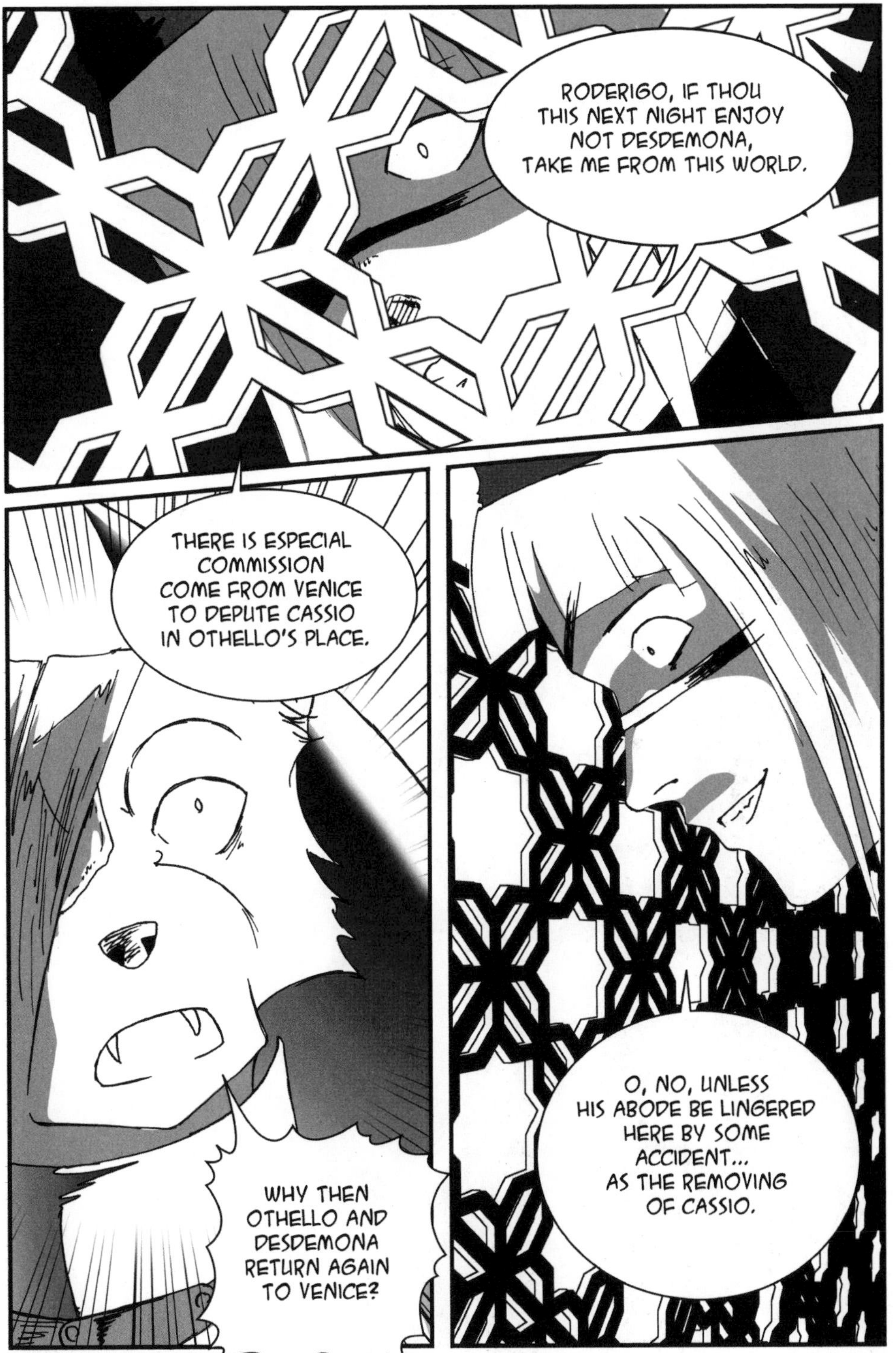
RODERIGO, IF THOU THIS NEXT NIGHT ENJOY NOT DESDEMONA, TAKE ME FROM THIS WORLD.
THERE IS ESPECIAL COMMISSION COME FROM VENICE TO DEPUTE CASSIO IN OTHELLO'S PLACE.
WHY THEN OTHELLO AND DESDEMONA RETURN AGAIN TO VENICE?
O, NO, UNLESS HIS ABODE BE LINGERED HERE BY SOME ACCIDENT... AS THE REMOVING OF CASSIO.

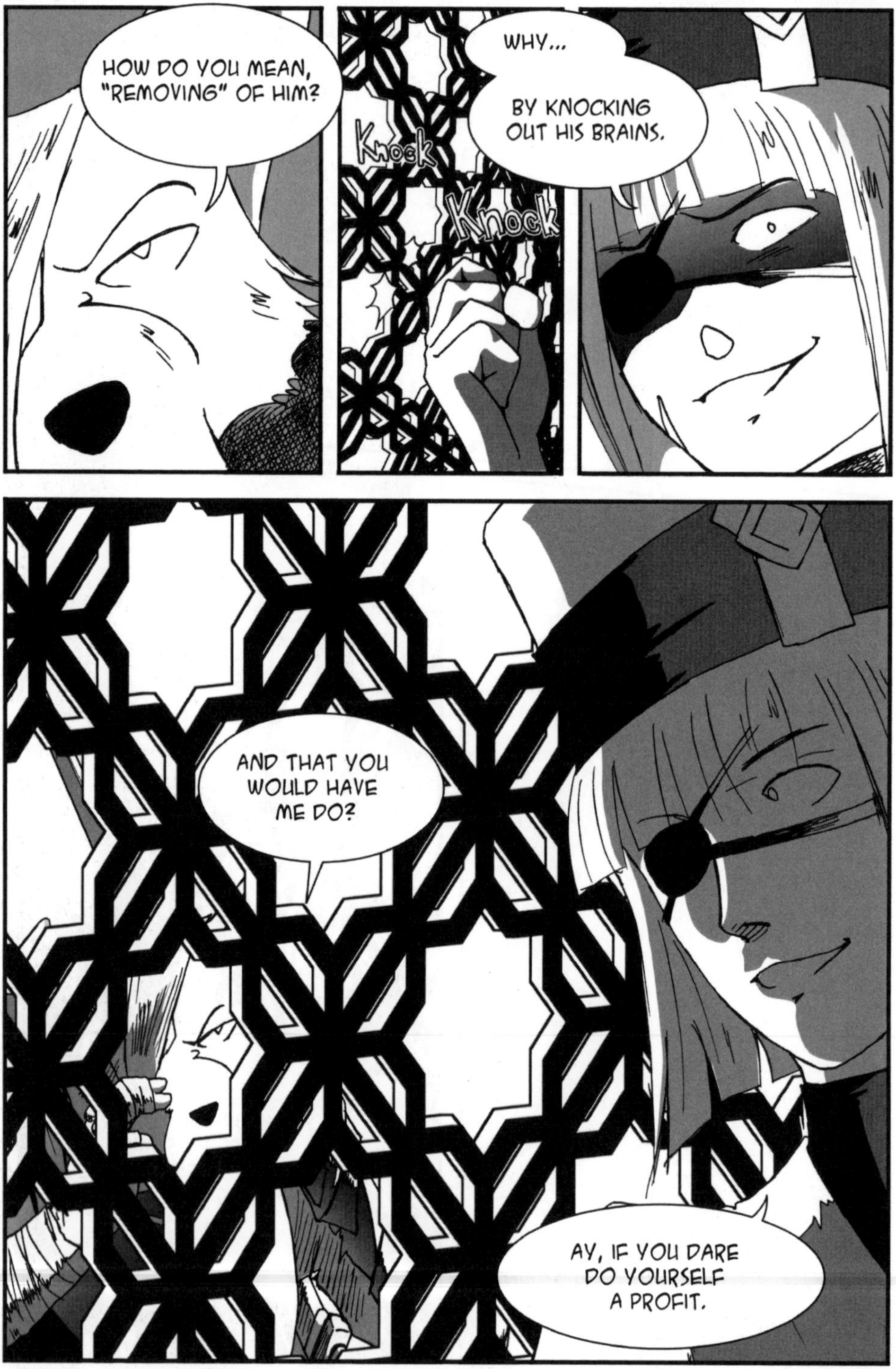
HOW DO YOU MEAN, "REMOVING" OF HIM?
WHY...
BY KNOCKING OUT HIS BRAINS.
Knock
Knock
AND THAT YOU WOULD HAVE ME DO?
AY, IF YOU DARE DO YOURSELF A PROFIT.

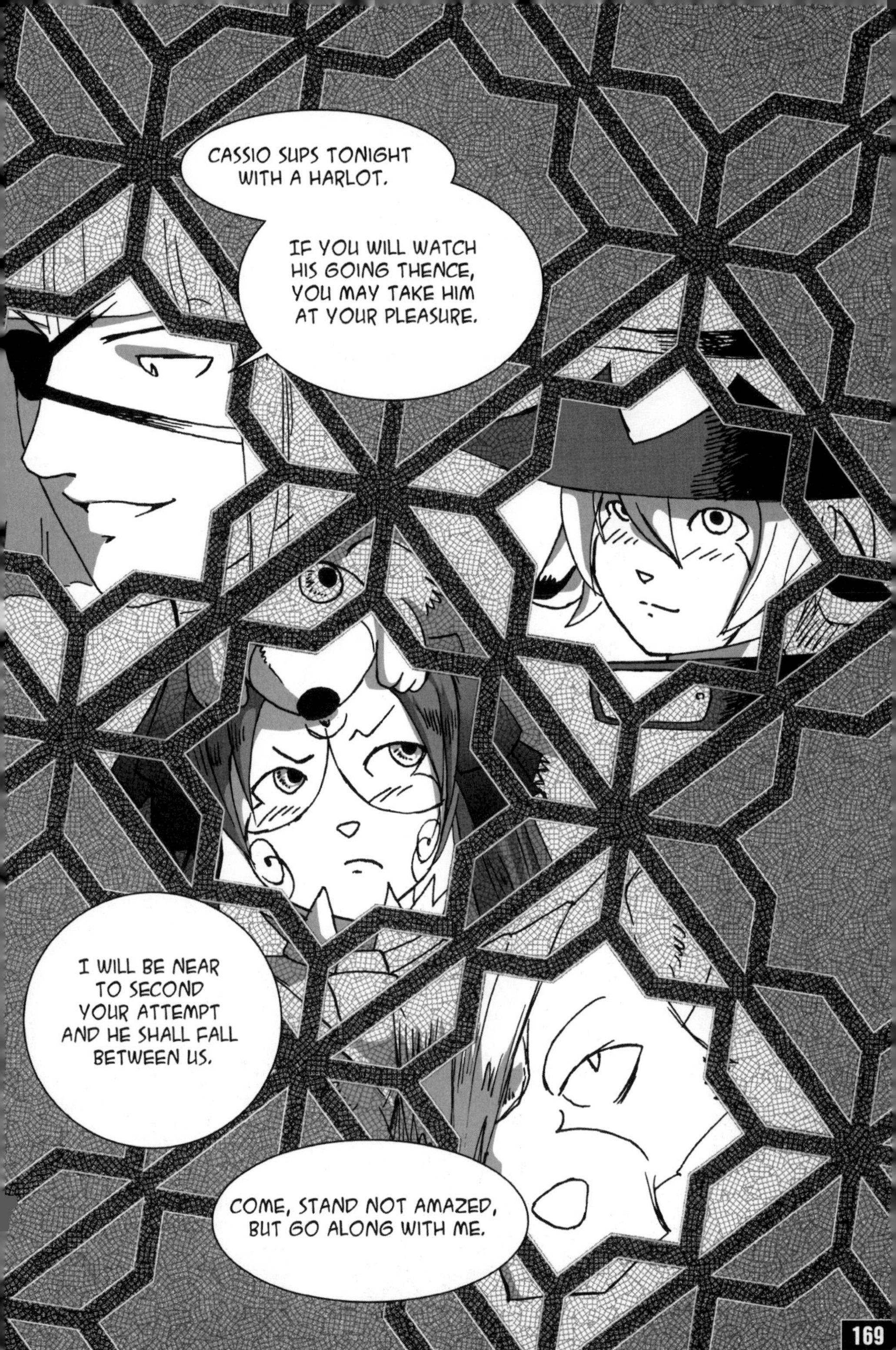
CASSIO SUPS TONIGHT WITH A HARLOT.
IF YOU WILL WATCH HIS GOING THENCE, YOU MAY TAKE HIM AT YOUR PLEASURE.
I WILL BE NEAR TO SECOND YOUR ATTEMPT AND HE SHALL FALL BETWEEN US.
COME, STAND NOT AMAZED, BUT GO ALONG WITH ME.

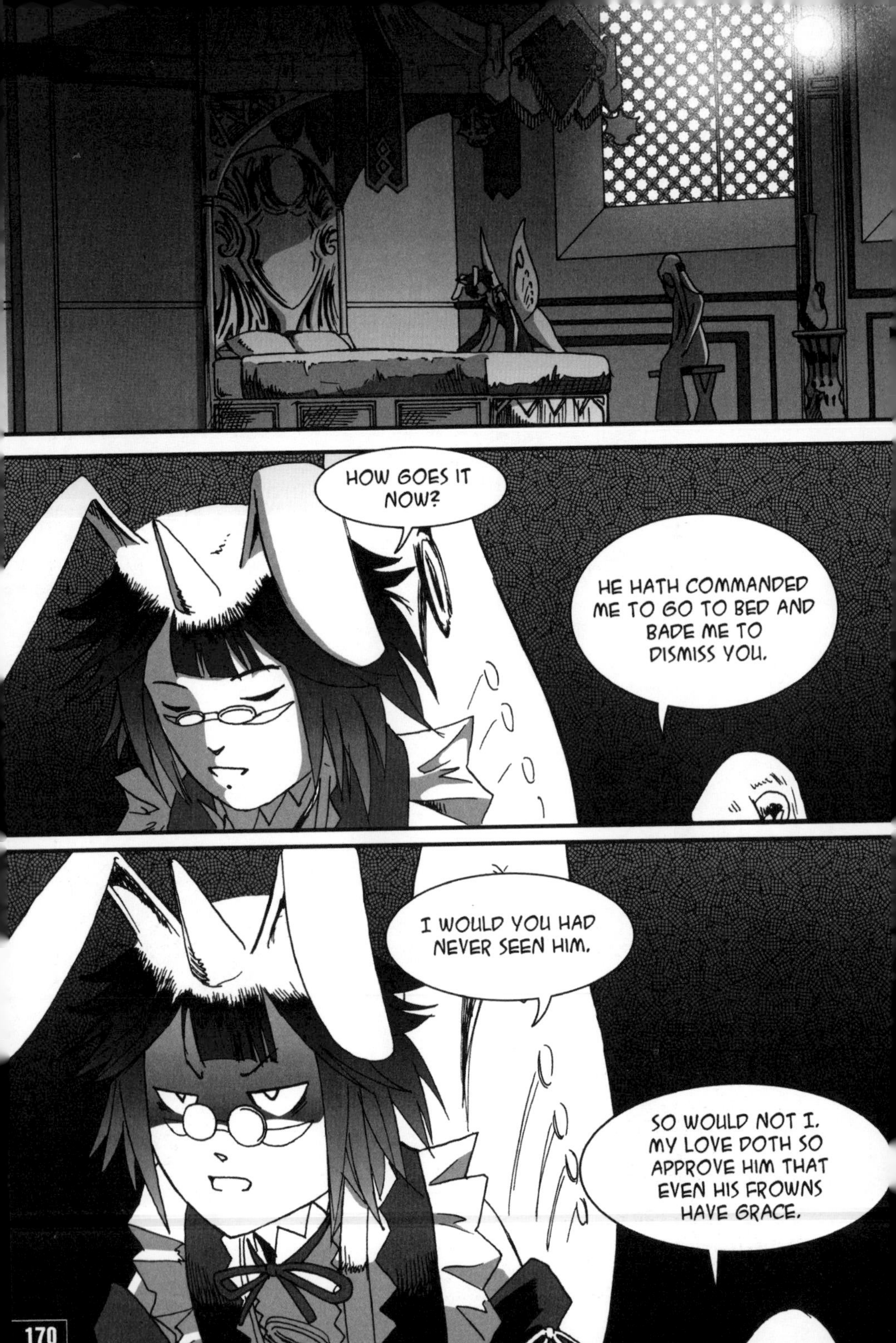
HOW GOES IT NOW?
HE HATH COMMANDED ME TO GO TO BED AND BADE ME TO DISMISS YOU.
I WOULD YOU HAD NEVER SEEN HIM.
SO WOULD NOT I. MY LOVE DOTH SO APPROVE HIM THAT EVEN HIS FROWNS HAVE GRACE.

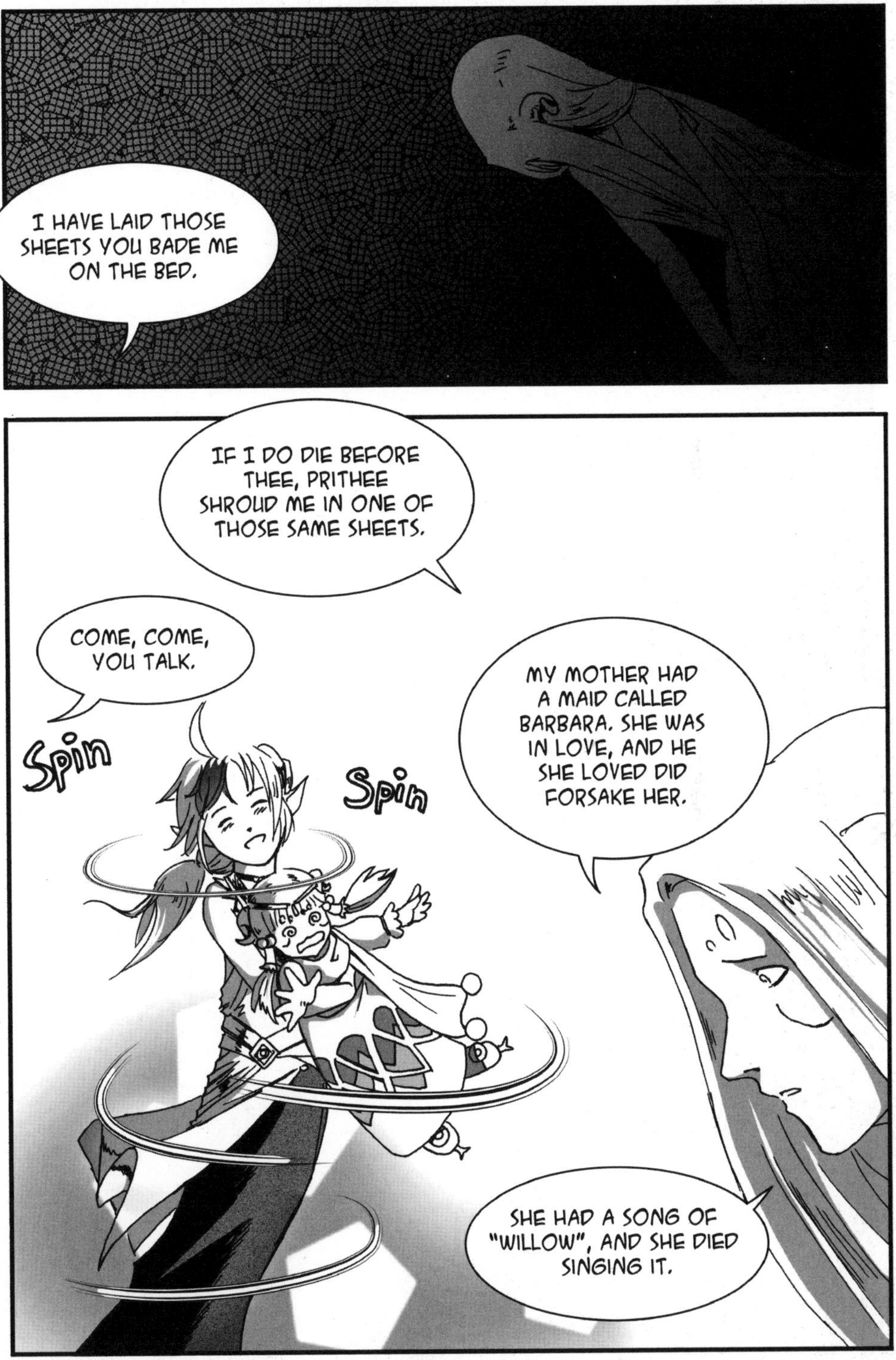
I HAVE LAID THOSE SHEETS YOU BADE ME ON THE BED.
IF I DO DIE BEFORE THEE, PRITHEE SHROUD ME IN ONE OF THOSE SAME SHEETS.
COME, COME, YOU TALK.
Spin
Spin
MY MOTHER HAD A MAID CALLED BARBARA. SHE WAS IN LOVE, AND HE SHE LOVED DID FORSAKE HER.
SHE HAD A SONG OF "WILLOW", AND SHE DIED SINGING IT.

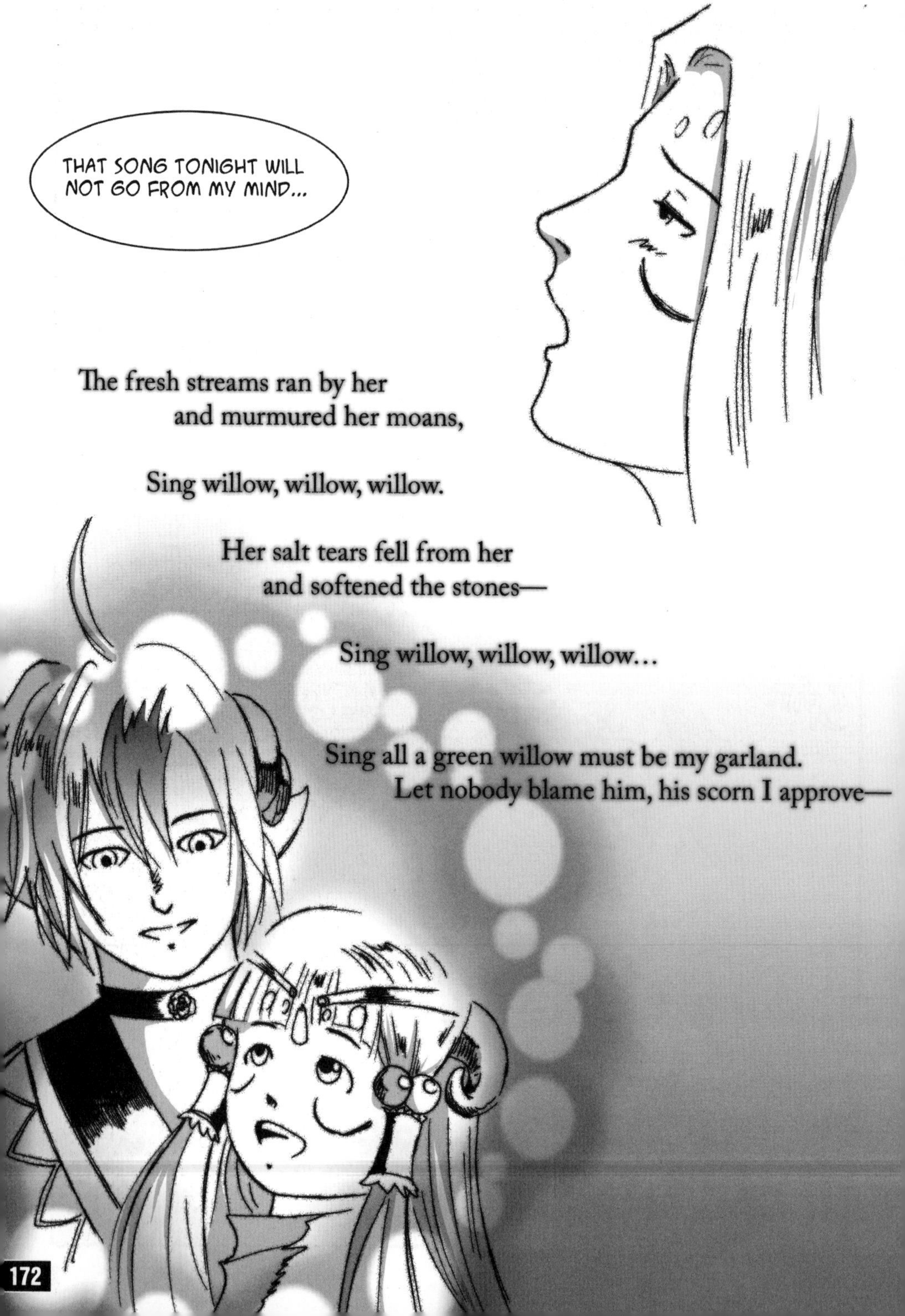

THAT SONG TONIGHT WILL NOT GO FROM MY MIND...
The fresh streams ran by her
and murmured her moans,
Sing willow, willow, willow.
Her salt tears fell from her
and softened the stones—
Sing willow, willow, willow...
Sing all a green willow must be my garland.
Let nobody blame him, his scorn I approve—

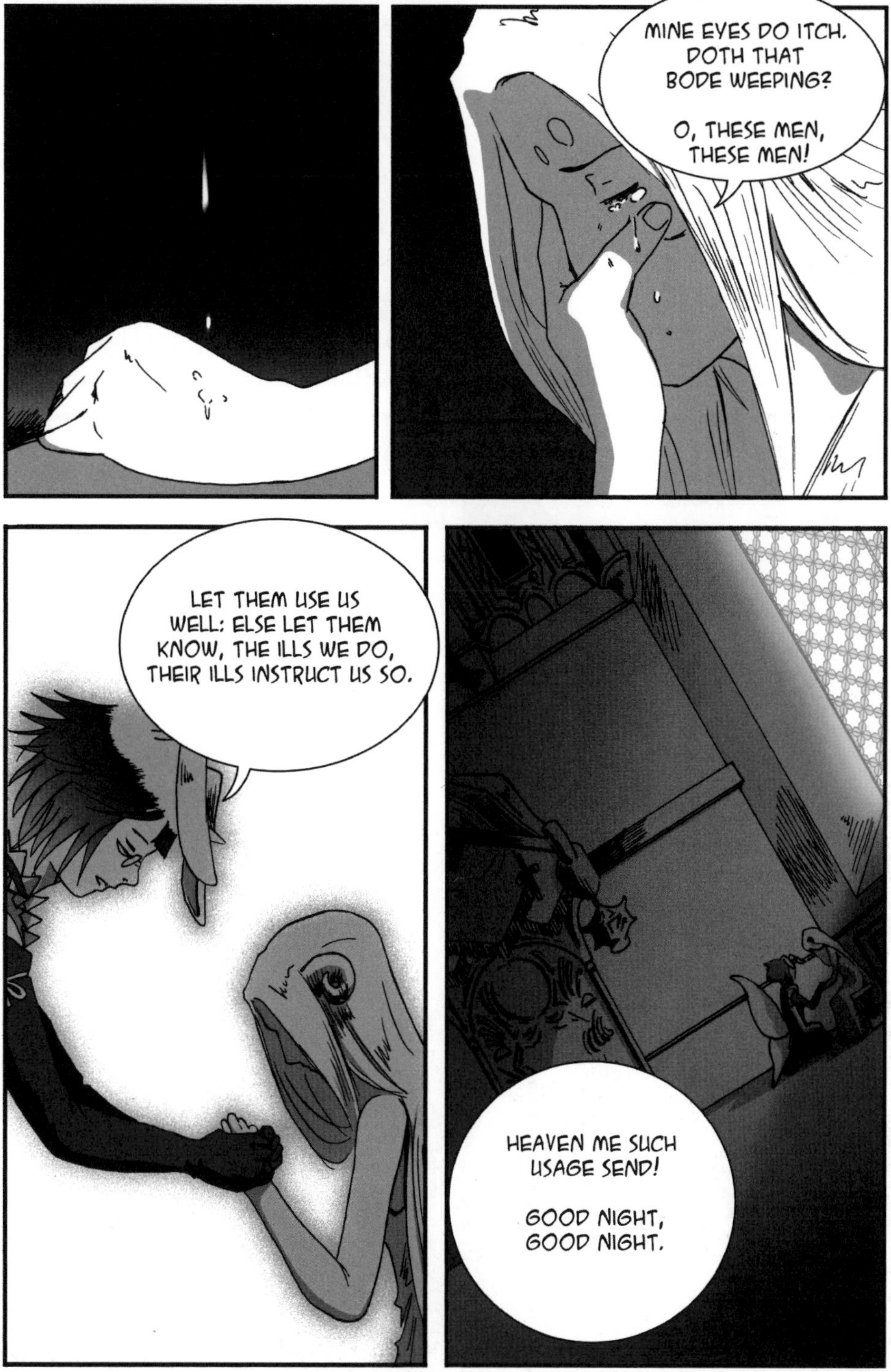
MINE EYES DO ITCH. DOTH THAT BODE WEEPING?
O, THESE MEN, THESE MEN!
LET THEM USE US WELL: ELSE LET THEM KNOW, THE ILLS WE DO, THEIR ILLS INSTRUCT US SO.
HEAVEN ME SUCH USAGE SEND!
GOOD NIGHT, GOOD NIGHT.

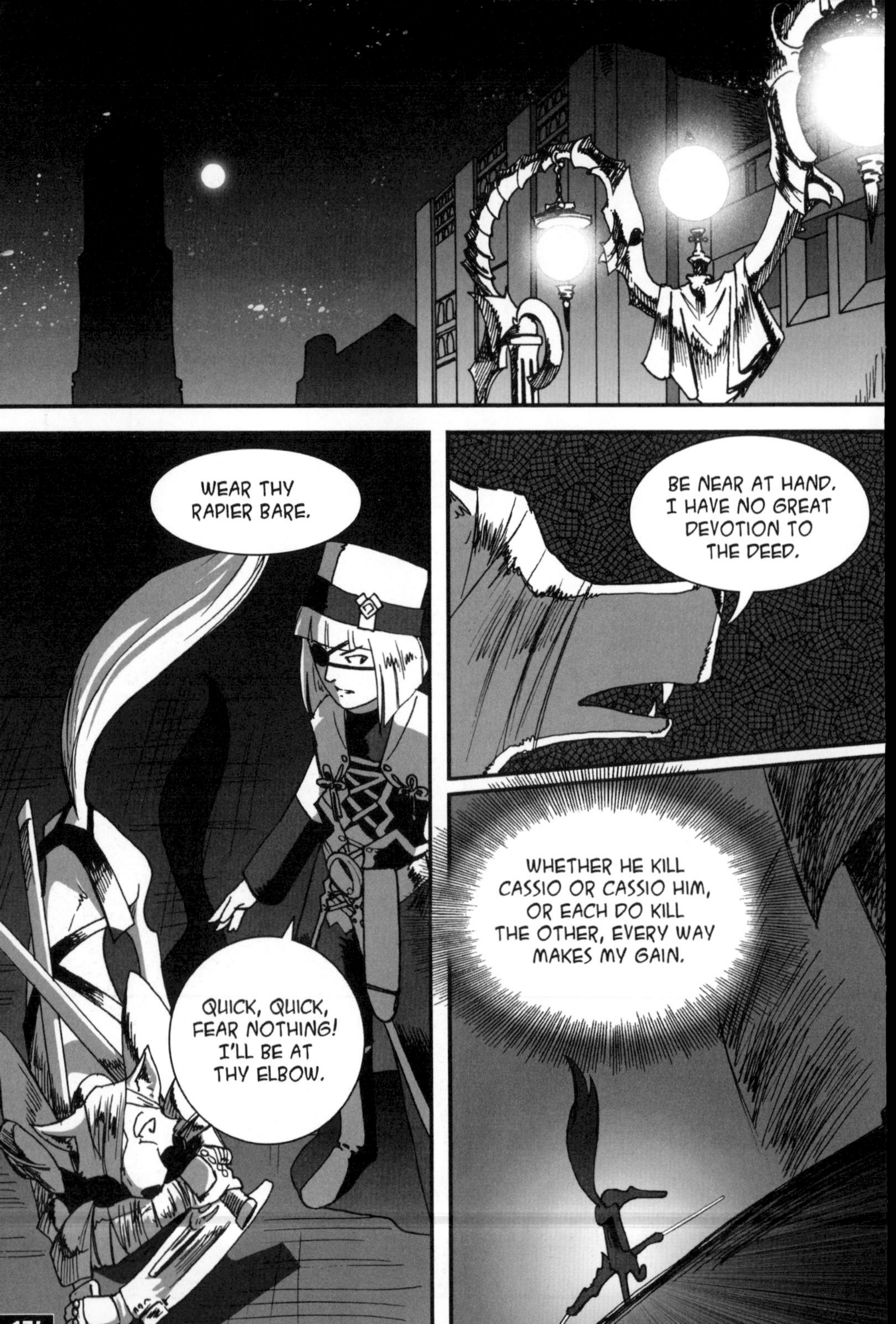
WEAR THY RAPIER BARE.
QUICK, QUICK, FEAR NOTHING! I'LL BE AT THY ELBOW.
BE NEAR AT HAND. I HAVE NO GREAT DEVOTION TO THE DEED.
WHETHER HE KILL CASSIO OR CASSIO HIM, OR EACH DO KILL THE OTHER, EVERY WAY MAKES MY GAIN.

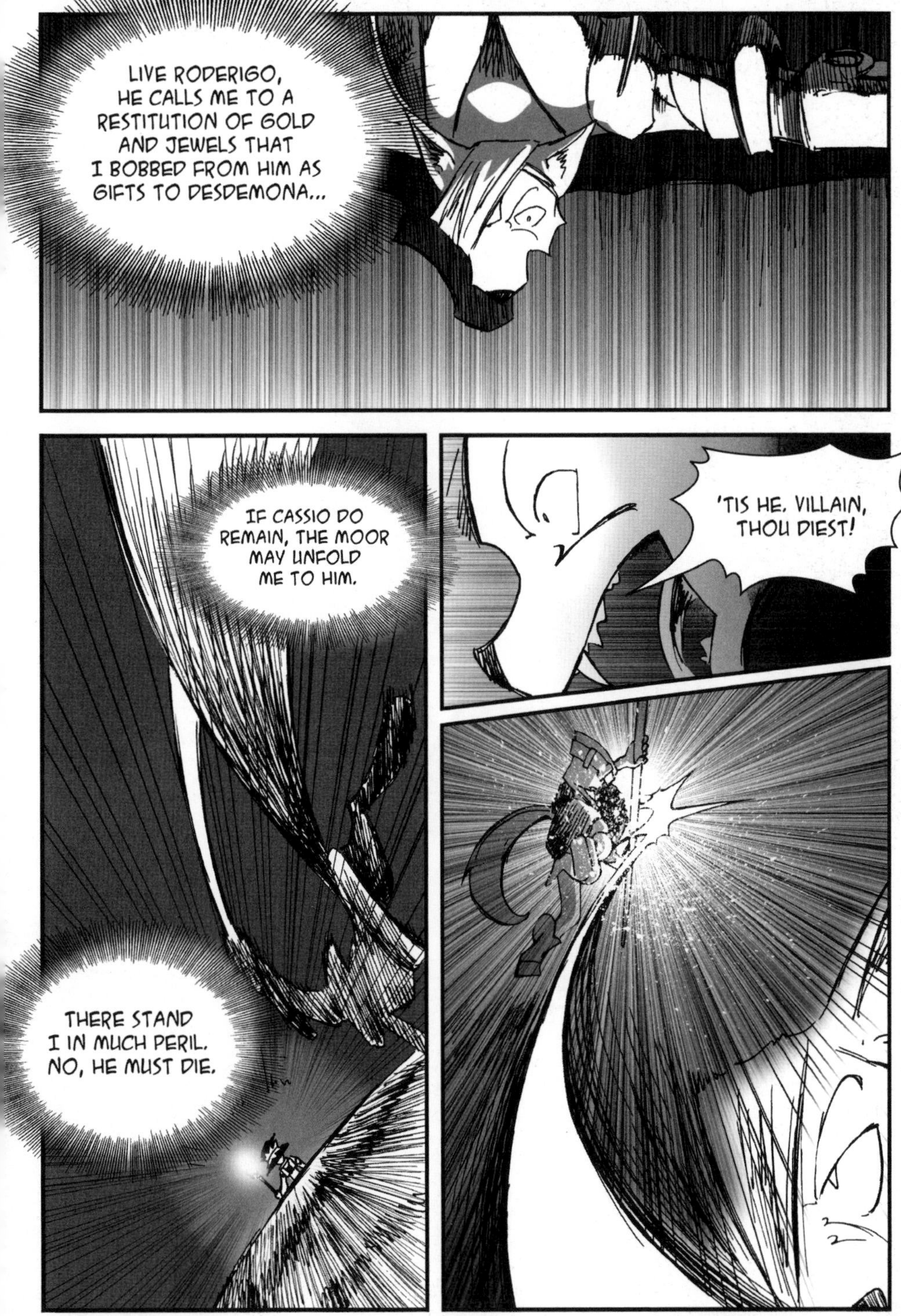
LIVE RODERIGO, HE CALLS ME TO A RESTITUTION OF GOLD AND JEWELS THAT I BOBBED FROM HIM AS GIFTS TO DESDEMONA...
IF CASSIO DO REMAIN, THE MOOR MAY UNFOLD ME TO HIM.
THERE STAND I IN MUCH PERIL. NO, HE MUST DIE.
'TIS HE. VILLAIN, THOU DIEST!

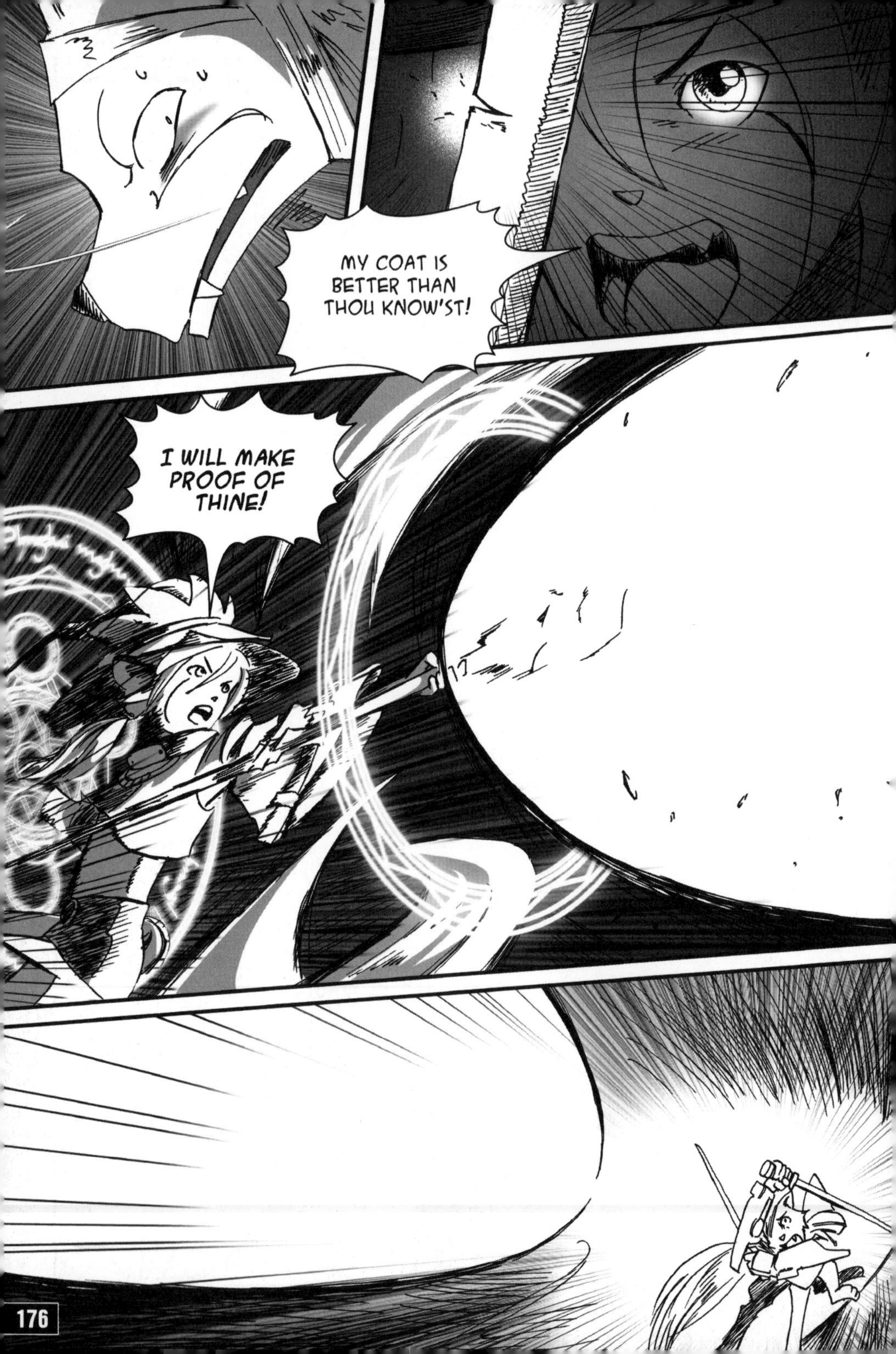
MY COAT IS BETTER THAN THOU KNOW'ST!
I WILL MAKE PROOF OF THINE!

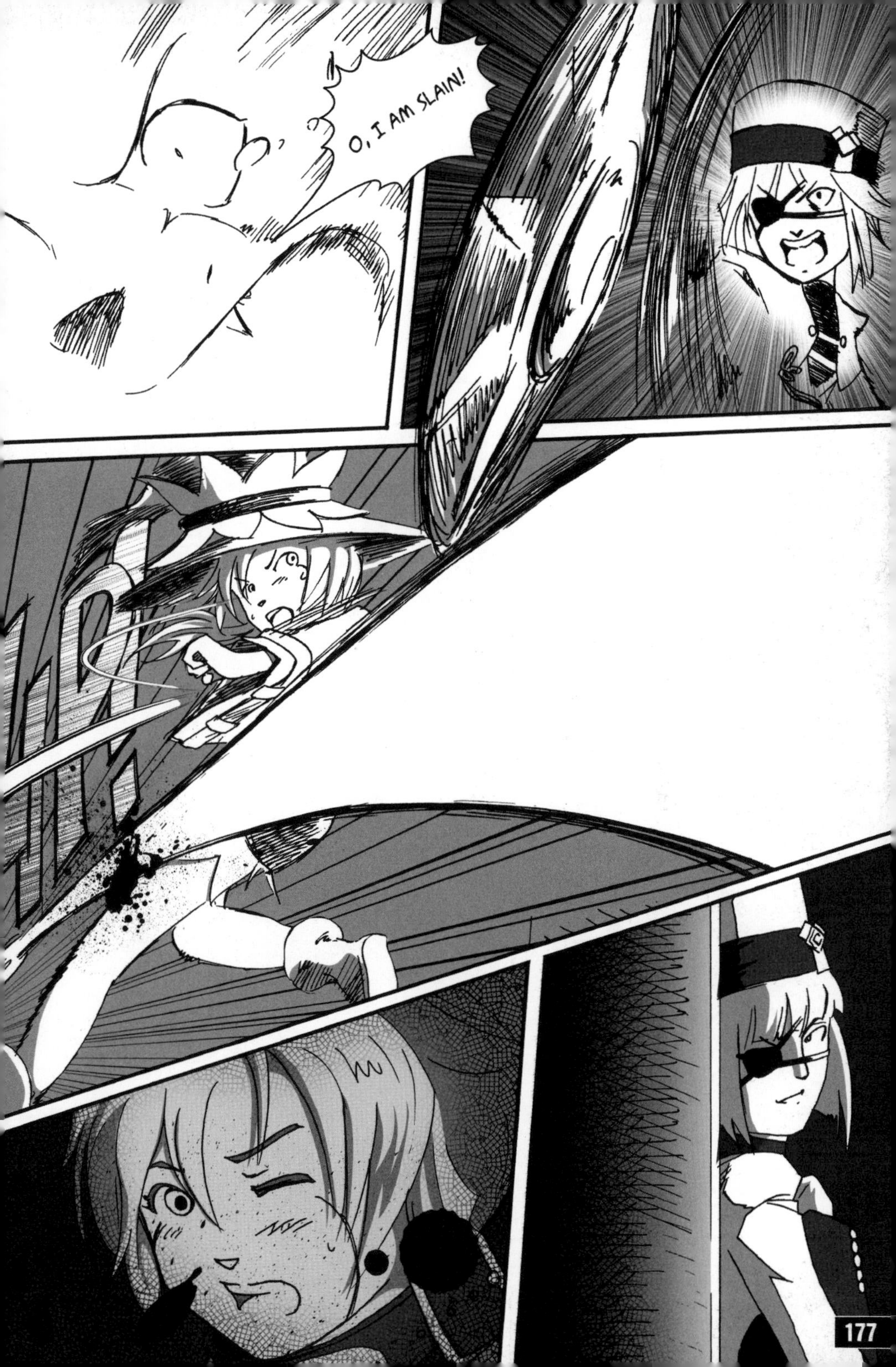
O, I AM SLAIN!

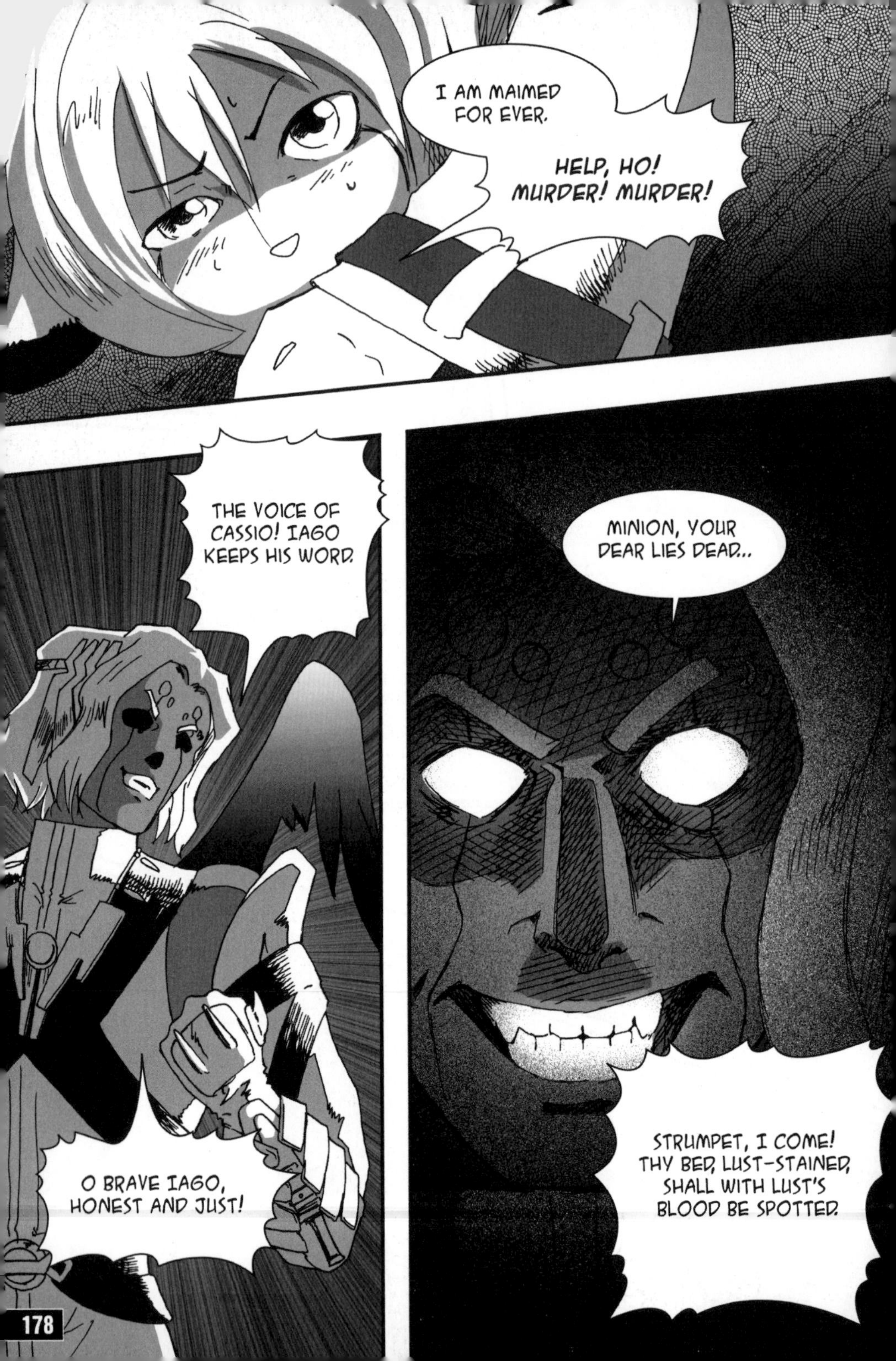
I AM MAIMED FOR EVER.
HELP, HO! MURDER! MURDER!
THE VOICE OF CASSIO! IAGO KEEPS HIS WORD.
O BRAVE IAGO, HONEST AND JUST!
MINION, YOUR DEAR LIES DEAD...
STRUMPET, I COME! THY BED, LUST-STAINED, SHALL WITH LUST'S BLOOD BE SPOTTED.

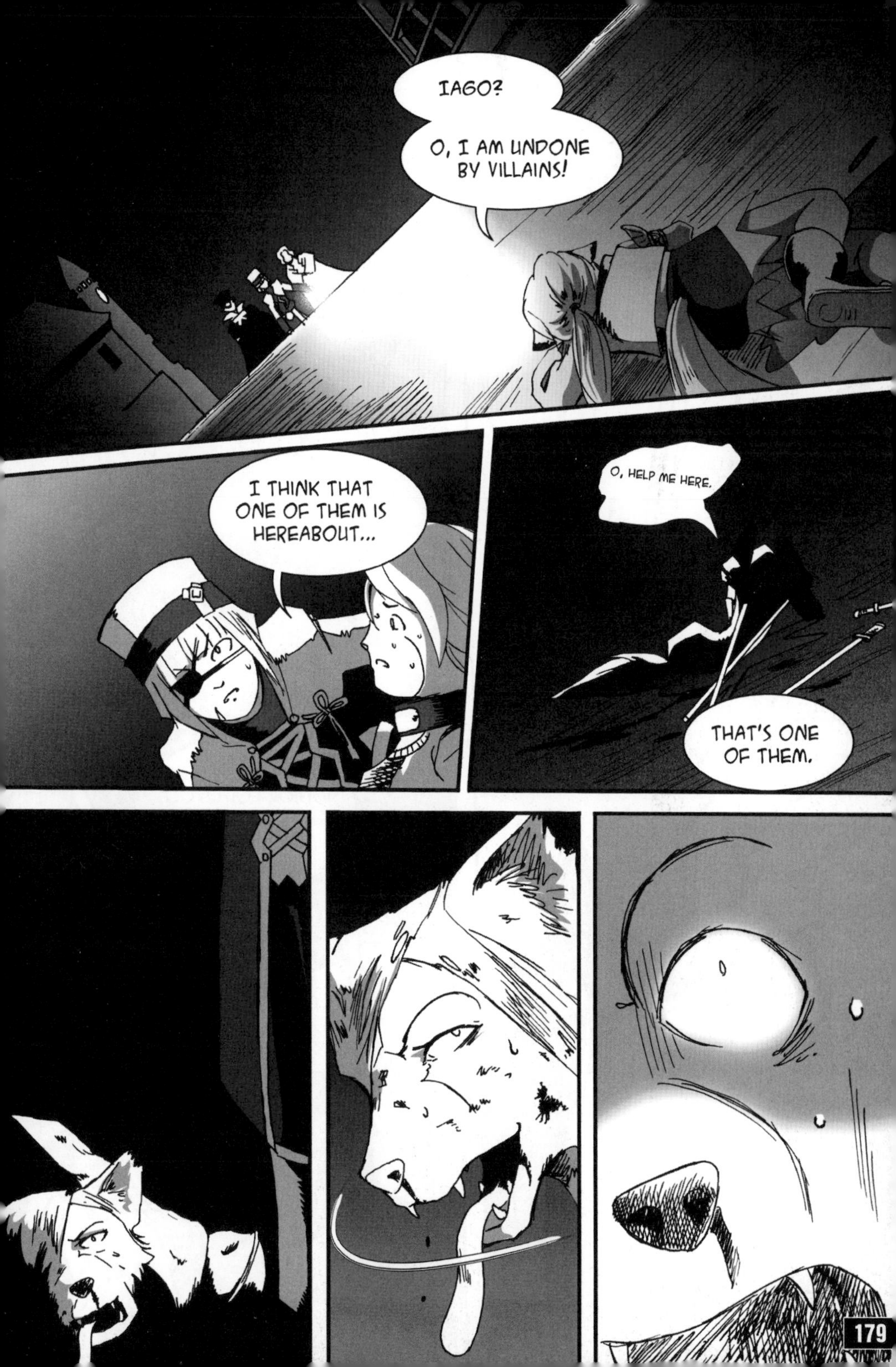
IAGO?
O, I AM UNDONE BY VILLAINS!
I THINK THAT ONE OF THEM IS HEREABOUT...
O, HELP ME HERE.
THAT'S ONE OF THEM.

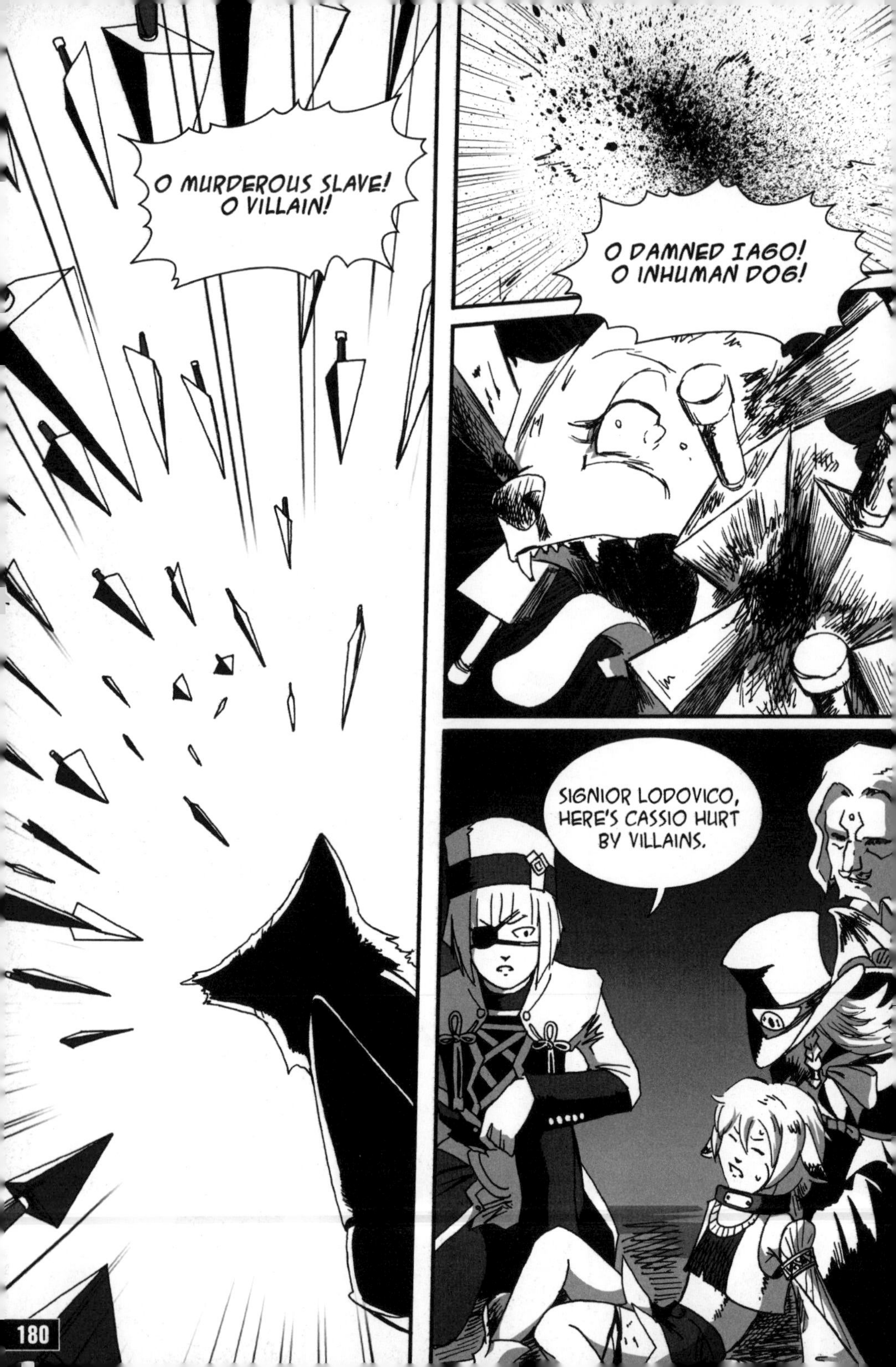
O MURDEROUS SLAVE! O VILLAIN!
O DAMNED IAGO! O INHUMAN DOG!
SIGNIOR LODOVICO, HERE'S CASSIO HURT BY VILLAINS.

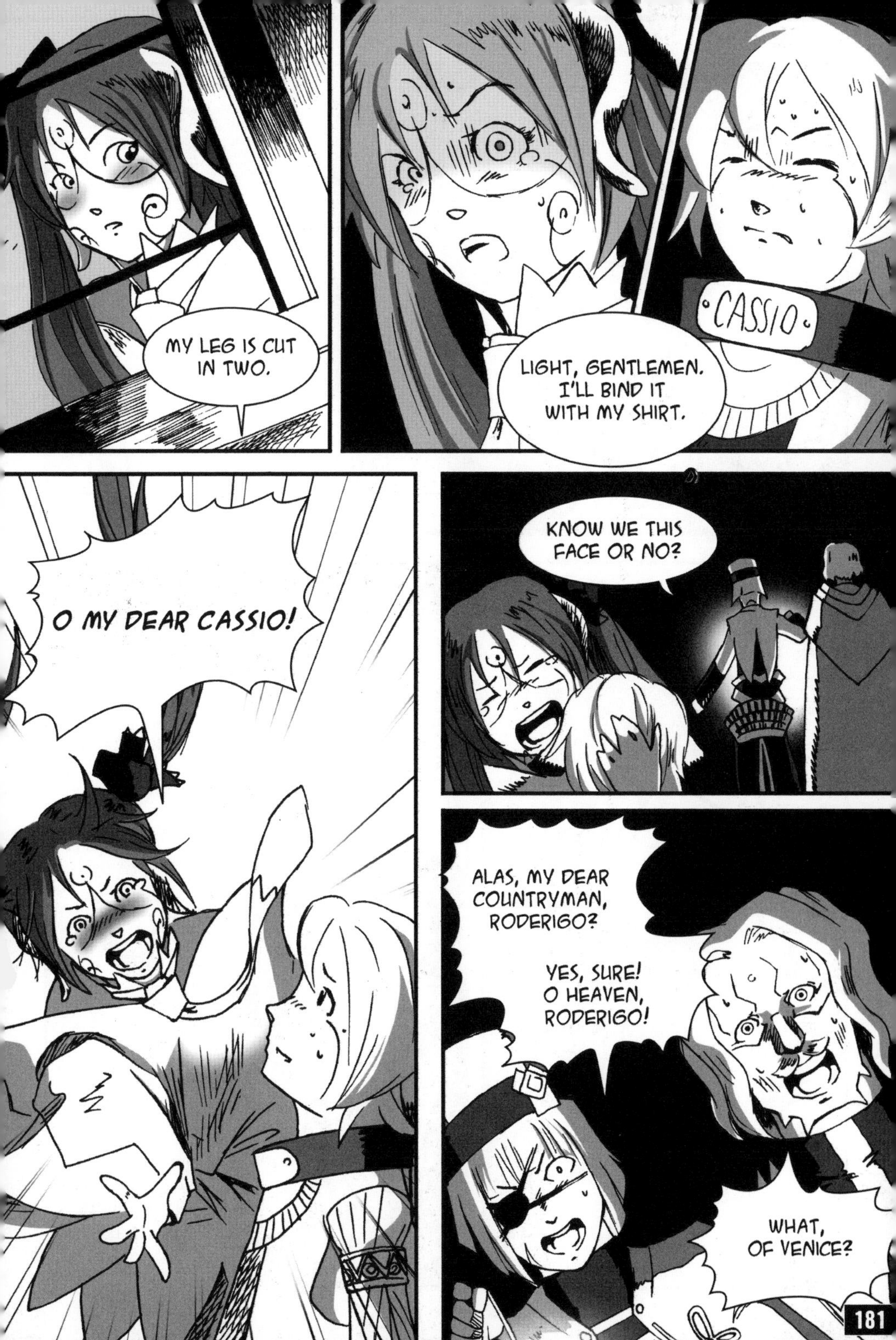
MY LEG IS CUT IN TWO.
LIGHT, GENTLEMEN. I'LL BIND IT WITH MY SHIRT.
CASSIO
O MY DEAR CASSIO!
KNOW WE THIS FACE OR NO?
ALAS, MY DEAR COUNTRYMAN, RODERIGO?
YES, SURE! O HEAVEN, RODERIGO!
WHAT, OF VENICE?

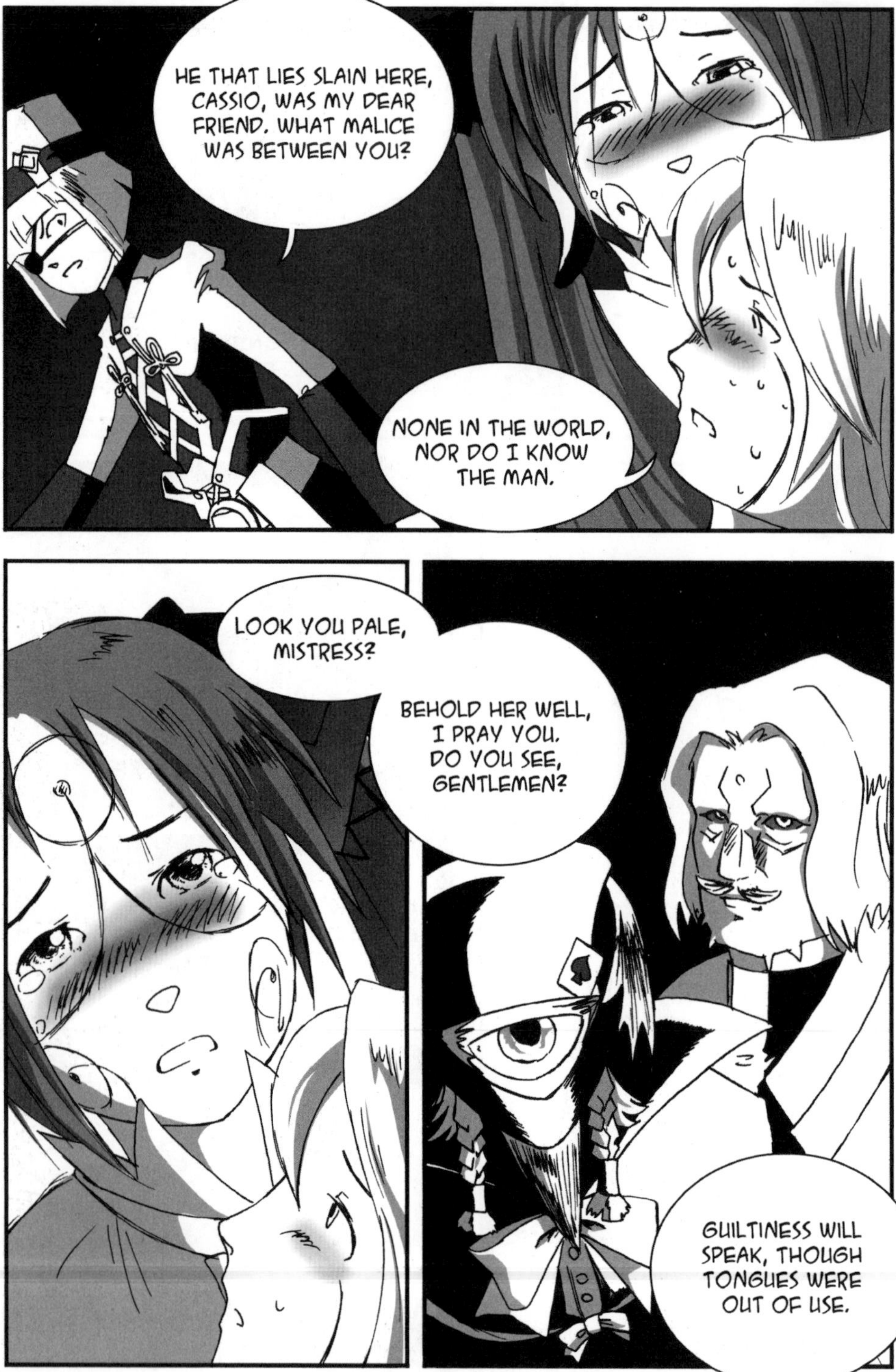
HE THAT LIES SLAIN HERE, CASSIO, WAS MY DEAR FRIEND. WHAT MALICE WAS BETWEEN YOU?
NONE IN THE WORLD, NOR DO I KNOW THE MAN.
LOOK YOU PALE, MISTRESS?
BEHOLD HER WELL, I PRAY YOU. DO YOU SEE, GENTLEMEN?
GUILTINESS WILL SPEAK, THOUGH TONGUES WERE OUT OF USE.

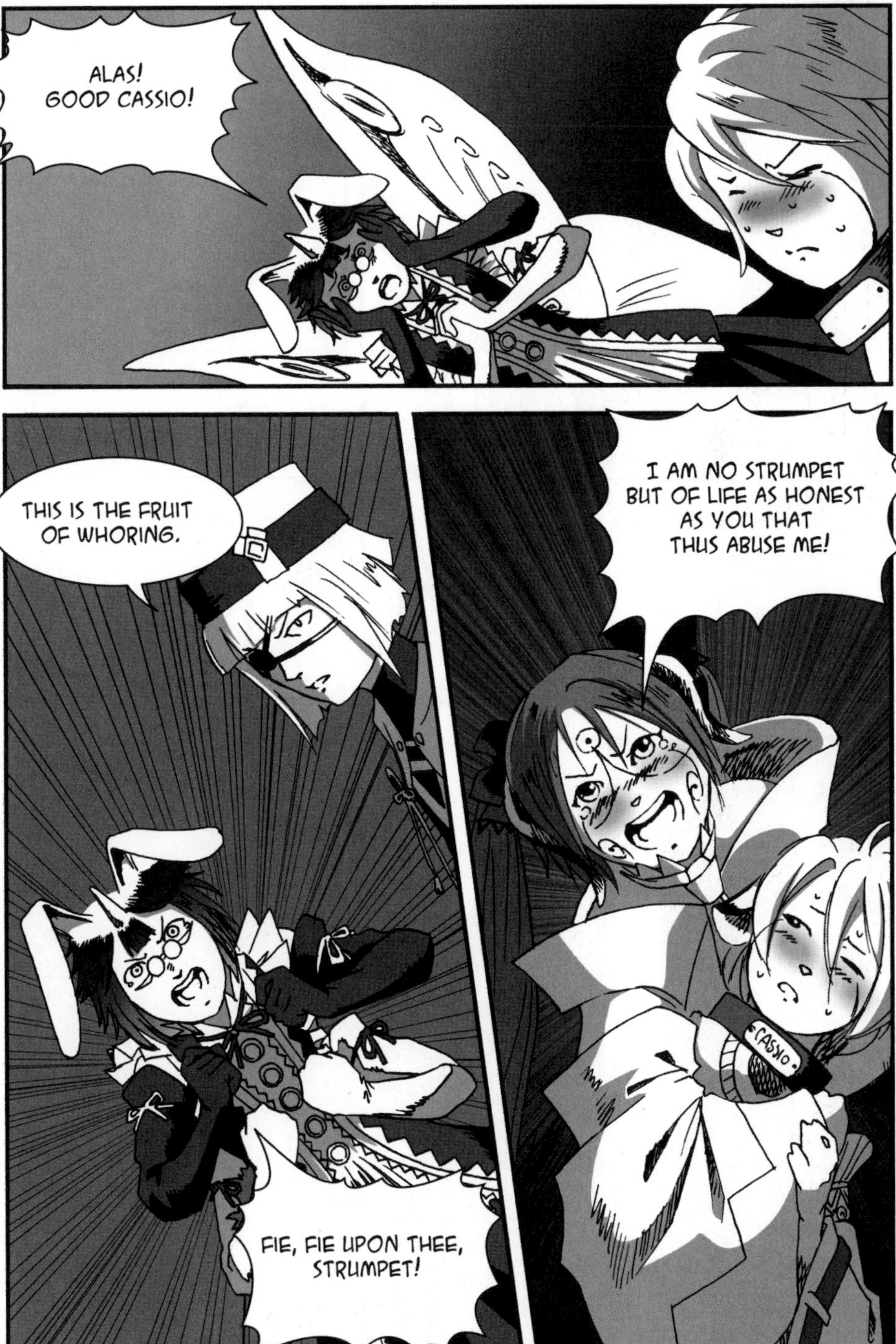
ALAS! GOOD CASSIO!
THIS IS THE FRUIT OF WHORING.
FIE, FIE UPON THEE, STRUMPET!
I AM NO STRUMPET BUT OF LIFE AS HONEST AS YOU THAT THUS ABUSE ME!
CASSIO

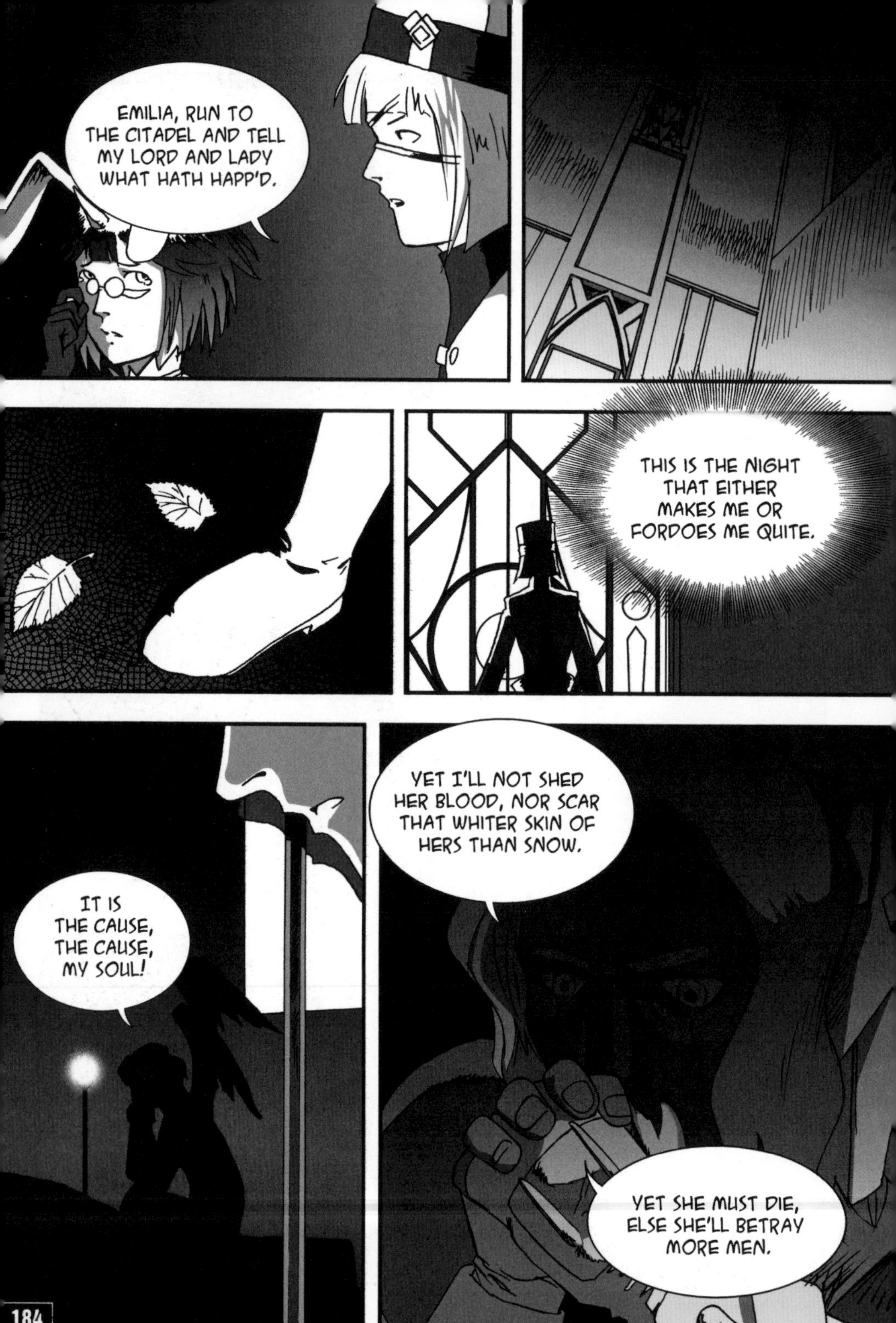
EMILIA, RUN TO THE CITADEL AND TELL MY LORD AND LADY WHAT HATH HAPP'D.
THIS IS THE NIGHT THAT EITHER MAKES ME OR FORDOES ME QUITE.
IT IS THE CAUSE, THE CAUSE, MY SOUL!
YET I'LL NOT SHED HER BLOOD, NOR SCAR THAT WHITER SKIN OF HERS THAN SNOW.
YET SHE MUST DIE, ELSE SHE'LL BETRAY MORE MEN.

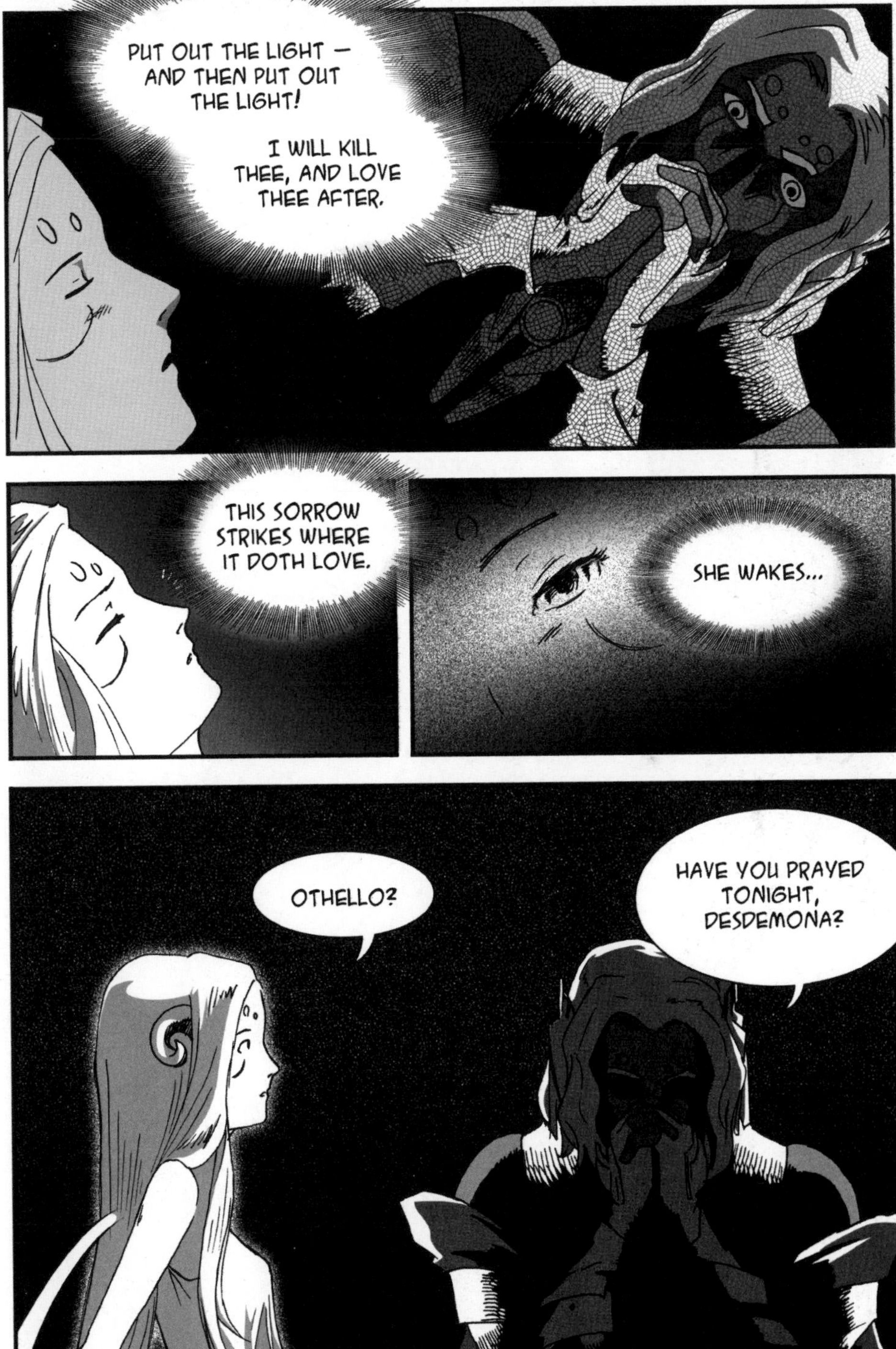
PUT OUT THE LIGHT — AND THEN PUT OUT THE LIGHT!
I WILL KILL THEE, AND LOVE THEE AFTER.
THIS SORROW STRIKES WHERE IT DOTH LOVE.
SHE WAKES...
OTHELLO?
HAVE YOU PRAYED TONIGHT, DESDEMONA?

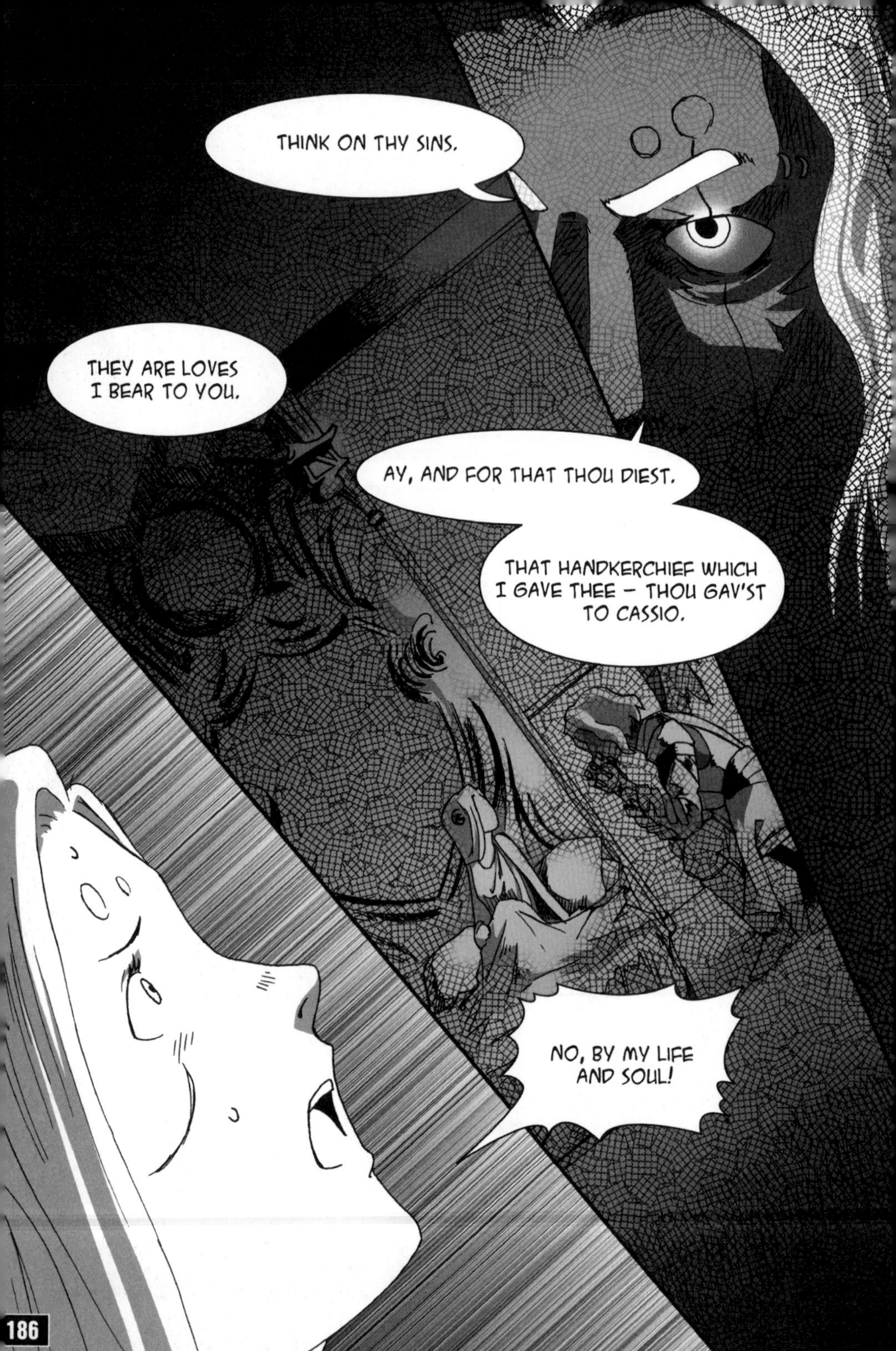
THINK ON THY SINS.
THEY ARE LOVES I BEAR TO YOU.
AY, AND FOR THAT THOU DIEST.
THAT HANDKERCHIEF WHICH I GAVE THEE - THOU GAV'ST TO CASSIO.
NO, BY MY LIFE AND SOUL!

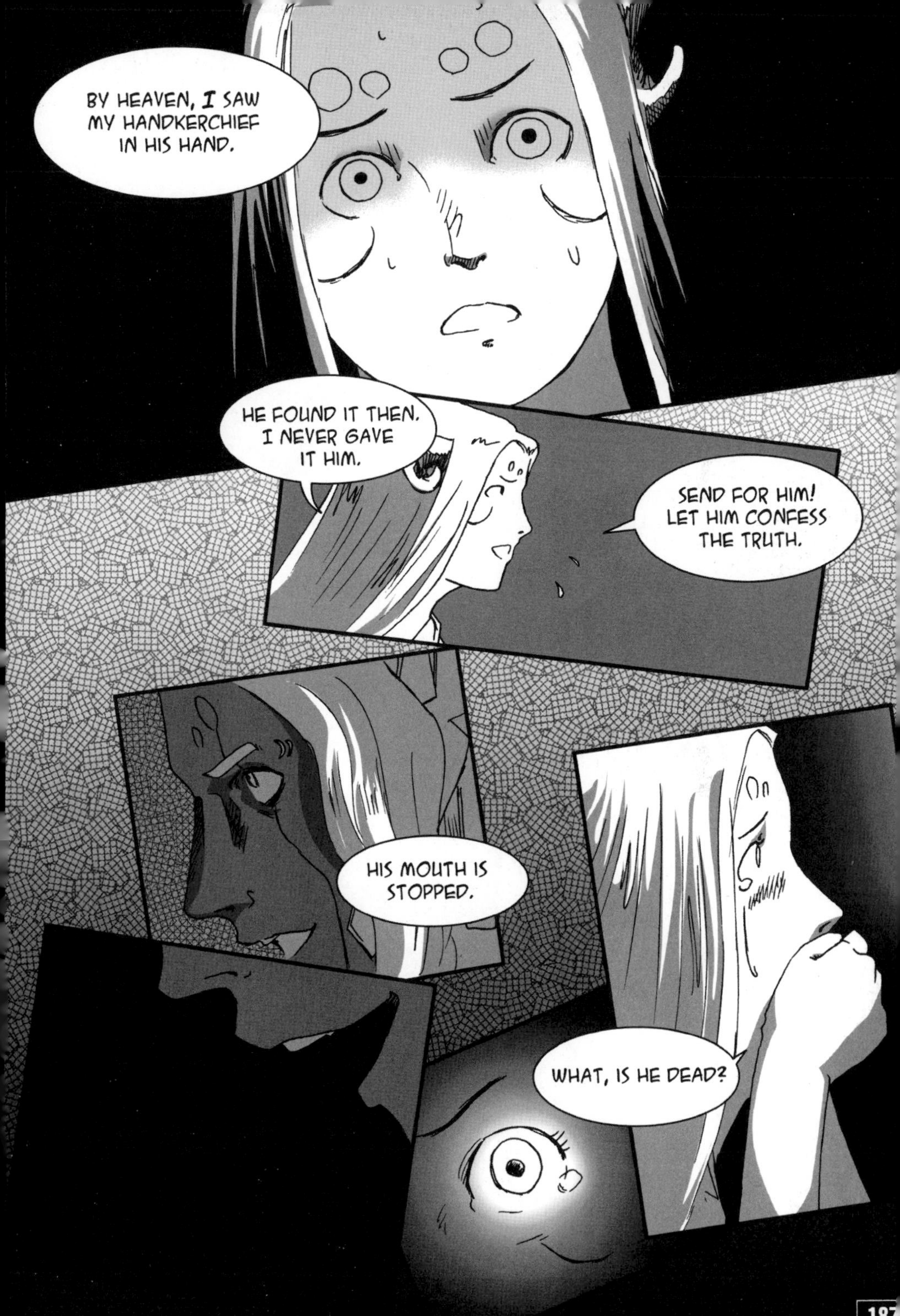
BY HEAVEN, I SAW MY HANDKERCHIEF IN HIS HAND.
HE FOUND IT THEN. I NEVER GAVE IT HIM.
SEND FOR HIM! LET HIM CONFESS THE TRUTH.
HIS MOUTH IS STOPPED.
WHAT, IS HE DEAD?

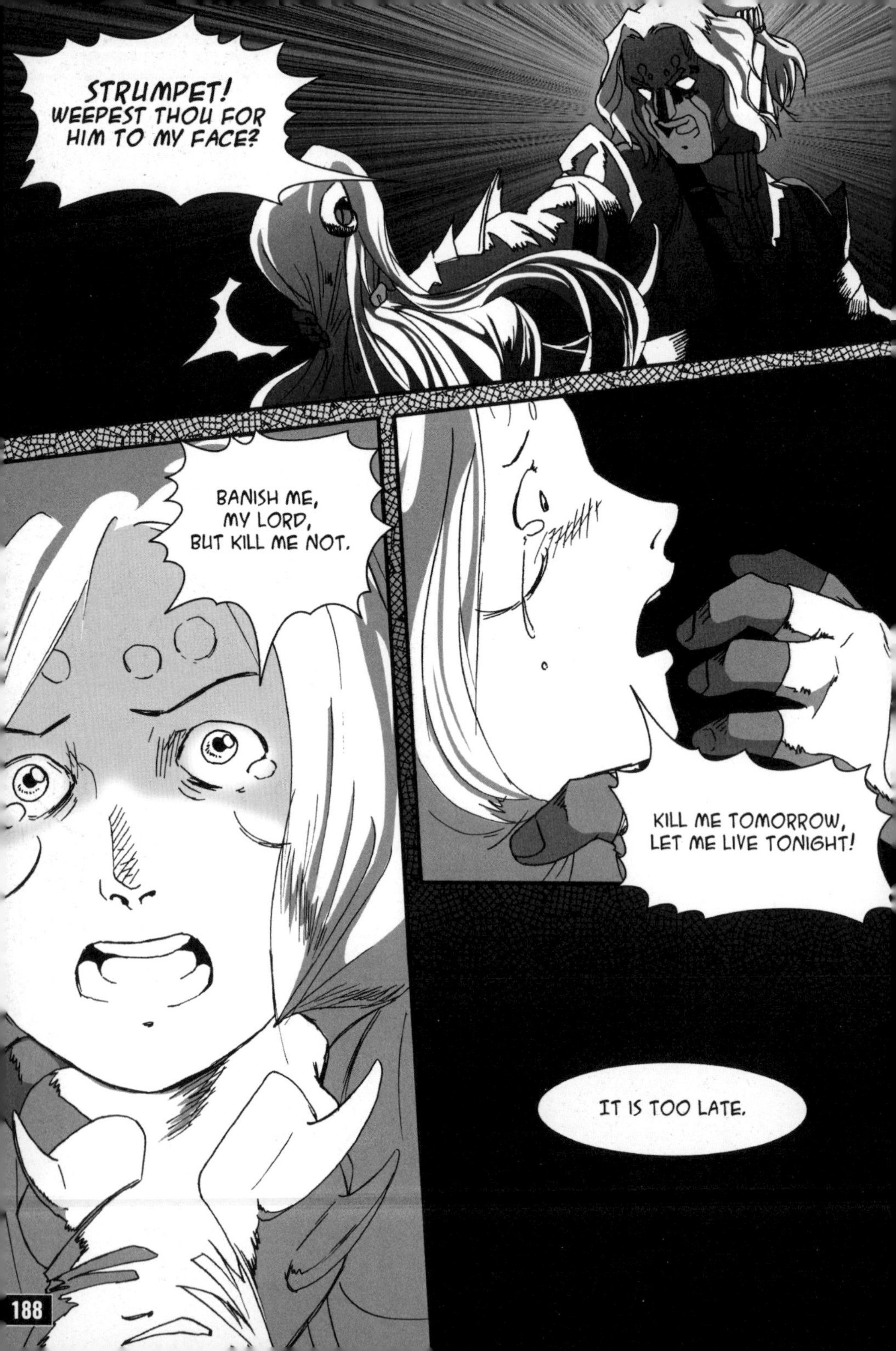
STRUMPET! WEEPEST THOU FOR HIM TO MY FACE?
BANISH ME, MY LORD, BUT KILL ME NOT.
KILL ME TOMORROW, LET ME LIVE TONIGHT!
IT IS TOO LATE.

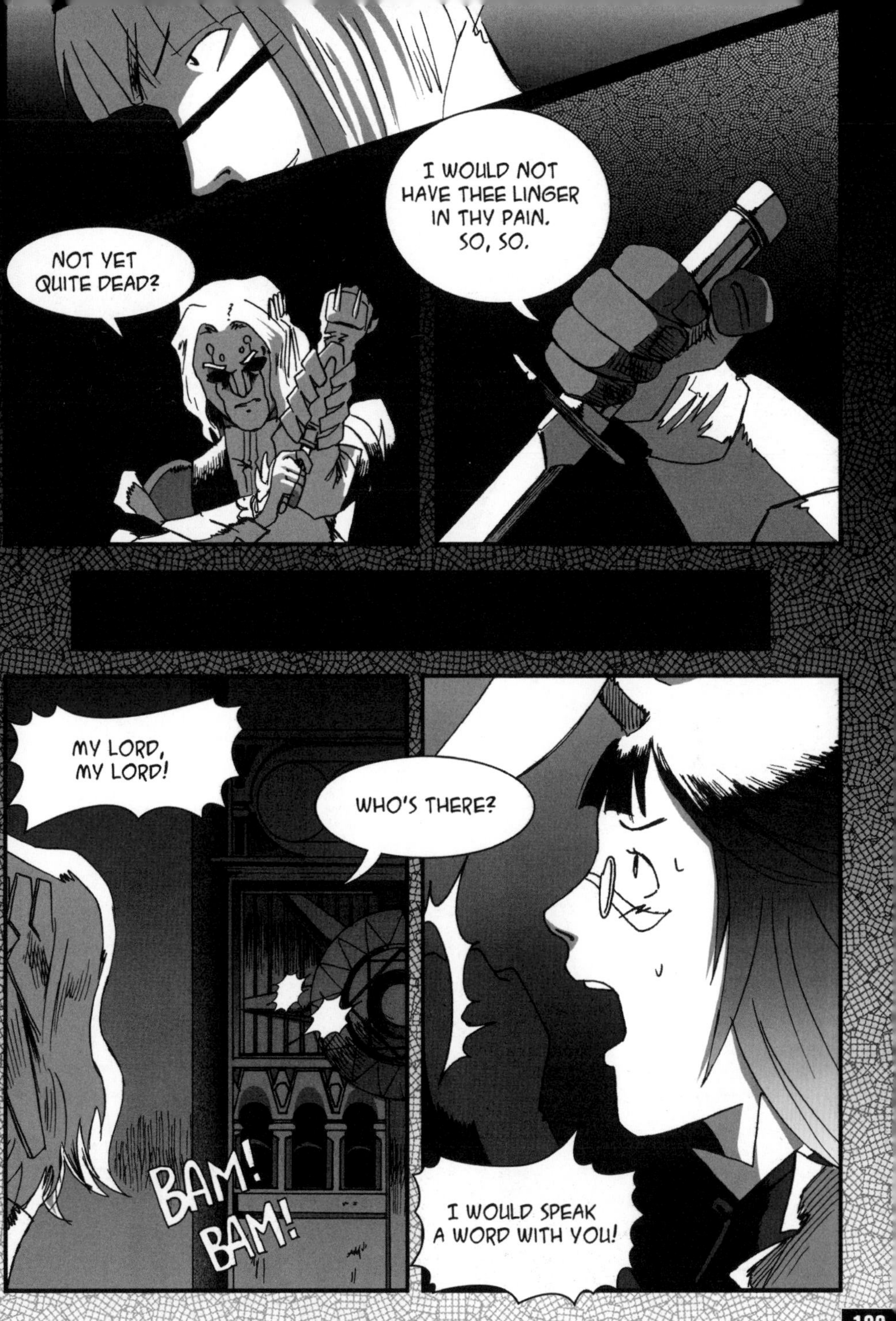
I WOULD NOT HAVE THEE LINGER IN THY PAIN. SO, SO.
NOT YET QUITE DEAD?
MY LORD, MY LORD!
WHO'S THERE?
I WOULD SPEAK A WORD WITH YOU!
BAM! BAM!

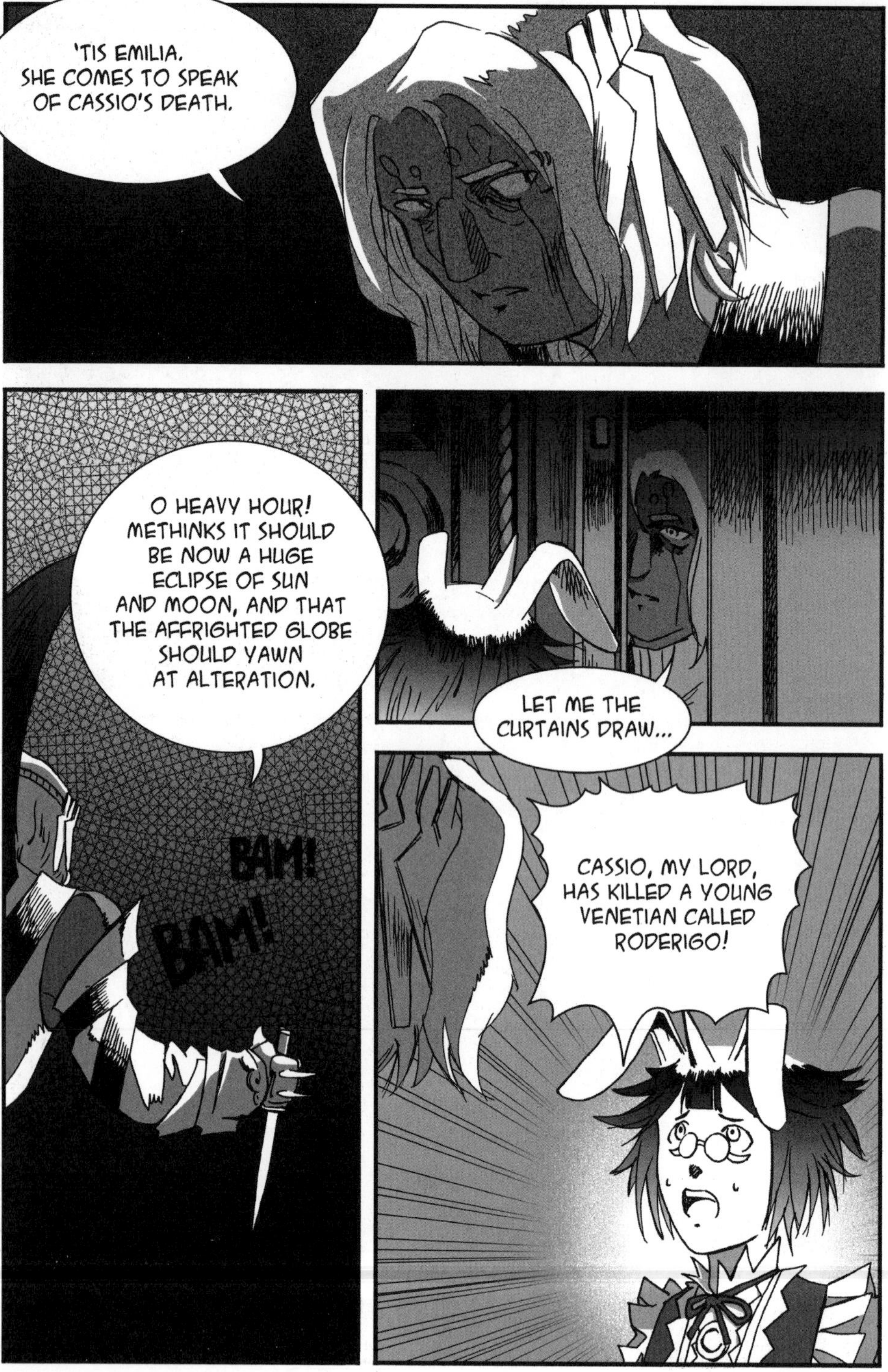
'TIS EMILIA. SHE COMES TO SPEAK OF CASSIO'S DEATH.
O HEAVY HOUR! METHINKS IT SHOULD BE NOW A HUGE ECLIPSE OF SUN AND MOON, AND THAT THE AFFRIGHTED GLOBE SHOULD YAWN AT ALTERATION.
BAM!
BAM!
LET ME THE CURTAINS DRAW...
CASSIO, MY LORD, HAS KILLED A YOUNG VENETIAN CALLED RODERIGO!

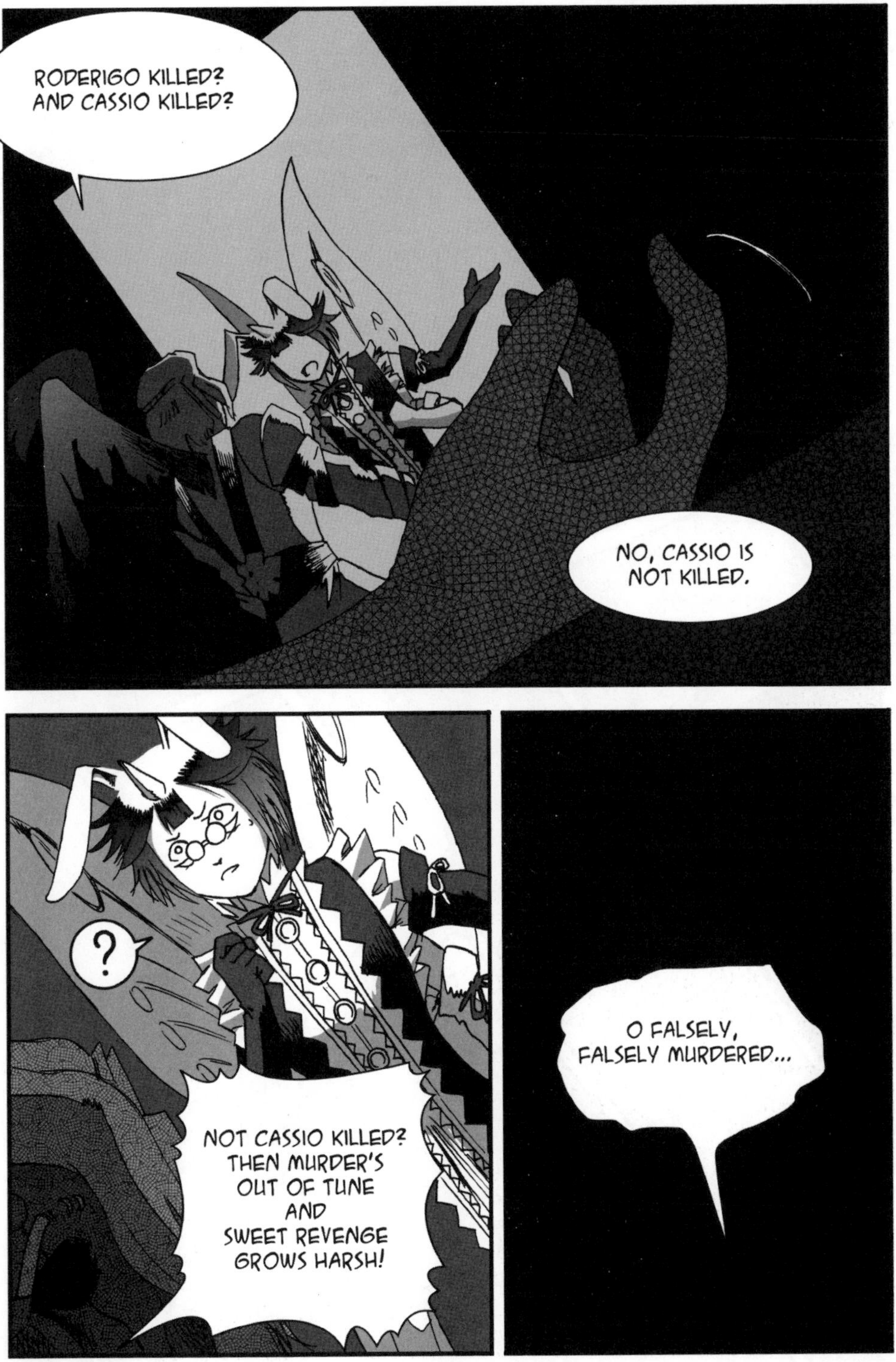

RODERIGO KILLED? AND CASSIO KILLED?
NO, CASSIO IS NOT KILLED.
?
NOT CASSIO KILLED? THEN MURDER'S OUT OF TUNE AND SWEET REVENGE GROWS HARSH!
O FALSELY, FALSELY MURDERED...

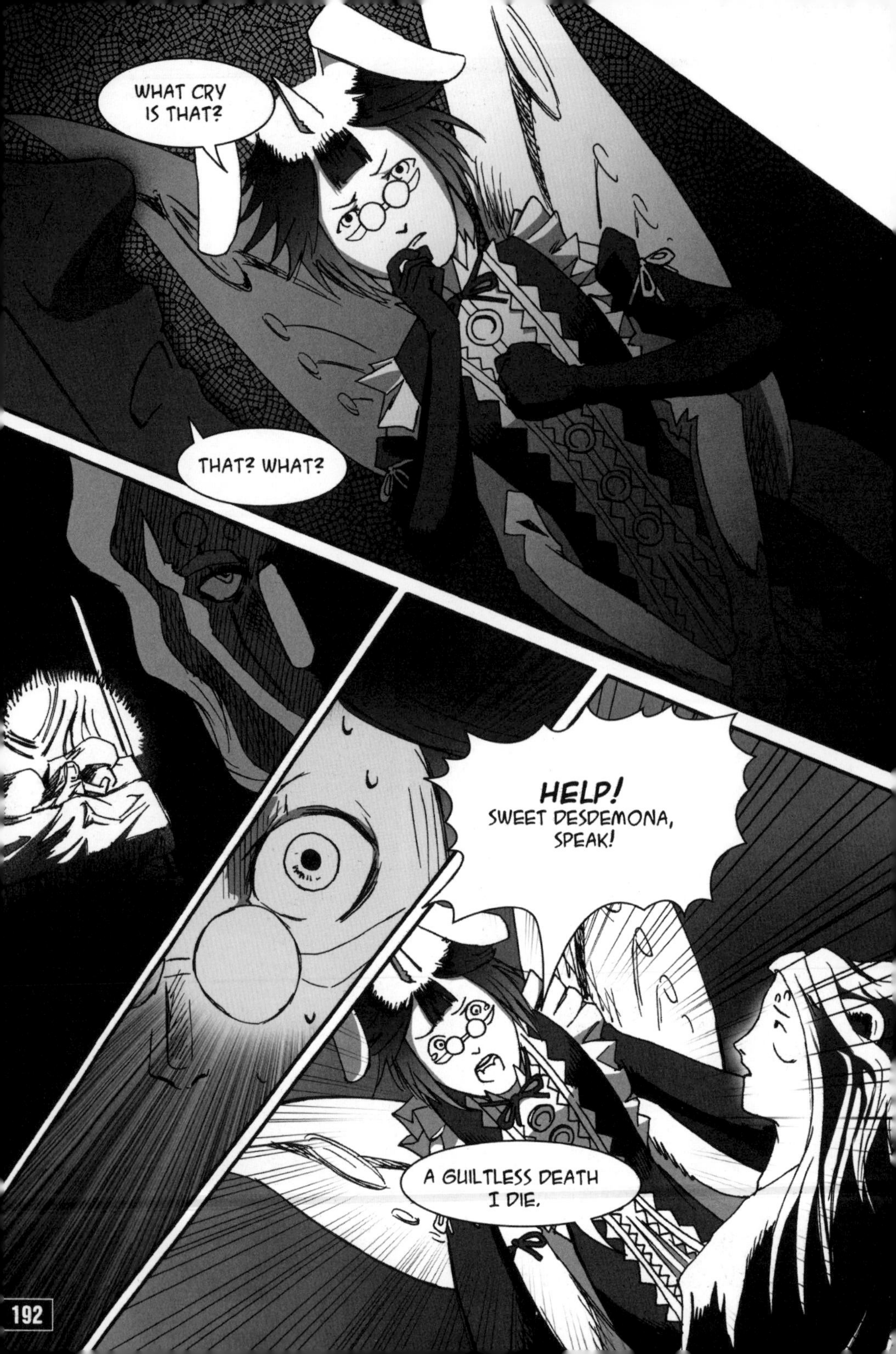
WHAT CRY IS THAT?
THAT? WHAT?
HELP! SWEET DESDEMONA, SPEAK!
A GUILTLESS DEATH I DIE.

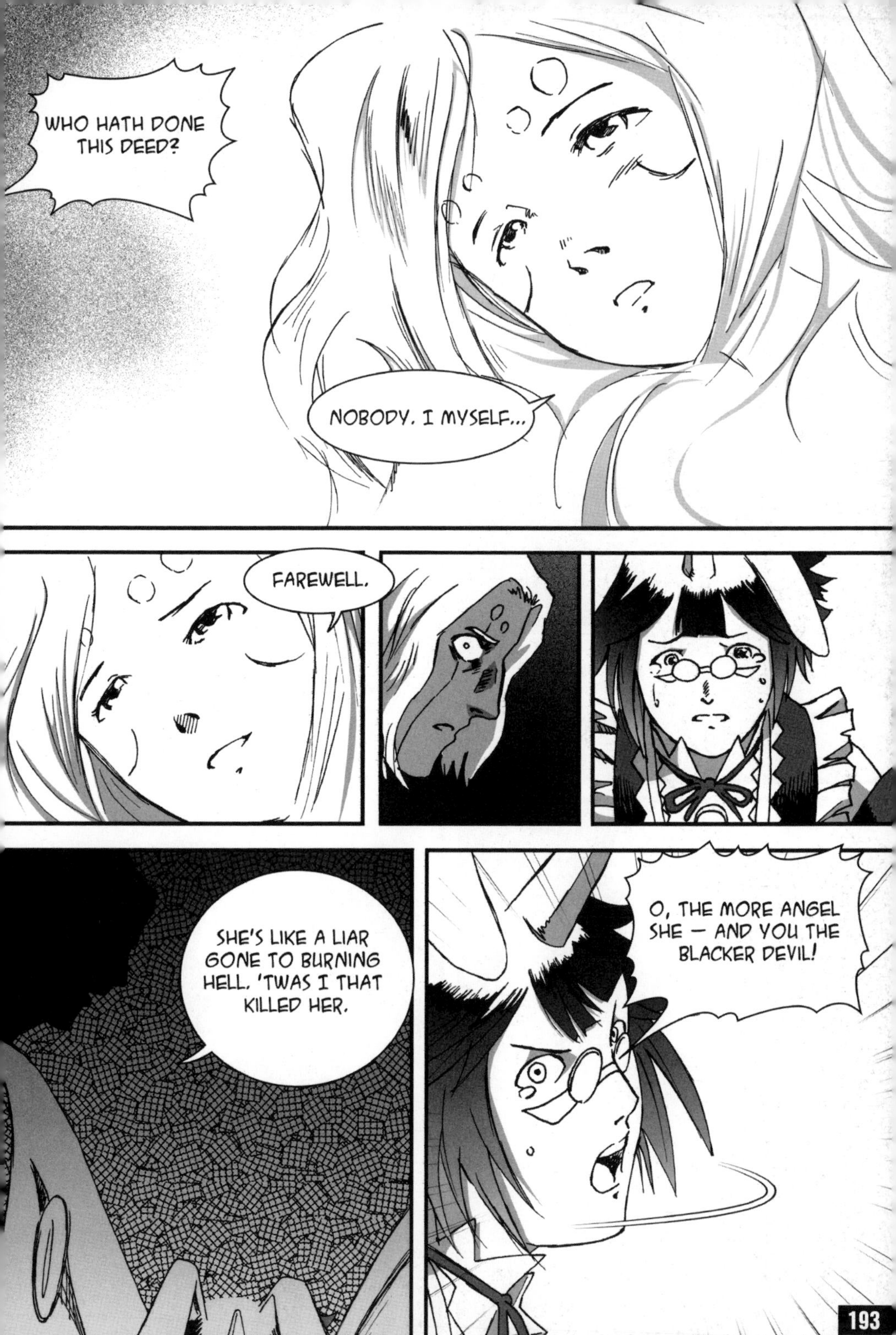
WHO HATH DONE THIS DEED?
NOBODY. I MYSELF...
FAREWELL.
SHE'S LIKE A LIAR GONE TO BURNING HELL. 'TWAS I THAT KILLED HER.
O, THE MORE ANGEL SHE — AND YOU THE BLACKER DEVIL!

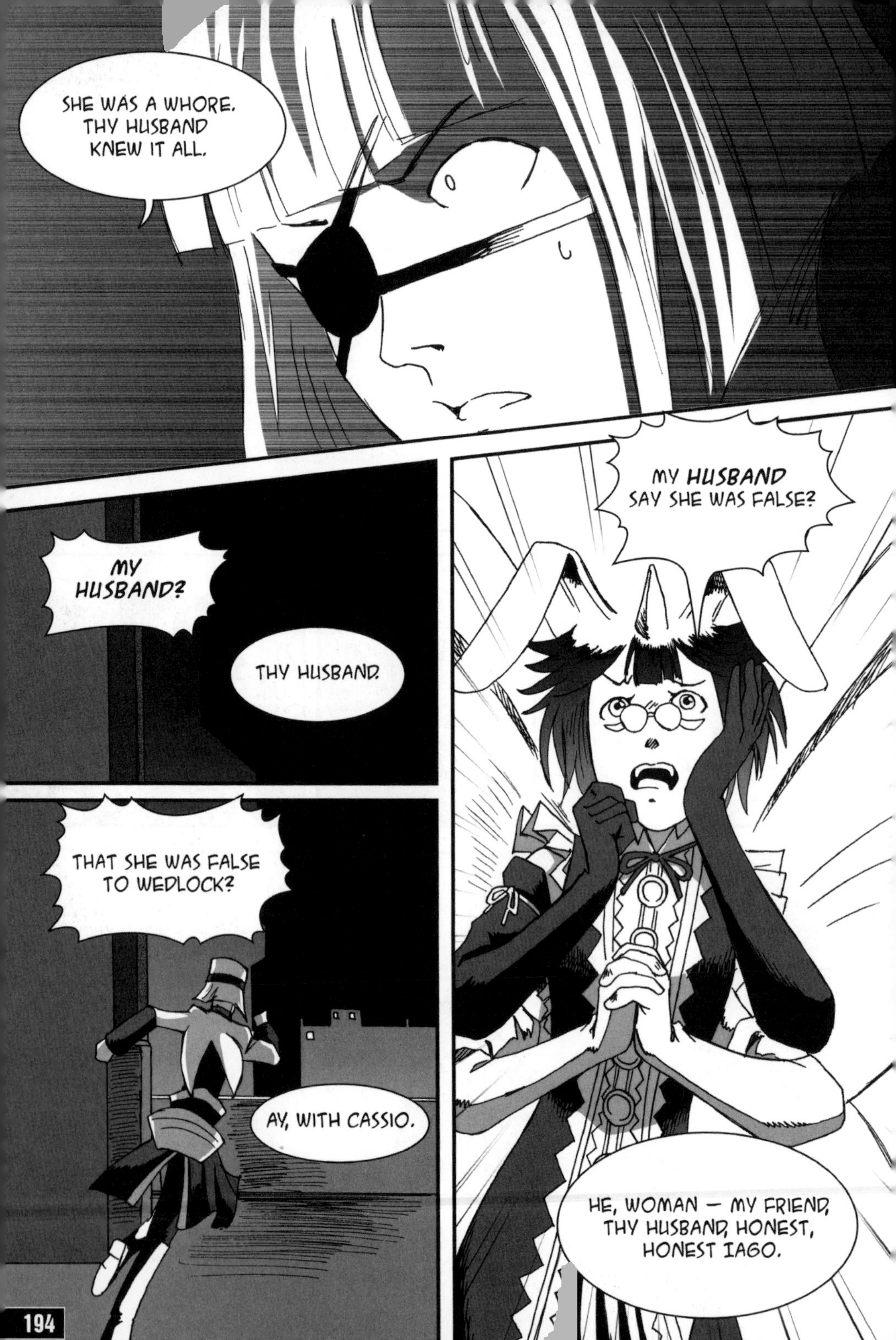

SHE WAS A WHORE. THY HUSBAND KNEW IT ALL.
MY HUSBAND?
THY HUSBAND.
MY HUSBAND SAY SHE WAS FALSE?
THAT SHE WAS FALSE TO WEDLOCK?
AY, WITH CASSIO.
HE, WOMAN — MY FRIEND, THY HUSBAND, HONEST, HONEST IAGO.

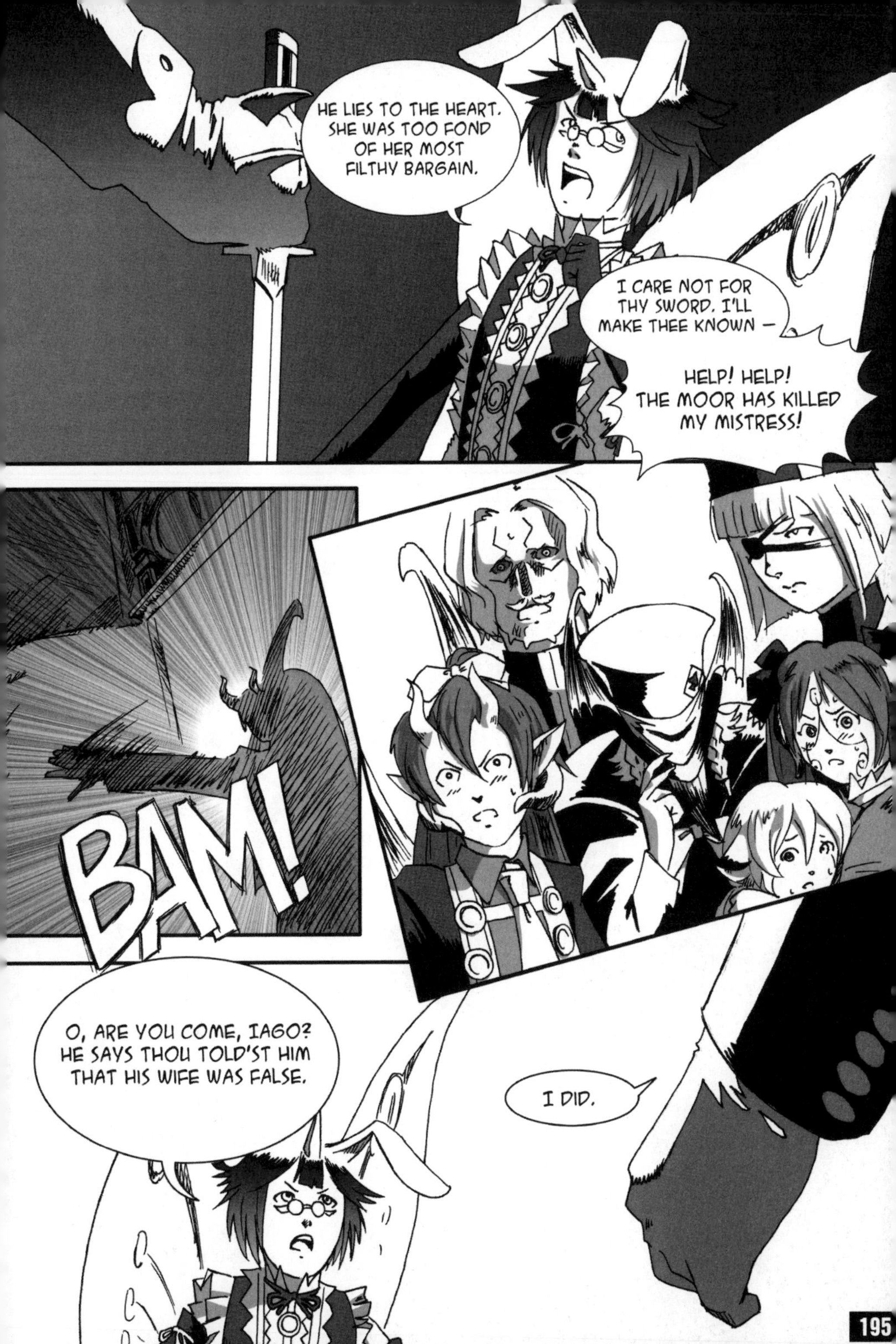
HE LIES TO THE HEART. SHE WAS TOO FOND OF HER MOST FILTHY BARGAIN.
I CARE NOT FOR THY SWORD. I'LL MAKE THEE KNOWN —
HELP! HELP! THE MOOR HAS KILLED MY MISTRESS!
BAM!
O, ARE YOU COME, IAGO? HE SAYS THOU TOLD'ST HIM THAT HIS WIFE WAS FALSE.
I DID.

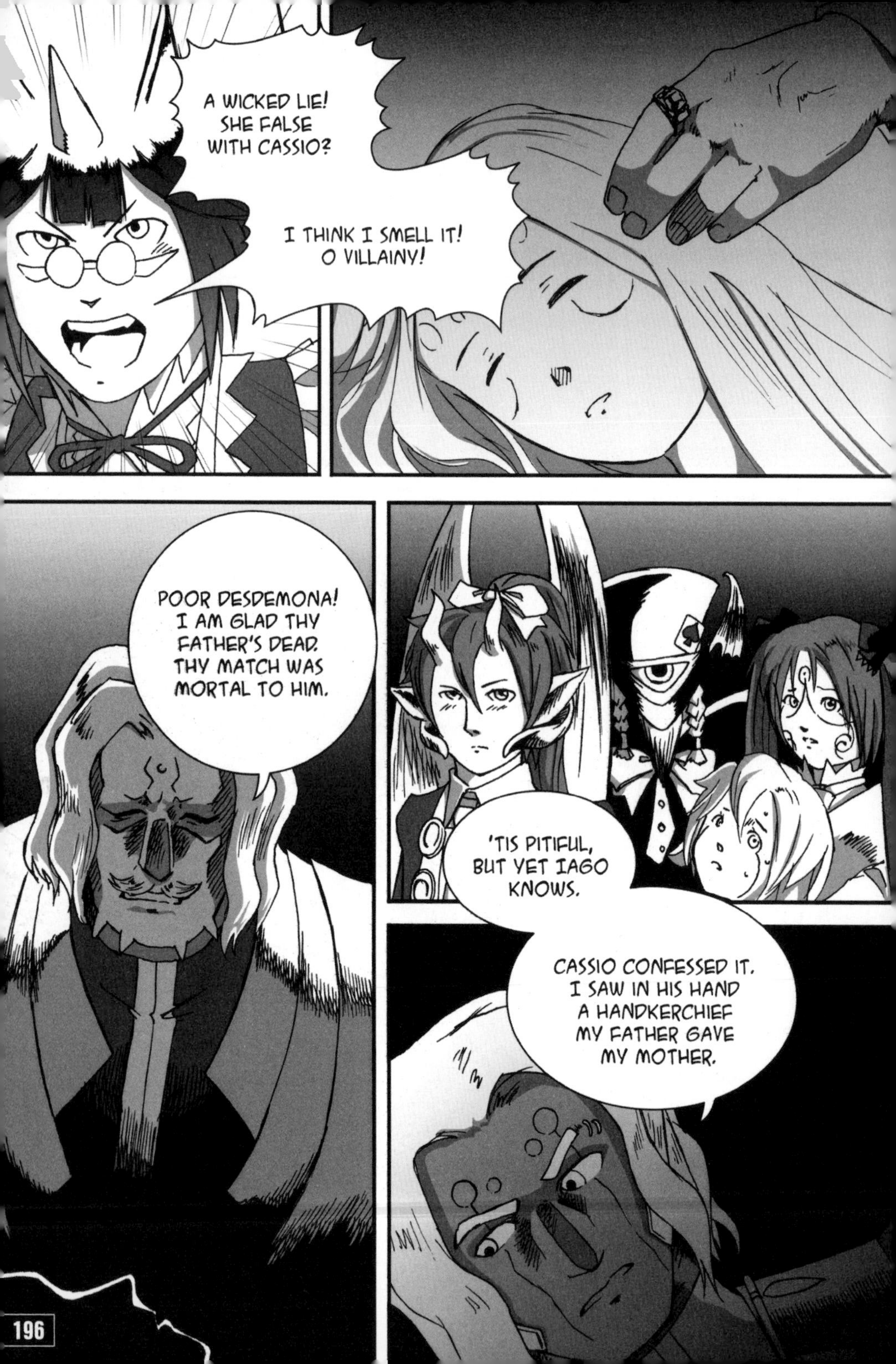
A WICKED LIE! SHE FALSE WITH CASSIO?
I THINK I SMELL IT! O VILLAINY!
POOR DESDEMONA! I AM GLAD THY FATHER'S DEAD. THY MATCH WAS MORTAL TO HIM.
'TIS PITIFUL, BUT YET IAGO KNOWS.
CASSIO CONFESSED IT. I SAW IN HIS HAND A HANDKERCHIEF MY FATHER GAVE MY MOTHER.

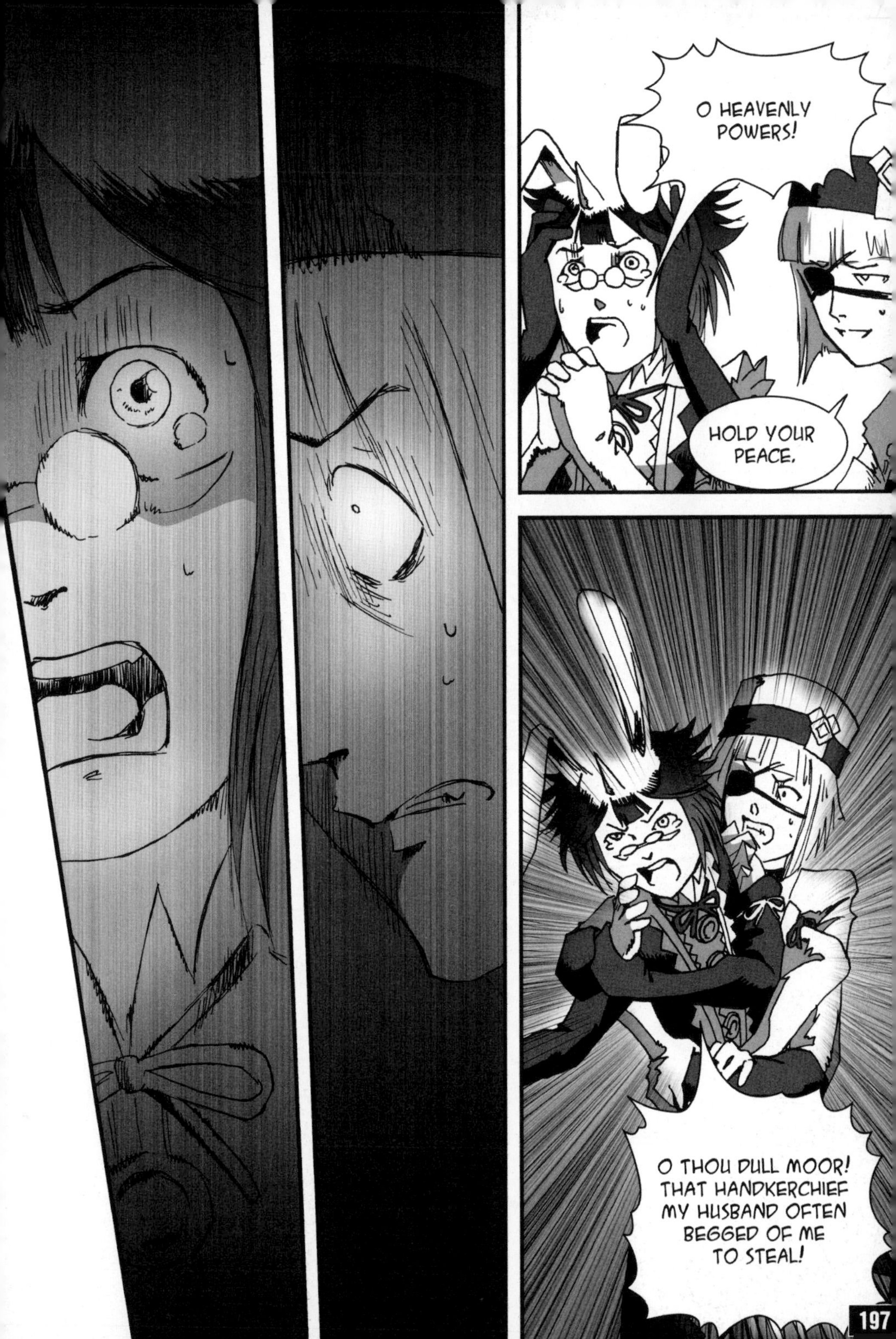
O HEAVENLY POWERS!
HOLD YOUR PEACE.
O THOU DULL MOOR! THAT HANDKERCHIEF MY HUSBAND OFTEN BEGGED OF ME TO STEAL!

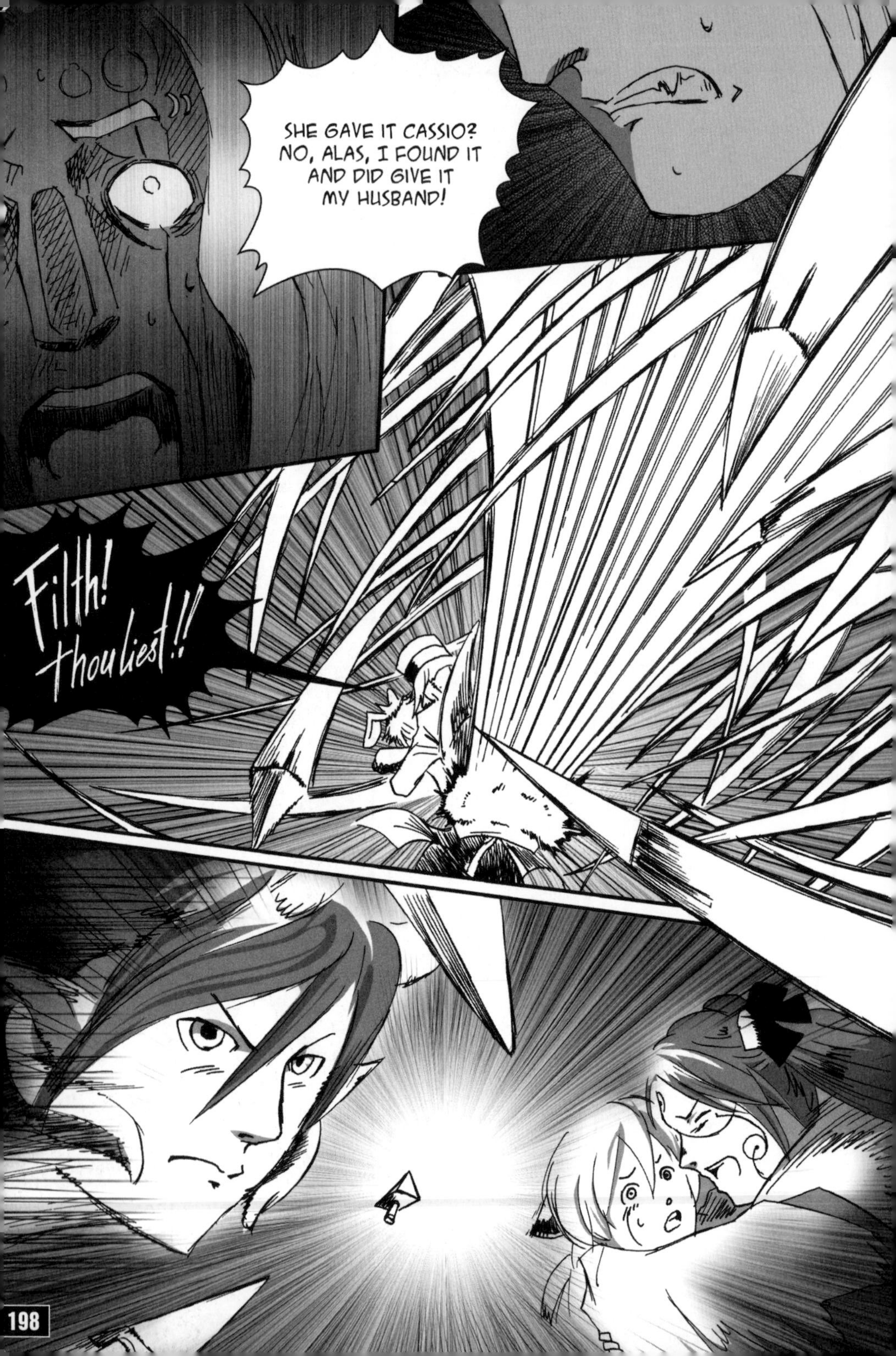
SHE GAVE IT CASSIO? NO, ALAS, I FOUND IT AND DID GIVE IT MY HUSBAND!
Filth! thou liest!!

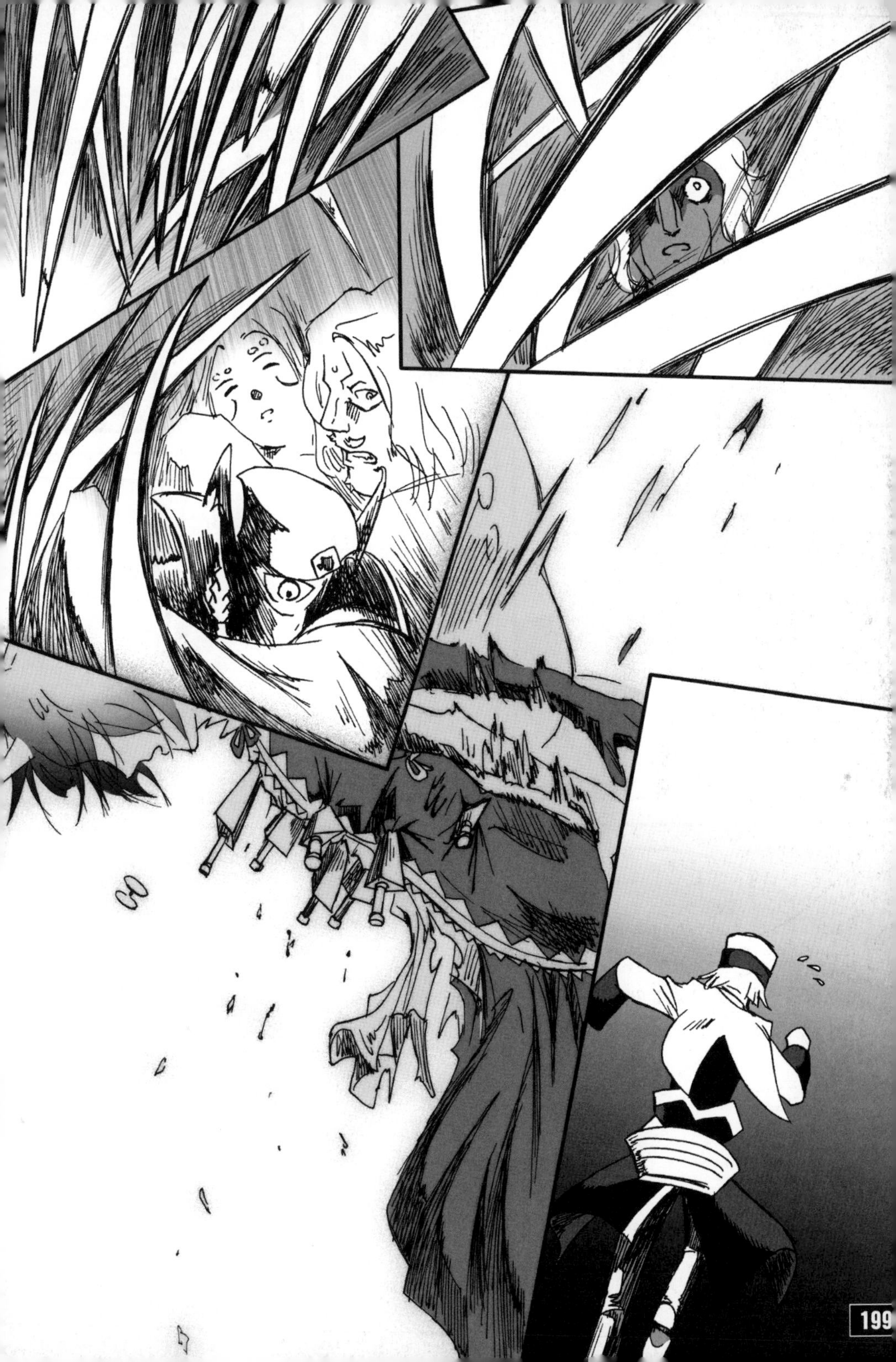

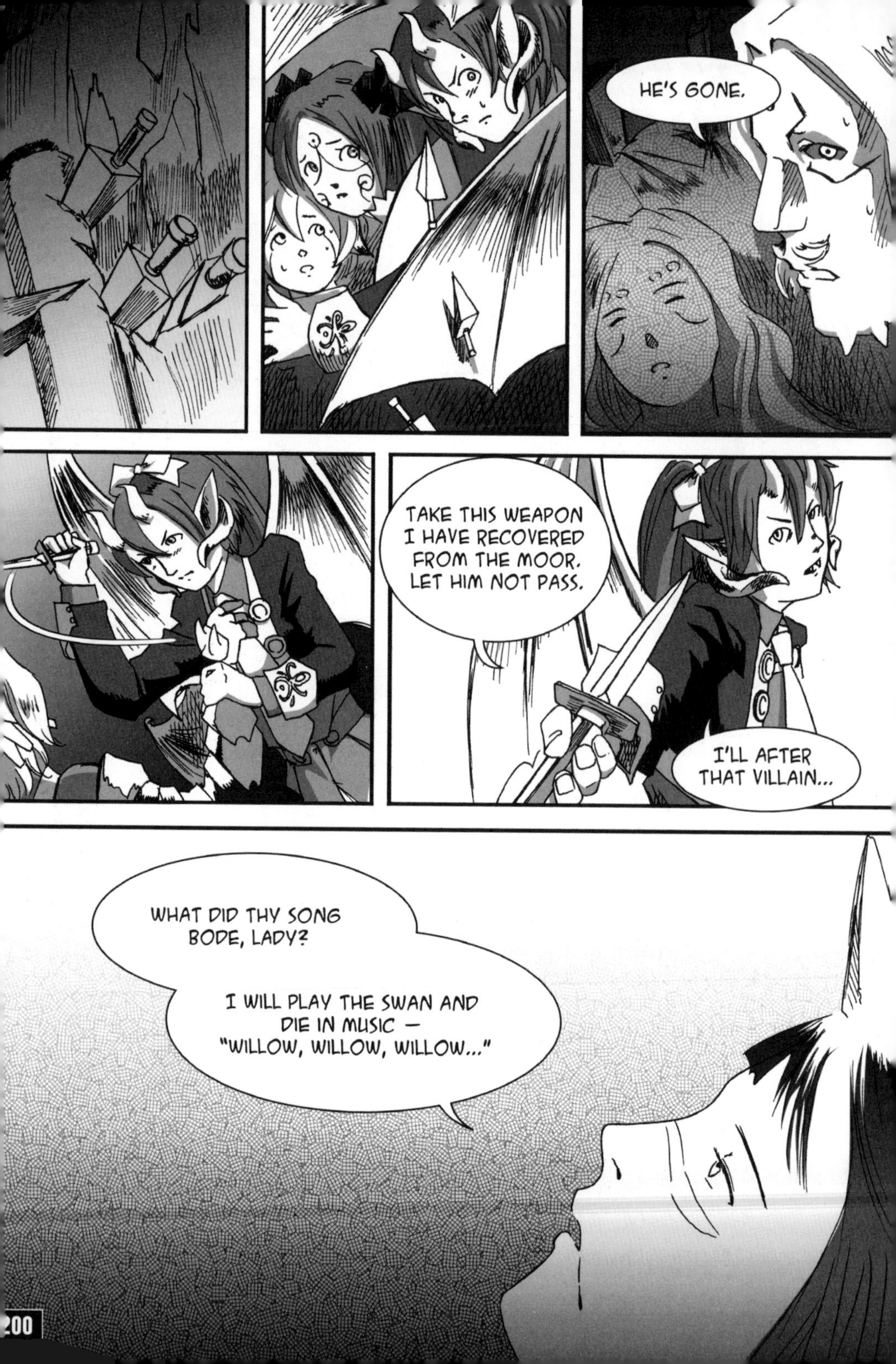
HE'S GONE.
TAKE THIS WEAPON I HAVE RECOVERED FROM THE MOOR. LET HIM NOT PASS.
I'LL AFTER THAT VILLAIN...
WHAT DID THY SONG BODE, LADY?
I WILL PLAY THE SWAN AND DIE IN MUSIC — "WILLOW, WILLOW, WILLOW..."

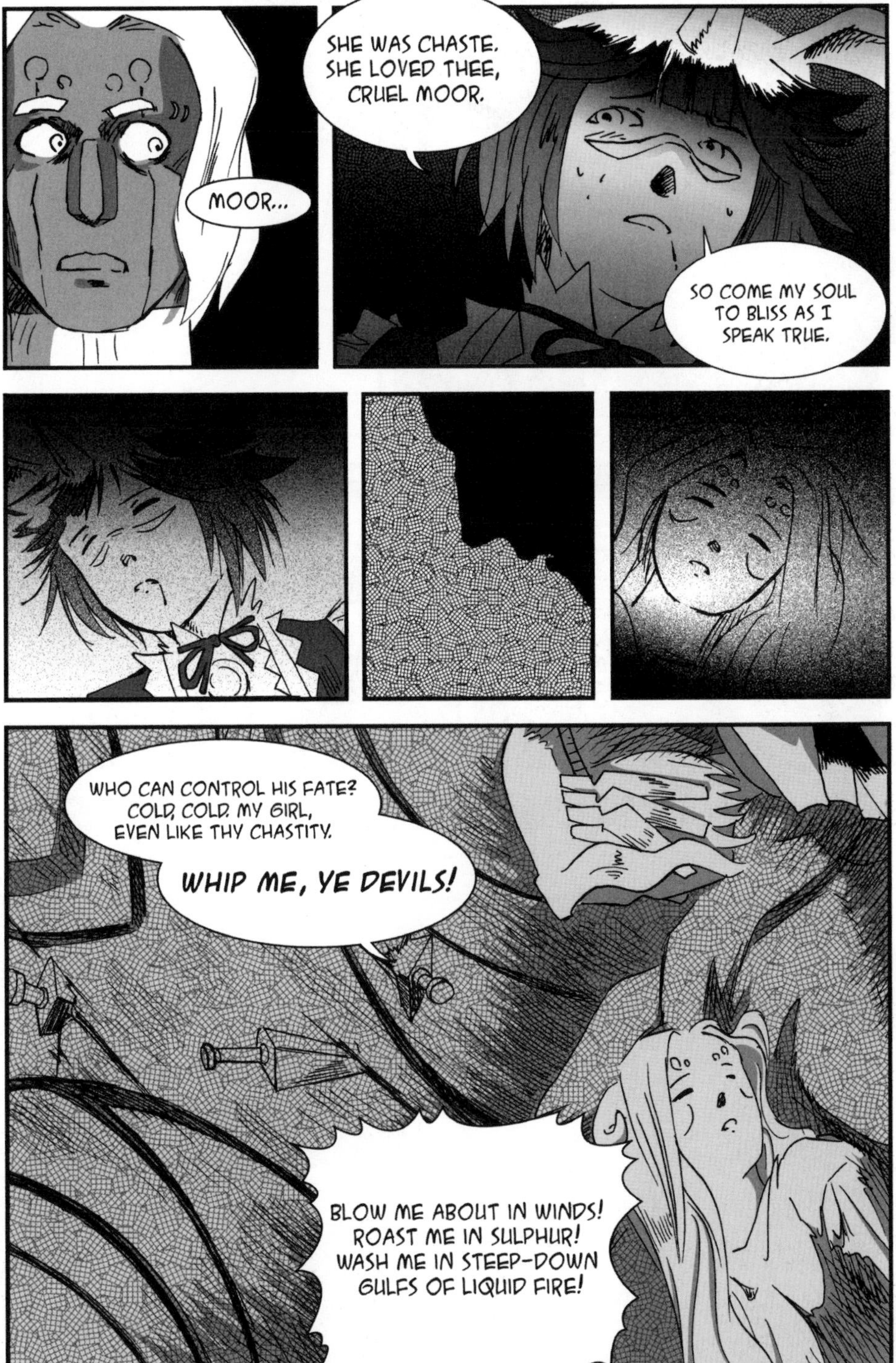
SHE WAS CHASTE. SHE LOVED THEE, CRUEL MOOR.
MOOR...
SO COME MY SOUL TO BLISS AS I SPEAK TRUE.
WHO CAN CONTROL HIS FATE? COLD, COLD, MY GIRL, EVEN LIKE THY CHASTITY.
WHIP ME, YE DEVILS!
BLOW ME ABOUT IN WINDS! ROAST ME IN SULPHUR! WASH ME IN STEEP-DOWN GULFS OF LIQUID FIRE!

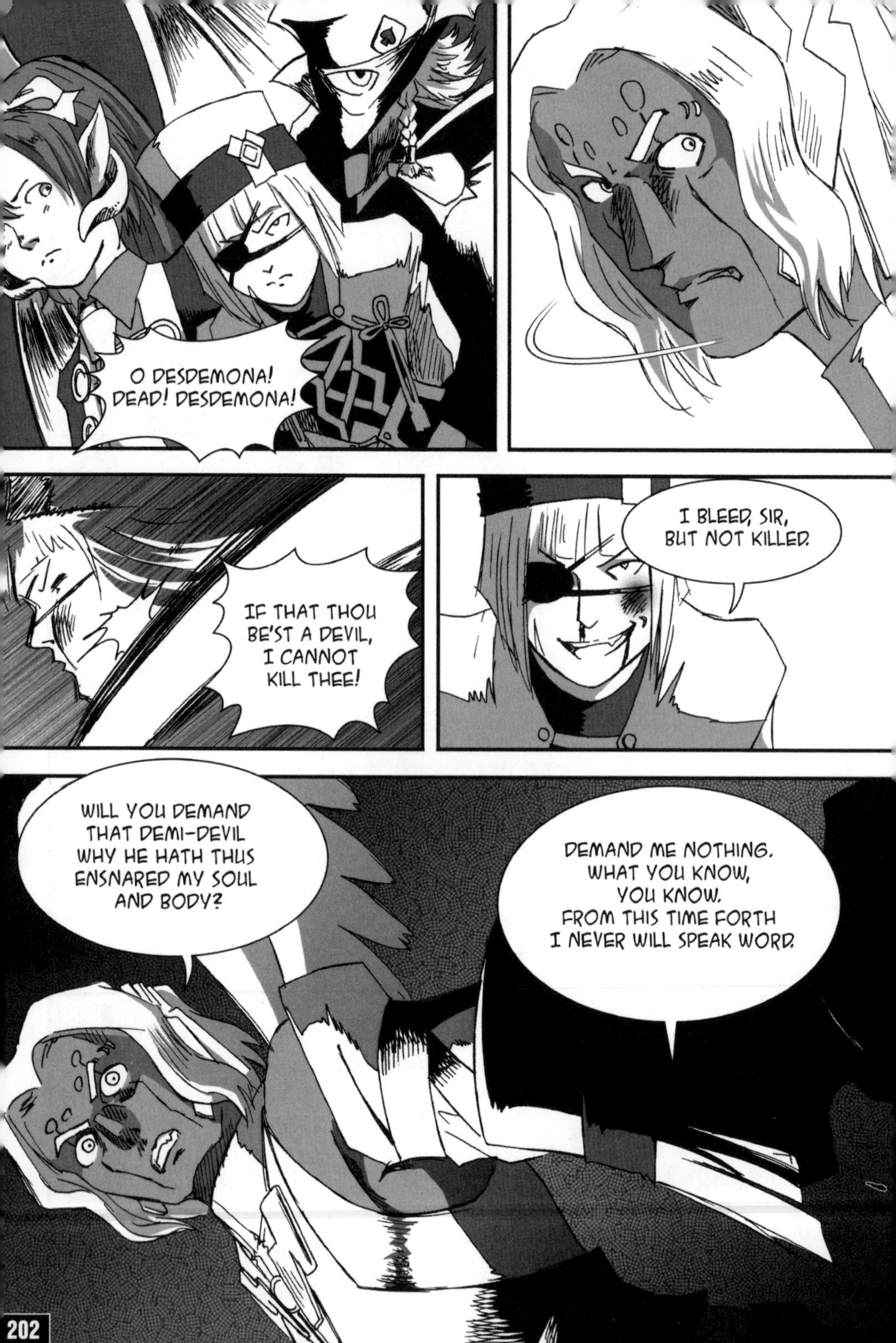
O DESDEMONA! DEAD! DESDEMONA!
IF THAT THOU BE'ST A DEVIL, I CANNOT KILL THEE!
I BLEED, SIR, BUT NOT KILLED.
WILL YOU DEMAND THAT DEMI-DEVIL WHY HE HATH THUS ENSNARED MY SOUL AND BODY?
DEMAND ME NOTHING. WHAT YOU KNOW, YOU KNOW. FROM THIS TIME FORTH I NEVER WILL SPEAK WORD.

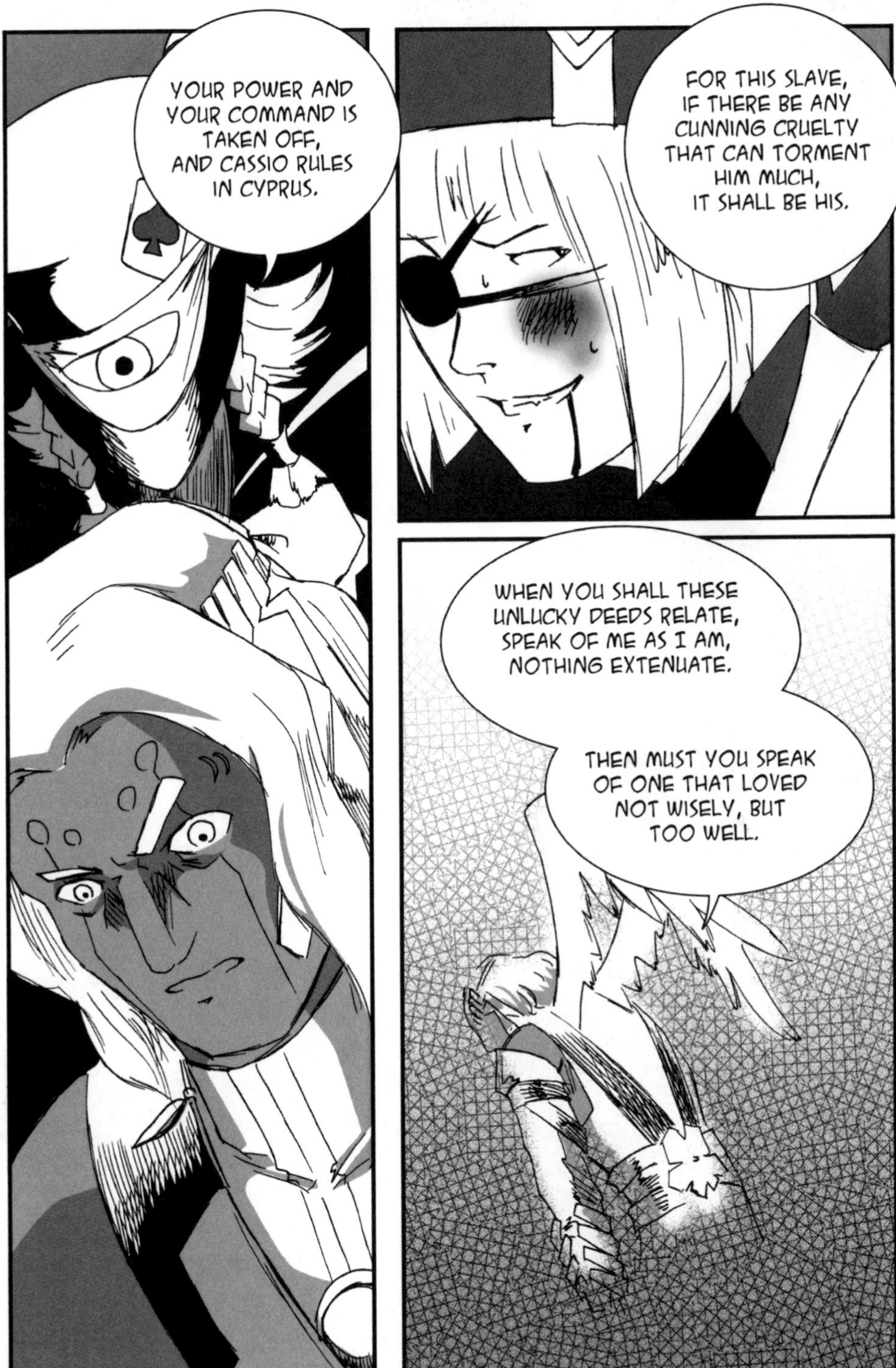
YOUR POWER AND YOUR COMMAND IS TAKEN OFF, AND CASSIO RULES IN CYPRUS.
FOR THIS SLAVE, IF THERE BE ANY CUNNING CRUELTY THAT CAN TORMENT HIM MUCH, IT SHALL BE HIS.
WHEN YOU SHALL THESE UNLUCKY DEEDS RELATE, SPEAK OF ME AS I AM, NOTHING EXTENUATE.
THEN MUST YOU SPEAK OF ONE THAT LOVED NOT WISELY, BUT TOO WELL.

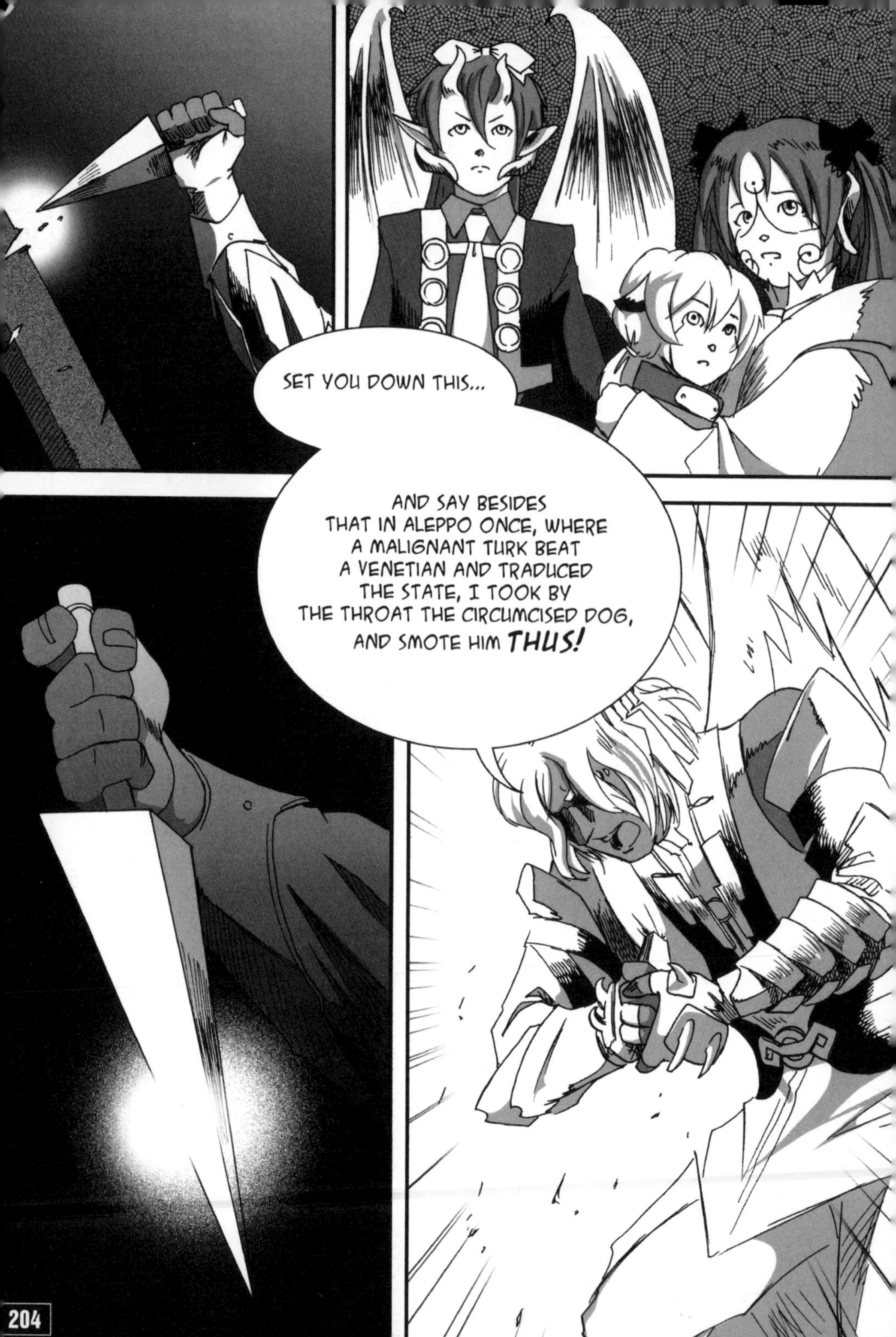
SET YOU DOWN THIS...
AND SAY BESIDES THAT IN ALEPPO ONCE, WHERE A MALIGNANT TURK BEAT A VENETIAN AND TRADUCED THE STATE, I TOOK BY THE THROAT THE CIRCUMCISED DOG, AND SMOTE HIM THUS!

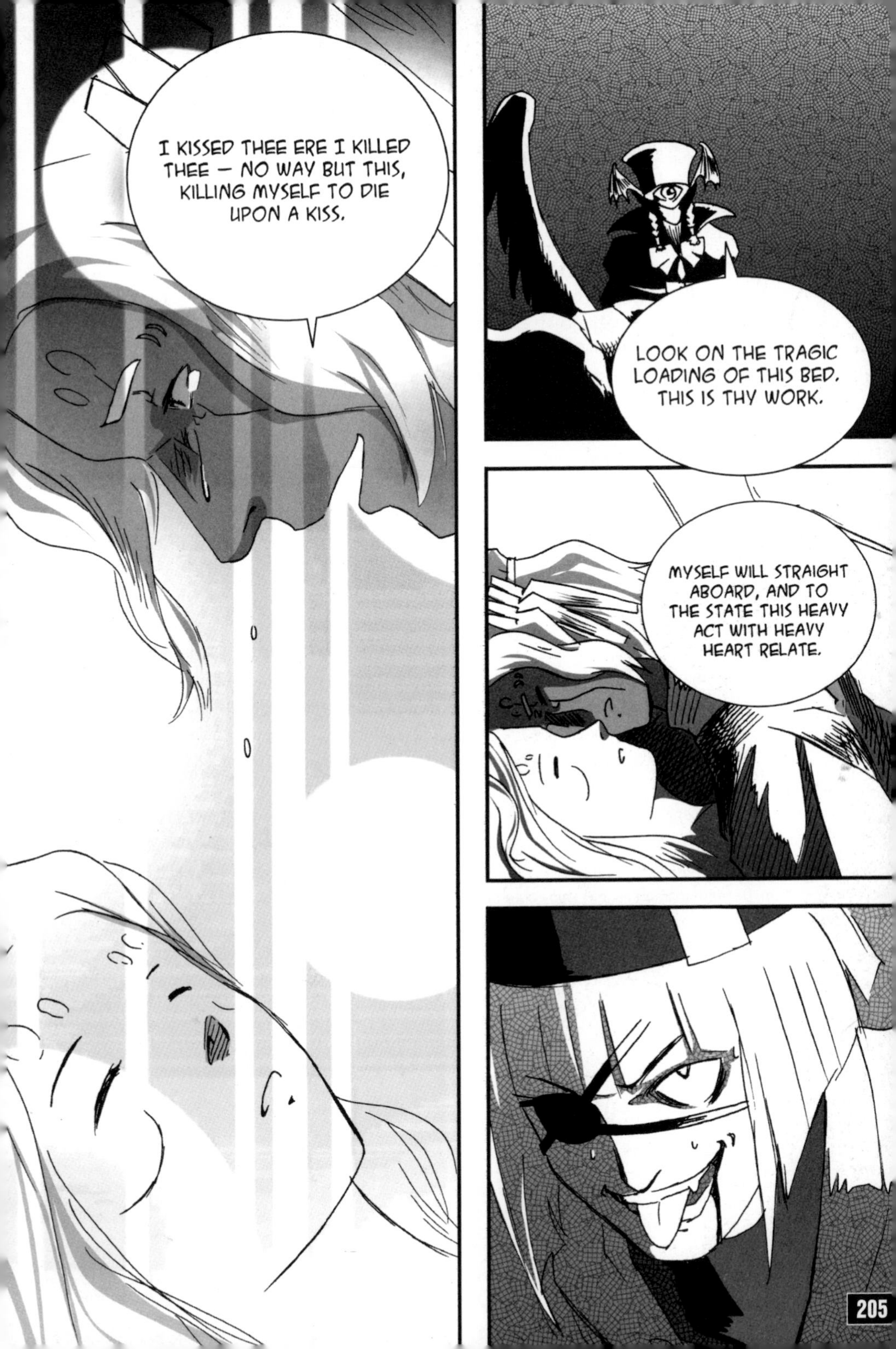
I KISSED THEE ERE I KILLED THEE — NO WAY BUT THIS, KILLING MYSELF TO DIE UPON A KISS.
LOOK ON THE TRAGIC LOADING OF THIS BED. THIS IS THY WORK.
MYSELF WILL STRAIGHT ABOARD, AND TO THE STATE THIS HEAVY ACT WITH HEAVY HEART RELATE.

PLOT SUMMARY OF OTHELLO

The scene is Venice during Carnival time when masks, costumes and fantasies take over from normal life. Othello – a former slave, now commander-in-chief of the Venetian Army – has eloped with Desdemona, the daughter of local dignitary Brabantio. But Othello has made a dangerous enemy: by promoting the loyal Cassio to be his Lieutenant-General, he leaves his junior officer Iago deeply resentful at being passed over.

Iago plots his revenge, persuading Roderigo (an unsuccessful suitor to Desdemona) to inform Brabantio of Othello's marriage to his daughter. Meanwhile, the Duke of Venice requires Othello's services: the Turks are sailing for Cyprus. Othello sets sail at the head of a task force, with his wife and staff. By the time they arrive, though, the Turkish fleet has shipwrecked.

Seizing the opportunity, Iago contrives to dupe Othello into thinking that Cassio is having an affair with Desdemona. He plies Cassio with drink, persuades Roderigo to pick a quarrel with him, and looks on as Cassio attacks the Governor of Cyprus, Montano. Cassio is disgraced, and Othello discharges him from his command. At Iago's suggestion, Cassio approaches Desdemona to persuade Othello to forgive him. Desdemona agrees, but Iago ensures that her pleas will be misconstrued, by insinuating to Othello that she and Cassio are lovers.

Othello, maddened by jealousy, needs proof of the adultery. This Iago supplies in the form of the handkerchief Desdemona accidentally drops and which Emilia, Iago's wife, retrieves. Iago leaves the handkerchief in Cassio's rooms – and Cassio in turn gives it to his girlfriend Bianca. Iago now stages a meeting with Cassio, knowing that Othello will overhear and misinterpret their words about Bianca as references to Desdemona. Then Bianca arrives, complaining to Cassio that the handkerchief he gave her was from another woman. Apparently confirmed in his worst suspicions, Othello vows to murder Desdemona, and Iago promises to murder Cassio.

Meanwhile Lodovico brings news that Othello has been recalled to Venice, and relieved of his command by Cassio. Enraged, and suspecting the worst, Othello publicly strikes Desdemona. Iago seeks to tie up his plot by inciting Roderigo to kill Cassio. But the ambush goes wrong and, after covertly wounding Cassio from behind, Iago kills Roderigo to shut him up. Iago's intrigues are unravelling – but not before Othello has strangled Desdemona in her bed.

Emilia arrives with news of Roderigo's death, but cries out for help when she sees Desdemona dying. Montano, Gratiano and Iago arrive and Emilia explains how the handkerchief was lost. Iago kills Emilia and flees, but is captured; having discovered his plot, Othello wounds Iago, then kills himself.

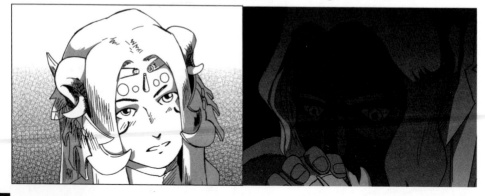